Wildcatting

Wildcatting

Shann Nix

Doubleday

New York
London   Toronto
Sydney   Auckland

Published by Doubleday
a division of Bantam Doubleday Dell Publishing Group, Inc.
666 Fifth Avenue, New York, New York 10103

DOUBLEDAY *and the portrayal of an anchor with a dolphin*
are trademarks of Doubleday, a division of
Bantam Doubleday Dell Publishing Group, Inc.
All of the characters in this book are fictitious, and any resemblance to
actual persons, living or dead, is purely coincidental.

Library of Congress Cataloging-in-Publication Data
Nix, Shann.
  Wildcatting / Shann Nix.
    p.   cm.
  I. Title.
PS3564.I935W55   1993
813'.54—dc20   *92-19020*
                                           CIP

BOOK DESIGN AND FAMILY TREE
BY CLAIRE NAYLON VACCARO

ISBN 0-385-42411-6
Copyright © 1993 by Shann Nix
All Rights Reserved
Printed in the United States of America
April 1993
10 9 8 7 6 5 4 3 2 1

FIRST EDITION

To Sir.
I will always love you.

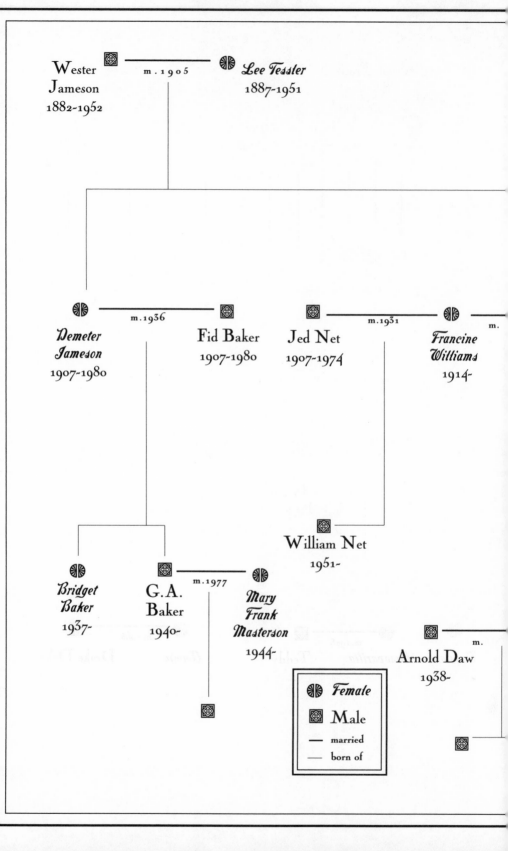

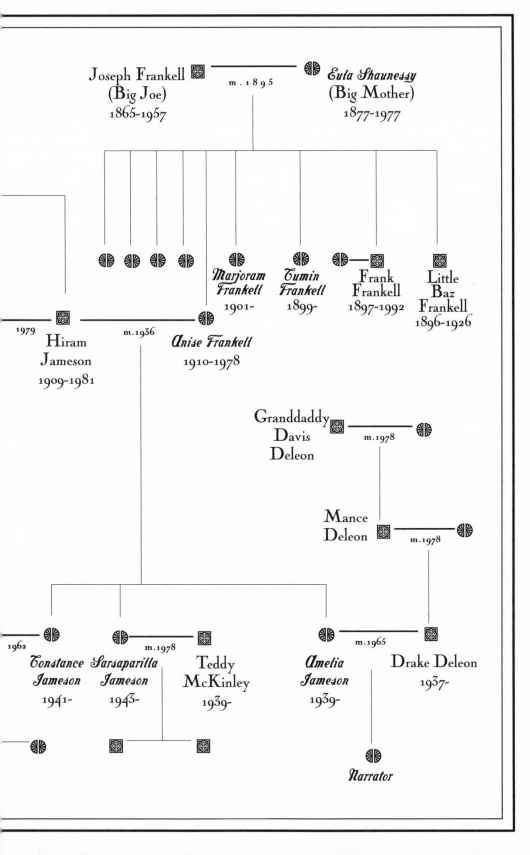

Joseph Frankell (Big Joe) 1865-1957 m. 1 8 9 5 Eula Shaunessy (Big Mother) 1877-1977

Little Baz Frankell 1896-1926

Frank Frankell 1897-1992

Cumin Frankell 1899-

Marjoram Frankell 1901-

Hiram Jameson 1909-1981 1979 m.1936 Anise Frankell 1910-1978

Granddaddy Davis Deleon m.1978

Mance Deleon m.1978

Constance Jameson 1941- 1962

Sarsaparilla Jameson 1943- m.1978 Teddy McKinley 1939-

Amelia Jameson 1939- m.1965 Drake Deleon 1937-

Narrator

The trainer of a racehorse once said this to me: "When you walk down the road and see a turtle sitting on a fence post, you know he didn't no way get there by himself."

So here's to the folks who gave me a leg up:

My beloved husband, Bill, without whose unwavering, unflappable support this book would never have been finished, or begun.

Ann and Don, the artists and parents whose stunningly graceful life is an artwork in itself. They have given me everything, again and again.

Bonnie Nadell, agent and lovely lady of steel who held my hand the whole way.

Peerless teachers Ebba Jo Spettel, Cynthia Rufty, Bernard Taper and Isabel Allende, who taught me to love words, and fear them.

My editor David Gernert, the man who believed from the beginning.

And most particularly my Texas family, who graciously loaned me their legends, and never asked for them back.

I would also like to acknowledge the marvelous work of J. Frank Dobie and the Texas Folklore Society, particularly the books *Cow People* and *Texas and Southwestern Lore*, on which I drew heavily for this book. Also the books *Wildcatters*, by Sally Helgesen, and *Folklore of the Oil Industry*, by Mody Boatwright, provided invaluable insights and factual anecdotes.

The life of Big Joe was inspired by a biography of my great-grandfather Willis Day Twichell, entitled *Pioneer Surveyor: Texas Was His Land*, by my great-uncle Fred M. Truett.

Contents

"Alas, we were all ignorant and only at the time of our death was it proved that whatever we had seen was all a dream, and whatever we had heard was a short tale."

—EAST INDIAN FOLK SONG

"If a story brings out truth, why let facts interfere with it?"

—J. FRANK DOBIE

1. The Palm of the Sky

It is said that we kill each other in my family, and it may be true. Certainly we inflict wounds on each other that cannot be borne, and cause irreparable losses. These things are too horrible to speak of afterwards, but they are not too horrible to do, and sometimes we die of them.

It may be because we are from Texas. The long alkali flats, and the oil boiling beneath them, make people mad. That is what happened to my family.

Or it could be that we are simply grown together under the bone too tightly to move without drawing blood.

In any case, no death occurs without suspicion and the laying of blame. "After that, he just died," we tell each other, secretly. "He thought you might have found a way to get in touch with him. It just broke his heart, and he died."

These rumors of guilt are passed in the club over lunch, because now we are an oil-rich family and have certain appearances to maintain. We wear white Chanel suits to pass these rumors among the heavy cut-glass goblets, between the floral arrangements, over the shining tables in flat Dallas homes. We trade speculation like the survivors of a hurricane, and crumple heavy linen napkins in our hands.

Most of the whispers lead to my grandfather Hiram. He broke many of the hearts and caused a few of the deaths, and may have died of a broken heart himself.

He was a sonofabitch, a wild man with a white widow's peak and eyes the dry blue of the Texas sky. He could jump six feet straight up in the air with weighted heels, ride two horses bareback with a foot on each, drink a bottle of whiskey upside down, whoop like a devil and tame a wild bronc just by staring into its eyes. He once sucked honey from the hummingbird throat of an Indian princess. That's what he told me.

I was the last of the many women whom he loved. Women surrounded him with their bodies, reflecting him like a pool. They showed back to him the man he wanted to be. They paid for that, in the end.

I was fifteen years old when he died. I never told him goodbye. When he died he left me a desk that had belonged to his mother. It was dark and polished, with long curves. I left it behind me for ten years. After that I went back to see if I had killed him.

It is rumored that my grandfather Hiram killed his mother. Her name was Lee, and she didn't give a damn for anything but God and horses. Her love was a great white stallion named Traveller.

Lee's hair went white at the age of nineteen, and she hacked it off and wore it short like a man's. She wore nothing but riding trousers and tailored men's shirts on her fragile, dauntless body.

She ordered her clothes direct from Marshall Field's in Chicago. The clothes came in candy-striped boxes, wrapped in white tissue paper. The matrons would cluster at the local post office and prod the boxes curiously when they came in, with their silver string and foreign stamps. They thought Lee might have been a witch. She had a degree from a university.

She had met her husband, Wester, at the university. He was a round-faced boy with spectacles and a kind look, with something firm inside him. She was small and ruthless, and chewed her pencils. He fell passionately in love with her when he noticed that the insides of her wrists were soft as silk, under her scuffed knuckles.

He followed her down the hall one day after class, and asked her to accompany him to the church picnic the following Sunday. She said that she would, looking away. Her voice was low and a little rough.

He met her at her house. She stood behind the screen door, pressing rust into the ruffles of her dress. Her arms hung longer than the sleeves. The dress had pink flowers, and had been sewn for a girl with larger breasts. Lee had almost no breasts at all. Wester came in and perched on the shiny horsehair sofa politely. He met Lee's mother, with a pale neck under dark hair, and shook hands with her blustering father.

Lee and Wester walked through the woods to the picnic. The air was humming and the flowers that drooped by the side of the road were swollen and slick with pollen.

Lee began to gasp suddenly, pulling at his arm with one hand, grasping her throat and arching her neck. He noticed that there was a tender spot just where her throat sat into her straight shoulders. She spread her arms, trying to breathe.

He pulled her to the side of the road while a cart rumbled by, streaking the air with red dust. He sat her in the shade of a tree, and fanned her with his handkerchief. He touched her hand. It was icy cold.

He hadn't known that she was an asthmatic. It stirred his sex to see her weak, when she looked so strong.

When he proposed marriage to her, she accepted with relief and despair, still looking away. They were married just after graduation, on a sweltering day in June. Bees crowded around the punch bowl, and some of them fell in and drowned.

Lee wore a suit of silvery grey. Her short cropped hair glittered white in the sun. She looked made of metal. Wester's mother came to him after the ceremony, and wept in his arms. Then she pulled back and looked into his face, putting a hand on each cheek.

She said, "Well, she's not who I would have chosen for you, but there, you've always pleased yourself."

Wester kissed her on the forehead. She pulled a bag of old yellowed silk from her purse.

"I brought the pearls for her to have, but she doesn't look like the type to wear them somehow."

"Give them to me, Mother," he said, suddenly weary of her hot female stench and wafting perfume. "Perhaps she'll give them to the children."

He went whistling off to his bride, glad that they would be alone, eager for the fire she hid under the cool lips she offered him.

But he never had her, never the way he had hoped. She was more religious than he had known, and spent hours reading the Bible, or looking away, her grey eyes glazed with distance. She would saddle her great white stallion, Traveller, and ride away from the house in relief, staying gone all day.

Baffled, Wester tried to win her. He brought her a bedroom set of dark polished wood, a dresser, a bedstead and a writing desk with smooth, graceful lines and slender legs. He rigged her a pulley device to saddle Traveller, so that she could pull on a rope and drop the saddle on his back. She was so tiny that she couldn't reach high enough to saddle him alone.

She accepted all Wester's gifts with the same cool gratitude. She smiled with such remoteness that he despaired.

When he knocked shamedly at her door, she let him in, but she met his furtive lovemaking without interest. Afterwards she would spend long periods at the window on her knees, the moon on her gown, her lips moving in prayer.

Lee discovered not long after their marriage that she was pregnant. It hindered her movements around the house, and kept her from the stable, as Wester became suddenly forceful and insisted that she not risk herself with the horses. He was joyful, painfully pleased with the thought that children would round her, and make her soft.

As the child began to knit itself inside her bones, Lee became very still. She imagined the child shining like silver, making itself out of her like wire, small hair and fingers, a tiny silvery thing like a fish. She looked out the window, and dreamed, and was as remote as ever.

When the time came to give birth to the child Wester was frightened and wanted to go for the doctor. But Lee refused, and bit her lip almost in two, pulling on the sheets. "God will provide," she repeated until her voice grew rough and stopped.

Wester ran out of the door into the wind, and brought back the midwife, who was waiting. Wester had arranged things with the midwife secretly, ashamed to speak of women's things. Together he and the midwife nursed Lee through the night as she raved in a harsh, strange voice.

There was one moment when Wester thought that Lee had died. He was holding her hand, and it clenched on his and then turned, and he looked at her face. Her eyes were rolled up and there was blood on her lip. The child nearly killed her, because her bones were so small and firmly knit, the midwife said.

But Lee never screamed, only made short, hoarse pants, and finally the child was born. It was a girl, tiny with dark hair and a whiplash look to her already.

Lee was pleased. A girl she could make in her own image, strong and sure, like wire, to cut her way in the world. Wester watched at the door, dreaming the world the way it would be now, with the child.

But nothing changed. Lee's breasts were small, and hard, and dried up quickly. The child, whom they named Demeter, had to be fed goat's milk. She was small and delicately made, like Lee. She learned quickly and was alert.

Soon Lee took her out on Traveller, galloping, holding the child in her wiry small arms, and Demeter laughed and waved her fists in the air. Lee and Demeter became a unit, as if there were skin stretched over the two of them, in which the blood ran finer and faster than in other people.

Demeter was still in her crib nine months later when Wester came up the stairs one night to find Lee's door bolted against him. He stood still while the blood went out of his face. Then he walked back down the stairs and out of the house, lurching slightly to the side.

When he came back the air was pale, and the birds had started to call. He was very drunk. He took the rifle from behind the door, climbed the stairs and bashed in the door with the butt of his rifle. Lee was lying very still under the covers, with her hands pressed flat on top of the sheets. She looked at him, her grey eyes reflecting the light from the window. He could hear the birds calling outside, mocking.

The stillness of the room pressed on him. He tore at his clothes and pushed himself on her, ripping the blanket away, fumbling until he found the dark space between her legs and thrusting himself into her in a rush, his voice gathering in his throat. He cried out once.

When he was still, he could feel her eyes on him. She had lain unresisting. He pulled himself to his feet, adjusting his clothes, and stumbled from the room, wiping the tears from his chin.

Two weeks later Lee discovered that she was pregnant again. Silently, she smashed the fine white china her parents had given them for a wedding gift into long pointed shards. Wester found her there in the unlighted kitchen, curled into a ball among the glass, her blood running into the floor.

He picked her up and carried her to the sofa, bathed her face and hands, and left her. When she recovered, she was kind to Wester. She spoke distantly but evenly to him, served him dinner, but her door remained locked. He had been holding her soul into its flesh, with his awkward fumblings in the dark, and she was glad to be free of his touch.

Wester took it hard, as he was still a young man.

This time as Lee's body swelled, she felt nothing for the child, except a ravenous hunger that woke her up at night, to claw the chalk from the walls of the spring cellar with her fingernails. She ate it hungrily. She baked loaves of brown bread, and ate hunks of it with her hands. So she thought it would be a boy.

Wester was amazed, to see her eating so steadily. She was always absent and uncaring about her food. He watched, and said nothing.

And Lee felt inside her only a dim blankness, a vagueness. Where Demeter had filled her with a light vision of nerves connecting like wires, and tiny bones knitting in the hot blood, this baby felt empty to her, a hole that sucked light. She felt a little afraid of it.

But she went on with her tasks, and rode Traveller, because Wester had lost the power to forbid her anything. She lay down along Traveller's back, her spine running along next to his spine, her head on his smooth strong haunch, as he slept at night in the stable. She heard his breath as he shifted from foot to foot, and breathed the clean smell of the hay in the bin.

The stable rested her more than the house. When she was inside, Wester followed her with his dark eyes, always wanting something, pressing her.

When it came time to have the child she lay down as if on her deathbed. Wester was struck with the thought that the twisted sheets looked like a shroud. The midwife was there waiting, this time, and Lee didn't object, but lay passively, ripped by the pains, but as if she were somewhere else.

The baby tore her, and she bled, but in the end she sat up and demanded to see it. They laid it in her arms—a boy, regularly made. She looked down at it, searching for the deformity that made the blankness in her. She saw only the child, and its helplessness made her love it, so that she nursed it, and Wester was relieved.

But there was always a seed of that blankness, a loss in that space where she should have felt for him. She felt it in her heart as guilt, and she did for him things that she never would have done for Demeter, to atone.

They named the boy Hiram, from the Bible. Hiram felt his mother's regard on him, cool and firm like a coat. But he felt the seed of blankness, and it made him afraid. It drove him, with a nameless fear. He learned to please Lee. He was careful, and learned to charm. Part of him always hung back, assessing the thoroughness of the surrender in his audience.

When Lee had two babies, she was trapped, fevered by being inside all day. They were quiet babies. Lee absently dressed them in smocks, little dresses with belts, easy to whip off over their heads and bleach.

Soon she could take them outside with her. She sat them on blankets in the sun, and taught them to pray. They rode Traveller with her, and had their own ponies as soon as their legs could grip.

They were almost identical until Demeter was five, with round faces, level eyes and the same blunt haircut.

When Hiram was five and Demeter was seven, Lee began to leave them alone. The children had started to separate from their unconscious twinhood. Demeter's hair grew long and dark, and she wore it plaited on either side. Hiram wore short pants and boots with buttons. But both of them still had the same nose, the same flat, practical stare.

They lived in Oklahoma, near a town that would later be named Jameson, after them. They lived in a long wooden room called the Batch, exactly twenty feet wide by eighty feet long, with a fireplace at each end. The whole family slept on a sleeping porch with mesh walls. In winter they woke with snow on their blankets.

Lee would sometimes ride away all day on Traveller, leaving the children alone to eat rice pudding from the Dutch oven.

Hiram and Demeter didn't care that they were left alone. They were sturdy children, used to caring for themselves. They brought their ponies into the Batch to saddle them, where it was warm, and drew treasure maps on the dust of the floor.

Then they rode out onto the wasted hills. They chased the armies of the clouds. Demeter was the commander, and she gave instructions over the telegraph set with the Morse-code book. She commanded Hiram to scout the armies of the clouds, and attack them, and kill them.

Hiram raced down the side of the huge flat hill, the wind in his teeth like foam, and chased the shadows of the clouds as they ran across the flattened grass. Demeter wired instructions and commands over the telegraph wires. Hiram subdued the clouds, and whipped them until they were his creatures. He always sent back messages of victory.

Demeter belonged to the plain. She ordered the miles of flat dirt, commanding it to rise to her fingertips and swell beneath the hooves of her small roan pony. She marshaled the fields, dividing each into square lots, peopling them with orderly ranks and regiments. When she sent Hiram onto the plains to charge the cloud shadows, it was mastery of land she was after, wide expanses of churned earth.

For Hiram, it was not the land. In the blue of his own eyes in the mirror, he saw tossing spars and whitecaps, bleached bones floating in a fathomless dark sea. He kept this secret close to his bony chest. When he galloped over the plains it was the ocean he saw, foaming and crested, his pony's head the rubbed gold of a figurehead, soaked with salt and surrounded by doves.

He looked back at Demeter on her hill. She looked to him like a cannibal woman on a desert island, her skin glistening with animal fat. They were alone in the vastness, alone with the sky pressing down on them like a great dry hand.

Demeter's figure suddenly seemed unbearably fragile to him under the weight of the sky. The frothing dream water around him subsided and soaked back into the Oklahoma dust. He was left stranded in the wastes, with only his sister in the world to watch him. He turned his pony slowly and rode back to her.

When he put his arms around her waist and pressed his face into her shoulder, she pushed him away almost absently. He let her go abruptly, roughly, so that she fell, and turned his back on her. He sat down on a knoll, whistling, and tipped his head back to look at the sky. Surprised, she knelt for a long moment on the ground where she had fallen.

Then she looked up at the sky as well. For a few minutes it was only the familiar sky that greeted her every morning, the vast dryness of it curved like a silver bowl, tarnished at the far corners, hot and baking blue. As she watched, she began to see what her brother was seeing. She shuddered. She watched the sky resolve itself into a great hand thrusting down on them, pinning them to the hill, alone in all the world. She went to sit beside him, humbled.

She kept her eyes fixed on the unblinking sky as he slid his hand under her sweat-soaked shirt to feel the fine white skin there, the puckered nipple on her flat boy's chest. Afterwards, when he lay his head in her lap and sobbed, she stroked his hair dreamily, her eyes still fixed on the sky.

Racing home, Hiram's pony stumbled on a hillock and threw him, kicking a bloody crescent into his forehead. Demeter rode up behind him. She saw the silhouette of his pony against the sun a little ways off, and Hiram lying still, almost covered by the grass.

She loaded him onto her pony, and whipped it with the knotted ends of the leather reins, and took him home.

When she got back to the Batch, she dragged him up onto the thick wooden table, and sat down next to him. She sat there all day, as the shadows slanted across the planking floor. She watched his face bleach as the blood trickled down his temple and into a pool next to his head. She clenched her thighs tight to the chair and waited.

Lee clattered up on Traveller at the end of the day, and threw herself down, and strolled across the courtyard. Her hair stuck up where she had run her fingers through it.

She came inside, and saw what had happened, and gently pushed Demeter away. She bathed Hiram's forehead, and clasped his limp hand in hers, and prayed over him. She prayed all night, until in the early morning he opened his eyes. Then she went to bed.

That night, Hiram dreamed of the sea. He dreamed that he walked along a beach, over piles of sand so fine that each step sent up puffs of powder, sucking his feet deeper and deeper. To his right he saw the ocean, dark and curling, fringed with foam. The bluffs behind him were covered with bruised moss, rust-colored in the fading light.

As he walked down the beach he could see ahead of him a shape against the horizon. He came nearer, wondering if it was the hull of a ship or a forgotten pile of bones. Then he saw that it traced a pure, curving line against the sky. It was a piano, upended, its lustrous surface pocked with grains of sand.

The wind blew and sounded the strings. The ivory keys were clogged with sand. On one side the salt had weathered the wood, cracking the varnish to expose the bulging wood underneath. Standing on the strange beach, Hiram felt irretrievable loss, and longing.

Later, when he was a man, he would take his family to the public beach at Galveston, and stand for the first time knee-deep in the real ocean. He would watch his young wife moving awkwardly beneath the red umbrella, her body loosened by two childbirths, her white joints tender under the ugly bathing costume.

He would listen to the shouting children, and look down at the grey water, and feel betrayed. No ocean in his life would ever equal the silver frailty of the ocean in his dreams, the night after he had seen the palm of the sky, and held the shallow curve of his sister's breast in his hand.

2. Nakomas Sorrel

His sister Demeter was the only person in the world who was luckier and tougher than my grandfather Hiram. When Lee died many years later, and the children tossed a coin for all her things, Demeter won. She always won.

When Hiram was a young man, he and Wester went to cut the horns off a red spotted calf on a June morning. The sun was hot, and the calf bawled and tossed his head. They made a fraying cut with a blunt tool once, but the calf screamed and kicked. After an hour, they decided to go to town for a sharper tool.

Demeter wandered over, her hair braided in each side and her hands stuck in the back pockets of her dusty jeans. "I can do that," she said.

The two men laughed at her, and left.

When they came back, they found Demeter with the calf's horns in her hand. She was covered with blood. They never asked her whose blood it was.

I have reason to believe that my grandfather Hiram lost his virginity to an Indian princess. Her name was Nakomas Sorrel. Her father ruled the Creek tribe of Oklahoma.

She had long, perfectly black hair down her back like water. Her eyes were slanted, and knew things. There was a faint blush along the top part of her cheekbone, but her hands were as hard as a man's.

On Saturdays in Wapanucka, where Hiram and Demeter went to school, Indians with yarn braided into their hair sat on the street corners, their blankets spread beneath them. They drank, and traded for bullets.

A man named Pawnee Bill lived there, and managed the remnants of the old Buffalo Bill Wild West show. He ran the show out of a battered old circus wagon, with dirty canvas stapled to the side and falling down in lazy loops. He hawked elixir, and love potions, and gems to heal the sick, cure the blind and make the lazy long to work. Girls visited him at night for vials of foul-smelling liquor to win the wish of their heart, and he cut their unborn children from them for an undisclosed fee.

Pawnee Bill was a large man of mixed blood, with a greasy ponytail and a red face. His voice was like Elijah calling his trumpets from the mountainside, full of the glory of God and joy in all His creatures. He ran a girly show sometimes behind the wagon, in a small space he cleared of stumps and ringed with smoky fire. He charged a quarter apiece for the men, but he never let in the young boys.

The girls danced in their underclothes, blowzy shifts with corsets and garters that made them pant for lack of air, and sometimes faint. Hiram was there one night, having sneaked past Pawnee Bill's vigilant eye. He was drinking cheap whiskey that tasted like smoke. He was a hard-faced boy with a smooth uncaring air, fifteen years old. He had a car, but he had never had a woman.

He was restless at home, and had started taking risks. He worked as a powder monkey on his father's construction site, dropping packets of black powder and short fuses into holes drilled in the rock. He craved the violence of the explosion, the death in the rough bundles, the building power of the blast at the tip of his rope torch as he lit the fuses, tearing from hole to hole.

At the foreman's yell he would run with the other powder monkeys to crouch beneath the bulldozer shovel, sweating in ecstasy and fear as the boulders rained down around them. At such moments he could close his eyes to emerge wet and gasping, his face purged and pure.

At Pawnee Bill's wagon the night of the girly show, there was a redhaired Samantha that had her eye on young Hiram. She was a woman with firm shoulders, who had in mind some education for the handsome boy. She wore a white-flounced petticoat and perfume like a thousand dead violets.

She danced at Hiram, smiling and twirling her shawl, showing how her heavy breasts hung provocatively inside the thin fabric. He watched her and drank the whiskey. He thought it was time that something happened to him.

Then he saw through the faint mist that trailed the town a figure, straight and cool as a spade. She walked through the damp night unhurriedly. It was Nakomas Sorrel, princess of the Oklahoma Creek, and she was going to the Indian powwow on the other side of town.

Hiram followed her as though he had no choice. He got up and left the smoky hot circle of men, trailing the still figure as it floated through the mist, leaving no sound. In the distance he could hear a humming, like bees. As they grew closer, he could see a flickering light, and hear a beating on the earth. It was a circling sound like no other sound he had ever heard. It was the sound of all the things that he had ever known and forgotten. He let himself be pulled to it through the cool air, following Nakomas Sorrel.

When they reached the edge of the light she turned around and looked at him. She had known all along that he was there. She put her hand up to her head and pulled out the leather clasp that held her hair, and let it fall to her back, as smooth and heavy as oil. She looked straight at him and did not smile.

She shook out her hair and went into the dance. Women were clapping and stomping and whirling, their heads tilted back and their eyes vacant, a keening sound coming from their throats. They wove into one another with a pattern, crushing the ground under them as they moved, until their feet were so heavy that Hiram thought they would sink through the earth. They pounded with the weight of a thousand seasons as they spun with their arms in the air.

He watched the girl and saw how the others made way for her. She danced, but it seemed that she danced more lightly, and she made no noise at all. She wore a bright red scarf and he watched as it wove through the crowd, the girl's arms white in the firelight.

Hiram followed her and forced his way through the ring of people sitting around the fire, who hissed at him and tried to push him back. He forced his way through and finally stood breast to breast with her, where she danced.

He looked down and saw her feet shining in the dust, her toes like nacreous pearl. He saw how they stepped—heel, toe, toe, toe, heel. Then the other foot. She shifted her weight, bent as if in a wind. Toe, toe, heel, toe. His own feet followed hers. Toe, heel, toe.

He lifted his arms and began to dance with her. She smiled at him briefly, and danced off. He followed her through the dance, drunk and dizzy with the drums and with the movement. His blood pounded in his ears. He flexed his fingers, and felt them grow stiff and full of blood like sausages. He laughed, and danced with another woman that he found in the circle.

The new woman frowned and hissed at him, gesturing with her head that he should leave. He looked outside the circle and saw the cool night air, as if it were a place he had left far behind. He couldn't go back there. His home now was the curling vapor of the open fire, and the dancing.

He kept dancing, until one by one the women dropped out and he was left there alone. He stopped dancing and felt foolish, looking around for the girl who had led him in.

She was behind a tree, watching. She laughed from the corners of her eyes, and looked at him sideways. He took a step towards her, feeling his feet as heavy as walking through sand. The women stood around watching, and frowning.

And then Nakomas Sorrel relented, and shook her hair back and came to claim him. Maybe she did it because of his bold look, or the way he held his shoulders. Maybe it was the hair that met in a sharp widow's peak, exactly in the middle between his two eyebrows. Maybe it was because a woman never left him standing, ever, in the middle of any circle.

He would never lack for soft hands to cover his mistakes. She was only the first.

She told him later that it was a sacred women's dance that he had interrupted, and that the Indians believed the failure to complete that dance would curse the luck of the next year, and blight the harvest. Yet she let him do it, and laughed.

She took him away from the dance and led him to a shack where the sheepherders rested at noon. Inside it was full of shadows that cut in clean angles across the dirt floor. There was a cot, and a water dipper in the corner with a gourd in it.

She stood looking at him for a long time. Finally he put out his hand and touched the notch on her chin. He thought that it was like the place where the sculptor chips the statue, to keep it from perfection.

She put her hands on his wrist, and stroked the hair on his arm where it gleamed silver in the light from the window. She had never touched light-colored hair before. It was very soft, softer than the hair of her father or her brothers. His hands were too large for the rest of him.

She put his hands up to her forehead, and he ran his fingers hard into her hair, feeling the roundness of her skull like a bird's. She trembled a little under his hand.

But she pulled his hands down her sides firmly, as if she felt no doubt. She had been bred never to show fear.

He loosened her wrap, and pulled it impatiently over her head. Some of the beadwork fell to the ground with a tinkling sound. He touched the curve of her hip, under the shadows, and bit his lip until it bled; he didn't notice until he found his lip bruised and swollen the next morning in the shaving mirror.

The next night and many nights after he drove to Wapanucka and took the dusty path down to the shack, bumping over the ruts. He would kill his engine and turn out the lights, and come gliding to a stop in front of the shack.

And Nakomas Sorrel would blow out the candle, and close the book she had been reading, hunched over the thin flame, and come out to greet him. So for many months to Hiram she had teeth and eyes of silver, like a festival doll. He never saw her in the daylight. He only saw her by moonlight and sometimes hardly at all, because she would never allow him to relight the candle once they were inside the hut together.

He saw her in the daylight only once.

His family came to Wapanucka on a Saturday. Lee wanted to do some shopping, to buy needles and some buttons and a new girth for her saddle. Wester walked beside her, looking around him mildly. They went into the dry goods store, leaving Hiram waiting outside, leaning against the hitching post.

As he waited he saw a man in a wheelchair, being pushed by a white-uniformed attendant. The nurse left the man outside the store in the sun and went inside to shop, adjusting the plaid afghan in his lap carefully before she left.

Hiram noticed the rich leather and chrome on the wheelchair. The man saw him looking and laughed, crooking a finger at him to come over. He had pale skin stretched over sharp cheekbones and a long, lazy gaze.

"Come here, young man," he said. His voice sounded odd to Hiram, rich and slightly nasal. He was English.

"Fancy a game of pitch?" the man said.

Hiram moved closer, watching the man's practiced, narrow fingers spreading the cards over the silver tray bolted to his wheelchair. The sun flashed on a thick gold ring carved with a black lion that the man wore on his thumb.

"High, low, jack and game," the man explained, riffling quickly through examples. "Got it?" His eyes narrowed as he watched the flush rise on the boy's face. Hiram took the hand of cards held out to him and squinted at the numbers.

They played for almost an hour on the curb while the rest of the family shopped. Hiram sat on the curb beside the wheelchair. He had a run of good luck. People drifted out of the stores, fanning themselves, to see.

The sun shone on the Englishman's quilted jacket, and sweat trickled down the back of his neck. He slapped a fly away from his face and concentrated harder on the cards, making them fly from hand to hand as he shuffled. He eyed Hiram.

"There, I have it," the Englishman finally said, slapping his hand down on the tray. "High, low, queen and game." Hiram laughed, and looked at him.

"That's not what you said," Hiram said. "That's not the rules. You said high, low, jack and game. Jack, not queen."

"Queen," said the man. "I said queen."

"Did he say jack, or didn't he?" Hiram asked the butcher store owner, standing next to him in his bloody apron. The butcher shrugged. The crowd began to break up silently, and drift back to work. In a few minutes the street was empty, the man and the boy alone in the harsh sunlight. The man flipped something in the air that landed at the boy's feet. It was the missing jack.

"Keep it," the man said with a harsh laugh. "A boy like you, you're going to need it."

Hiram picked the card up off the ground, smoothing the dust from it. He watched the back of the man's head disappear as the attendant wheeled him off. Hiram's eyes were thoughtful.

Lee and Wester and Demeter came along. Hiram fell in with them. Demeter watched his face, but said nothing. They were like twins, without knowing it. They had grown into each other like two trees that lean together.

Wester turned aside at one of the blankets where the Indians sat, to look at the smoking tobacco that was spread in dark wet sheaves. He squatted amiably on his haunches to talk with the man selling the tobacco. Hiram, standing behind his father, watched when the girl sitting next to the man lifted her head. It was Nakomas Sorrel.

She looked up at him and looked away quickly, a flush spreading up her neck. She bowed her head and continued with the beadwork she was holding in her lap. Her hands did not shake.

Hiram watched her, feeling his legs under him. He felt hot, and wanted to loosen his tie. He saw the curve of her cheek over his father's shoulder. He couldn't breathe. He thought of the night he had last been to see her, with her legs locked around the small of his back and her head thrown back, a fall of black hair on the rough pillow behind her.

He thought of the times when she laid her head into the hollow of his shoulder while they waited for the sky to grow light, and how she traced each of the sparse silky hairs on his chest with her forefinger.

He felt that he should say something to her. He pictured himself saying the words, shaping with his mouth the way the vowels would sound. He wanted to touch her. Then he imagined his mother, his father, his sister sitting at the dinner table, the clatter of their silverware. He put his hand in his pocket and felt the outline of the jack, and said nothing to the girl.

When Wester rose to go, brushing off the knees of his trousers and looking up with an inquiring glance, Hiram went with him. He didn't look back.

He didn't go to the shack that night, or for many nights after that. When he finally went again, she was there. He saw the familiar flicker of the candlelight against the window. He wondered for the first time if she waited for him every night, and what she told her father.

He had seen her father in the marketplace, a man with skin like roughened mahogany, with deep creases beside his mouth. He was a king. He wore his dark hair in braids on either side, and dressed in deerskin breeches and tunic. Many of his tribesmen wore clothes of brightly colored fabric, and carried guns. But the king carried no gun, and drank no alcohol. He was surrounded wherever he went by a gang of young Indian men, who stalked the streets of the town like cats.

Hiram walked in the door of the shack, and stood looking down at Nakomas Sorrel. For the first time, she didn't blow out the candle. She sat cross-legged, with her book in her lap. He could see her throat move as she swallowed. She looked lost in the shadows, like a wild young animal.

He knelt beside her, and stroked her forearm. She said nothing, only looked at him. He could smell her, a faint sharp scent like crushed sage.

She took his hand, and put it on her belly. She looked at him defiantly.

"It will be a boy child," she said. "He sits high."

Hiram stared at her for a long time without speaking. Then he walked out of the door, got into his car and drove away. He drove all night, drove the streets of Wapanucka and out into the stretch between towns, clenching his knuckles on the wheel and retching, bending over where his stomach cramped shut.

He drove in the open country, where the moon drew a fragrant mist from the trees. The shadows were blue, and the grass was damp. He pressed the pedal to the road, riding the ruts with abandon. The moon raced him over one shoulder.

He drove all night. Towards daybreak he entered the limits of Okmulgee. The sleeping houses looked tired and grimed with dust. He thought of the shack, and Nakomas Sorrel's black hair. He swung the wheel and drove down the main street of the town, putting his hand on the horn and holding it there, as the Model T brayed long, hard wails of sorrow and shame.

Windows opened and lights came on in the houses. When he reached the end of the road, his hand still pressing down on the horn, he saw the night constable standing square in the middle of the road, blocking his path. The constable was wearing his uniform, covered with polished brass. He carried a rifle.

Hiram stopped the car and waited. He knew the policeman—it was Officer Davis. Hiram's father Wester affectionately called the constable Stormy, and played poker with him every Thursday night. Hiram called him Officer Davis, and "sir." Many times when he was younger the policeman had given him hard peppermint candies from the bag he kept in the pocket of his blue suit.

Officer Davis came to the side of the car and looked in. His breath smelled of peppermint.

"What's the matter with you, boy?" he said, looking into the dim interior of the car. "Somebody witch you?" He laughed at his joke.

Hiram got out and stood patiently with his arms against the car as the officer patted up and down his legs in search of weapons. Finding nothing, he stared at Hiram bemused.

"Well, you ain't carrying no weapons, and you don't look drunk. Your pa's a fine man, and I sure bet he wouldn't like you out like this. Does he know where you're at?"

Hiram said nothing, only looked back at the policeman. Officer Davis leaned over and spit into the dust, and looked back at Hiram, considering.

"I can't have you driving about at all hours, speeding," Officer Davis finally said. "All the boys will be doing it, if I let you off. And your pa would never forgive me if I let you go off and get in more trouble. You better come with me."

He got into the driver's seat of the Model T and Hiram slid into the passenger's side. Officer Davis drove slowly to the jail, and parked in front. They went inside and he motioned for Hiram to step into one of the three cells.

Inside was a cot with a blanket, a bucket with a water dipper and a slop jar, unemptied. Hiram wrinkled his nose at the stench.

"I'll call your pa soon as it gets light," said Officer Davis. "Meantime you see if you can't get some sleep." He settled himself at the desk in the corner and put his feet up. In a few minutes his head wagged to the side and he began to snore.

Hiram sat on the hard cot looking out the front window at his car. He watched the light change as the shadows crept toward the front wheel, then away, then disappeared. He waited until Officer Davis woke with a start and poured himself a cup of coffee. He added a slug from a bottle he carried in his uniform pocket. He poured a cup and offered it to Hiram, ceremoniously adding a slug from the bottle.

"Boy old enough to be out that late must be up to no good, I figure," he said as he handed over the cup. He winked.

"Well, we better call your pa. He'll be wondering where you are."

He made the call from the telephone on the desk. Hiram listened to hear his father's voice, but couldn't hear anything.

Two hours later his parents came in. They had left Demeter at home. His father looked frazzled and wrinkled, as though he hadn't tucked his shirt in properly. Lee looked crisp and ironed as always, hard as metal.

Officer Davis put the key in the door and turned it, letting it creak open. He started to say something, but stopped when he saw the look on Lee's face. She strode into the cell and stood looking up into Hiram's face. He could look down on the top of her head. She smelled of cinnamon.

She swung her arm back and struck Hiram across the face. It left a white mark. She turned on her heel and went out of the jail. He heard the car door slam.

His father looked at him, with his hands in his pockets. He hadn't shaved, Hiram saw. Wester gave his son a tired smile.

"Come on, boy, best we be getting home." He shook Officer Stormy Davis' hand in his courtly way.

"Stormy, we're sorry to be a bother to you. You won't be seeing this young man around anymore."

"Glad to hear it," said the officer. "He's a good boy, I figure. But look," he said uneasily, "the judge is going to have to pass sentence on this ticket I issued."

"That's fine," said Wester, steering Hiram out with a hand on his elbow. "You just let me know when."

That night, Lee served them mashed potatoes and roast beef, with gravy. She was silent. Hiram could feel the angled sweep of her scorn, like a cloud bank. She passed everything to Wester to pass to Hiram. Demeter sat with her ankles folded together under her chair, making herself small, looking from one to the other.

On the day of the trial, Wester took Hiram to the courthouse. Hiram had his hair slicked back, and he was wearing his good dark suit. They sat at the bench. Mr. L. L. Cowley, the City Attorney, was settling his papers on his side.

Before the judge could tap the gavel down, Wester stood and met the judge with his gaze. They played together in the Thursday poker games, along with Stormy Davis and a few other gentlemen.

"Judge Carpenter," Wester said, "I figure that we could save the court a whole lot of trouble here if you and me and Mr. Cowley were to just put our heads together and figure out how to punish this boy. He's not a bad boy, and I don't think we need any official ruling here, do you?"

Judge Carpenter let his gavel fall, and then put it aside.

"All right, Wester," he said. "Let's see what you have in mind."

The three men talked at the judge's bench for a while, heads together. Hiram stared at the back of the uniformed guard in front of him. His belly lapped over the sides of his shiny black belt, and his neck was red.

Wester turned around and looked at Hiram sitting on the bench. He saw his son as if he were a stranger, from a great distance.

Hiram was sitting absolutely still, white in the face, but calm. He didn't fidget. Wester sometimes wondered about the boy. Already at fifteen he had a ruthless air under his laughing ways that Wester didn't see in himself.

"Stand up, son," Judge Carpenter said. Hiram stood.

The judge banged the gavel down. "This is the punishment, as decreed by this court of Okmulgee. This is legal, so far as I know, Wester, but God help me if the circuit court hears of it. The defendant shall not drive a motorcar of any kind, for any reason, during the next thirty days without having first gained the permission of this court. I set his bond at fifty dollars. Who will stand bail?"

"I will," said Wester.

"Done," said Judge Carpenter. He banged his gavel again, and the court was adjourned.

A reporter wrote the case up in the Okmulgee *Times* with this headline: "Youthful Speeder Deprived of Auto: Unique Penalty Imposed by Judge Carpenter in Police Court."

The story began, "High school boys who are prone to convert Okmulgee's streets into race tracks will do well to heed the punishment meted out yesterday to Hiram Jameson, 15, by Acting Police Judge W. E. Carpenter."

Hiram cut out the article and put it in his wallet. It was all he had left of Nakomas Sorrel.

After she watched Hiram walk out the door, Nakomas Sorrel blew out the candle and sat for a long time in the dark. Then she went out to find Pawnee Bill.

She found him in front of the wagon, hawking his elixir to the men waiting to get into the kootch show. The elixir came in a small blue bottle. Pawnee Bill made it himself, in a small still hidden behind the greasewood trees on the edge of town. He gave it color with tanning acid.

"This here elixir of life will save your lives, gentlemen," he said. "This will ease your liver and salve your conscience. This will soothe your heart, fade your pain and make your blood run smooth and fast. You drink three swigs of this, you be more man than most bulls. Come on now, who wants a bottle of the miracle cure?"

A few of the men bid halfheartedly for bottles. They were waiting for the girls.

Nakomas Sorrel stood in the shadows until the men had filed back behind the wagon into the flickering firelight. The wagon creaked back and forth as the girls inside put the finishing touches on their costumes.

She stepped forward into the light for Pawnee Bill to see her.

"Nakomas Sorrel," he said, frowning, "what you doing here? Your pa don't allow you here." He looked around him quickly. "He kill me if he catch you here."

"I need your help," she said. She looked him in the eye.

The blood drained away from his face as he understood her.

"I think you better come in here," he said. He opened the flap of the wagon for her, and she stepped inside.

"You speak with Samantha here," he said, nodding at the bosomy redhead who was bent over a piece of mirror in the dim space. "The rest of you gals, get out there and start the show."

The girls jumped out of the wagon, one at a time, and went out into the firelight, laughing and shaking the jingle bells sewn into their petticoat linings.

Red-haired Samantha looked up from her mirror, where she was lining around her eyes with a stick of coal. The wagon was littered with underclothes, garters, ribbons and dirty lengths of lace. It smelled of women's sweat, and violets.

Samantha looked at the girl, not unkindly. She patted the floor beside her stool.

"Come sit here, where I can get a look at you," she said. The girl stood stiffly. "Oh, come on," said Samantha impatiently. "I won't hurt you. You can't do business with Pawnee Bill 'less you tell me the trouble first. He thinks it more fitting that way."

Nakomas sat down. Samantha took her chin and tilted it up into the faint light coming through the crack in the canvas.

"You carrying something you don't want to be carrying," she said knowingly. "Ah, I know how it is."

"You been witched by a man," she went on, looking dreamily into Nakomas Sorrel's eyes. "You had a piece of your soul stolen, and you got back for it a life. And now you don't want the life. But no good—he'll never come back to you, this man."

Nakomas Sorrel jerked her chin out of Samantha's hand. "I don't need my fortune told," she said.

"Oh, I wasn't telling your fortune, honey," Samantha said coolly. "That costs extra. No, I was telling what any fool could see."

She settled to business. "Now, it's going to cost you plenty cash. You got it?"

Nakomas Sorrel nodded yes.

"Pawnee Bill's no doctor, but he washes his hands first, and that's more than you can say for most. How far along are you?"

"Five months," Nakomas said.

"Five months, my!" Samantha whistled mockingly. "You must really thought this boy would do right by you. Well, we see plenty your kind, here. You come back tomorrow night with the money, and we'll be ready for you."

Nakomas Sorrel was walking. She had been walking for a long time. Her feet were very heavy. She picked them up and put them down, one by one. Where her feet had been, the tracks were blood.

When she reached the edge of town, she paused, not knowing the way. Her feet drew her on. She walked out of town and into the fields, up and across the plain onto the narrow track that stretched out of her sight.

She walked and walked. She walked across a broad, swelling hill. The dust under her feet was soft, and it rose in little puffs. It sucked at her feet. She felt as if she was swimming through powder. The dark tracks she left behind glistened in the moonlight.

She came to the crest of the hill, and looked down to see the Batch. She could see light coming from under the door. She went to the door and knocked on it.

Lee answered the door. She stood, shocked, looking at the Indian girl standing there, clothed in blood from the hem of her dress to her feet.

"Here," said the girl. "Here is your son." She put the burden that she carried, wrapped in a blanket, in Lee's arms.

She swayed forward, and Lee put out a hand to steady her. Nakomas Sorrel pulled herself upright, and turned away without looking behind Lee to see Hiram, sitting at the table with the candle flame reflected, doubled, in his eyes.

Nakomas Sorrel began to walk again. She staggered slightly, as if drunken, but her back was straight.

It was Hiram that she had come to see. But Hiram sat motionless, and did not follow her. It was Lee who followed the girl into the garden, Lee who held out a hand to stop her and then let the hand fall, watching with a strange kind of pride the way the girl held her thin shoulders back. It was Lee who bent down and touched the dust, wet with blood, and rubbed it between her finger and her thumb, wondering how far the girl had walked that night.

It was Lee, finally, who took the shovel from behind the door, and buried the tiny bundle in the garden, and prayed over it.

It was Lee who stood outside, with her hands clasped loosely on the shovel handle, watching Nakomas Sorrel disappear slowly into the darkness, and the rising mist.

I write on the desk my grandfather left me, Lee's desk. I imagine her sometimes sitting there as I do, scrawling lists of things to do in a mannish hand, with her boots propped to the side. Perhaps she sprawled in the chair—there was a chair to match, also left to me in Hiram's will. My grandfather's widow has the chair now. She has refinished it to match her living room furniture. But I have the desk. It is sleek and grace-ful.

I imagine Wester buying it for Lee, early in their marriage. He would have screwed the back piece, with the small raised drawers, onto the body for her. She stood in the doorway, perhaps, in her riding trousers and shiny boots, watching, impatient to be away.

For the first ten years after my grandfather's death, I left the desk where he died. It was distant, in a place where I never went anymore. I wanted to forget it.

I worked hard to forget my grandfather. I was fifteen when he died. I remember staring out the window at a row of town houses, tiny and colored like hard candies, as my mother told me of his death. I remember staring at those houses, as if there was something I needed inside.

My grandfather Hiram was high-waisted and elegant, with hair that went silver at the temples, and glasses. I called him Sir. His hands were gentle. There was hair on the backs of his knuckles, which were broad and rough. To me, he sanctified what he touched. Airports, the smell of hay, stunted oaks and the sounds of cicadas were fractured with light because he made them that way.

When I left his house, I left him in it, trusting. When I went back to find him, he was gone.

The years had not been as good a caretaker as I might have wished. They had erased him from every corner.

I found some of his hats in a black plastic garbage bag in my aunt Constance's attic. They still smelled of his sweat. I found a picture frame he had carved, and the spurs he had given me. I fought with my aunt Constance for some sepia photos of him. She reluctantly parted with a folderful.

I have these things, and I can lay them out in front of me. I have a saddle with one tassel missing. Sir tore off the thong and used it to tie my hat more firmly onto my head, one day when we rode through the brush. I was amazed, when I saw it again, to see how small the saddle is. I must have outgrown it long ago.

I have a picture of Sir with his dog at his feet, my grandmother Anise matronly and firm, clinging to his arm. I have the spurs he gave me, and some old rusty horseshoes from his barn. I have the nails to the horse-shoes, and some old letters. I am bitter, when I touch these things, for the things that are lost.

But before I went back for these things, I had nothing. I woke one morning with a huge emptiness in my chest. I felt the future slipping out of my grasp as invisibly as the past, all pierced to nothing. It pressed the air out of my chest.

I called my mother Amelia and told her it was time to go back.

She cried, but she came with me. Some things there I found were empty, and some full.

I came back with my great-grandmother Lee's desk. I had it crated, and shipped. I paid for it with money I didn't have, praying that the check wouldn't bounce. It didn't.

When the desk arrived at my house, the deliveryman and I wrestled it down the long narrow steps, chipping the crate off to get it in the door. The man left, cheerful with his tip.

I tore off the brown paper, suddenly impatient. The desk came out like a dolphin, rising lustrous from the crumpled wrapper. I had not known it would be so beautiful.

I screwed the back on, with the screws that Wester had used. I knelt as he must have done. I ran my hands over it to feel the silkiness of the wood, and looking so that no one would see me, I checked the drawers for some secret message from my grandfather, some letter.

I almost believed that this is what he wanted, that he had waited until I was strong enough to bring back the desk. I imagined a letter with no address on the envelope, just my name, the inside filled with his tall, slanted handwriting.

There was nothing. The drawers were dark and empty. The desk was my message, the only one I would get. I sat behind it.

I loved it more than I had known I would. It had sat in my mother Amelia's room as she had grown up, with a china cup painted with violets. Lee had written on it. The women of my family had touched it, had looked in its drawers, had hidden things in its secret crevices.

But my grandfather had given it to me. It had meant something to him. It was the only thing he had inherited from his mother. His sister Demeter had gotten everything else, in the coin toss. But I would never know what he had meant by the gift. There was no one to tell me. I held the edge of the desk, and rocked back and forth with the weight of it.

He had remembered me when I had thought myself forgotten, and now the desk was mine. But it spoke no words that I could understand. It was not enough.

3. Hardpan

My grandmother Anise was born on Amarillo hardpan. There are many other facts to her life, but this one is the most significant.

There is a picture of my grandmother, taken when she was five years old. She is sitting outside, in the dust of Amarillo. There is nothing around her but the hardpan, and the sky. She is alone. Her eyes are empty, but behind them already the walls are building.

Amarillo hardpan makes two kinds of people. One kind is bent by the dust, and conforms to it. They ride in rodeos, and live in trailers. They eat dust and breathe it. They breed children in it, who run around the rodeo lots with stringy hair and running noses.

They break their arms and legs and hips, horses roll on them in the lots, smashing the softness out of their bones, and they live on welfare after that. The housing there is the cheapest in the nation. There is nothing to plant in Amarillo, and nothing to do. These people when they die are buried under sheaves of the dust that trickle onto the graves like shifting sand.

And then there are the ones that form apart from Amarillo. My grandmother Anise and my father Drake are two of these. They build walls behind their eyes, and where others see the baking dirt, these people see waterfalls. They see distant trees, and stony castles with flags. Their dreams are elaborate, with sharp edges. They pull themselves out of the sucking sand with their dreams, like broken bottles.

Later their dreams will cut them, and they bleed. For these refugees, nothing will come easy. They offer up their blood to escape, and their blood is taken. They remake the world as they had rather it would be, and the real world yawns up and takes them back in the end.

Anise's father, Big Joe, left his home in Ohio when he was very young. One day his parents went for a train ride to visit a cousin, leaving Joseph to take care of his younger brother Edgar. Joseph was fourteen and Edgar had just turned eleven.

Their parents never came home. A neighbor came to tell them that their parents were dead. They sat for a while on their mother's bed, thinking what to do. Then they packed all their things into one pigskin suitcase, and lugged it to the train station, carrying it between them. They paid for a train ticket to New York with the money they had taken out of their mother's blue-striped ticking mattress.

They had ten dollars left over, and with some of the money they bought a hot apple pie from the vender. It went into greasy flakes in their laps as they ate pie and stared out the window, waiting for the land to start to move. People stood on the islands and waved goodbye to the other passengers, but no one waved to them.

In New York, the two boys got out and walked until they smelled burnt sugar. It was a bakery. The woman who worked there, a red-faced woman with plump arms covered in flour, gave them more greasy pastries, clucking over their motherless state and clear eyes. She told them they could stay in the room upstairs until they found work.

They were good boys, able-bodied and clean, with strong bones in their faces. They were not too young for the jobs New York offered them. They lived there together above the bakery for many years, and became like two halves of one man.

Edgar was mild, with pale eyes and an easy laugh. Joseph became firm and rigorously hardened to the glance, but with something inside his character still liquid, leaving it unfinished. He felt a calling, but did not know its direction. He worked furiously at his job of loading boxes, and tossed in his sleep.

When Joseph was seventeen and Edgar fourteen, Joseph decided that they should go to college, and learn. He worked the first year, and paid the money it cost for Edgar to study. Then Edgar worked and paid for Joseph's studies. In this way they passed eight years.

Edgar began to pore over the fine colors in the paintings he saw in the college library, bending close for his nearsighted eyes to see. He began mixing egg temperas for his own paints, finding the balances of colors and shades. He grew a flowing mustache to cover his weak mouth. He drank rum and hot water behind his easel, wiping his mouth with the back of his hand, smearing his face with the colors of robin's eggs and spring moss. He hid his bottle when Joseph came in with his books, and chewed mint to hide the taste on his breath from his sterner brother.

Joseph scorned art. He learned the ruthless edge of mathematics, and the cut of geometry. He learned the stars, and felt the heavy rhythmic sweep of them. The hard pointed lights wheeling in patterns spoke to him of order, and clarity.

He committed the stars to memory, and Edgar painted the night sky of winter over Joseph's bed, sanding down the rough stucco to make the painting precise. Before he slept, Joseph would lie in bed with his arms behind his head, gazing at the sky. The train outside roared by with its passes of light and darkness until he dreamed that it was the stars, unfolding their secrets on his eyes.

Joseph learned Greek, and Latin. He studied numbers, and the ways in which they went together. To him they were all systems, cool and firm. He filled notebooks with his tiny, exact writing.

As Edgar grew looser in his ways, Joseph combed his hair back more severely and wore a black knotted tie and a plain coat. He was small, only five feet six inches tall. He spent his nights in the library, hunched over books, unraveling the patterns.

Joseph took a surveying class, and was appalled by the sloppiness of the methods men were using to draw tracks in the frontier. Some surveyors dug stacks of dirt to mark their boundaries, which blew away in the alkali storms. Others would sit in their offices and chart unseen parcels hundreds of miles away, never leaving their desks. Sometimes they measured using a method called "north three cigarettes on a burro," in which the surveyor sat on his burro and held his cigarette up against the horizon, squinting his eye to estimate the distance.

Even the more accurate methods, Joseph found, did not take into account the curve of the earth. The surveyors laid out flat plots onto a sphere, and expected them to come straight. He marveled that men forgot so quickly what they had known so long ago. The Greeks would not have been so stupid. He wrote in his notebooks, breaking the sharp points of his pencils in his fury.

Joseph devised a system of surveying by the stars, orienting on Polaris. He pawned his father's gold watch, and bought shining surveying instruments in wooden cases. He polished them with a velvet cloth. While others slept, Joseph sat by the window with a telescope trained on Polaris, measuring angles and writing notations in his notebook.

He presented his new star surveying system to a professor, who studied the figures and shook his head in amazement. The professor left to confer with a colleague, and returned with a job offer for Joseph to survey the High Plains of Texas after his graduation. Joseph accepted.

At the end of eight years, Joseph and Edgar graduated together in the class of 1882. At the ceremony, they wore their caps and gowns and stood to the side, alone, as the families of other classmates beat around them like brightly colored moths.

They boarded the train headed west the next day. After three days of travel, Edgar got off in Dallas, a busy rail crossroad, to stay with distant cousins until Joseph was settled. Edgar carried his paints off the train, leaving Joseph feeling light and empty.

Joseph rode on alone, staring out the window. The train jostled him, moving at twenty-five miles an hour. He saw brown grass, taller than any he had ever seen. The prairie surged under the train like water, covered with patches of mesquite and bushes he couldn't name. In the far distance he saw strangely shaped, flat-topped hills dropped like eggs from a skillet. They were mesas.

Along the railway sidings were piles of white buffalo bones. Beside them stood stoop-shouldered men with streaked faces, and women in dirty bonnets, pointing at the bones and waving at the train.

Joseph turned and asked his seat companion what the people wanted. The man next to him had a narrow, weaselly face. A dusty black hat was sitting on the seat beside him. Joseph noticed a band of pale skin across the top of the man's forehead, where the hat had been.

"Homesteaders," said the man. "Figure they're going to sell those buffalo bones for a little cash, to tide them until their first crops come in. Don't know who they think wants their filthy trash."

The ground under Joseph's eyes swelled and roared. He felt the flatness of it come over him, pressing him back against the rough fabric of his seat. There was a vast and fragile grace to the land, like a benediction.

His seatmate looked at him appraisingly. Joseph's face was round and young. He had grown mustachios like leaping fish on his face to make him look older for his job. Instead they made him look surprised.

He was wearing corduroy pants, a wool shirt and work shoes, a heavy outer coat, and a cap with earflaps that buttoned on top. The man looked amused.

"You're new here, ain't you?" he said. He put out his hand. "My name is Bean. Roy Bean." He offered his flask of whiskey.

"Pleased to meet you," said Joseph. He shook the man's hand, and refused the whiskey. "I'm Joseph Frankell." He stood up. "I believe I'll ask the conductor how much further we've got to go."

Roy Bean looked him up and down. Joseph's head barely reached the top of the compartment doors. "My, you're a big un, aren't you?" he said, lifting an eyebrow. "I believe I'll call you Big Joe."

Joseph flushed. He held on to the edge of the door. "Call me what you like," he said stiffly, and left the compartment.

"Hey, boys," Roy Bean called out as Joseph walked down the aisle of the train, "we got a tenderfoot aboard here. Sing howdy to Big Joe, the toughest five-footer in all these hereabout parts."

The men in the next compartment heard, and whistled and stomped. "Tenderfoot. Hey there, Big Joe," they called. "Welcome to the Devil's back yard."

The name stuck, and Joseph became Big Joe. He went straight to work correcting the errors of surveyors that had been before him. The work suited him. He traveled the brown face of the land carrying his charts and pencils like a priest, alone in the shimmering heat, submerged in the waves of distance.

He learned to ride a horse, but he never wore cowboy boots or a cowboy hat, preferring his own tall lace-up boots and a felt hat. He never carried a gun.

There was madness in the reaches of the High Plains that Big Joe surveyed. The sun baked the earth until alkali boiled up like a storm. Once he saw a man he knew from town, riding with his team of mules about half a mile away. Big Joe stopped and waited for the man to catch up with him. He watched as the man and the mules jogged along for nearly half an hour, never coming any closer. Finally they faded away altogether, leaving only the hard light glinting on the ground.

Later that day, Big Joe got off his horse and staked it, walking a few feet away to take a measurement. He heard a pounding sound, and from around the corner of a nearby mesa saw a herd of wild mustangs, manes tossing in the heat, their hooves coated with dust. They were stampeding in a tight bunch, close to thirty of them, eyes rolling like frightened children. While he stood and watched, they swept down on his horse like a thundercloud. When they passed, his horse was gone with them, dragging the stake behind like a broken wing.

Forty miles from a settlement, alone and on foot, Big Joe began to walk. He walked all day and all night. He recited psalms out loud as he pulled his feet through the dust. When his tongue swelled from thirst and shut his throat, he recited the psalms in his head.

When he awoke, he was wallowing in mud and water at a spring. His head ached, and he had no memory. When a wagon stopped for water, and agreed to take him back to town, he found that three days had passed. The wagoner heard his story and remarked that rolling in the spring had probably saved his life—he had recovered enough water through his skin to save him from bloating and dying like a steer from the water he drank in his stupor.

After that, Big Joe never traveled alone. He put out notices for an assistant. A stranger applied for the job, a man with an English accent and an old tweed hat pulled down around his ears. He carried a small bullwhip at his belt as his only weapon. He said his name was Diggory. Big Joe hired him.

The next morning a brisk north wind was blowing. It lifted the edges of Diggory's hat, and then blew it off entirely. He rode back cursing wildly, chasing it, knees and elbows flying, but the hat was gone.

Next the wind pulled off his toupee. He worked on, silent with shame. Underneath the toupee, he was completely bald. The sun shone on his head, splitting into rays. Big Joe laughed under his breath but said nothing.

So far from town, Diggory had no choice but to work on without a hat. The heat made him dizzy and ill, and he sat down at times beneath the shelter.

Diggory's head burned, blistered, and peeled. Then it burned, blistered and peeled again. At night he scratched it like a dog. A week later, he sprouted a full head of hair. He never wore a hat again.

Diggory was a useful man, stoic and uncomplaining. He carried on his horse the first-aid kit for their trips: kerosene for cuts, Epsom salts, turpentine, paregoric, spirits of camphor and axle grease.

He didn't speak much until they were two weeks from the reaches of town. Then he began telling tales, and after that Big Joe could hardly get him to be quiet. He listened to Diggory sometimes, sometimes shouted at him to hush up, and sometimes just ignored him, but Diggory talked on through all the baked miles of the Panhandle.

He had been a cowpuncher, he said. He had herded all the kinds of cattle in Texas—from the runty little cows called swamp angels or saddle-pocket dogies, all the way to the coastal cattle called sea lions, so practiced were they in swimming.

He had ridden all the way across the state, from the driest desert to the wettest, soggiest marshes. He told Big Joe that he had ridden once on a coastal prairie so boggy that his horse could hardly pull out one hoof after another, when he had seen a buzzard hanging in the sky like a kite on a string.

When Diggory rode closer, he saw there was a huge mud puddle underneath that buzzard, and the buzzard's shadow was bogged in it, so that a prairie rat could have run up the shadow and taken a ride on the buzzard. Diggory felt sorry for the buzzard, flapping there at the end of his bogged shadow, so he spurred his pony through the puddle and turned that shadow loose. The buzzard flew away—so grateful, he said, that he dipped twice around Diggory's head in farewell and later brought him a prairie rat, to put in his stew.

Diggory talked of whores he had known and his favorite cow pony, the loss of which he still mourned. He had lost it in a poker game. The pony was so clever, he said, that it could recognize brands on cows and would rustle out only its master's cattle from the herd, leaving the rest alone.

Diggory had farmed for a while, and picked cotton. He hated picking cotton so much that he swore to God on a Bible that if he ever planted another cotton seed, he would boil it for three days first to make sure it would never come up.

While they crossed the Indian ranges, Diggory told Big Joe about a partner he once had named Skunky. Skunky had earned his name when he was bitten on the nose by a skunk as he lay sleeping, in the middle of the night. He woke Diggory with a yell, and they rubbed kerosene oil on the bite, as it was all the medicine they had.

Then they considered another problem. All cowpunchers knew that only rabid skunks ever bit people. The only cure for rabies that either of them knew was to gallop at top speed towards a mad stone, and they didn't know where one was. Or what one was, for that matter.

So all they could think of was whiskey. Skunky started drinking all the whiskey he could find, while Diggory whipped up the horses and drove him towards Shallow Water, where they thought a doctor might be.

About midday the pair ran across another group of cowpunchers, who were eager to help and offered more whiskey. Skunky drank so much that he staggered down to rest by a woodpile. He had no sooner sat down than a rattlesnake bit him, right on the knee. He goggled at the snake, and shouted for help. He showed his new bite to Diggory, but the only cure any of them knew for snakebite was whiskey. So they loaded him with more liquor.

Skunky left the camp with three bottles in his breeches, three bottles more in his coat pockets, and one bottle in each hand. Diggory whipped up the horses again and headed for Shallow Water. Skunky sang out the words to a melancholy tune, keeping time with himself by beating an empty whiskey bottle on the side of the wagon.

By the time they found the doctor in Shallow Water, who was actually a dentist and knew a little about treating horses, Skunky was pretty well drunk. But everyone thought it was for the best, since the only cure the doctor knew for anything was whiskey. Folks in the town seemed eager to help the poor bitten gentleman, and anyone else who seemed thirsty.

After a while they lost track of who was the patient and who was the doctor, and things got a little bumptious, as Diggory explained. In fact, Diggory forgot about Skunky altogether until the next morning.

Then he crawled out of the shed where he had slept to find Skunky, who was sleeping under a tree. He woke Skunky up and asked him how he felt. Skunky said indignantly that he felt fine, and demanded to know what he was doing in Shallow Water. He had no memory of being bitten by anything—just wanted to know where in hell a man could get a drink.

Diggory always said that if Skunky ever died, he had never heard of it. It was Diggory's opinion that Skunky had been saved by judicious application of the right medicine at the right time. But, he told Big Joe solemnly, "I myself haven't had a taste of whiskey from that moment to this."

After that, Diggory said, he had been driving a herd through the Cherokee Strip when they spooked in a rainstorm, and stampeded and drifted for seven straight days. He rode day and night, drowsing in the saddle, and followed the herd all that time.

On the eighth day Diggory longed for a good night's sleep so heartily, and the herd seemed so quiet, that he took the risk of skinning off his outer wear and staggered to sleep on his horse blanket, wearing his red flannel underwear.

At about eleven that night, he wakened to a sound like thunder, and knew the herd was off again. So he stomped on his boots and pulled on his hat and swung back into the saddle, still wearing his red flannel underwear.

He rode with the herd for two more days. He was dreadfully hungry, and thirsty, and once he passed a cabin with smoke coming out of the chimney, and the good smell of coffee and bacon coming out as well. There was a woman with a baby outside the cabin, pinning clothes on the line, but Diggory was a naturally modest man, and would rather have starved right to death than accosted a lady while wearing only red flannel underwear. So he kept galloping on past, and left that lady staring after him with her mouth hanging open. He rode those cows in his underwear right to the end of the line, he said.

That was Diggory's last run on the cow trail. When he ran the cows into town, his big boss took sick and died by the railroad tracks. The man had been kind to Diggory, so Diggory buried him and waited around for three months, seeing to the cattle and settling his boss's affairs.

Then word arrived that the boss's wife wanted his body back with her, a thousand miles away, so she could bury it in the family burial ground. Diggory and the other cowpunchers dug up the coffin, and argued over what to do with it.

There was no way of putting the body on the train, after three months, and no one else would volunteer to ride with the boss's body back all that way. So the job fell to Diggory. He set out with the coffin in a new Studebaker wagon and a pair of good mules, with his horse tied to the back of the wagon. The trip took him exactly forty-eight days and nights. He had a little bottle of medicine to put on the coffin so it wouldn't smell too strong.

But at night, when the breeze lay still and the smell of dust rose up around him, Diggory would hear a scratch-scratching sound that sat his teeth on edge. Half asleep, he would stagger up and bang his fist on the coffin and shout, "Hush up, damn you!"

"And whether it was wild animals, or whatever it was," he said, "it shut up."

He had stored the gold from the sale of the cattle at the head of the coffin, figuring that it was perfectly safe there. And when he reached the end of the line, and safely delivered the boss's body and his gold to the widow, he quit cowpunching forever and turned his pony out to pasture.

"I figured," he said, "that I'd had about enough experience in the cowpunching line." So he had offered himself as a surveyor's apprentice, and that was how he had come to work for Big Joe.

Diggory rode in a strange way, looping the reins around the horn of the saddle and letting his hands hang at his side, touching the reins only to turn his horse. When Big Joe asked him about it once, Diggory said he didn't dare touch the horse because he had "too much electricity" in his hands and it would spook the beast too badly. Big Joe only raised his eyebrows and didn't say anything. But he doubted Diggory's word until one time when they were joined for a spell by a mail carrier, who was headed the same direction.

The man took an unfriendly shine to Diggory, and twitted him about his funny suit, his odd accent, and his bizarre boots, which were English riding boots, black-topped with brown straps. Diggory bore it for a long time with patience, until the man got around to insulting his horse, an ugly paint of whom Diggory was particularly fond.

Diggory said, "I've had about enough of your lip, now," and he struck the man once on each cheek, knocked off his hat and slapped him on the forehead. The man's skin seemed to stick to Diggory's hands, and the man cried out in pain.

But the odd thing to Big Joe was that the handprints on the man's face never healed up, just kept watering and watering. Finally he was in such misery that he turned and went back the way he had come.

"I hated to do it," Diggory remarked. "People I hit, they never heal up. It's all the electricity."

Not long after that Big Joe and Diggory finished the job they were on. Diggory took Big Joe to the Two Minnies Saloon, to celebrate. It was located in an area that would later be called Hell's Half Acre, and would come in time to be surrounded with other saloons and whorehouses. But in the time that Big Joe and Diggory went there, the Two Minnies Saloon stood almost alone in the midst of the plain, its red light shining out on the hard-packed dirt.

From inside came the melancholy strains of Mexican waltzes. The place was run by two sisters, both named Minnie. They hailed from Paris,

France, and wore silks and feather-lined satins in the latest French styles. Once a week the two Minnies would drive up in an open carriage and collect the earnings, and drive away again.

When Big Joe entered the Two Minnies, he went past a burly black man who felt along his sides brusquely and asked for his chaps and gun. Big Joe told him he had neither. Diggory had already squeezed past the doorman, into the brightly lit room beyond.

The room was filled with leather-cushioned chairs and marble-topped tables, sent all the way from Spain. The trimmings of the room were dark green velvet, and everything sparkled. A bartender wearing a necktie, his hair greased close to his head, asked the two men for their pleasures. They ordered two glasses of sweet sarsaparilla, as neither of them drank spirits. A casual survey of the room assured Big Joe that there were no women to be seen anywhere. Men were drinking quietly, with none of the brawling noise he knew.

But when Big Joe threw back his head to drink off his sarsaparilla, he choked and sputtered and had to be patted on the back for several minutes by Diggory, who was grinning widely at the joke. The ceiling of the Two Minnies was completely made of glass, and there were forty women walking around up there, each of them as naked as she had been on the day of her birth.

Big Joe watched them, fascinated. The women were comporting themselves quite as genteel women might. Some of them knitted, or sewed; some of them drank saucers of tea, or played at a game of tenpins. A few women strummed long-necked stringed instruments with their soft hands. There were long banquet tables set up there, covered with white cloths and festooned with grapes, and plums, and all sorts of exotic fruits and cheeses. The women feasted on these all day, dropping them languidly into their swollen mouths, or feeding each other the juice of oranges.

Black men in chamois-soled shoes padded around the glass floor, cleaning and polishing it constantly so that it shone like spilt diamonds. There was an orchestra of Mexicans who played waltzes without ceasing. Some of the women swayed dreamily around the dance floor alone, their pink and dimpled elbows showing in the dim light, or lounged on velvet couches. From time to time one of the women would look down through the glass floor and smile gently, or mouth some words to a man below.

But mostly the women were apart there, in their own dream. They sailed across the floor as if clothes were a barbarous invention for men alone. Their skins shone pink and white, fleshy like falling petals. They rubbed their skin with scented creams, so that they glistened, and combed oil through their unbound hair with long, absent strokes.

Big Joe could see only one man up there, among the women. He looked to be a wealthy old cattle baron, with a grizzled mustache and burnt skin. He was naked as the women, and dancing in the center of a circle of ten of them, lifting up his elbows and striking strange attitudes. The women made much of him, waiting on him and competing to bring him a match or a drink, clapping and laughing and teasing him to come and bet on their game of tenpins.

Dark-skinned men in uniforms went up from time to time to serve fine meals at one of the banquet tables, and the women would eat carelessly, handling their knives and forks with grace, wiping their mouths with silk napkins and drinking wine out of long-necked glasses. If they ran out of a delicacy, they would have more hauled up from the floor below in a dumbwaiter. The women conversed in low, twittering tones. From time to time a burst of laughter would come from the table.

They lived behind dark green velvet curtains that were drawn all along the walls, each in her own compartment. While they worked there they could never leave the glass-floored palace. Diggory told Big Joe that there were never any women allowed in the barroom itself. None of the girls upstairs could come down, and no outside women were allowed in. No man could go up into the glass-floored compartments unless he took all his clothes off and paid five dollars to stay until 10 P.M., or ten dollars to stay until morning.

The girls kept half of the five-dollar fee and six dollars out of the ten, with their board thrown in. Of course, they saved on clothes, since they needed nothing to wear from the time they came to work at the Two Minnies until the time they left. They also got to keep 10 percent of the money from drinks sold in the bar, and half of what they stole. Once they lifted a thousand dollars off a cotton man who came in and foolishly fell asleep with the proceeds of his cash crop in his pocket. He never complained or pressed charges, lest his family find out that he had been there.

The girls were all from exotic places, Diggory said, from New York or Paris, and they were highly educated. They could speak to a man of philosophy, or history, or tell any number of amusing and delicately bawdy tales. He had also heard that they were unparalleled in the arts of love, practicing perversions and contortions never before heard of in this part of the world. There was one woman there, he had heard whispers, who had a full set of tiny razors, each with an ivory handle.

Diggory had never been up to the glass apartments himself, but he had known some men who had. It changed them, he said. After a night up there, a man was never quite the same. It was as if he had sucked some subtle poison that worked very slowly through his veins. Most men could never afford to go back—ten dollars was a month's pay. But they would never be satisfied, afterwards, with the frank embrace of a Texas girl, and so they would drift to the Two Minnies every night, to watch the chosen woman of their affections, the red tresses or the brown or the blond floating over the glass floor.

These were the men on whom the women would sometimes look down, to laugh, or blow a kiss. Sometimes they would break a blossom off from one of the vases, and toss it down, to watch the men scramble. But they remained forever out of reach, drifting like pale sea creatures under a foreign ocean. Bitter men cursed them for soul suckers, or sirens.

Big Joe had money in his pocket that night, but he thought it better not to try his luck. So he and Diggory had another drink and went out, into the clean night. Big Joe had a shiver down his back as he rode away, and he and Diggory whipped up their horses and rode quickly, as if something behind were chasing them.

Big Joe noticed that Diggory was fascinated by the rattlesnakes that swarmed the High Plains, sliding over the ground and leaving their skins behind like the gloves of loose ladies. Diggory was once quiet for an entire memorable afternoon, while he watched a brood of young snakes hatch from their eggs. Diggory dreamed of them at night, fluting like death angels, rattling with a dry, delicate grace. Once a rattlesnake slid by their fire at night, displaced by their noise. Before he thought, Diggory shot his hand out and picked it up by the tail.

He held it out in front of him in horror, watching the ripples slide up and down its body. If he swung it to gather enough momentum to throw it, it might curve up to bite him. If he dropped it, angry as it was, it would be on him before he could run three steps.

He stood for a long time. Big Joe watched him from across the fire. Then Diggory smiled, fondling the bullwhip at his waist. He lifted his wrist and snapped the snake like a whip. Its head racked sharply, with a snapping of bone, and flew off into the darkness. Diggory, whistling under his breath, brought the snake to the fire and skinned it for soup, cutting off the rattles. He strung them on a piece of twine and wore them around his neck.

After that he picked up every rattlesnake he saw, and snapped it. His necklace of rattles grew thick as a cannibal's, and sounded when he moved.

Big Joe was giving directions for the day's surveying trail as they packed up the camp one morning, when Diggory absently picked up another snake.

When he looked down, he saw that he was holding the snake's head, instead of its tail. The snake looked up at him for a long moment, eyes glittering, and sank its fangs into his thumb. A drop of blood, dark with venom, came from the bite. Diggory dropped the snake and it slithered away.

Diggory laid his thumb down on the wagon tongue, picked up an ax and brought it down on his thumb, severing it. He tossed the thumb into the brush, and rolled the stump into some fine dirt to stop the bleeding. Then he reached into the first-aid container, scooped out some axle grease, smeared it on the wound, got on his horse and rode off to start the day's work.

Big Joe never heard him mention the incident again, or complain. But when he was packing the camp one morning, he found Diggory's small, stained travel Bible sitting on a rock. When he picked it up it fell open to reveal sheets of foolscap writing paper. Every sheet was covered with drawings of snakes, long quivering ones with wings and eyes like coals.

Months later Big Joe and Diggory came to a washed-out creek gully they needed to cross to mark a boundary line. Fearing the horses would break a leg, they decided to dismount and cross on foot. Diggory went first, backing up for a running start and leaping from the close lip of the gully.

When he was in midair he looked down on the other side of the gully, and cried out. Below him, directly in the path of his landing, was a ball of mating rattlesnakes, ten or twelve of them wound into a globe three feet across.

He descended towards them, his arms outspread, the time drawn out into a thin thread. On the other side, Big Joe watched in horror. Diggory fell closer and closer, his face pale, and as he fell, his eyes rolled up in a kind of ecstasy. He fell into the ball, face first.

Big Joe stood still, unable to move. He could see Diggory jerking, the snakes swarming over him in a frenzy, shining wetly in the sun. Then Diggory put his hands against the ground and pushed himself upright. He walked, staggering a little, to the edge of the gully and stood with his arms spread out like a Christ. He smiled at Big Joe. Hanging from his eyelids, his cheeks, his arms, his breast and his legs were rattlesnakes, writhing and hanging by their fangs. Big Joe counted at least ten of them.

Then Diggory fell back onto the ground. Startled, the snakes poured off him like water and disappeared.

Big Joe shook himself back into motion. He took the first-aid kit and leapt the gully. He knelt beside Diggory and shook him.

Diggory's eyes were turning up in his head. In the air above him he saw bright-feathered serpents, rolling lazily in loops, leaving trails of flame in the still air. They sang to him like women, flickering their sweet forked tongues, humming a song he'd never heard before. He reached his hand out to touch their scales like peacock feathers, but the edges were sharp as razors, and made him bleed. He cried out, begging them not to leave him behind when they went wheeling back to their nests, curled on the edge of an endless sea.

"Stay awake, old friend," said Big Joe. "Don't go to sleep on me now." He took out a tiny razor, held it in the flame of a Lucifer sulphur match that he carried carefully wrapped against the damp, and burned the edge of the blade. Then he started to cut Diggory.

He cut fast and hard, two cuts near every fang mark. He stripped off Diggory's clothes, afraid he would miss a mark. Diggory's skin was pale and cold to his touch. Diggory bled into the sand, humming, his face set in a smile and his eyes fixed unblinking on the white heat of the sky.

Diggory lived. Big Joe took him back into town, and gave him into the care of twin sisters who ran a convalescent home for range riders who had fallen ill, with the tick fever or the flux from bad water.

But Diggory never rode again. Big Joe would stop by to see him sometimes, on his way through town for supplies. Diggory sat always in the same chair on the porch of the convalescent home, rocking back and forth gently in the sun. His eyes remained fixed on something Big Joe couldn't see.

Big Joe brought Diggory things he had once liked to eat, tomatoes and sometimes a rare shipment of golden-skinned fruit that came up from Mexico. He would lay it down beside Diggory's chair, and touch his cold fingers.

"How are you today, old friend?" he would say.

Diggory never answered. He just sat smiling into the sun, fingering the necklace of snake rattles that still hung around his neck. He rocked and rocked slowly, humming a tune that Big Joe couldn't name.

4. Barbed Wire

Big Joe was thirty-one years old before he ever saw barbed wire. He heard from the owner of the drugstore one day that John Warne "Bet-A-Million" Gates had ridden into town, with a scheme mad enough to tickle the back teeth of every man, woman and child in town. It was wire, the drugstore owner said. Wire to fence the range, and to keep the cattle from running over the farms.

Bet-A-Million had come into town with a fast yellow-haired city woman in a lavender dress, and had hired the best room in the only hotel in town. He was going to show everyone his wire at sunset.

Big Joe had heard that Bet-A-Million Gates was only twenty-one years old, fast as a monkey and slick as a snakeskin. There was bound to be a good show.

In the plaza Big Joe saw that bleachers had been hammered up. A crew of silent-lipped men were ignoring catcalls from bystanders, and driving mesquite posts into the ground in the center of the plaza. To each post they attached eight long strands of silvery wire, glinting in the failing sun.

Big Joe went closer to have a look. The wire was toothed with little spikes, wrapped around and poking out every six inches or so. It looked strange against the red dirt, shining like something that didn't belong. It was lethal in the way of new things, fragile and cruel as a blade.

Ranchers and their wives were starting to drift into town and stomp the dust off, dickering for a place on the stands. Houston had even sent a newspaper reporter, a wiry young man missing a tooth in front.

Gates had borrowed a small herd of longhorns to test his wire, and penned them in an arena about a hundred feet from the wire enclosure itself. Longhorns were the toughest, meanest, most ornery beasts on the Plains, wild-eyed things that hated the stench of all men. This herd milled restlessly, smelling trouble.

One rancher went over to the arena, and looked them over. He spit into the dust, and said, "That man don't know dung from wild honey. Them longhorns gonna rip that wire to pieces."

Sunset had come and gone, and the dusk drifted in. The crowd shifted on the hard wooden boards, and someone started calling for Bet-A-Million, jeering at him to get it over with.

He came out with a flourish, wearing a theatrical cape, and a flower shipped all the way from Houston in his buttonhole. He climbed up on top of a wooden crate, and lifted his arms for silence. He had thick arms and slicked-back hair, and the magnetic, lightly drunken air of a spieler.

"Ladies and gents," he said. "This here is the finest fence in the world. Light as air, stronger than whiskey, cheaper than dirt, all steel and miles long. The cattle ain't been born yet that can get through it, or my name's not Bet-A-Million Gates."

There were shouts and catcalls, and a few boos. Bet-A-Million turned to the arena men and called, "All right, boys, let 'em loose." Chased out of the pen into the barbed-wire enclosure, the cattle stampeded in ten directions, throwing their heads and kicking up clouds of dust. One mesquite post snapped, and the audience gasped, but the wire held firm.

Then a man on horseback rode in with two flaming torches, thrusting them at the longhorns. He twirled the torches in the blue dusk, throwing trails of sparks and whooping at the top of his lungs. The cattle screamed with rage and threw their bodies against the wires with such force that the ladies screamed back and gathered their skirts, and the men grabbed their rifles and snapped the safeties off their guns.

But the eight strands of wire, shining in the dimness, held and held. They pinned the cattle in, drawing on them long stripes of blood until the winded animals finally halted and gathered together in a nervous, blowing clutch—defeated.

There was a long moment of silence when they had done, and the only sound was the wind sweeping the plains behind. Big Joe had a shiver up his spine like a death, and he knew he had seen the end of something familiar, and dear to him.

The ranchers and their ladies left silently, two or three at a time. Only one man went up to touch the wire, sagging in loops, and whistled his breath out between his teeth and shook his head.

Bet-A-Million stood in the middle of the trampled red dust, after the cattle had been herded away, watching the people leave. No one looked at him. He stood alone there, until everyone was gone.

Finally the yellow-haired lady in the lavender dress, her feet in thin dancing slippers, came out to him where he was standing. She picked up the crumpled opera cape from the ground, and draped it gently around him, and led him back to the hotel.

John Warne Bet-A-Million Gates made four hundred kinds of barbed wire, before it was all over, and fenced the High Plains. In the city, Neiman-Marcus plated six-inch lengths of barbed wire with pure gold, and sold them as swizzle sticks for ladies to stir in iced drinks.

After he saw the wire, Big Joe went out again onto the Plains, to finish his work of cutting the land into squares. But the heart had gone out of it for him. The barbed wire was behind his eyes, and in his mind. Without knowing it he had grown to love the burnt, edgeless horizon, the endless days dimmed with dust, the hugeness of it, the sweep of the land before God. To bite into this, he thought, was sacrilege. And yet this was his trade, and his duty.

He was thinking of sacrilege when he went into the Second Baptist Church for an early Sunday service. The death of the land curdled in him, and he went to sing the hymns. Although he belonged to no church, he sang tunefully and well, in a clear baritone, and he was welcomed at all the services in town.

This Sunday he saw at the piano a wasp-waisted woman with red hair, her neck transparent as glass. She wore a white dress. He could see the blood beating through her skin. He watched her through the service, seeing how her slight fingers touched the keys hesitantly, her neck bent down dumbly over the piano, as if the shining weight of the hair was too heavy.

He asked to walk her home. Her name was Eula, she told him, and she taught at the schoolhouse. Her fragility made him think of sugar-spun angels in a Bible picture book he had seen long ago, when his mother was alive. His mother would turn the pages for him, and point out the pictures of the angels, and tell him how they sang. It gave him a warmth, and a feeling of home he had lost long ago, when he looked at Eula.

Eula sang hymns when she played the piano, in a thin sweet soprano, and he would close his eyes and tilt his head back and let the purity of her voice ease his conscience.

He imagined that her lowered eyelids covered a fierce and romantic heart. In fact, her blankness was a genuine lack of eccentricity, mixed with an occasional salty pragmatism that was odd for a young lady of her day.

But despite her lack of imagination, she fell quite sincerely in love with Joseph. When he proposed marriage to her, she accepted him at once. She had been in Texas for only six months, but she well understood the impossibility of an unmarried woman surviving for long.

"Texas is a good place for men and dogs," she wrote to an aunt in Kentucky. "But it's hell on women and oxen."

Eula had come from the South in a wagon, with her parents and five sisters. They came from low-lying cropland, warm and fertile, where they lived gracefully. They dragged with them their piano, its black curve sharp as satin against the dust of the road.

Even in the sands of Amarillo, Eula and her sisters wore starched white dresses. They stood around the central room of the house, their long hair curling to their waists, ironing their white dresses and singing like sirens.

Once a group of Indians came to the house and walked in through the unlocked door. They prowled like panthers around the room, sniffing at the women who stood poised, their irons lifted.

The Indians poked at the grandfather clock, and one sat down behind the piano, but could not make it play. Their skins shone with oil, and they smelled rancid. Their muscles were long as ropes under their shining skin, and their faces were perfectly smooth, like stones.

Eula and her sisters stood still, and watched the Indians. Finally the chief Indian made a sign and pointed to his mouth. They understood from this that they wanted food. Eula's oldest sister walked, swaying in her petticoat, into the pantry and brought out a salted side of bacon and a sack of flour. She handed it to the Indian.

One of the Indians walked up to Eula and lifted a lock of the flaming red hair that hung over her breast. She held her breath and looked directly up, into his eyes. His eyes were dark, and ringed in the middle with a color like smoke. He smelled of crushed grass. She felt dizzy, as if the floorboards were tilting beneath her, making her lean toward him. She felt that she could drift through him like air.

He stood there for a long time, watching her, smiling. Then he dropped her hair and turned away. The Indians left.

Her oldest sister crossed over to Eula, who was watching the muscles of the Indian shift in his back as he walked out the door. She held Eula's face in her hands and dealt her two sharp, swift blows, one on either cheek.

"Don't shame us," she said.

For weeks afterwards, Eula's dreams had been disturbing and vivid, and her temper short around the house. Then she met Big Joe, and became engaged to him, and the family was relieved. They thought it was high time that Eula married.

Eula and Big Joe said their vows at the Second Baptist Church, where he had first seen her playing the piano. The whitewashed church had no underpinning, and the ground space beneath the floorboards was a favorite gathering place for the hogs that ran free through the center of town. They scratched their backs against the boards, snorting and shaking the church and causing great embarrassment to the preacher during dramatic pauses in his sermons.

The hogs also contributed to the church a large number of their fleas, which kept the faithful in agony, as it was forbidden to scratch during the service.

Fortunately Eula was a member of the Ladies Aid, and her fellow members came in before her wedding and sprinkled powdered cinnamon on the carpeted aisle to protect her dragging train from the fleas. Big Joe looked very distinguished in his mustachios and frock coat. The town paper reported the wedding as a lovely affair.

Eula, who never did learn the trick of preventing pregnancy, began having children immediately and went on having them for many years. My grandmother Anise was the youngest of nine children. By the time Anise was born, the whole town referred to Eula as Big Mother, and Big Mother was tired.

Big Mother bore all nine of her children sitting astride her husband's knees. She was completely dressed for each labor, except for underclothes. She sat on her husband's lap, facing him, and gave birth to one baby each year for nine years.

The chair was a straight-back chair with strong wooden armrests. Big Joe rested his forearms on the armrests when he tired of holding the small of Big Mother's back during the births. Behind the chair was a spice rack that he had made for her as a wedding present, out of ash wood that he had rubbed with a cloth until it was smooth as satin.

Big Mother filled the spice rack with spices from India and the East, purchasing them from a traveling slant-eyed peddler who stopped once a year at the nearest town. She opened the bottles of spice and rubbed pinches between her fingers, closing her eyes to smell them. They smelled to her of voices in infidel tongues, of dancing girls with eyes like heifers, of silver goblets buried in the sand and tents of many colors, ragged silks stitched together like the flying balloon from the fair, lifting in the hot wind. It was the only dream she had, for she was a woman of little imagination.

She stared at the spice rack as she waited for her babies to be born, Big Joe's hands firmly on the small of her back. She chanted the names of the spices again and again to herself as a litany against the pain. Turmeric. Oregano. Anise. Cumin. Thyme. Sweet Basil.

She wrapped the children in clean cloths, warm from the hearth, when they were born. She named as many of them after the spices as Big Joe would allow. He put his foot down after she named the first son Basil, and the only other boy was named Frank. In her secret mind, Big Mother thought of his name as short for Frankincense.

But the girls she named as she wished, and then washed her hands of them. So my grandmother Anise was born with a wanderlust, and the scent of spices in her nostrils.

Big Mother's first son, Basil, was born with a disease of the spine, and only grew to be thirty inches long. The family called him Little Baz. They carried him everywhere with them on a velvet pillow with fringed ends, and they told him their secrets.

Little Baz was wise, although he was no bigger than Anise's doll with the china face. His small slanted eyes gave him a foreign look, and his mouth turned up in a silent smile. He received the confessions of the family, each in his hour of the night, and forgave them with his tiny, twisted hand.

Little Baz was ten years old when Anise was born, last of all the children. Big Joe gave her a red wagon. It was her only toy on the vast, flat plain. When a wind blew up she rigged her wagon with a sail, and the wind drove her across the prairie. It carried her far, far away, until she was out of sight of the house and the rutted dirt streets.

She took Little Baz with her, on his pillow, and tucked him into the wagon with a blanket. He laughed at the motion, and the distance. When they had been gone so long that the clouds no longer left shadows on the grass, then Anise would get out of the wagon and pull it back, panting and sweating, her socks falling down around her ankles and her skirts stained with the fine red dust that seeped into everything and blew in clouds across the plain.

Little Baz lived to be twenty years old. When he died they buried him in a hatbox, on his velvet pillow. Anise hung a string of jingle bells over his grave, and listened to them ring when the wind blew.

When Anise turned eleven, Big Mother told her the story of the piano brought from Kentucky, carted over the ruts of a thousand miles, shielded by the sisters' best white dresses ripped to rags, forded across rivers that swelled and roared beneath the ivory keys. In one town they had cut a team of dying oxen away from the wagon carrying the piano, and hitched in another to go on. It was the only story Big Mother told.

Anise dreamed of the piano sometimes, in the baking heat. The keys seemed to her like chips of ice that she could peel off and suck in her mouth. The piano in her dreams would give a cool smoky vapor into the air, like the beginning of a storm.

Married life was a disappointment to Big Joe. He quickly tired of the sight and smell of babies, and allowed his work to lure him again out onto the plains.

He was like a god there, the small man on the brow of a hill. He laid out towns, and settled arguments like a Greek deity, waving his finger to draw lines in the dust that became maps.

He made Tascosa, Mobeetie, Hartley, Channing, Vega, and Amarillo, once called Old Town and Rag Town—names that strummed by his ear like dried beads, names he fingered like coins in his pocket and felt that he owned.

When Anise was born, the last of all the children, Big Joe looked at his wife and saw that she was drained. After all the births, and the death of Little Baz, she had nothing left to give the tiny dark-haired girl child.

So out of pity, he took an interest in Anise. She was well behaved, and quiet, and sometimes he would take her out with him on the buckboard to do a nearby surveying job. She watched the shining rumps of the horses move in front of the shafts, and listened to him talk. She asked him questions, about words, and where they came from, about the burning holes in the sky, about the things that fell to earth. It seemed to her that he knew everything.

At night he gave her strong black coffee, with grounds floating in it, and baked sourdough pan biscuits over the fire, from the sourdough starter that he carried with him. He always brought tomatoes, to suck in case there was no water, and to ward off the scurvy.

The story Anise loved best was the tale of Tascosa, the town that lived only twenty years. Big Joe would tell how he made the town of Tascosa on tracing linen, laying out where each thing should be. The map he made was six feet long by three feet wide, and he colored in the water, the trees, and the residences with different shades of ink from his office desk, drawing them precisely in the lines.

There were thirty-three residences in Tascosa, three drugstores, three saloons, one blacksmith, one wagon yard, one livery stable, one jewelry store, five merchandise stores, two restaurants and one hotel. Big Joe did not draw in the dance halls and houses of ladies of dubious reputation.

Everyone thought Tascosa would become a great city. The editor of the weekly Tascosa *Pioneer* called it the Chicago of the Panhandle. It was filled with Indians, cowboys, nesters, murderers, thieves, fortune tellers, Scottish and Irish noblemen throwing away their inheritance on dusty tracts, Yankees and Confederates playing cards, businessmen, gamblers with high collars and their women, soft and ruffled as bright birds.

Big Joe told Anise how Billy the Kid once came to Tascosa to lose a shooting contest to Sam Houston's son, Temple. At the end of the contest, while Billy the Kid's men lounged in their greasy hats, Temple Houston performed a trick that was ever afterwards known as Temple's cutter. He shot the star out of a plug of navy chewing tobacco tossed in the air from twenty paces.

Billy the Kid said, *"¿Quién lo haya mejor?"* (Who could do better?), kissed Temple on both cheeks and bought him a whiskey with his own hands.

Big Joe told Anise about Dr. Henry F. Hoyt, the first doctor who came to Tascosa. Dr. Hoyt was a man from Minnesota with traveling feet and the blind heart of a mystic.

Dr. Hoyt was one hundred miles away from Tascosa when a Mexican rode up with red and silver trappings on his saddle, leading behind him a fine saddled palomino. He bore for the doctor a message from a wealthy Mexican inhabitant of Tascosa named Casimero Romero.

Casimero Romero's daughter Piedad was the most beautiful girl on the High Plains. She had dark hair burnished with blue, and slanted eyes, with lashes that swept down. Her father never allowed her out of the house, for fear of the cowmen who rode for days to sit under her window. She combed oil through her long black hair and looked in the mirror all day, fogging it with her breath.

Now beautiful Piedad was dying of smallpox, and Casimero Romero offered his fortune to the doctor if he could save her life and her face.

The doctor rode through the night, and arrived at the girl's bedside. The windows were closed, and the room was smoky with incense. Through the girl's sweat, the doctor could see that she had the pale carved face of a Madonna. He fell to his knees to pray that he could save her beauty, and the candles blew out.

Then he opened the windows, cleared the room of anxious relatives, and set to work on the girl.

He bathed her face and cleaned her sores. He packed her body with ice, wagon-drawn across the plains wrapped in straw, and then piled blankets on her until she sweated green fluid out of her pores.

Her face tossed in her long black hair, and he could see the sickness evaporating around her in the dark and rising like swallows. He stayed at her bedside for many days, and fell in love with her while she slept in the fever.

She opened her eyes once, and he took her hands and swore to marry her. She smiled at him and turned on her side, her cheek on one hand, and fell asleep again. When she woke up she found her father had, in gratitude, given her to the doctor to be his wife. Their marriage was the talk of the plains. Her father built them the finest adobe house in Tascosa.

Around this time the editor of the Tascosa *Pioneer* wrote an editorial to advertise the town's wholesome climate, hoping to draw more settlers. He wrote, "Boot Hill burying ground has only two occupants who died unnatural deaths. One of these died from drinking too much whiskey and the other died from not drinking enough."

Big Joe showed Anise the newspaper clipping, and told her that the man who died of too much whiskey shot himself in the foot with delirium tremens, and died of the infection that crept into his blood as he slept propped against the horse trough, the ends of his hair tangling in the green water.

The man who died of not enough whiskey was an Italian fiddler, who was locked in the jailhouse without his bottle. He woke up during the night, and died of shock to find himself sober. They found him in the morning with his eyes wide, his hands curled around an invisible shot glass.

There were two other markers in the Tascosa graveyard on Boot Hill that Big Joe liked to visit, before the town died. One said "Rubein Juice," and the other "Apple Ax."

Rubein Juice was a chuck wagon cook, and such a bad one that the men of the Frying Pan Ranch shot him dead through the heart one morning after breakfast. Apple Ax was his hoodlum, or assistant, and as he stepped out from behind the wagon to avenge his master, he was caught in the cross fire, and shot in seventeen places. He died with biscuit in his mouth and a frying pan clutched in his nonshooting hand.

When the railroad bypassed Tascosa in favor of Amarillo, the town began to die. It died of apathy, of drunkenness and the Texas tick fever, which stopped the trail drives. Mostly the town died of the new barbed-wire fences that were strangling the cattle runs across the plains.

It was a black day when county officials removed the county seat from Tascosa to Vega. Then Dr. Henry F. Hoyt died of a fever and his wife Piedad buried him in the Boot Hill cemetery. She lived on in the crumbling adobe house with a small fox terrier, her ivory profile faded by the glare off the hardpan. Townspeople left gifts of food on her doorstep. Piedad waited steadfastly to join her husband in the afterlife, while the town crumbled around her and the dust blew.

Finally everyone left Tascosa. The buildings cracked and came apart, drying back into the earth under the sun. Only the courthouse stood against the coyotes, with the jail and the burglarproof vault carved from solid stone.

The wind went down the streets, and tore the shutters from the adobe. The hardpan blew, and rubbed the ruts from the road, and covered over the bottles and tins in the yards, until it was all smooth again, like painted glass.

Anise would dream late at night, with her head on a hard pillow pointed to the west, that the voices she heard in the distance were the people of Tascosa, come scudding across the plains in the night to take back their town.

5. The White Buffalo

Big Joe had grown prosperous enough by this time to hire an entire surveying party, though he never found a man as stolid and uncomplaining as Diggory. But the three men he hired to take Diggory's place were all levelheaded men, and good in a pinch.

The point man, Kelly Boothe, who held the mirrors for messaging and rode ahead to plant the flags, carried a rifle. He was the only one of the men who was armed.

The party was riding to the next point when they heard a thrumming sound, a faint throbbing like thunder ahead. They were on the staked plains, and it was summer, when flash floods could come over the dust and take a man, twist his legs back over his shoulders and drown him dead, leaving his hat behind and disappearing without a trace. They stopped to listen.

The noise got louder. Squinting their eyes and looking to the north, they could see what looked like a rain cloud. As they looked, the cloud got bigger, and louder. Kelly Boothe saw it first, and snapped the safety off his rifle. "Buffalo," he said.

The men were standing directly in the path of a buffalo stampede so broad that it spread across the horizon as far as they could see. It swept forward like a cloth for a picnic, like ants thick on a foundered cow. It came toward them with a clean surgical edge, leaving nothing behind but the pulp of mesquite pounded into mats and ground into dust.

Big Joe gave orders. "Single file, behind Kelly Boothe. Hold the horses." They dismounted and formed into a line four men long, each holding his horse and standing slightly in front. They moved with dreamlike slowness, watching the dust boiling towards them.

"Kelly, wait till they get real close. Then shoot," said Big Joe.

They stood in silence, as the herd came on. Soon they could smell the fierce musk carried ahead on the breeze. The noise became louder and louder until it poured around them like cream, making them dizzy, taking their breath. They were near now, near enough to see the legs moving like pistons and gleaming in the sun with sweat, near enough to see the soft red skin in the nostrils and the rough shag of the horns, floating in the flood.

Kelly Boothe readied his rifle. He was having trouble focusing his eyes, and found himself swaying slightly to the thunder of the hooves, watching them come on in a daze.

"Shoot, man," screamed Big Joe, who stood directly behind him. "For Chrissake, shoot!"

Kelly shook his head to clear his gaze and swung his rifle to his shoulder, sighting on the bull directly in front of them, only fifty feet away now. He would have one shot and no time to reload.

He held his breath and shot for the rolling eye. The bull went on with the momentum of his rush until he was only twenty feet away. Then he heeled graciously to them, bending his front legs first, and died on the ground.

The herd parted for his body, parted clean as a comb in dark hair. They stayed parted, exactly the width of the dead bull's body, as they swarmed around the men and their horses, their eyes looking front with the rage of the rush.

The men stood still, holding the horses, who were wild with fear.

They stood silently as the herd surrounded them, screaming and thundering, going on and on. Big Joe turned his eyes up and watched the sun move, feeling the sweat trickle down the back of his neck. He figured later that they stood for two hours in the center of the stampede, until it disappeared behind them.

They stood silently in the aftermath of the rush, breathing deeply and feeling their ears still ringing.

"Hold on, boss," said Kelly. "We're not through yet." Big Joe squinted to see what he saw. Riding towards them, in the wake of the churning dust, was a group of about twenty Indians. They rode wild-caught ponies, and were painted, not for war, but for a religious ceremony. Big Joe knew if Indians from these parts were caught off the reservation, they would be hanged. They weren't likely to take kindly to witnesses.

Kelly reloaded his gun, loud in the silence. The Indians seemed quiet. They rode up until they faced him directly. Big Joe rode forward, to show that he was the leader. The Indian leader, who spoke passable English, told him that they were looking for a white buffalo.

"White buffalo?" Big Joe scratched his head, considering. "I think I saw one in the stampede, just a flash," he said, pointing at the retreating herd. The Indians looked at him quizzically, and said nothing. "It was a big one," Big Joe said, holding his hands apart to show size. "Leading the herd."

The Indian leader looked at him for a long moment, and Big Joe felt the Indian knew he was lying. Then the Indian motioned that Big Joe and his party should go on their way. They rode very slowly to the rise of the next mesa, the skin between their shoulder blades itching as they waited for the rain of arrows. But no arrow came.

When they topped the mesa and were out of sight, all four men whipped their horses with the knotted leather reins and rode as fast as they dared until the horses were lathered and exhausted.

Big Joe had meant to lie to the Indian chief, but strangely enough, he did see a white buffalo that day. It was towards the end of the day, when they were preparing to make camp, and the men had fanned out to find the buffalo dung that they burned for the cooking fire.

The sunset streaked the alkali dirt blood red, and Big Joe crouched by a huge red stone boulder to rest for a minute before he started back to the campsite.

He heard a noise behind the boulder, and climbed cautiously up the side of it to look.

Beneath him was the white buffalo. It looked pink in the light, its rough white coat matted with red dust. It looked up at him and swung its head, shaking the horns as if they weighed heavily. He was mystified by its presence here alone. Thinking back, he realized that the Indians had known, somehow, that the white buffalo would be apart from the herd. He supposed they needed it for some ritual.

He looked in its eyes and saw himself perfectly reflected there, like a fly trapped in amber. Its eye looked mild, like a horse he remembered when he was small, and its breath hissed roughly in and out of its flared nostrils. He had an overwhelming urge to slide from the boulder down onto its back, and ride to where it would take him.

When he looked again, more closely, he saw that the animal's legs trembled with age, or sickness. Its muzzle was frosted with silver hairs that shivered in the light.

It let out a long breathy sigh as he watched, and slid to its knees, bowing its head until its horns pointed directly down at the ground, tracing a pattern in the dirt as it shuddered. It stayed like that, perfectly still, until he saw a ripple run through its body and it stiffened, flinging its tail straight. Then it collapsed on its side, with a wheeze, and lay still. Excrement oozed from its vent, and the flies buzzed suddenly in the silence. A cloud of red dust rose and settled over the white scruff, blending it into the side of the rock.

Big Joe knelt on the top of the rock for a long time after, until the light had faded from the sky and the night came down around him, chilling him. When he rose, his knees were stiff and he was surprised, when he touched his face, to find that it was wet with tears.

That was the first omen of death that night, and later there was another. When he returned to the camp, he said nothing about the white buffalo. All the men were shaken and exhausted from the aftermath of the stampede. The stars were particularly bright over their heads. They broke out a bottle of brandy saved for first aid and drank silently.

Kelly Boothe looked up smiling, about to say something, and then stared into the shadows outside the fire, the smile leaving his face. "There is a man's skull," he said.

They looked, and sure enough, it was a man's skull, studded with thick teeth and still smiling, sitting on the ground just outside the circle of light.

There were three brass buttons lying next to the skull. Big Joe picked it up, examining it closely. He had studied medicine in school, and wasn't afraid. He opened the jawbone and looked inside.

"Perfect teeth. No cavities," he said, "and wisdom teeth intact. Our guest was a young man."

The men laughed, and leaned back into the fire, relieved. Big Joe brought the skull back close to the fire, and turned it in his hand. "From the shape and thickness of the skull, I'd say it was a Negro," he said. "Brass buttons say he was a soldier. Only Negroes around these parts were the soldiers from Fort Concho. General Mackenzie used them to try and chase down Quanah Parker and his tribe back in the seventies."

He looked down a moment more. "They died from thirst, the whole troop," he said. "All the San Angelo boys. This one made it further than the others."

They buried the skull with honor when they left, laying the three brass buttons in the shallow hole, and marking it with a rock.

So Big Joe knew there would be a death, but he didn't know whose it would be. And he was never to know, because what happened next seemed to him at the time like a stroke of great luck.

What happened was this: In the spring of 1925, Big Joe got a call from a businessman in Greenwood, asking him to survey a certain oil-producing area in the neighborhood. He was to look for a "vacancy" in a particular tract, a slice of land that had been incorrectly surveyed earlier. The businessman, whose name was Aaron Henshaw, said that he couldn't afford to pay Big Joe cash for his work, but told him he could have a cut of the oil-producing vacancy, if he found one.

It was a gamble, but business was going well and Big Joe accepted. He easily found the vacancy, and proved it in court. He took his share of the land. It turned out to be part of the Yates Oil Field, one of the richest in the world. When a well was drilled on Big Joe's portion, it blew in at 68,000 gallons per day.

More than sixty years later, that well is still producing. In fact, just after my grandmother Anise's death, the drillers worked through a thin layer of shale, and a whole new load of oil shot up, tripling the well's output and bringing in about $9,000 a month.

Big Joe was pleased. He could leave the well to his children, a legacy that would give them lives of ease, and smooth the way for them. To him, the oil was black, and rich, and good.

To his descendants, that well would mean nothing but corruption, and death. It was found in lost land, never meant to be. It would drive us down that track until we were too far from the light to see. It would twist my grandfather and kill him, and take a price, finally, from us all.

But when Big Joe gave the well to his children, it was in innocence, as a gift. And nothing after that would ever be the same.

6. The Saints

Anise kept growing, and she grew delicate and rigidly pure, like a flower carved from white bone. Big Joe brought her books from his travels when he came home, and she read them. She became paler, and more still. With every year that passed she seemed to resolve into herself.

She had dark, fine hair and large eyes. She was kept from beauty only by her mouth, which was thin and pressed together. But her brows were thin and penciled high, and the skin under her brows had a tender arch, so that she always looked surprised and a little breathless.

She spent much time alone, as the youngest child in the family. Her oldest sister, Cumin, was almost a grown young lady now, and wanted to go to college in Austin. The next-oldest sister, Marjie (for Marjoram), was to go with her—the girls would lodge in a respectable boardinghouse, run by an old friend of Big Mother's from her days in the Ladies Aid. The oldest boy, Frank, had graduated from law school and had established himself as an up-and-coming young lawyer in town. The rest of the children fanned out over the state, making their way as best they could.

When Big Mother had run out of attention for Anise, Cumin had stepped into the breach and provided as much offhand mothering as she was able. She tied ribbons into Anise's braids, and brushed her dark hair, and taught her how to put it up into a smooth bun when Anise was old enough.

Cumin had a starchy way about her—she was well meaning and concerned, but with a cutting edge to her that made people afraid. She was tall and straight-backed, and very particular about the details of her dress. She had great industry and energy, and could fly around a room and make it straight in no time.

She didn't have many beaux, and this was perhaps why she wanted to go to Austin. She was pragmatic and fair-minded, with no illusions on the subject of her own feminine appeal. She knew that to find a husband, she must go where there were plenty of men and not so much competition. The city, not a small town, was the place to do it.

Big Mother was distressed by Cumin's decision, and by her cool resolve to leave. Big Mother's red hair had become more pale and faded every year, and she had grown to depend on Cumin so much that she couldn't think of running the house without her.

Big Mother didn't weep, because she was not a woman who went on about her sorrows. Instead her dismay stimulated her mind and made her think. And although she was a woman of few ideas, she had one now: why should she not go to Austin with the girls and open her own boarding-house? After all, Big Joe traveled so much that he would hardly notice whether his home was in one place or another, and her boardinghouse could be quite a respectable place, with home cooking and preserves that she put up herself.

Big Joe, however, was unexpectedly stubborn in opposing the idea. Amarillo was a town he had laid out himself—he had built his house, every board and timber of it, and he had no intentions of giving it up to live in a crowded city with strange people he didn't know.

The truth was that the recollections of early days in the city with his brother Edgar as a young man, the grinding poverty and the dreadful work, stayed in the back of his mind and gripped him with fear.

After much thought, Big Joe ruled that Big Mother might go to Austin and open the boardinghouse while Cumin and Marjoram were in school, and return after that time was over. The other children had scattered and settled elsewhere, and need not be worried over. Anise could stay with Big Joe in Amarillo and keep house for him in the meantime.

So it was settled, and Big Mother and the two oldest girls left on a Thursday morning in November 1926, driving the family Model T, its high black fenders already smeared with dust. They turned pale faces against the upholstery and waved with hands like dead leaves. Anise and Big Joe watched them until they were out of sight, and then turned silently to go back in the house.

Big Joe soon went away on another trip, leaving behind him a stack of books for Anise. She arose each morning in the unnatural silence, ate breakfast alone and wiped the dishes with only the trickling sound of the water in her ears.

She had never been alone before. There had always been nine children, their friends, their animals, screams and sharp sounds, smothered laughter and feet on the stairs and explosions.

Now she felt panic as the silence closed over her head, as cold and green as glass. She kept the silence at bay as long as she could—tidying the house, running the water, humming hymns until her voice was hoarse.

But the silence followed her from room to room, seeping into her footsteps inevitably as ice, so that she felt she was trudging across a tundra, with each step crushing down the blades of grass beneath her feet so that they would not grow again. She began to move less and less, spending days wrapped in a crocheted afghan on the hearth of the fireplace, reading the books Big Joe had left for her. She ate very little, and slept almost not at all.

One of the books was about the passions of the Catholic saints. She read it in horror and wonder, turning the pages slowly, her eyes fastened on the pale, suffering faces, the bloody weals, the empty and flaccid skin hanging from the hand of the skinned saints. Her own Baptist church, with its honest whitewashed wood and hearty worshippers in their best bonnets, was nothing like this.

She came on one picture of a female saint, who leaned back against the ledge of a window, her back arched and one leg drawn up, her pale beautiful face transfixed with ecstasy. Anise stared at the soft folds of the cowl that surrounded the saint's face.

Staring into the mirror, she arranged the folds of her afghan the same way, and tilted back her head at the same angle, peering from under half-closed eyes to see. Yes, she thought, she looked a little like that woman—very pale skin and eyes invaded by darkened, swollen pupils.

She looked at a photograph of a Catholic church that was far away somewhere, on the other side of the world. The dark soaring pinnacles of stone and flaming tints of glass seemed to her the very colors of the Lord.

When she closed her eyes she could see the same colors imprinted on the back of her eyelids. They surged and flared before her eyes. She felt suddenly that she was falling, and she cried out and reached out her hands, but they met only air.

And then she felt that she was falling through the darkness, falling past all the things that she knew into a seamless black void where no light had ever been.

And the void was filled with screaming. It was the howling of the saints with blood running down their pale faces, their tongues like crystal and their suffering eyes turned up in misery. And then the saints became all the stenches and hungers of the world and she felt that she was looking down the shaft of an endless well with the rime of old dampness on the walls, and roiling below her were all the wicked and evil thoughts she had ever had, the hatred of her mother and the anger at her sister, all the hot and wicked thoughts that visited her alone when she touched herself in her narrow bed at night. With fingers like knives the saints waited for her to fall into their embrace. The screaming went on and on, until she realized that it was her own screaming.

And then her downward rush was suddenly caught, and held, and a voice said to her out of the darkness, "You must not fall."

And she sobbed with relief, and opened her eyes to see the familiar things of her own house, and promised the voice that whatever happened, she would not fall. She promised it that no wicked thoughts would ever enter her mind, that she would keep her eyes forever fixed on the good things, and the light, that she would keep herself pure of the blackness that churned there at the edge of her soul, only waiting for her once to slip.

When Big Joe came in the door from his trip he found Anise curled on the hearth. At first he thought that she was sleeping, but when he looked closer he realized that she was in a dead faint, her face and hands so white that he felt he could almost see the floor through them. He wondered how long she had been there. The house was cold and dark, and he was suddenly afraid. He pulled her up into his lap, rubbing her hands and looking into her face anxiously. "Anise?" he said. There was no answer.

He laid her back down gently and went to fetch the smelling salts that Big Mother always kept in the linen closet for just such an emergency. He waved them under her nose, and was relieved when she opened her eyes and coughed.

"Daddy," she said, smiling up into his face. "The saints came here."

Alarmed, he looked around. "There's nobody here, angel," he said. "Just you and me. Now let's get you to bed."

Big Joe picked her up to carry her into her bedroom, and was shocked to see how light she was. She must not have eaten for days. He looked around the empty house as he trudged up the stairs, and felt remorse. He should never have left her here all alone, such a young girl. She took impressions like the silver papers the photographers used. Heaven knows what dreams she must have had, what things stroked cold fingers down her spine. He would take her to Austin. He had been wrong.

Big Mother and the girls welcomed them to Austin with open arms, though they secretly wondered what had come over Anise. She was thin, with the bones of her hands standing out, and terribly pale. She was determinedly cheerful, never mentioning or, for all they knew, even having a dark thought, speaking only good words and reporting problems only after they had been solved, to celebrate. When before she would have argued or been angry, she only pressed her lips together in a thinner line and left the room.

"Heaven help us, she's become a saint," said Cumin to Marjie. Marjie threw her hands up.

"I liked her better before," she said. "Surely she can't be like that forever. She'll explode."

But Cumin only pursed her lips, and looked thoughtful.

As Anise regained her strength she began to paint and draw a little, as she had done before, but mostly she read. She had become fascinated with the Bible, and with all religious books. She read the works of Mary Baker Eddy, and the stories of the Mormons, everything she could find. She turned the pages slowly, reading intently, holding in her breath.

"It's not normal," Big Mother fussed to Big Joe. "A child her age should have better things to do than hang about reading books all day."

"Send her to college with Cumin and Marjie," he suggested. "She's bright for her age. It would get her out of the house, at any rate."

Big Joe himself was feeling restless. His sensibilities were offended by the ugly lodging house with its big dark beams, by the smell of cooked cabbage that permeated the place, by the movement of foreign people and the cries of strange children.

He absented himself with the excuse of work, and spent longer and longer hours in his office, sharpening his pencils to fine points and tracing them over the maps of towns he had designed. The fragile sweep of the land that had first shocked open his eyes had been fenced and trampled now until there was not much left. But it stayed in his mind, the burned roll of it. If he tipped his head back, closed his eyes and put his boots up on the edge of his heavy brown desk, he could see it still. His partner found him that way more and more often.

7. Dirt Farms

My grandfather's second wife was named Francine. She was a strawberry blonde, with soft hair such an unusual shade of pink that when it was piled on her head it looked like cotton candy. She was very vain about it, and when in later years it started to dim, she had it dyed back to its original brilliance.

She had green eyes, and a charm that mystified those who didn't know her, as well as those who did. Her face was pale, with a long, narrow slant, and she had an odd habit of tipping her face to the side and laying a hand along her jaw.

She was the daughter of a dirt farmer who ran a hundred head of starved cattle on his ranch—sad creatures with ribs showing through their lank hair and large, mournful eyes.

Francine remembered her mother fighting the endless red dust that soaked in through the windows and cracks in the doors to cover the floors and the chairs. The dust lay in lines along the dishes like the marks of the tide, and blew to pile softly into the corners of the house. Her mother walked the rooms in a stained blue apron and slippers, weeping slow tears and wiping uselessly at the dirt that stirred whenever the wind blew.

In bad years, when the cattle died of the tick fever and the wasting disease, and the alfalfa rotted standing in the fields, the neighbor from the next ranch over would bring them crates of canned food and discarded clothing, silently unloading the boxes from his cart onto their stoop.

The neighbor's wife was a city girl, who affected long lavender dresses with ruffled cuffs and shiny taffeta silks. She read fashion magazines, and always tucked a few into the bottom of the charity cartons. The magazines were yellowed with age and marked with wet, the corners turned down.

Francine wore the absurd lavender dresses because there was nothing else for her to wear. They dragged the ground behind her. She would roll the long sleeves up above her elbows and carry the magazines back to her room, where she read them carefully, lying on her stomach with her feet kicking the air slowly, her head propped in her hands, her green eyes thoughtful.

She was a long way from the girls in the magazines, she could see that. She stood up and walked to the mirror. She saw the ridiculous gown and ripped it off impatiently. She stood naked, looking at her reflection critically.

Her shoulders were broad, and she was tall for her age. She had narrow hips and almost no bosom. Her hands were awkward, and too large.

But her hair was good—bright and soft. She put her hands under it and piled it up on her head, looking at herself sideways. Her eyes were pale, but there was an angular slant to her jawbone a little like the girls in the magazine. It wasn't much to escape with. She would just have to do the best she could with what she had.

When her family went to church that Sunday, Francine dressed carefully. She didn't have stockings, but she draped a piece of cheesecloth around her shoulders and tied it in front over her dress, so that it framed her face, and wore her best hat.

The preacher, Jed Net, was a young man with black hair and blue eyes, ruddy skin and a wide, infectious grin. He had come to the church only two months before, fresh from the seminary.

Francine watched the preacher as he gave his sermon that day, gesturing with energetic sweeps of his arms, his shoulders straining under the cheap suit like those of a football player. He was different from her father, who sat next to her caved in on himself, holding his hat in his lap, his face carved by the weather into lines of submission.

The preacher was powerful, persuasive. She could see it from where she sat. The world would make a place for him, and his wife. She suddenly felt dizzy, and she put a hand on her ribs. Then she sat up very straight, opened up her eyes wide, and listened intently to the rest of the sermon.

The preacher looked over his flock that day, his eyes scanning the pews as he talked. He tallied absences in his mind. Mrs. Matthews was gone again—she had the wasting disease and he would have to visit her after the service, taking a covered dish from the Ladies Aid table and the comfort of the Word. She was always so thankful when he came, holding his arm with her hands, her eyes starting out of her poor withered face.

Jed hated and feared illness with superstitious terror. He himself was possessed of a vigorous animal health and excellent digestion. He had played football in college, and ran the ball down the field with the same dedication with which he saved the fallen. He could suffer smiling through almost any trial, in fact, except the odors of a sickroom. The fact that his chosen profession required him to spend much of his time in sickrooms was an irony that escaped him. He was an earnest man, and firmly suppressed his squeamishness in order to minister to his flock. He bore the shrinking of his skin as a personal scourge.

He noticed the Williams girl in the third pew today, sitting quietly next to her bowed father and her mother, who was, as usual, wiping away seeping tears with her pocket handkerchief.

His eyes came back to the girl. She was sitting up very straight, trying hard to pay attention. She had some ridiculous rag tied around her —perhaps he should ask the Ladies Aid to take up a fund for the family. It had been a bad year for them, he knew.

His eyes rested on her smooth upturned face, and something stirred in him. She was very young, not more than seventeen. Just a child. Lately he had begun to turn his mind to the problem of finding a wife. An unmarried preacher could be a lightning rod for gossip in the small towns, and a woman with a strong back and a willing hand would be a welcome addition to his ministry.

This girl, though—she was too young, and certainly not wise enough to be the helpmeet of a preacher, with all the sacrifice that entailed. He brought his mind back to the service, and lifted his hand. There was a rustle as the congregation stood to sing the final hymn.

"Number twenty-nine, please, 'Jesus, Lover of My Soul,' " he said, and wiped the back of his hand across his forehead. He was sweating.

After the service, he stood at the door to shake hands and smile into the faces of the congregation, promising visits and prayers for the needy. When almost everyone had gone, he noticed Mrs. Williams standing nearby, crumpling her handkerchief into her hand. Her eyes were red and her face puffy.

"Reverend Net, we'd be most honored if you'd come to take dinner with us this afternoon," she said, snuffling a little. "We've got some new veal and I made the potato fritters that you like so."

He smiled and grasped for a polite excuse, his mind sorting through the things yet to be done that afternoon. Then his eyes fell on Francine standing just behind and to the left of her mother, her eyes on the floor. He saw the graceful droop of her neck, and the rounding of her young breasts at the front of her dress. He was startled to hear himself say, "Well, now, I'd be proud to dine with you today, Mrs. Williams. How kind of you to think of me."

Francine looked up at the sound of his voice and her cat-green eyes fixed on his face. She smiled, a warm, tilted smile that lit her angular face and made her suddenly beautiful. He felt himself flush, and composed himself with an effort. Ridiculous. Just a child. Her mother was still talking to him.

". . . and we'll be ready for you about then, is that all right?"

"That'll be just fine," he said. "Fiveish?"

"Well, sure, if you like," she said, looking surprised, "but I thought we said six o'clock."

"Of course, that's what I meant," he said, turning his charming smile on her. "Of course, six o'clock. I'll be there."

At the time of Francine's wedding it was discovered that two black cats had made a nest in the back of her father's old broken-down truck, and had a litter of kittens. Her mother considered it a good omen, and wept for joy. Francine wondered.

She was very beautiful coming down the aisle of the tiny old church, her sugar-red hair piled high and her green-gilt eyes glittering. She would leave this place, and she would never come back. She shook the red dust daintily off her white satin wedding pumps, got in the car with Jed Net and drove away to the city. She waved goodbye as her mother wept, growing smaller and smaller in the rear window and finally vanishing altogether.

Under Francine's urging Jed had agreed to give up his small church and apply for something that would be more fitting for an ambitious career. She caressed him with her soft voice and white hands. He promised to speak to the church official.

With Francine sitting next to him demurely in a blue dress that exactly set off her bubble-gum hair, the church official found himself agreeing to all kinds of proposals. He promised Jed a church in Austin, a small place, but one that was certainly on its way up. Things were happening there. Francine thanked him, and gave him her hand with lowered eyes.

The church official wondered why he had never seen before just how promising young Net was, with his dark hair and blue eyes and penetrating, spiritual gaze. And the young wife was extraordinary.

Francine was jubilant on the ride home. "Won't it be wonderful, Jed?" she said, curling up next to him and squeezing his arm. "Your own church, right in a town that's on its way up, with all kinds of people to come to it. And I'm going to help you so much, you'll see."

Jed nodded, his eyes on the road as they bumped along, his mind already busy with the strands to weave, the net cast to catch those foundering souls who had drifted out of reach of the Word. There would be so much work to do in a new church, so many hands to shake, so many patients to pray over, so much loyalty to win. He realized with a start that Francine was speaking to him.

". . . And in the winter I thought we could entertain a little, just a little, just for people in the church, don't you think?" Her voice faltered when she saw he wasn't listening. "Jed?"

"Yes indeed, honey," he said, turning his smile on her. "That would be just fine."

When they had settled into their new house, Jed gave Francine a white dove that he had found injured by the side of the road. It had soft, downy feathers and round eyes. She called it Baby. She nursed it carefully, binding the wing with strips of cotton towel. Jed showed her how to splint it straight with a tiny stick of shaved kindling. She fed it broth and soaked bread.

The bird became very tame and ate from Francine's hand, leaning its head against her leg, and arching its neck to be scratched. When Francine wandered through the empty rooms of the new house, she took Baby with her in a fold of her apron, with only his two eyes showing out of the pocket.

On long evenings when Jed was out tending to church business or sitting up with the ill or the dying, Baby sat on Francine's shoulder as she sewed or tried to read a book. The noises around the house were strange and unfamiliar. The trees scritched against the planks of the house, with a shrill hissing sound that made her sit straight up. The hollowness of the house spread out in front of her like a pool of tar, and retreated as she shone the lamp around the room.

She tried to be patient and brave, to be worthy of Jed, who was out doing the work of the Lord. But she was seventeen, and her foot tapped on the floor to an invisible dance tune, and inside her head the lights were brighter than anything she had ever seen. She smiled politely when the Ladies Aid Society came to tea, casting their curious sideways eyes around the room and running their glances under the sofa for dust.

They carried the tale away with them that "the new preacher's wife is only a child, and a little slatternly at that. She has hair like a new penny. It's plain to see the preacher dotes on her, but I don't know—she don't seem practical to me, somehow."

Some curious and some sympathetic, the Ladies came with casseroles and tea cozies. They tried to make her at home, but their prying ways made her nervous and unsure. She wasn't accustomed to belonging to people as she did here.

Jed lived on a stipend provided by the congregation, and the good Ladies considered that his square, ugly house belonged to them. They poked through dresser drawers, handled silver without shame and criticized freely anything that they considered "undue expense" in Jed's lifestyle, until Francine thought that she would go mad and chase herself around in a circle like a dog until she died.

"Jed, honestly," she complained one day, "Mrs. Jimpson has been harping on me for wanting to buy new china when she knows very well that we only have four cups and three saucers, and what am I supposed to serve with when the whole Society comes over at once? Now honestly, Jed, do you think I'm extravagant?" She made her eyes wide and smiled at him in a way she had.

But he was on his way to a meeting with the deacons, and he only kissed the side of her forehead absently and said, "I'm sure it will all be fine, sweetheart." The sound of the door slamming behind him made her feel hollow inside.

She went into the bedroom and lay down full length on the bed, even though she had just made it and her shoes were getting dust on the eiderdown, and cried. Then she combed her hair and blew her nose, and had a long talk with Baby. She carried him around the house with her, although she hid him in a box whenever she heard the doorbell. His round eyes forgave all her troubles. He would lift one wing and spread it over her shoulder while she buried her nose in his feathers. He smelled of sweet grain, and the carrot tops she fed him.

"Baby," she said, "nobody tells me nothing. I mean, anything," she corrected herself. Jed was always nagging her to mend her grammar. She missed other girls her age. At home, although her friends had been few, there had been other girls to laugh and talk with. Here she was isolated as the preacher's wife, and no one ever gossiped with her or told her things, for fear of darkening their neighbor's reputation with the preacher.

She only heard the stories in the case of congregational disputes brought to Jed to settle, and then he kept the details from her for fear of making her coarse. She learned to multiply the little hints that anyone gave her into a full story, and became adept at reading between the lines. She longed to walk outside sometimes and plow her feet into the dust, or

make a noise, bang her pot lids together, anything. She thought sometimes she would go mad.

Francine was pruning the one rose bush she had planted, with Baby
tucked into her apron and making soft sounds, when the dogs began
prowling close to her. They were huge, bony dogs with foul breaths and
hanging mouths. She hated them, but Jed had grown up with dogs and
said they were necessary to keep the house secure, since it was God's
property that he was protecting.

One dog came up to her and sniffed at her apron pocket, where Baby
was. She could see the yellow roll of the dog's eye, and wondered if Jed had
fed it that morning. She looked for Jed, and could see his silhouette in the
window. He was having an important meeting with a church official, and
shouldn't be disturbed, she knew.

The dog pawed the ground and whined softly, thrusting its nose
harder against her apron pocket. Baby chirped with alarm, and she spread
her hands across her apron to distract the dog, kicking out at it to make it
go away. The plain gold band of her wedding ring caught the light, and she
watched the puffs of dust kicked up by the other dog as it trotted towards
them.

The second dog nudged at her elbow and then snapped at the air. She
jumped, and tried to push it away. But it leaned against her hand and
didn't move, setting its weight against her. Both dogs were standing now
between her and the door, and she measured the distance with her eyes.
She heard a low growl and looked down. The first dog had its nose almost
in her apron pocket now, and was voicing long, low sounds that edged
along her spine. Baby was cowering in the bottom of the pocket, and the
dog snapped at him, its jaws closing on a tail feather. Baby shrilled in
alarm.

Francine scooped him out of the pocket and stood with him cradled
against her chest, one arm wrapped around him protectively. She started
to walk towards the house. But one of the dogs stood squarely in her path
and growled more loudly, baring its teeth in a snarl, its head hanging down
between its shoulders. Slaver fell from its mouth to the ground, and she
wondered if it was mad. Each time she tried to move, the growls rose to a
bark, and it lunged in place, holding her where she was.

She felt the skin around her eyes grow tight with tears of frustration.

It was too absurd, that she was penned in here, her own yard, by these dogs. She looked with increasing anxiety towards the closed window where she could see Jed's dark profile, his hands steepled, index finger pressed against his full red lower lip. She saw him nod his head once, gravely.

Suddenly one of the dogs crossed to where she was standing and leapt up so that its teeth closed just underneath where she was holding Baby. She kicked at it and it fell back, with a snarl, and then leapt again. She held Baby up above her head now, as both dogs came at her, leaping and throwing the weight of their bodies against her as she turned and turned, trying to keep them both in view. The decayed breath of the dogs hit her face in waves as they leapt past her, and she heard herself scream, from far away.

She turned to run into the house towards Jed, but one of the dogs dashed in front of her and she fell full length into the dirt. She felt herself moving very slowly, as though she was under water. She watched as Baby fell gently from her outstretched hands. The muzzle of the dog dipped down toward Baby. There was a crunching sound and the muzzle rose again, glistening.

She screamed and crawled towards Baby. He was still alive, she could see, and his round eye was looking at her, his white feathers soaked with blood, and the jaws of the dog closed around him and shook him, so that drops of the blood flew towards Francine and spattered down her white housedress with the blue flowers, spotting the dust on her face.

The dog trotted away with Baby in its mouth, and Francine lay in the dirt, completely motionless. She felt the heat of the sun beating down on her thin dress, and a slight breeze lifted the edges of her hair. She couldn't see Jed's face in the window. All she could see was the ground next to her eyes, which had two small grey rocks and a black ant that labored to move a piece of something. She stared at it until it blurred in front of her eyes.

Jed stood up, rubbing his hands together. It had been a good meeting. He was hungry, and called to Francine, but there was no answer. He wondered where she was, and what had happened to delay dinner.

He would have to speak to her about the punctuality of meals. He had married her thinking that he could have a hand in her formation, and bring her up to be the kind of wife a successful preacher needed. But he had little time for training lately, and he feared she felt the loss of a firm hand, so far from home.

He wondered for the first time if she was homesick here, and was suddenly struck with guilt. He had been so busy, and hadn't even thought to ask if she was happy. She had been looking pale, now that he thought of it.

When he didn't find her on a quick tour of the house, he looked out the window to see if she had gone out to prune the rose bush. He saw a still white figure lying in the dust. He ran outside, and dropped to his knees beside her.

"Francine, honey," he said urgently, "are you all right?"

Her face was bloodless, he saw, and her eyes were rolled up into her head until they showed a sliver of white, like an egg. He stifled a feeling of revulsion, and cradled her head on his arm, trying to feel for a pulse. Had she fainted? Was she expecting, and hadn't told him, or was it a woman's complaint? He knew nothing of such things.

He noticed her dress was spattered with blood, and that blood dotted the dead white of her skin. She was like a wild woman out here, lying in the dust and covered with blood. He looked around quickly to see if any of the neighbors were looking out of their windows, but saw only blank glass. He gathered her up into his arms with a grunt—she was surprisingly heavy, for such a thin girl—and took her into the house.

He laid her on the bed, took off her shoes and bathed her hands and face. Not knowing what else to do, he sat in a chair and opened the Bible at random and began to read aloud from Micah 3:1.

"And I said: Hear you heads of Jacob and rulers of the house of Israel! Is it not for you to know justice?—you who hate the good and love the evil, who tear the skin from off my people, and their flesh from off their bones; who eat the flesh of my people, and flay their skin from off them, and break their bones in pieces, and chop them up, like meat in a kettle, like flesh in a cauldron. Then they will cry to the Lord . . ."

Francine opened her eyes. "Please don't read any more," she said. Her voice was perfectly calm, as if she had only been resting.

He hurried over to the side of the bed.

"Sweetheart, are you all right? What happened to you out there?"

"Nothing," she said.

"Nothing? Why were you lying there? Did you trip? Did you faint?"

"Yes, I tripped," she told him, and watched the lines in his forehead relax.

Her eyes were glittering strangely, although her voice was very flat. He wondered if she was quite stable, and made a mental note to check into the possible existence of emotional illness in her family. She was flushed, and her breathing seemed harsh in the stillness.

He stroked her bright hair as it lay spread out on the pillow, noticing with distaste that it was streaked with dust.

"You just rest now," he said, shifting nervously on the bed. "Will you do that for me?"

She nodded. "Would you stay home tonight, Jed? I—" She looked up, and licked her lips. "I would like it."

He withdrew his hand gently. "You know I'd like nothing better, but Mrs. Phelps has asked me to come and sit by Mr. Phelps's bedside tonight. He's not long for this world, she said, and I feel I must be there. You do understand, don't you?"

She nodded again. Her eyes looked peculiarly flat, like two stones.

"That's my girl." He drew the covers gently up to her chin, and left her.

Francine lay very still, and finally she slept. She dreamed that she was walking through a deep forest, where the trees sprang up green and rough along the path, and her footsteps kicked up piles of needles. The sky was as blue as when she was a child, with only the tiniest pieces of cloud floating through. She walked and walked, and gradually the light faded until the air was dark.

She walked until she came to a house in a clearing, ringed with red rock. The house was grey, of stone and faded wood. She knocked on the door, to ask for a pinch of lemon peel. The door opened, showing a slice of the blackest dark that she had ever seen.

Swimming up out of the dark like a fish was a face that looked familiar to her. It was the twisted, misshapen face of a woman at least a hundred years old. When Francine looked closer, uncertain, she saw that it was her own face, her hair faded to a burnt orange, her eyes bitter and watchful, her skin wrinkled as crags and hanging from her bones like washing, all alone.

The face looked at her, its eyes widening for a moment, mocking her own. Then it laughed, and laughed, throwing back its head so that its hair fell down its back, long brays of laughter that bared the thing's yellow teeth like ankle bones in the dimness. It laughed and laughed, as if she was the funniest thing it had ever seen in a hundred years of fearsome loneliness.

When she looked down, she saw that the figure was wearing grave clothes, a long white gown that fell to the ground in ripped shafts. Trimming the gown were white feathers, all crusted in dried blood, drifting in the air behind the figure and floating before it, pinned in a single dusty shaft of light so that she felt she could see the interlocking barbs of each feather. She saw that the dress was her own wedding dress, which she had wrapped carefully in tissue paper and laid in an attic drawer. Blood marked it and was smeared down the front of it like a baptism.

The figure brought one hand out from behind its back, and slowly opened up its hand. The fingers were stuck together with something dark.

"Is this what you wanted?" it said to her, struggling to open its fingers.

The fingers opened and Francine saw the body of Baby lying crushed there, with bones showing, the round eyes still looking trustingly up at her through the matted feathers. "Is this what you lost?"

Francine opened her mouth to scream, and the thing brought up its other hand to her face. She saw that its hand was only bones.

"Fool," said the figure. "Feel nothing." It reached up to touch her cheek and instead of stopping at her skin, the thing pointed its long finger bone at her and pushed it right through into her jaw.

She woke screaming, her pillow wet and her jaw aching. Jed was still gone. She lit a candle and crept to the mirror to look at her face there, tilting it until the wax dripped down and burnt her fingers, trying to see that awful figure in her face, in the gathering flesh underneath her chin, the lines beside her eyes, the teeth she thought might be yellowing ever so slightly.

At some moments she could only see her own familiar face, and she knew that she was being foolish. But at other moments the ancient face was there as well, horridly real, lying in the planes just underneath hers. She thought that if she sifted through she would find it like lead under her skin, waiting to poke through. When she woke in the morning her eyes were ringed, and her cheek was swollen and hot. When Jed came home he was alarmed to see her looking so ill, and he called the doctor.

The doctor proclaimed that she had an abscess in her gum, and he lanced and drained it, and pulled the infected tooth. The slight hollow that it left in her cheek made her look more than ever like the figure in her dream, and she dreaded going to sleep at night lest she should see that lonesome face again.

8. Swimming the Flood

After the night that the Indian girl brought her unborn child to the house, Hiram's family left him strictly alone. Lee looked at Hiram sometimes with a blank stare that made him uneasy. She remembered the empty feeling she had when she carried him inside her. Sometimes when she looked at him, she saw her own death.

"People are fools," she told him once, in a rare moment of confidence. She stroked the russet head of the hound at her knee, and looked sharply up at her son. "They'll try to make a fool out of you. See that you fool them first."

Wester became more abstracted and drawn into the miracles he created with tiny lights and electrical cogs. He would disappear into his workroom sometimes and work through dinner. His business, oddly enough, prospered without his intervention and he gave Hiram contracting assignments to complete on his own, sales calls to make and complicated deals of shipments, pipes and supplies to arrange.

Sometimes Hiram went ahead to ready a work site, or lay in a detail of tools that would be needed on the building job. He was still green, but he had an uncanny knack of making the right things turn up at the right time.

He had become a laughing young man, with something hard in him, and an ebullient charm that drew people. He was a fence leaper and a car racer. As he grew older he cultivated the look of a scoundrel. He favored finely cut jackets and crushed fedoras, slanted down over one quizzical eyebrow. He blacked his shoes with printer's ink, and buffed them to a high shine with a special rag every night before he went to sleep. His ears stuck out a little.

He dismissed schooling as irrelevant. His closest friend was named Fid, a tall and lanky, laconically silent boy. The two traveled in Hiram's black low-slung car with the swelling wheel wells. It was a company car— Wester and Hiram were contracting for Conoco at the time.

Hiram and Fid spent much of their time in the car, whistling, riding the roads. The wind from the open window tossed Hiram's black hair. They chewed on straws and thumped on the sides of the car, keeping time with tunes in their heads, heading for the next town.

In September they were stationed in a tiny town outside Austin, settling contracts for a new filling station. It was hot and dusty, with a buzz of cicadas over the fields, burned gold and smelling sweet. There was a dance in town that night, at the University of Texas. They both had dates.

Hiram was taking a girl he knew, Helen, a brassy blonde who wore dresses that came down tight over her breasts, with a way of cocking her head to one side that Hiram found charming. Fid was taking a new girl, whom he had met at the library.

Hiram and Fid knocked off work and drove back, powdered with dust, to the room they rented together. It was a small furnished one, with striped wallpaper hanging discolored on the walls. Fid went to shave again —his hair was dark and showed on his skin in the afternoon. Hiram rolled back his sleeves and washed in the basin.

"So who's the girl?" he said, wetting his hair until it stood up in points. "Do I know her?"

Fid smiled his rare slow smile through the shaving cream, and twirled the brush on his chin. "Not your type at all. Very quiet. Dark-haired. Thin, a little young."

"What's her name?" said Hiram. He leapfrogged over the bed and jogged his friend's elbow so that the shaving brush stuck in his ear. "Something you're not telling me."

Fid took a swipe at him.

"No mystery. Name's Anise. Like the spice. And stay out of my cologne," he warned.

But Hiram was already dosing his hair with the cologne. He stuck a stick of gum in his mouth and dodged his friend's heavy hand, out the door into the stairwell, singing "Darlin' Anise" to the tune of "Clementine."

They were late, and Hiram drove too fast, waving and shouting greetings to townspeople they passed. They left the town limits and drove into the green and sagebrush country on the outskirts, the road wrinkling under them as they went. Austin was twenty miles away, a long drive, part of it over a bridged gully.

As they neared the gully they heard a wet rushing sound, a booming under wood like thunder. Hiram stopped the car a few feet from the bridge. The usually dry creek bed was filled with water the color of dark beer, foaming on top with sticks and debris. The midsection of the bridge was missing, so that the planks on either side gaped with a hole like a pulled tooth. The water spit through the gap, making the boards there slick and dark.

Hiram was already out of the car and walking up to the creek bed, his eyes squinting. He held up a thumb for measure. Fid waited in the car.

Hiram got back in, bringing a waft of cologne with him. He grinned into Fid's eyes. "I figure we can make it easy. The gap can't be much better than three feet, and if we're going at top speed, we'll jump it like it wasn't there."

Fid sighed heavily, slumped down into his seat, braced his feet up against the dashboard and pulled his hat down so that it covered his eyes.

Hiram backed the car, his forearm braced against the passenger-side seat, carefully avoiding the ruts in the road. He backed until the bridge was barely visible, then let the car run while he cracked his knuckles and looked at Fid, who was still slumped with his hat pulled down.

"Want to drive, doc?" he said, and cracked his gum. Fid just moaned.

"Here we go, then," Hiram said, and gunned the engine. The car gathered speed as it bumped down the road. Hiram whooped, and ran the car at the bridge. The car strained, and lifted, and for a wrenchingly bad moment

Fid felt the road fall away from under it. Then it came back down on the other side of the bridge with a thump. Fid sat up and pushed his hat back. He was pale and sweating.

"You okay, doc?" Hiram said. Fid punched him on the shoulder, hard, then adjusted his hat. They grinned at each other and drove off down the road, whistling. Hiram put another stick of gum in his mouth.

Helen met them at the soda shop, as always. Her father didn't approve of Hiram's arched eyebrow and natty suits, sensing that he was a trouble-maker.

Helen's dress was a shade of blue that exactly matched her eyes, and nipped in to a tiny waist. The bright gold of her hair curled under a new hat with a dyed feather. She stood at the corner, oblivious of the cloud of dust that the car raised as it stopped suddenly in front of her.

Hiram jumped out and bowed, doffing his hat gallantly as she giggled and picked her way around to the passenger side. She waited for Hiram to help her into the car. Hiram opened the door and glared at Fid, who glared back.

Finally Fid got out of the front seat and climbed, grumbling, into the back. Helen slid into the seat with a triumphant air and a smell of lilac. She came as close as she dared to Hiram and slid her arm under his. Fid directed them through town until they stopped at a lodging house, a respectable-looking building with heavy dark shutters and a carefully planted flower garden outside.

Fid got out and rang the doorbell. It was answered by an older gen-tleman, very short, with white hair and mustachios that leapt on his face like fish, making him look surprised. He had level eyebrows, wind-burned skin and a stern, steady stare. He looked up at Fid. Fid shifted uncomfort-ably, introduced himself and stuck out his hand.

The white-haired man asked him a few brusque questions, which were apparently answered to his satisfaction. He stepped back and a girl came through into the early-evening light.

She was dressed all in white. Her hair was soft and dark, bobbed short to her head, and she tilted her chin up. Her shoulders were thin but she held them straight. There came from her an almost aggressive purity. It was in her slim ankles and wrists, in the unforgiving arch of her eyebrows, and her stern mouth. There was something very much like Lee in her, Hiram thought, and shuddered to see it.

Fid handed her into the car and they drove to the dance without saying much. Helen snuggled close to Hiram in the car, and he felt her breasts brushing his arm as if by accident. She suddenly looked cheap and coarse to him.

He could feel the girl in the back, Anise, as if she carried with her a cold cloud. He thought for some reason of his mother's breath, scented by the fennel she chewed. They pulled up in front of the college gymnasium and the girls and Fid got out. Warm pink light came from the cracks of the brick building, and noise.

Hiram parked the car and walked back to meet them, the two veins by his temples pounding with the beginnings of a migraine. He was feeling very strange, almost dazed. Helen took his arm and they walked in to the dance, leaning over to greet friends with high squeals that made his head hurt. Anise and Fid disappeared into the crowd.

As soon as Hiram could decently rid himself of Helen he did so, and went into the back room, where the boys were passing bottles of thin brown liquid. He hesitated, knowing that the rotgut was flavored with tanning acid, but the pounding in his temples was getting louder, and there was no chance now of getting back home for his painkillers.

The boys welcomed him—some of them he knew from the Conoco building site—and someone put a paper cup into his hand. He tilted his head and drank it quickly, feeling the acidic burn of it down to his groin. He drank another one, and another, and the pounding began to subside, and he sat back to enjoy the party.

He shot a game of snooker, and went dutifully to dance with Helen, who was pouting and looking neglected. Her curls had wilted and were stringing across her back. He surrendered her when someone came to cut in, and left her looking at him over her partner's back, her eyes faithful as a dog's.

In the back room now they were laying out hands of cards, chewing cigars, acting like old dandies and looking foolish, with their hair pushed wet off their bright, soft faces. Hiram looked around and felt revulsion, but he sat down, pulling out a straight-backed chair with a red velvet seat. A boy was at the door, watching the dancers and making remarks.

"There's Fid! He's got a live one," he said, opening the door a crack further. "I'd like to get a hand around her."

Hiram came to the door and looked out over his shoulder. He saw Anise, her face lit in the faint pink of the air, looking up at Fid and laughing, her white dress floating around her like snow. He thought she should be somewhere else, and not in this place.

He turned back to sit down. The boy at the door said, still watching, "Tits like fruit. I bet Fid gets those legs apart tonight." Hiram leapt from where he was, across the room, making a thin noise in his throat. He landed on the boy with his arm locked around his neck, bringing him down onto the table, sliding cards and smashing bottles onto the floor.

The boy lay stunned for a moment, his eyes popping. Then he started trying to take Hiram's hands from around his neck. Finally he managed a short jab into Hiram's stomach, and Hiram let go of his neck and began to beat him, rhythmically and scientifically. He beat him until the boy lay still, and blood ran from a corner of the boy's mouth. A teacher rushed in and seized Hiram, pulling him up roughly. The boy opened his eyes and wiped blood from his mouth stupidly, looking at Hiram as the teacher held him back.

"Why'd you do that?" the boy said. But Hiram only shook his head and looked away. The teacher, a dark-haired man with a thick mustache, let go of him with a shake.

"Look at you, the both of you. What's going on here? You got liquor here? The headmaster's going to hear about this. And you," he said, looking at Hiram, "I don't remember your face from school. If you're an outsider, I better never see you around these parts again, understand me?"

Hiram shrugged him off easily and held a hand out to the boy, who was still lying on the floor. He pulled the boy to his feet and wrapped his arm around his shoulder.

"Let's go," he said, half carrying, half dragging the boy.

They went out of the room that way, and the dance fell quiet to look at them as they passed, pale and spattered with blood. The boy's feet made a hissing sound on the ground, over the tinsel.

Anise looked up and saw them coming out of the dark doorway. She thought that Hiram looked for her and held her eyes as he came out, dragging the boy with him like a crucifixion. She shivered, feeling something on her spine. Fid's friend was drunk, she speculated, from the flush on his thin cheeks and the way his hair was disordered. But he had saved a boy, maybe from a bully. She smiled at him.

Hiram, under the burden of the boy, saw the smile. His face went very still. Then he smiled back at her, just for a minute, a crooked, charming smile that made his eyes squint.

Fid looked down and saw the attention in Anise's eyes, and followed her gaze to Hiram's face. Fid's arms were still around Anise, where they had been arrested in the dance. He felt that her body was moving away from him, that she was receding faster and faster until he could hardly see her. He let his arms fall away from her. She didn't notice.

Hiram caught Fid's eyes then, and jerked his chin toward the door. Fid and Anise left the dance floor and moved toward the door obediently. Helen came out of the crowd, her eyes wide. When she saw the blood on Hiram's shirt, she wrinkled her nose.

"Where are you going with him?" she asked Hiram.

"Taking him home. Gonna bandage him up," he said briefly.

"In the car, with the blood on the seats?" she said. Her voice, shocked out of its kittenish purr, had a nasal whine.

"Stay here, then," he said, and went by her, the boy's feet still dragging. She stood looking after Hiram uncertainly, the fingers of her right hand pulling on one long uncurled lock of hair.

Anise went out with Fid, not looking at Helen. Helen turned and went slowly back in to the dance.

In the car Fid took his usual seat in the front, and Anise sat next to the boy in back. He was conscious but still. The blood from a cut on his scalp soaked slowly into the upholstery where his head was thrown back onto the seat.

She touched him with a white finger, and then asked Hiram softly, "Who beat him?"

"I did," he said, looking up to catch her eyes in the rearview mirror. He saw her startle, and her look of shock.

"Were you drinking?"

"Looks that way, don't it?" he said neutrally, swinging the wheel and looking out the window. Then he looked up in the mirror again and smiled.

But she looked away, angry. He was drunk, and filthy, and stupid. She had thought he was different, but he was just like the other boys she knew. How ridiculous, to beat up a boy and then insist on taking him home to bandage him. Drinking, and fighting, and acting absurd. She sat in stony silence the rest of the way home.

They got out at the rented rooms. Hiram went in and turned on the light. The room was spare, she saw, just two twin beds with blankets pulled straight over them, an unshielded light bulb, a stack of magazines, a pile of blueprints. Hiram carried the boy in slung over his shoulder, and put him down on one of the beds.

Anise was ashamed to see the beds. She shouldn't be here, she thought, in these boys' rooms alone, one of them bleeding and lying still. It was wrong. She felt naked and ashamed. But the turn of the evening, the dancing and the lights, then the darkness in the car and the blood soaking into the upholstery, had left her dizzy, and she couldn't object. She went along, like a child led by the hand.

She followed the lift of Hiram's eyebrows and fetched the basin, taking it outside to fill it with clean water. Then she ripped up an undershirt he handed her into even bandages, the way her father had shown her. She held the boy's head as Hiram sponged his cuts. The worst one was under his left eyebrow.

Hiram saw Anise's firm, pale hands. They were steady and didn't shake. As she bent her head over the boy, her hair fell in a dark shining bang over her forehead. Her neck was white and thin. He wanted to stroke her, to keep her like a ferret in his pocket. Fid stood back and watched Hiram's eyes on the girl, his hands helplessly jingling keys in his pocket.

After the boy was cleaned up, Hiram and Anise went outside, leaving Fid to feed the boy a cup of coffee. They stood on the rickety wooden porch, watching the yellow light of the lamp pool on the dusty road. Crickets sang in the darkness. The air was warm and buoyant as salt water. Hiram teased her and made her laugh, watching the dark circles of her eyelashes go down on her cheeks. She had a beautiful smile, he thought, something wrenching in the line of her jaw. She should smile more. It made her lips not seem so thin.

"Why did you hit him?" she asked, looking at him.

"I had to," he said easily. "He said something about my mother."

She frowned. "You shouldn't fight. Or drink," she said.

"I won't anymore," he promised her, and almost meant it. "Would you like to see a show with me on Friday night?" he asked.

"No, thank you," she said, and went back inside.

Hiram followed her. Fid looked sharply at his face. The boy was walking around now on Fid's arm, looking dizzy and hanging his head down.

Hiram said he would walk the boy home, and Fid took Anise back to the car. He drove her home and walked her up the path in silence, only stopping at the door to clasp her hand and look at her with an odd, intense stare that she didn't understand.

She climbed the stairs to her room, hearing the roar of the car fading away, the headlights sliding across her wall. She undressed down to her shift, then slid into the cool white sheets and lay staring at the ceiling. She thought she was awake, thought she would lie awake all night, but she slid into a sleep that closed over her head like water.

The next day Anise woke feeling tired, with an ache in her jaw as though she had been grinding her teeth all night. She lay and watched the shifting light coming through the window, and finally got up reluctantly when her mother called, her voice thin with irritation.

She came downstairs, dragging her hand along the dark banister, and ate her toast points and eggs in silence. Her mother chanted an unbroken stream of complaints in the background about the lodgers, how far behind they were in their rent, how thoughtless they were to track dust through the house. Anise spooned up the last of the egg yellow and left the white.

"And you watch out, walking to school," her mother called after her. "I heard from Mrs. Matthews last night that there was a real big fight at the school last night, some troublemakers in from out of town. You hear me?"

"I hear you, Ma," Anise said, and she drifted out of the house onto the street, carrying her books hugged close to her chest.

She had only walked a block when she heard a car behind her. Without turning around she knew who it was.

"Want a ride?" said Hiram, poking his head out the window. For once Fid was absent. Hiram had detailed him for the early shift on the site.

"No, thank you," she said, and walked a little faster.

"Give a fellow a break," he said, still leaning across the passenger seat to look up at her while he drove slowly alongside. She noticed how tan his forearm looked, with the lighter hairs sprinkled on it like gold.

"I'm sorry about last night," he said earnestly. "I didn't mean to scare you."

"You did," she said, not relenting. "Where's Fid?"

"I took care of Fid," he said, grinning up at her.

"Look out," she said, and pointed at the kid on the red bicycle whom he had overtaken and nearly hit. Hiram swerved neatly around and pulled up next to the walk again.

"See, I almost killed myself for you," he said, laughing. "Now won't you just let me give you a ride to school?"

She refrained from pointing out that if anyone would have been killed, it would have been the child on the bicycle.

"All right," she said, and smiled down at him suddenly. "You can." She waited while he got out and hopped across the hood of the car to open the door for her.

"Isn't that better?" he said, rolling up the window and settling her books on the seat. "Wasn't it kind of an exciting dance last night?" He looked at her, and his eyes were very blue and warm, and crinkled at the corners.

She laughed, admitting that, in fact, it had been a strangely exciting evening.

Anise brought Hiram home to dinner on a Sunday night two weeks later. He wore a dark grey suit with a light shirt and a polka-dotted tie. Anise showed him into the parlor, and waved him to sit down, a little dubiously, on the horsehair sofa. He looked stiff and out of place here in her parents' house, surrounded by all her father's books and surveying instruments. She realized suddenly that she didn't know who his folks were or if he had even finished college.

Her mother came bustling in, with the fussy manners she put on for company.

"Now, Mr. Jameson," she said, "will you have port or sherry?"

"Neither, thanks," he said, looking awkwardly sideways at Anise. "I'm fine, thank you."

"Neither?" said Big Mother. She was slightly suspicious of gentlemen who didn't partake.

"Not at the moment," Hiram said. "I'm—working on a big job tomorrow, need to be fresh for the early morning. I'm sure you know how that is, Mrs.—"

He stopped, appalled at the realization that he had never asked Anise's last name.

"Frankell," Big Mother put in. "It's a strange name, but there, it's the only one we've got."

A silence fell.

In the middle of it, Big Joe came in. Hiram seemed to shrink further in Big Joe's stocky, demanding presence. Anise wondered, irritated, what had possessed Hiram to wear such a ridiculous tie.

Big Joe shook Hiram's hand in a grip like iron, looking him up and down.

"You from outside town, are you, boy? Hear there was a bit of trouble with some outsiders not too long ago."

"I heard about that, sir," said Hiram smoothly. "I'm afraid it may even have been one of the men from the Conoco lot. They're a rough crowd."

"They are, are they?" said Big Joe, still looking him over. "You go to school around here?"

Hiram smiled warmly. "We sure do move around the country a lot, as I'm sure you understand, sir. But I'm just about to complete my degree from the University of Texas here—only a few credits that I'm lacking from where I went to school before."

Anise's mouth twitched. That, at least, she knew to be untrue. She looked down at the tips of her shoes, planted neatly together under the hem of her skirt. Big Joe looked sharply at his daughter, and back at Hiram.

"And what is it that you study?"

"Sales and communication, sir," said Hiram gravely. "It's useful for a man in my line of work."

"The pot roast will be getting cold," interjected Big Mother, and they followed her into the dining room, which was carefully laid for company. Hiram walked after her, his eyes on a level with the faded coppery bun of Big Mother's hair. He wondered what she had looked like when she was young, this wiry-boned woman with the hands red from soaking, and her eyes clouded with disappointments.

During dinner Hiram performed well, answering Big Mother's endless questions with grace, his head charmingly tipped towards her. Anise felt anxious and hollow at her center.

Anise found herself thinking of things she never considered when she and Hiram were alone together. She wondered suddenly what it was they did together—how did they pass all that time? Talking or laughing over one of Hiram's wild escapades, she supposed. He never listened to music. He had no interest in the classical phonograph records that her father played, or even the new jazz coming in from the East. He was quickly bored when she talked of religion, or the life of the mind. His conversation was pragmatic, filled with tales of practical jokes he had played, or adventures he planned.

When she was with him she felt light, as if nothing could go wrong. And nothing ever did go wrong, for him—she called it his "light touch." He escaped from the most absurd situations with never a scratch or a bruise, and when Anise was near him his magic extended to shelter her. With him, she shed the stiff skin that kept her movements small and her voice muted. She could be wild and brazen, like the book heroines she had always admired.

But these feelings withered under her father's eyes. She pushed the green beans around on her plate. All she could think of was the time she had wanted to talk about Proust, and Hiram had asked innocently if it was a kind of sausage.

Hiram courted Anise persistently, with all the charm at his disposal. He needed her. He hardly knew why. But he could feel her presence like a cool thing in his life, below him and around him. She was the cloud, and he shone against her like bright copper.

Anise's friends were enraptured with him. "He's so handsome," they told her. "And such a good dancer." There were many of them who would have happily taken him for themselves. Young ladies languished over him, secretly sighing when he passed, and throwing soft looks at him.

But Hiram devoted himself to Anise, persisting in spite of her distance. She was class, and family. His own family was so odd, and so far from everything. He hungered to belong. Anise fit so effortlessly, while he scavenged around the edges. All of his charm could not win him into the circle where she rested in her white linen dresses.

They went boating on Lake Austin, with a party of young people. They rented leaky rowboats, and went out to the shore. The girls wore soft dresses that caught the gleam of the starlight. They tucked plaid blankets around their knees and rowed out into the current, drifting and talking softly. Off to the right there was a small island, crowded with brush and small trees.

"Look at the moon," Anise said to Hiram. "Isn't it lovely?" It rode, a narrow crescent, just over the horizon. He looked down at her upturned face, and a shiver ran up his spine. He squeezed her fingers, curled in her lap.

Through the still air there came a sudden noise, loud and dreadful. It sounded like a horse that Anise had once heard with its leg broken, screaming and thrashing on the ground. After the noise had faded they heard a strange music.

"Sh," said one of the girls in the boat ahead. "Listen."

The boats drifted silently, with only the sound of the ripples splashing against the sides.

They all listened, mystified. The music came up from behind them, impossibly distant and yet very close, so that Anise felt she could touch it with her hands. Looking around, she felt as if the music were rising out of the water, and then thought that it was coming from the air, down to the boat.

It was the saddest, sweetest, most impossibly melancholy thing she had ever heard, and Anise both wanted the music to go on and on, and longed for it to stop.

"What is it?" she said. Her heart pounded and she felt afraid.

"Not many people hear it," said a girl in the boat with them, holding her finger up mysteriously. "It's the hermit of the island."

"What hermit?" said Anise. "I've never heard of a hermit on the island."

"It's a terribly sad story," said the girl. "Just the saddest thing you've ever heard. My mother told it to me. It happened a long time ago—at least twenty years, I think. There was a young musician, the handsomest one in the town, my mother said. He played the fiddle. Of course, it wasn't such a big town then, just a tiny settlement. But this young man had black hair and flashing black eyes, like a gypsy. And he fell in love with the daughter of the richest man in town. She had beautiful long yellow hair, they said, and her name was Imogene.

"Of course, the handsome young man was poor. Aren't they always?" She looked archly at Hiram. "He hardly had a dime. But he gained her father's permission to marry her by playing his fiddle at a party.

And he played so beautifully that he melted the hearts of all the ladies. And everyone at the party cried, because his song was so beautiful.

"So the fiddler and Imogene were going to be married, and they say they were so happy! And then"—she lowered her voice dramatically— "they say Imogene came to this riverbank, this one just here on the left, to pick a white water lily to braid into her hair for the wedding. But when she reached for the flower, a horrible snake leapt up out of the water and bit her on her white, white neck. And she fell down dead into the river. Her lover just went insane with grief. He became a hermit and moved to the little island there, to be near her ghost. And he just played the fiddle, all the time, sad songs, and ate fish he caught from the river. No one knows if he's alive or dead—if he still plays his fiddle for her or if it's his ghost, longing to go home." The girl leaned back, satisfied with the effect of her story. Anise was shivering, and even Hiram was looking a little unsettled.

"Shoot, I don't believe that," he said loudly.

"Suit yourself," said the girl. "But how do you explain that music?"

They all listened again, intently, but there was nothing to be heard.

"Just nothing," Hiram said. Anise wasn't so sure. She had looked over, as they passed the island, and thought she saw a face peering out like a memory, very pale among the dark roots.

A few weeks after the outing on the lake, the dam near town broke. A cresting wall of water came down the river, carrying with it pieces of broken trees, ladies' hairpieces, dead dogs and children's schoolbooks.

Hiram talked his two friends, Fid and Bake, into swimming on top of this wave as it passed through the riverbed in the middle of town. He persuaded and teased them, and finally shamed them by calling them cowards.

Anise was working for the college newspaper. Someone ran in to order her to cover this story—that the dam had broken and three fools were swimming the flood. She knew immediately who it must be. She picked up a notebook and a pencil, smoothed her hair in the powder room and ran to the riverbed.

When she arrived, she saw that a huge wave was running over the river like a solid wall toward the bridge. The three boys were lazing above the foam, and the people on either side were screaming.

Hiram's two friends looked ahead and saw the grey stone bridge coming. The wall of water would hit it directly. They swam to the side, and were dragged out of the water to be fed root-beer floats by the scolding townspeople.

Hiram was waving to everyone, and didn't notice the bridge. He finally looked ahead and saw the fringed heads of the townspeople leaning down over the bridge, just a few feet away.

He took a deep breath and dived, as deep as he could. He dived past the debris and the sticks, down through the tumbling water to where it was green as glass. He dreamed as he swam, of a mermaid with pearls around her pale arms, and a piano shipwrecked on a beach, its bright black curve gleaming.

And then he came up again, on the other side of the bridge, and the townspeople rushed from one side to the other to see if he was alive. They called it a miracle.

Anise and Hiram became engaged in the spring of 1929, when Anise was nineteen years old. She hardly knew how it had happened. They went out for a picnic on a Sunday, after the dam broke. Anise packed a basket with a red-and-white cloth, filling it with cheese, fresh fruit and sharp knives, cherry soda and a loaf of bread for sandwiches. She put in a tiny vase of fresh flowers, pink ones shaped like stars.

Hiram came to pick her up in his black Model T, knocking carefully at the door. He looked very handsome in his light suit and straw hat, knocked rakishly to the side. His eyes were blue under the hat.

They drove down the road, with the windows open so that Anise could breathe, in great gulps, the daisies and sage bushes standing by the side of the road.

Steam started to come out from the front of the car, and Hiram got out, cursing under his breath. He reached in with a rag to unscrew the radiator cap, and steam shot, hissing, into the air. Anise watched it rise and thought she had never seen anything so beautiful, the white steam arcing up into the air, cutting a clean curve, with Hiram hidden behind it as though it were a veil.

After the steam subsided, Hiram reached in again with the rag and removed the radiator cap. It was bent, hopelessly melted until the edges turned in. He tossed it up in the air and put it in his pocket.

"My good-luck piece," he said. "Looks like we'll be here for a while."

She got out of the car and he hoisted her up onto the roof in one lift. He handed up the picnic basket and she laid out the picnic on top of the car. He jumped up to join her, with his jacket off and his sleeves rolled above his elbows.

They ate the bread and cheese, and drank the soda, and laughed at the cows that came up to poke their noses through the wire fence. Hiram turned backflips and walked on his hands in the dust by the side of the road, and after they finished lunch they sat in the car, singing old songs that they knew and holding hands until a delivery truck came and picked them up to take them back home.

When he pulled a ring with a tiny diamond chip out of his pocket and slipped it onto her finger, she wasn't surprised. She only looked at it, turning it in the sun, looking up to see the lines crinkling around Hiram's eyes as he smiled at her. There in his eyes she thought she saw a flickering shape, like a candle flame reflected double, but when she blinked and looked again it was gone.

B ig Mother was thrilled to hear of the engagement. Hiram had long ago charmed her out of her initial suspicions. Big Joe was more reserved.

"He can marry you," Big Joe said, "but not until he's proved that he can take care of you by setting up a house first."

Money was tight and jobs were scarce, so Hiram went on the road, chasing contracting jobs and organizing the hauling of great logs of steel from one place to another. He never worked as a powder monkey now—he was too big to fit under the bulldozer shovel as the dirt and boulders rained around him. But it came sometimes in his dreams, and he woke up sweating.

He didn't think too much of Anise when he was gone—there were many young ladies of loose reputation in the towns that he visited, who were eager to oblige him. But Anise's distant hold on him changed him, made him more removed. He philandered, but considered his hand and his heart pledged. He warned the young ladies with whom he dallied not to expect anything from him.

Each time he came home, he and Anise would stack up the money that he had saved, and make an order from the Sears catalogue. They sat on the parlor sofa, with the glossy catalogue spread out on Hiram's knees, and Anise traced her thin soft fingers over the household things until they found what they wanted. They decided on a set of china, with a blue-and-brown border, and bought one plate at a time. It took them seven years to outfit an entire house.

Hiram stowed the dishes, and later the silver and the pots and pans, in the back of his Model T. The clinking reminded him of her when he was on the road.

One day without warning Anise woke up feeling desolate. She couldn't breathe. She sat up and looked out the window. The distances outside the town seemed to be calling her, just outside of her hearing. The closeness of the houses around her house pressed her in, until she thought that the ceiling might squash her head as flat as the heads of natives she had seen in her father's *National Geographic*.

She went to the bookshelf and pulled out a *National Geographic* dated November 1934, turning the pages to marvel at the people, the looks and the ways of strange people that she would never know. She traced her finger down their white paint, and wondered if they believed in God.

She put her hand up to the space between her breasts, and pushed in, onto the bone. She could feel her heart beating, and wondered why. What was it that drove the heart, why did it beat so fast? She ran her hands down the spines of the books in the bookcase, feeling the heavy embossed leather, smelling the faint, musty smell that came from the pages.

She could feel her life pouring away into nothing. She wanted to make a book, something that would have mass and weight and heft in her hand. She wanted to write a book that would stand on these shelves, something with her name in gold initials on the front. She knew she could do it. People often did. She had worked at the college newspaper, writing about tea parties and social events, and she knew how to turn a phrase. Gasping for air, she determined that she would go away and study journalism. And then she would write a book.

Big Joe's well had come through, and the family was flush with money. Big Mother had never been so well turned out, and her Sunday hat was heavy with maroon velvet bows. Cumin and Marjie had stocked their wardrobes as well, buying smooth gloves and stockings to lay with tissue into their drawers. A shiny new motorcar stood in the driveway. Big Joe had a new horse, a rangy chestnut with a white blaze down the front of his face.

Only Anise had not asked for anything, not knowing what she wanted. And now she knew—she wanted escape, to go away and learn the things that writers needed to know. She wanted to see the lights and hear the music she only knew from stories, and from the yellowed big-city newspapers that sometimes came into the college journalism office.

She wanted a real city, a big city, where the people were bright and beautiful and loved ideas. Dallas was full of people and money, but they were only oil ranchers with shiny boots and big belt buckles. She wanted to go further than that, so far that her family could never find her. She wanted to go to New York, to the Columbia School of Journalism. She would ask her father that night.

This time when Hiram came back from his trip, Anise had something to tell him. She sat down with him and held his hands. She was going to New York, she said, to study and learn. She didn't know how long she would be gone.

He looked at her, trying to understand. New York was a place he had never been. No one that he had ever known had been there. She was going there, and leaving him like a fool with a load of china in his car?

They were sitting in the darkened parlor, with the curtains drawn down against the hot air outside. The room smelled faintly of the wood polish Big Mother used. The parlor was empty and spare, with paper covers on the lampshades to keep them from the dust. There were tatted doilies everywhere. The horsehair sofa was pale blue, the same color as Big Mother's watery eyes.

Anise said nothing, only looked at him. She was as resolute as he had ever seen her, her mouth pressed to the thin line that made him squirm, her eyes wide and her jaw set. He could see a blood vein throbbing, very small, on her temple. Her thin dark hair clung to her forehead.

"Sure," he said, leaning back and bringing up one polished boot to rest on his knee. "You do what makes you happy, honey."

They spoke no more about it. In the days before her departure, while Anise packed and washed, Hiram thought her eyes were lit from behind in a way he had never seen before. He was twenty-six this year, and Anise one year younger—but she seemed old to him, gone from his grasp, blown by a bright wind of expectation.

The two of them were together only rarely, and never alone. There were always crowds of people blowing through the room, shaking out clouds of lace underthings or running tape measures up Anise's sides to fit her for her traveling dress.

Hiram went away with Fid. They fished, rode horseback and drank gin out of a tin cup, playing cards late into the night, laying them on a dark table grooved with knife cuts.

Fid watched Hiram in the days before Anise left, and waited for him to speak. Hiram had set Fid up with his own sister Demeter, in payment for taking Anise away. That was all right with Fid. Fid liked Demeter. He liked her smooth mass of dark hair, and her determined chin. She never prodded or poked him to make him talk, only fell in step beside him, looking up at him sometimes and smiling. She was tough, he thought, for all her small bones, rangy as a little mare with neat hooves. She could outthrow and outjump her brother. And she was lucky.

Fid found himself bringing Demeter things. He thought about her, in his silent way, and picked up things he thought would please her. Once he brought her a shell that he found in his mother's attic, at the bottom of one of the old trunks.

He knelt in the dust of the musty-smelling attic, sifting through the broken rose-colored brocade, and old shoes, with their heels beaten by use into tiny points. He saw the shell at the very bottom, wrapped in tissue, its curve as pinkly satin and precise as the working model of the human ear he had seen once in a science class.

He picked it up and cradled it in his hands as though it were a living thing, feeling the weight of it and its creased, rough surface with brown knobs poking out. Inside, it was smooth as cream, seeming to gather all the light in the room to itself. He held it to his ear and he could hear, far away, the washing of the ocean waves over a beach he had never seen, a foreign place where stallions ran on the sand, perhaps, their forelocks wet on their heads from the waves. He sat there, a big man on his knees in the attic, listening to the ocean in the shell, for a long time. He went down-stairs and asked his mother if he could have it.

She wiped her red hands on her apron and took the shell from him, laying it to her ear and listening, smiling gently and nodding her head as if to an old dance tune. Then she nodded abruptly, gave it to him and turned back to the dishes.

Fid brought the shell to Demeter on a Sunday evening. She had come to keep house for Hiram in Austin, when it seemed that he had made it his home. They rented a small furnished house with white shutters. It had a porch covered with honeysuckle and a porch swing with peeling paint.

Fid stayed in the spare room. He left it almost as impersonal as a hotel. Sometimes Demeter arranged wildflowers in a jug for him to set on the dresser, to brighten things up. The only thing he had put up in the room was a pen-and-ink drawing of an ocean liner.

Fid was fascinated with the big boats, their heavy grace, the way he imagined the ocean peeled around them as they passed, leaving foam in their wake. He found a book in the library of great ocean liners, with colored plates, and he took it home and looked at it every night before he fell asleep, turning the glossy pages carefully, looking at the boats and closing his eyes to see them in motion, to feel the great slow rocking under his feet. One night one of the prints came out, loosened from the thread of the binding, and fell at his feet like a lady's glove.

He picked it up and laid it on the dresser, wondering what to do with it. Should he take it to the librarian and try to explain? She was a formidable woman with iron-grey hair. He cringed at the thought of facing her. She might think that he had cut it out on purpose. Finally he took a tack and pinned the picture to the wall above his bed, feeling a guilty pleasure in having it hang over him while he slept.

That Sunday, when he brought Demeter the shell, he thought of that print over his bed, of the delicate coloring and the tiny pen lines that went together to make the image. The shell was heavy under his arm, like a child. His mother had given him some white tissue to wrap it in. He watched his footsteps in the sinking dust, against the sun. The town was quiet, wrapped indoors with the promise of supper, and sleep.

Demeter was sitting in the porch swing, slowly pushing herself back and forth with the balls of her feet against the splintered wooden floor. The swing creaked in the dusk. She smiled up at him and patted the seat beside her, and he sat down gratefully, sliding across through the smell of honeysuckle that surrounded her, and the lighter, milky smell that was her skin. He laid the shell in her lap. As she opened it, he smiled. She unwrapped the shell, letting the paper fall into her lap and held it up to her face, burying her nose in the coolness of it.

"It's perfect," she said, looking at him. She laid her hand gently on his knee, and the shell gleamed like some precious alien thing between them. They rocked together on the swing in the darkness, listening to the sounds of the evening, the smell of the flowers rising around them.

Hiram took Anise to the train the day she left for New York. She had said all her goodbyes to the family. She wore a plaid traveling suit, trimmed with red, tailored over her waist. It made her collarbones look very fragile. Her hat was red, and her new gloves were fine grey kid, so tight and smooth that Hiram could see the perfect ovals of her fingertips beneath them. Her eyes were wide and excited. He had never seen her skin so pale. He thought that he could almost see every vein, every pulse.

They waited on the platform surrounded by her luggage, matching pigskin of a gold-brown shade. The cases had no stickers or stains from travel yet, every edge sharp, every corner creased. Hiram wore his hat down over his eyes.

She looked at him thoughtfully, holding the handle of her purse exactly in front of her. She traced with her eyes the line of his face, the angled sweep of his jaw, his eyes, the faint downward parenthesis already forming on either side of his mouth.

She had loved him now for five years, watched for his moods and known his silences, waiting to be his wife. She had studied his laugh, his harebrained ideas. He took her out of herself. With him, she felt her hands and feet as things in space, moving and floating, swinging with weight and dimension. Before him, she thought sometimes that she was only a head on a stick, going through the air.

She had promised to marry him. She knew she should feel tied to him. But as she looked at him now, she felt only release and a light-headed soaring free, an unshackling. She could talk now, to people who knew things, who knew more words than she did, who would part and divide for her the magic of symphonies, of books and shining things, of crystal and carpets and the life of the mind.

She could be there at the wells where such things were born, and nourished. She could make these things herself, with words, trading ideas with young men in gloves, who would hand her round the dance floor. They would admire the whiteness of her skin, the smallness of her ankles, the cleverness of her remarks. She would drink champagne, and go to foreign restaurants with strange food. She had never had champagne before. She imagined a red dress, and snow, and the dark brown eyes of a man filled with light.

Then she looked back up into Hiram's eyes, filled with love and worry. His eyes were blue, not brown. His booted foot seemed to sink into the wooden train platform like a root, it was so solid. She saw the crease between his eyebrows, and felt a surge of love for him, for his magic touch and his rash, charming ways, and the pull of his magnetism.

"Don't be sad," she told him lightly, putting the tip of her gloved finger between his eyebrows to press out the crease. "I'll write you every day, I promise. In my journal. You can read it when I come home, and know what I've been thinking and doing all along. I'll be back in no time at all."

He smiled, and kissed her hard on the mouth, ignoring the outrage of the ladies in traveling coats who had gathered to wait for the train.

The train was coming, swinging around the long curve, painted dark green with brass trimmings and a blackened smokestack. Anise and Hiram waited quietly as the other ladies stepped on board, until she was the last. Hiram handed her luggage up, and she climbed onto the steps, turning to face him and holding on with one hand.

She said something to him, but he couldn't hear through the whistle and the huffing as the train gathered speed. Her words were blown out of the air by the steam, and he couldn't bear it that he had missed the very last thing she said to him. He ran foolishly beside the train, just like in the movies, looking up and shouting, "What? What?"

But the train had gathered speed and was away from the platform now, becoming long and pointed as it moved away from him, and all he could see of her was the pale grey flag of her glove, waving.

9. New Wine

Until I came to write this story, I had never heard that my grandmother Anise kept a journal of her trip to New York. No one in the family had ever spoken of it.

But my mother Amelia came back from a trip to Texas and, without explanation, put a very battered black book into my hand.

It was a three-ring notebook covered with leather, weathered and cracking. On the inside it said: National Mogul No. 4651, University Co-operative Society, Austin, Texas. On the front cover my grandmother's name, Anise Frankell, was embossed in gold letters.

The spine was metal, quite rusted. I took it with me to a favorite cafe, and laid it on the table in front of me. I looked at it for a long time before I opened it.

The paper inside was fragile and yellowed, falling out in places. The early entries are neatly typed, the later ones written in ink, hurriedly, scrawled in a flat looping script. On one section divider, before her school notes, a note is written in pencil: "Be careful with spelling. Your notes are neatly organized. B+." She was twenty-five years old when she wrote those pages. I had just turned twenty-five as I read them.

As I read the journal an unfamiliar picture formed in my mind—a girl, very young, with dark hair and fair skin. It made me cold, reading back into the past of a dead girl, a girl that I had never known. She was a stranger, a giddy, proud young woman who danced down the streets of New York, who drank water upside down to cure hiccoughs, who ran through the snow in high heels, who bartered with the brass salesmen in the shops of the Bowery and had her fortune read in the tea leaves.

Time had closed over that girl's head as seamlessly as ice, leaving no trace of her except the battered notebook in my hand, its rings rusted closed. Who is there now to care which play she attended on what night, or that she loved Tommie, the brown-eyed soldier from West Point?

And yet I knew the woman—she was my grandmother, her blood is in me, some of her phrases and maybe even her gestures. I saw her face at Christmas every year, watched it age and fold in on itself. I grieved for her death.

But the woman I knew was not the girl in the journal. The woman I knew was crumpled and frustrated, desperate. Her story weighs heavily on me.

I know how the story ends. I know that she purged Tommie from her journal, when the letter she expected never came. I know she went home brokenhearted to marry my grandfather and take up the life she thought she had escaped forever. And she never complained, not until the very end. She had extraordinary discipline, my grandmother. She closed her lips and her eyes forever when she came home from New York, as if to open them would bring forth an intolerable rush of yearning.

I only saw her afterwards, in the kitchen with an apron strapped firmly around her, cutting fruit salad alone while my grandfather rode with his horses and dogs, or came in hungry for his dinner. I knew her wasted thin with yearning, her skeletal fingers clutching at my clothes. "Tell me what's happening in the world," she would say. "Talk to me."

I only knew her on her deathbed, yellow with frustration, looking away from my grandfather. But reading the words in the journal, I thought I could feel her standing over my shoulder, the brave, bright ghost of the girl she had been, with her hair falling into her eyes and a slender forefinger tracing over the stories she had written, so many years ago. "Yes," she could have said in my ear, "it was like this, this is what happened. I remember."

New York shook the ideas in Anise's neatly coiffed head like a windstorm. There was a gentleman at Columbia named Mr. Howell, who took journalism students on tours of the slums and the ghettos, eager to draw them from behind the doors of the college and out into the real streets, to make them indignant, and wise.

Mr. Howell was a sprightly man with stark-white hair and impressive mustachios. He carried, as a proud mark of his eccentricity, a tiny brass horn that he used to shepherd the students who were following him, and he danced backwards before them, tooting madly like a latter-day Piper. Some people that saw him shook their heads pityingly. Others murmured, "Poor man," and looked amazed. The children followed him for blocks, and Anise, dressed in a new suit and a bewitching little black cloche hat, thought herself perfectly happy to be following along in his trail.

Mr. Howell parted the dank air in front of her like a swimmer treading oily water, and Anise saw a sort of poverty new to her, for all the baked bleakness of her hometown. She viewed the sights with a pity that was no less sincere for being sentimental.

She saw tenements that had been condemned, where folks still lived, with dirty faces and racking coughs. The bathtubs, when there were any, sat in the cramped kitchens, and drafts played freely through the greasy walls. She learned that the houses burned like tinder once set alight, that even a stiff breeze could knock down the ancient, unprotected wood. She heard a story of two children burning to death just the week before.

She sweated with rage when she heard that thousands of people in New York were dying from "malnutrition," as the papers politely called starvation. She flirted briefly with the idea of becoming a Communist herself, but gave it up when she imagined Big Joe's face. There weren't the makings of a rebel in Anise, really. Her compassion was sharpened to a painful point, but she lacked the innards to split the expectations that she carried on her back, hardening like a locust shell every year.

Mr. Howell's group of students had their dinner at Bernarr MacFadden's One Cent Restaurant, where every item cost between one and three cents. Anise chewed on her tough bread and spooned up her watery greens, eager to feel herself in solidarity with the persecuted people she had seen. Spirits were high in the group—the students had the noisy sensation of being virtuously concerned with the poor, without actually having to touch them.

They were on their way to Box City in the Bowery when they picked up a strange man. He was about forty, cadaverously thin and very shabby, wearing a greasy fedora with two holes poked in it, as for a donkey's ears. He danced in the streets to the sound of Mr. Howell's little brass horn, and Anise remembered him later, the shaggy arms and legs moving under the rags, jerking like a puppet's as if by magic, for the man was so thin it was a marvel to her that he moved at all.

He scented in this gay group a possibility of food, and hid his starvation under a lively face, hoping that if he amused them, they would feed him. He trotted along to the music and talked all the time and always stepped over the fireplugs rather than going around them, asked Mr. Howell to play taps and said, "Now it's time to eat," suggestively, every time he could. The group thought him hilariously funny. But it didn't occur to them to feed him, being full themselves, and they left him outside Box City, bowed against the coming night, and silent.

Box City fascinated Anise. It was a couple of blocks in the Bowery where men—some of whom had once made good salaries, Mr. Howell said —built houses of dry-goods boxes, and linoleum, and furnished them from garbage heaps. Anise wandered along the rows of boxes, seeing a rough and awful beauty in the shades of the weathered corrugated paper in the twilight.

The stench horrified her, but there was an air about the place like playing dolls, and she thought that there might be a charm to living in a little place like this, a tiny box where you had your bowl and your spoon, and nothing else to trouble you. The faces of the men stared out at the wandering students like animals being watched in a zoo. Some of them slept and some of them tossed, wakeful; their faces were pale in the dimness, covered with beards that grew on them like moss on a tombstone. They eyed the students, indifferently, incuriously. They were past begging.

After Box City a strange silence came over the group. Mr. Howell asked Anise and her roommate Kay if they were tired. They were, drifting along in a dream of fluttering rags and smells, finally oppressed by what they had seen. They admitted to fatigue, and Mr. Howell advised them to skip, linking his arms with theirs and skipping with them brightly down the street.

Anise's exhaustion disappeared at once, under this strange exercise, and she tipped her head back to watch the stars dance crazily as they went by. She could never have been this way at home—it must be New York, she thought, that did this to you, let you out of your skin, demanded wild and rash things of you, passionate and violent things. She laughed at the amused stares of the passersby, and even boldly winked at one fellow who was shouting at them, although she was horrified afterwards by what she had done.

They ran into Little Italy, where there was a celebration with lights arching all the narrow, winding streets. The lights flickered, and Anise and

Cathryn wandered enchanted down the winding ways, boldly chewing their gum in public, crazed with sleeplessness and the foreign place.

Anise thought she might really be in Italy, the dark-eyed men with their ample, mustached wives, the dusky peddlers hawking their goods on pushcarts, selling dress fabric, kitchen utensils, strings of chestnuts, candied pumpkin and watermelon seeds. Mr. Howell's group admired the handsome children running about and bought bananas, which they peeled and ate on the spot. They felt vindicated, saved, as if they had come from a lonely purgatory into a heaven that smelled of sausages, garlic and lovely melting butter. A band played loudly and two singers screamed lyrics and gyrated their hips, and people hung out of all the windows.

Wild with the late hour, Anise suggested the students shout, "Down with Mussolini," but everyone ignored her. The girls danced with the Italian men, who greatly admired Anise's tiny feet and trim waist, and whirled her through the streets and tried to put their arms around her, until she quite forgot where she was. Cathryn and Anise danced until midnight, when they straggled home, leaden-footed and weary, feeling debauched, and very much women of the world.

It had snowed the afternoon that Anise met Tommie at West Point. It was an early November snow, and as she wasn't used to snow at all, she wasn't prepared. Her coat was thin plaid, and she had no galoshes. She went off across the West Point campus to take a basket of treats to Ron, a soldier she had dated, going along with Cathryn and her beau. Ron was in the West Point hospital with the flu.

It was a blue and sliding afternoon, full of shadows, though the sky was clear, and Anise took great breaths of the snow-washed air, thinking it was the most delicious thing she had ever tasted. She struck out bravely in her raspberry satin high heels across the path, which hadn't been shoveled yet. In moments she was stuck and floundering.

The wind had piled up the drifts, and she sank in one almost to her knees, and caught her heel on something. She was trying ineffectually to free herself without slipping or dropping her packages when she saw a pair of highly polished black shoes, placed neatly together, exactly in front of her. The shoes were standing on top of a drift of snow, without breaking through, and she was so amazed that she knelt there for a moment, bent down towards the foot she was trying to free, without looking up. Walking on water was nothing, she thought, a little hysterically. It was walking on snow that was the trick.

She saw a hand extend down in front of her, and heard a voice, deep and crisp. "May I help you?" it said.

She looked up along a pair of sharply creased dark blue trousers, a starched shirt and a blue jacket, trimmed in gold at the cuffs, and on up into the darkest pair of brown eyes that she had ever seen. They were flecked with gold, like a cat's eyes, and the face around them was tanned and creased at the moment into a smile.

"May I help you?" he said again, and without waiting for her answer, took her basket.

"Oh, well, it's lovely of you," she said, still struggling to free herself discreetly, breathless. "It's just that . . . something down here seems to have my shoe." She fought in vain a few minutes more, then gave up and sat down flatly on the snowbank, ruining her dress. "It's no use," she said, and looked up at him. His mouth was quirking dangerously close to a laugh.

"What seems to be the problem?" he said, and sat down next to her. She was horrified at the thought of what the snow was doing to his creases.

"I don't exactly know," she said, and laughed up at him. "My shoe seems to be stuck down there under the drift, and I can't get it loose."

"Well, I'm a scientific sort of guy," he said. "Let's apply some scientific principles to this problem."

He dropped to his knees and started digging, paying no heed to her protests. She thought it was probably terribly improper to be sitting on a snowbank while a soldier dug down in search of one's foot, but she couldn't think of any other solution. She folded her hands and laid them at her lap as if she was in a parlor.

"Ah," he said triumphantly. "Here's your problem, ma'am." He held up her raspberry-colored slipper, with a mousetrap neatly attached to the heel, severing it almost in half. "That's terribly dangerous, to leave those traps around," he said, frowning. "That could have been your foot."

"Well, thank goodness for heels," she said lightly, trying to cover her embarrassment. "Now, could I have my shoe, please?"

He held it up, examining it. "I'm not sure if you're safe to run around by yourself, trotting through the snow in these things. There should be a law."

"I'll never do it again," she agreed. "And look, all the dye's running off the shoe."

The sad, soaked shoe was dripping dye onto the snow, staining it a lovely pale pink. For some reason that struck them as tremendously funny, and he smiled, and then she did, and then they were both howling with laughter, trying not to roll on the snowbanks.

"Look, I think you should come into the commons room," he said, holding out his hand to her again. "They've got a fire there, and you need drying."

"But I don't even know you," she said. "How could I go to the commons room with a man I've never met?"

"Lieutenant Thomas Andrew McCovey, entirely at your service," he said, as he picked her up and slung her easily over his shoulder. She screamed and beat him with her remaining shoe, but he carried her resolutely through the drifts.

"Put me down immediately," she said.

"Absolutely not," he said. "Your shoe's busted, and you'd fall a dozen more times between here and the door, and probably catch pneumonia, and I'd have it on my conscience forever."

"But my basket," she said. "It's still back there."

"One thing at a time," he said, and true to his word, when she was ensconced in the commons room in front of a silvery fire, a plaid blanket on her knees and a thick mug of brandied chocolate in her hand, he trudged back through the drifts to retrieve her basket, and dropped at her feet with it, panting like a dog.

She looked down at him, his hair shaggy and sticking up from his exertions.

"Are all the soldiers like you?" she said.

"Only the very best ones," he assured her.

Her hand went out in spite of herself, and stroked the hair off his forehead, and he turned back to watch the fire. They sat there for a long time without speaking, both looking into the flames and listening to the damp wood crackle. It struck Anise that she felt she had been sitting here forever, exactly like this, with Tommie McCovey sitting on the floor at her feet, her hand resting lightly on his shoulder.

Tommie took Anise to her first football game. She thought she would always remember that day at the football game, the cracked and tender blue of the sky, sitting in the stands with Tommie. The dark shock of his hair falling over his forehead, his eyes, lit with amusement as he tried to explain the game to her, and she shouted at the wrong moments. She was fascinated by the amber flecks in his eyes. Later she put her hands on either side of his face and made him hold still so that she could look into them, and figure them out.

"It's the strangest thing," she told him. "You'd think that your eyes were as dark as they could possibly be, but then around the edges they're a little darker still, like a smoky ring. And then there's these lovely gold things, floating in them like they're suspended."

"It sounds horrible," he said.

"Oh no," she said. "It's marvelous." She kissed him, because she wanted to, because his face was so near hers, and because she loved the clean soap smell of his skin, and the faint roughness of the stubble under her hands. His lips were soft and harsh on hers at the same time, moving very slowly and gently, so that her breaths felt funny and strange, coming faster, and her heart beat so that she was afraid he would hear it. It was like drinking a new, brash sort of wine, made from grapes that grew up in far regions.

She imagined the grapes as she kissed him with her eyes closed, the vines climbing up over stony protrusions in the hillside, draping down over whitewashed stands and swaying in the faint breeze, mounting up over her head and closing around her, so that she fell back into the embrace of the leaves, twining around her arms and legs with the wild growth of new things. She felt his hands on her dimly, as from a distance, and cried out at the loveliness of the green light, filtering down through the vines.

10. Raspberry Satin

They danced, and watched each other's eyes, ate scrambled eggs in the middle of the night and drank brandy out of water glasses. Then it was December 28, and time for Tommie to sail. He couldn't tell Anise where he was going, or why, or when he would come back. There wasn't even a place that she could write him.

They drove together to Brooklyn, and she went on board the ship with him to wait until it was time.

He showed her his quarters. They were so small! And a tiny round window, but he couldn't open it, and anyway it only looked out on the endless, foaming ocean.

She set up the flowers that she had brought with her, bright white-and-yellow ones, on the little table. She fussed around them, arranging them, hiding her face. "They'll probably make you throw these out as soon as you leave," she said, trying to make her voice light.

She heard his footsteps rapidly crossing the floor towards her, and his arms went around her, crushing her tightly to his chest.

"You're messing my hair," she said, but he didn't let go, and she held on to him and cried a little, bitterly.

He put his hand under her chin and tipped her face up. She looked up at him, ashamed.

"Don't you think I'd tell you if I could?" he said. He kissed her eyelids, and the tip of her nose, and bent down to kiss her chin. "Do you think I want to leave?"

He kissed her for a long time, a very long time, too long. She pushed him away and straightened her dress, catching her breath.

"Don't sailors have a lot of girls, at every port?" she said. "That's what I hear."

"Dear God, give me patience," he said, rolling his eyes to the ceiling in mock prayer. "Look, do I have to spell it out for you? I can't ask you anything now, Anise." He took her hand. "Look at me! I don't have anything at all, I can't say anything to you now. Not yet."

She reached up and touched his face, laying her hand along the slant of his jaw, very gently. He took her hand and turned it up, pressing his mouth into the palm of it. He tucked her in close to him, her head under his chin, breathing into her hair.

"I'll write you," he said. "I can't say it, but I'll write you everything. That's a promise."

It was almost time to sail, and he walked her through the endless corridors. She had a pain in her side, and her jaw was aching from making it smile. The skin under her eyes stung. She longed to be alone, so that she wouldn't humiliate herself.

They came down the gangplank and through the huge docking hall, where men were busily pulling boxes and supplies on board, through the freight doors. Tommie's steps rang out sharply beside her.

"Look what I have," he said, reaching into the deep pocket of his greatcoat. "Just like Cinderella." It was her shoe, her old raspberry-colored satin shoe, battered and missing half the heel.

"Give that to me," she said, reaching for it.

"Not on your life," he said, holding it out of her grasp. "Not a chance. I'm going to need this shoe."

She gave him her hand, and he squeezed it tightly, so that the bones ground together. His eyes were very dark as they looked down at her.

"So long, soldier," she said, and turned around to walk away. She walked very quickly, and very firmly, one shoulder a little lower than the other, and he watched her small neat figure, in its blue suit, heels clicking on the pavement, until she was entirely out of sight.

Anise didn't do much after that except wait for the letter. She could see it in her mind, how the envelope would look, with its firm slanting capitals and looping *l*'s. She had gotten letters from him before—almost every day during the weeks when he was at West Point and she was at Columbia. He was only allowed freedom on the weekends, and so they had spent as much time writing letters as they had actually being together.

Tommie wrote lovely letters. In person he was elastic, unpredictable, and the marvelous flush of his nearness made her thoughts rush out of her head. The two of them were grandly ridiculous when they were together. Anise's clearest memory was dancing down the street with Tommie at midnight, loony on brandy and out in search of scrambled eggs.

But the tenor of Tommie's mind came out in his letters. The thrust of his thinking was sharp, and true—poignantly sensitive, pensive. He had ideas about the way things should be. He was concerned, as she was, about the impoverished, the ignorant and the destitute. They wrote to one another about politics, about the nature of friendship, about form and essence, about the meaning of true love, and what might be gained from it.

In his letters Tommie confessed his anxieties, his doubts, the fear he felt that he was not made to be a military man, that he lacked the proper heartlessness.

Anise secretly rejoiced when she heard that—she didn't fancy a spouse who would be tied forever to the service, moving every two years. But it didn't matter, it wouldn't have mattered a bit. From the first afternoon that she had sat with him staring into the fire, Anise's soul went into its place like a dog turning around and settling, with a sigh. She had never questioned it. If Tommie McCovey was destined to move every other week, she would move with him, and never count the cost.

She waited patiently for the letter, the most important one, the one in which he would ask her to join him. New Year's Eve came and went, and she was swept into the streets with her friends, each equipped with a tin horn. Anise blew hers until the tears ran down her face. The city was wild, and light as day, with cars of people racing down the streets blowing horns and flashing headlamps, screaming and throwing things. They stood for hours in a line to get into the Music Hall, and watched a stage show that was all silver and copper and gold, exactly the gold of the flecks in Tommie's eyes.

Anise laughed, and clapped, but there was a hollow at the center just above her stomach, and the champagne made her feel slightly ill. But she drank it in her decided way, determined to have a good time as one should in New York on New Year's Eve, doing what should be done.

When they left the theater, the ball on Times Square had just fallen to announce the New Year and light the 1936 sign and all New York was parading on Seventh and Broadway. People who had never seen each other before banded together and marched, blowing horns in unison. Peddlers sold Indian headdresses and "raspberry" whistles, and Anise linked arms with her friends and marched the streets until it was light, and she could finally fall across her bed and watch the ceiling with dry eyes.

The weeks lengthened horribly, and slowly. Anise's roommate Kay came back from her vacation. Watching Anise with shrewd eyes, Kay figured that something was very wrong. So she insisted that Anise come with her on outings, to try to stir her up a bit. They went back to West Point, watched wrestling and boxing matches, ate "boodle" at the "boodlers" and sat through the impressive church service, listening to the cadets sing the Alma Mater.

But it wasn't any use. All Anise could think was that the captain of the wrestling team had been trained by Tommie, that he stood and wrestled like Tommie. The singing of the Alma Mater, with its rough, sweet boy voices made her cringe because she knew that Tommie loved it so. She walked through a daze, smiling and nodding and trying to be polite to her date, who counted her a dismal failure.

As the weeks passed, she ceased to mention Tommie, to write about him in her journal or even to allow herself to look anymore for the letter. But no matter how strict she was with herself, how she chastised and berated herself for a fool, behind her eyelids lay Tommie's panther eyes, the golden sparks in them dancing like fish in the waves.

Wandering the streets to pass the time, Anise stopped curiously in front of a sign. "Have Your Fortune Told," it read in bold red letters. "At the Gypsy Tea Kettle. Madame Nedre Will Lift the Veil of Your Future."

Anise went into the place, opening a heavy door that rang with bells on it. She stepped from the icy light into a close muffled room. The windows were covered with red curtains and there was a curious, heavy smell in the air that made her slightly dizzy.

The woman who came forward to greet her was strange, tall and broad as a man, eyes deep and glittering under dark eyebrows. Whatever hair she had was tucked up into a turban dyed a vivid shade of saffron yellow.

She reached out to grab Anise's elbow and draw her in, just as Anise was on the verge of backing out the door. She found herself being pulled in through the cluttered shop. Madame Nedre apparently did her business in the back of an antiques shop, cluttered with doorknobs and broken headless dolls, wooden idols with leering faces, carved from trees, faded handkerchiefs and broken mirrors. It made Anise think of an old Irish ballad she had heard about the nest of the night mare, made of white horsehair and the golden feathers of birds that tell dreams truly, and scattered inside with the entrails and jawbones of failed poets.

Anise found herself nerveless and still under the eyes of Madame Nedre, who brought her into an alcove, and offered her a drink of very strong, honeyed wine. She never drank in the afternoons, but she took the heavy pewter goblet Madame Nedre gave her, without saying a word. The goblet was marked in places with dents that someone had tried to hammer out, and decorated with a row of tiny circles embossed into the cup just below the lip. Anise drank down the whole cup, even the lees, which looked dark and tasted bitter.

Then she looked up into Madame Nedre's left eye, which stared out of her strange, beaky face. It seemed to Anise that Madame Nedre's eye was huge, its darkness pleated with rust, the pupil expanded until it was a hole with blue sky on the other side of it. Anise squinted and leaned forward, trying to lift up her head, which felt very heavy.

She found herself dizzily falling through into that pupil, which became a dark tunnel with dry earthen walls, and white roots showing through. She fell faster and faster, and as she fell she dragged her fingers along the walls, digging her fingernails in to try to stop her fall. Her fingers went through into the earth and turned into roots. Her feet followed until she was cartwheeling through the tunnel, the tunnel rolling over and over until her feet were pointed downward, rooting into the ground with great speed, thrusting their way until they came to the edge of the dirt and out beyond. Her hands and eyes became leaves and twigs and branches, so that her feet were in the darkness and her arms were in the light. She felt her body pinned against the bark of a tree.

Then she was shrinking back into the wood, feeling the bark close up and around her, growing with scales over her face, covering her lips and ears until finally she closed her eyes and felt it run over her eyelids. She lay there very still, in the heart of the cottonwood tree. She thought she might be dying. Death was very dark, she thought to herself, and very quiet.

When Anise woke up she was lying with a scratchy piece of fabric bunched under her head. She reached back and touched it, and found it was a purple cloth, encrusted with sequins, the kind that circus performers wear. The red drapes had been pulled back to let in the light and Madame Nedre was looking down at her calmly, resting a palm on her forehead. She could see the wrinkles on either side of Madame Nedre's eyes, grained into her skin. The creases in her forehead were very faintly pink in their center.

"You fainted," Madame Nedre said matter-of-factly, and took her hand off Anise's forehead. She stood up, and sighed.

"I will get you a cup of tea."

She came back with a very thin cup of bone-white china, hot to the touch, and filled with a light tea, the leaves floating on the surface. "Drink it," said Madame, and Anise did. It had a smoky taste. She wondered if she had imagined what had happened. She thought of leaving, but her legs felt shaky, and she was afraid she would fall.

When she finished the tea, Madame took it and glanced into the leaves briefly, tipping them so that they sloshed from side to side. Then she looked back into Anise's face and tipped it up with a broad hand.

"Great pain," Madame Nedre said, "and great joy. You'll have to wait a time for the joy, though. It is strange," she went on dreamily, "to see so much pain in such a young face. But it is not the present pain, no—it is pain to come.

"You have a love, yes?" she said, looking sharply into Anise's eyes.

"Yes," said Anise.

"You must not forget him," said Madame. Her voice rose emphatically. "You must not forget him! You must wait for him. He is somewhere far away, is he not?"

Anise nodded.

"He is far away," muttered Madame. "But he needs you. He will come for you, and you must wait for him! If you do not, there is pain that you have not dreamed. You must be faithful. You must be patient. You must be strong. Are you strong?" She tilted Anise's face up to the light again.

"Maybe not so strong," she conceded. "Maybe not strong enough. Maybe too strong. You try to run everything your own way. It will take your life. You must be soft, like a petal falling, soft and patient. But you will not. I fear it. You will not."

She released Anise's face and sat back, shaking her head. The heavy skin under her chin shook, and her eyes were cast down.

Then she looked up at Anise from under her beetling brows.

"Go!" she said. "Go now. I am tired."

Anise reached into her pocketbook to pay. Madame shook her head.

"No money," she said, a hint of humor in her eyes. "You will not take my guidance, I do not take your money. Only fair for fair is a good trade."

She stood abruptly, and led Anise, still shaky, to the door. When she opened it, a blast of icy air came in.

"Don't forget," she said, catching Anise's arm shrewdly as she passed through the door. "Don't fall. Don't fail him. Don't forget."

"Don't fall," Anise repeated to herself, as she went out the door and into the blinding light of the February afternoon. The words rang familiarly in her ears, as if she had heard them somewhere before. She drifted out into the day, feeling as hollow inside as if she had been hung in a smokehouse. She could hardly feel her feet. The branches were iced, and they rang together like bells.

At 12:15 A.M., on Tuesday, May 12, 1936, the dirigible *Hindenburg* passed over the skyscrapers of New York. It went past Anise's window on its way back to Germany, from its anchorage in Lakehurst, New Jersey. Anise was curled into the window seat in her nightgown, watching the clouds, and she was fascinated by the huge ghostly thing, parting the air as it swung over the city.

Its round shape touched something in her that felt like hunger—she wanted to reach out and take it in her hands, to cling to the ropes, to wind her fingers through them and let it take her where it would, where it was going. She envied its passage through the cold air, the pure certainty of its motion. It might be going to where Tommie was. Tommie might be somewhere and see it, like a huge alien moon, swollen and bobbing in the night sky. She could order it to take her to where Tommie was.

She was so tired of waiting! Waiting and waiting, useless and stuck into the ground. Her pain drove her forward, made her want to cover long distances and swing free of the ground. Surely if she could only see him, only put her hands along his jaw and stare into his eyes, she would understand his silence! Surely if he could have written, he would have. She imagined her slipper, the raspberry satin shoe with the broken heel, being cast off the deck of the *Hindenburg* and falling, falling silently, turning over and over toward the ground and drifting with the breeze, now fading into shadow and now gleaming like a broken rose in the searchlight that passed over the city.

She imagined herself falling, the light nightgowned figure falling to the ground below without a sound, to lie crumpled and doll-like until the morning. Who would find her? Who would mourn for her? Would he be sorry?

She found herself leaning hungrily out into the cold air that smelled of wood smoke, gazing out into the far distances. Too far out, she was, too far for comfort. She pulled her head back in the window and barred it, locking the night firmly outside, padding back to her bed. She curled up against the empty spot just under her ribs.

Outside, the *Hindenburg* moved on steadily, with such speed that it was visible for only a few moments before it disappeared into the washing fog.

Anise slept and dreamed, strange scattered dreams. She dreamed that she was back in her old house, where they had salad every Sunday with cherries in it. The cherries, she remembered, were always kept in a bottle in the sideboard, gleaming with a hidden redness.

She saw the attic of her old house, where there were magazines with ladies in big plumed hats and long tight dresses; an armadillo basket; an old toy train that had belonged to her oldest brother, Frank, now broken; a dilapidated doll buggy; uneven floorboards; a stained-glass window, with light coming through the small colored panes.

She saw a mysterious tobacco box with a big fat man, which had once been in Little Baz's room. And then she saw Little Baz, curled on his pillow, smiling at her and waving his arm for her to come closer—such a tiny arm! She looked into his almond-shaped eyes, to see something she had forgotten.

She bent close to him, holding her ear close to his little mouth, curling like a rose petal, to hear his words. They were soft, almost invisible. She smelled the sweet wash of his breath.

"Don't cry for me," he said, touching a tiny wrinkled finger to the corner of her eye, where, indeed, there were tears gathering. "Don't cry."

She picked him up in her arms and took him, pillow and all, out into the garden, under the huge cottonwood tree where they had played their games—telegraph, and tea parties, and school with cats that they forced to sit upright in baby clothes.

She smelled the earth, coming up from between the roots of the cottonwood tree, and remembered how she used to eat the mud in the summer by the handful. She ate some now, picked it up and laid it along her cheek, swallowing deep drafts of it, and it was good to her. It tasted of the earth, the loam, the deep longing, and she took a handful and fed it to Little Baz, and he ate it, and smiled.

In her dream Anise rested her back against the trunk of the cottonwood tree, and looked up into the branches. Against their screen she saw things, scenes playing out: Cumin dressing like Gramps and hiding under the bed; Marjie in a terrible temper, cutting her sewing in two; the sweet-voiced blacks who lived out in the little servant house behind, and tried to make her go to bed, and gave her milk shakes with onion; the schoolteachers who brought her valentines that opened, with Christmas bell paper; tents made of chairs, tents of cards; the pans of butter in the pantry, screened against the flies; the window box she used to love to sit in, to cut out paper flowers.

She heard a sound, unearthly and high—it was Little Baz beside her, singing "Babies Boats" for her, as he used to. His voice soared up like frozen tears, delicate as the veined leaves that shook up over her head.

She pillowed her head on her arm and wept for the things that were gone, and would never come back. She grieved for things she had not thought of in years, which she thought now she had left underneath the cottonwood tree. She dug with her hands down through the roots, looking for them, forgetting even as she dug what it was that she had lost. And always Little Baz sat beside her, his withered body propped against the tree and his earth-smeared face shining, looking up, singing to her of peace and the cessation of sorrows, in a voice that trembled and clung to the leaves over his head.

She woke in her bedroom still digging, clawing at the pillow, tears wet on her face for lost Little Baz, his voice still drifting in her ears.

The next day Anise received a letter from Big Joe, telling her that Hiram was dangerously ill, that she must come home at once. It was the end of her year.

11. The Tree

Francine stood in front of the burnished hall mirror to put in her hatpins. The mirror was pocked with spots, so that her face looked out of it palely, like a fish rising in the dimness.

Today she felt young, and happy, and she tapped her foot and hummed a song as she adjusted the hat, tipping it slightly, lifting her chin and widening her eyes at the mirror. It was the harvest church picnic and the day was perfect, sunny with the slightest glaze of clouds in the sky. There was a cool, bright wind.

It was Jed's free day, his one day to take off and have fun. Jed had been sweet to her, really, after that day with Baby. She felt a little ashamed of herself for not telling him the truth about what had happened. She hadn't confided in him, hadn't laid her head on his chest to cry. It would have been better if she had, she thought now, and she regretted it.

But the habit of solitude had grown on her like a skin, and was growing on her still. What she saw seemed removed from what she felt, as if she looked at the world through a thick pane of glass that admitted no sound.

She had always been lonely. But she noticed the silence creeping around her more, since that day with Baby. Her own thoughts went on hotly, inside her head, but when she spoke, her words came out cool and spaced apart, heavy and deliberate, as if she had read them in a book. It was strange. Her interior world drifted further and further from the loud noises and colors of the outside.

She could sit and watch herself pour tea into the cracked cups, smile and nod and hand around the shortbread with her long, square-tipped fingers, and it seemed as if someone else was acting. The comments of the

Ladies hardly bothered her anymore. She just looked at them and smiled, a smile that froze them and made them spill their tea. She didn't know what it was in her eyes that made them rise quickly, with murmurs of other things to be done. She didn't feel mean towards them, not really. Only cool, drifting and cool in a place apart.

But she could still be charming and helpless to the men, the church officials and the important men. She knew how to slump slightly to the side as if the weight of her bubble-gum hair were really too much for her slender neck. They would rush in to carry her parcels, sit her down and find her a glass of water, lean over her and fan her and look into her eyes anxiously. She would make her eyes wide and watch the blood rush to the surface of their roughened skin, and they would be gripped with the urgent need to do things for her, anything at all.

She had gotten the plumbing in the old house fixed that way, and new curtains, white with a lace trim. And a coat of paint for the church, and shutters.

She exerted a nameless, wordless force on the men around her and they felt confused and powdery before it. It was just something that she knew how to do. It was all distant from the things just behind her eyes. She figured that she was growing up at last, growing up into just the kind of helper that Jed had wanted her to be all this time.

And he was pleased, there was no denying it—pleased with the new coat of paint for the church and the nice things for the house. With all the help they had now for lifting heavy things, setting up tables for the church bazaar and rolling the kegs of cider to the picnics—things that used to be left undone until Jed bent his own shoulder to do it—he felt almost that he wasn't needed. He would watch Francine sometimes, with a puzzled frown in between his eyebrows, and start to say something, and then stop.

He was an innocent man, concerned only with the machinations needed to run the church, to do the Lord's work. He couldn't understand the forces at work in Francine. She bewildered him, and yet she was as docile and pliant as a man could wish. He had been reaching out for her lately, she could feel him sometimes withdrawing from the maze of church business and reaching for her, trying to find her.

But it was too late. She thought it with a certain sense of triumph. She could laugh at him, and everyone, now, safe behind her wall of glass, and not be hurt when he left halfway through dinner or never came home at all, from the bedside of the dying.

At first she had lain in bed through the long, empty nights, her palms flat against the sheets, and stared at the web of cracks in the ceiling. Stained with damp, there was one that looked like a witch's broom. There was something else that looked sometimes like a starfish, and sometimes like a hand, reaching for her through the darkness.

But now she hardly ever lay awake anymore, listening for the sound of Jed coming in tiredly, the heavy boots clumping up the stairs, washing slowly in the next room with cold water because the hot took too long, the smell of the sickroom still on him. No, she hardly ever lay awake waiting anymore. She slept in the nest of new blankets that the church officials had given them, her palms turned up, her breathing soft and even as a cat's. She never even woke up when he slid in beside her. She was sorry, sometimes, for the puzzled look in his eyes. But she couldn't explain. She couldn't reach that far.

She shook her head to clear it. Today was the picnic, and she was determined to have a real good time, in spite of the Ladies. She stuck in the last hatpin and stood, considering her reflection. She was filling out, she thought.

She had been so young when she married that everyone thought of her as a girl. Now the lanky, awkward set of her wide shoulders and big-boned hands had solidified into a kind of chic that gave even her plain gowns style. Her skin was smooth and clear, glowing with the new life she had carried inside her for two months now.

She hadn't told Jed yet. It was her secret still, all her own. She smiled at the thought of it, and her smile was dainty and a little carnivorous, showing off her teeth, still childlike and small as pearls. She wetted the tip of her little finger and ran it complacently over the arch of one eyebrow. She had never looked better, really.

Men turned to follow her with their eyes down the street, but she was wrapped in the mantle of being the preacher's wife, and they didn't dare speak to her. She could walk by them and say hello to them and smile, knowing that all the time their hot eyes were on her. But they could never touch her.

She pinched her cheeks to redden them and applied a pale dusting of a translucent powder to her nose, which had a few freckles from the sun. She wished that she could darken her pale lashes, but didn't dare.

She turned and picked up her basket, which was filled with good things for the picnic: coltsfoot jelly and kidney pie, ham hocks and biscuits she had made herself, light and brown on top. When she heard the car horn she walked out the door into the warm October sunshine.

The Leesburgs were waiting for her in their big battered car. She handed in her basket and got into the back seat, settling her skirt around her. She greeted Mr. Leesburg, who tipped his hat and looked up to raise his eyebrows, smiling in greeting to her in the rearview mirror. Mrs. Leesburg exclaimed with malicious delight about Francine's lovely new hat, wondering aloud where she had ever gotten such a thing in this poky town. Must have cost a fortune . . .

"Reverend Net gave it to me," Francine said clearly, through the hot air of the car. She sat back in the seat, and fastened her green eyes on the back of Mrs. Leesburg's teased head. "It was a gift." Mrs. Leesburg fell silent.

Francine turned to greet Elena Leesburg, who sat beside her in the back seat—a pale, nervous girl who fidgeted. Elena's lank hair, curled into ringlets for the picnic, had given her red spots where it hung down over her forehead. "How are you, Elena?" she said, and smiled with genuine warmth. The girl smiled back, her homely face becoming quite pretty for a moment.

How odd, Francine thought suddenly, that she was actually closer to this girl's age than the old cat and her horrid husband up front. Francine might be a girl like Elena, going to the ice-cream socials and the dances, worrying about beaux and hair ribbons instead of organizing church affairs, flattering rich old men and hosting boring tea parties.

But Francine didn't feel young. She had never really felt young, and now she felt as old as a stone. She rested her hand lightly on her middle, where there wasn't even a bulge yet. She smiled to herself, and looked out the window, tapping her foot against the floor. If only they would hurry up, would drive faster! If she were driving this old car it would be there in a second.

When they finally arrived, she noted with approval that the picnic area looked lovely. The committee had done a fine job of decorating. They had wound strips of bunting through the branches of the lower trees, and spread bright blankets on the ground. Almost everyone from the church was there, dressed in their best. Francine numbered them off in her head. Where was Mr. Carver? she wondered. Probably getting drunk in the back room of the mechanic's shop. His wife was there, pale, with two red spots in her cheeks. Jed would have to be especially kind to Mrs. Carver today.

Francine spotted Jed standing with his back to her, his broad shoulders straining at the seams of his old blue coat. Surely the committee would understand new clothes were a necessity and not a luxury for Jed. Did they want their own preacher looking like a ragbag? But Jed always shrugged off her attempts to smarten him up, kissing her absently and reminding her that he was storing up his treasures in heaven, instead.

She was always a little shocked that he really believed all those things that he said from the pulpit. He expected her to believe them, too. She never quarreled with him about it, but underneath the coppery hair her brain ticked shrewdly. She had no time to waste on folderol. If God was there, it was all very well. He'd never done much for her, and she didn't see any particular evidence of Him in the world around her. He probably didn't favor mealymouthed whiners any more than she did herself.

But for Jed, the Bible and his religion were real things, vibrant, vital, full of mystery and meaning. She saw it in him, and was always a little surprised that a grown man could give such total attention to something that was just a bunch of ideas. It provided a living for them, certainly—but what an odd way to make a living, selling ideas and the breath of God! It all seemed quite unstable to her, as if it could go with a puff of wind. She had resolved to lay something aside, just in case. It would ease her mind.

Jed really was remarkably unconcerned about his appearance, for such a handsome man. She felt a surge of wifely pride as she looked at him, the sun dappling his coat under the shade trees. He was balancing a tiny plate of potato salad, ridiculously small in his huge hand, and looking around unsuccessfully for a place to put down his cup of punch. He was talking to Mr. Farley, probably concerning funds to hire the new choir director. Mr. Farley was looking unconvinced. She picked her way carefully through a patch of damp to avoid dirtying her shoes.

"I just don't believe that anything can be done without it, Mr. Farley," Jed was saying as she came up to him. His blue eyes were focused intently on Mr. Farley's somewhat shriveled person. "The church simply must be a pleasant place to be, or people will fall away. And we can't make improvements without funds, however hard we may pray."

Francine slipped up beside Jed quietly. She relieved him of the awkward punch cup and slipped her arm through his, turning the full battery of her green eyes on Mr. Farley. Farley was as sour and pinched as if he had been nursed on goat's milk, and looked as though he hadn't bathed since the last church picnic, she noticed with distaste. She held out her hand to him and smiled.

"Mr. Farley."

"There you are, darling," Jed said with relief. "I've just been telling Mr. Farley—"

"I'm quite sure Mr. Farley knows just exactly what needs to be done, don't you, Mr. Farley?" she said, caressing the words. "Mr. Farley has never been remiss in doing what needs to be done for the Lord's house, Jed. I'm ashamed to think you would imply it."

"I didn't—" Jed stammered.

"Certainly not," said Mr. Farley, mumbling into his mustache. "Certainly not re—remiss." His watery eyes fastened on Francine as he pressed her hand moistly. "Do all I can, of course."

"That's lovely, Mr. Farley," she said, with her brightest smile. "I just knew we could count on you. Now you men must stop talking business— this is a party! And I think I would like some barbecue—it smells just heavenly."

Mr. Farley offered her his arm, and she kissed Jed on the cheek lightly. Now she would be caught with old Barley-water Farley all afternoon, and he would edge too close to her on the picnic blanket, she was sure, and put his grubby hands on her shoulder. But it was a small price to pay for the new choir director. Perhaps she could manage a new carpet for the church lobby, as well.

"Now, Jed, don't forget to keep the punch going round, darling, we don't want the young men getting dry and slipping off for their own refreshments."

Jed nodded, as Francine went away on Mr. Farley's arm, bending her head down to him flatteringly. He heard the high crystal of her laughter over the noises of the picnic. He felt confused and uneasy, though he couldn't tell why. She had handled Farley beautifully—one of the richest and crustiest old sinners in the parish, who took a certain perverse pleasure in withholding badly needed funds from the church until Jed had humiliated himself to a proper degree. And here Francine had gotten Farley, light as meringue. It was quite a miracle. Still, Jed felt something strange.

He noticed Francine these days. She was growing up from a scrawny cat-eyed thing into a firm-fleshed and lovely woman, smoothing his path under his feet. He had much to be grateful for, certainly. And he had the oddest feeling sometimes, when she was near him—a warm sensation, like feathers. He watched her, and the curve of her jawline. She came into his mind at odd times, in the middle of day.

He felt sometimes an unaccountable thrill of apprehension, a wrinkling of his skin. She had become everything he could have asked for—lovely, demure, socially adept, untiring in her church work, endlessly patient, always willing to turn a situation, laying calm on it like a sheet of glass, hands like cream. Her voice was soft and reasonable, beguiling.

She gave herself to him willingly enough, but there was part of her, he was sure, that he did not touch. It frightened him, as though he had lost something he didn't know he had. He felt a rising hunger in him, as if he were hovering outside a window, where inside on a table lay a feast and his heart's desire, and he could only hang helplessly and look at it through the glass.

Later that afternoon, Francine slipped away from Mr. Farley, with relief. She walked quickly away, before someone else could drag at her. She just had to get away from the crowd, away from the crying babies and and pouting girls, the mothers determined that everyone eat their cheese pie.

She walked until the air was quiet, and sat in the grass with her back against the trunk of a tree, not caring if the bark marked it. She put down her plate with its red-stained barbecue and potato salad, barely touched. She looked off dreamily into the scrubby oak thicket around the clearing, playing with the blades of grass that she pulled up. She was planning a baby's dress, white with pink shirring, and shoes with ties of satin ribbon. She would cut up her wedding dress to do it. She had saved it for just such a thing.

She heard a rustling in the branches above her, and felt a shock. Her heart pounded. She leapt to her feet, her fists at her side, and looked up.

"Hello," said a voice from up in the tree. She saw a young man perched in the fork of the largest branch, eating an apple and swinging his free leg.

"Do you want to come up?" he said, and extended his arm to her enticingly.

She went white with rage. "I thought I was alone here."

"So did I," he said, unperturbed. "Do you want to come up, or not?"

"Certainly not," she said, working to keep her voice level. "I don't climb trees like a monkey."

"Have it your way," he said, and laughed down at her. His eyes were very blue—as blue as Jed's, she realized. His hair sprang from a perfect widow's peak.

She studied him as if he couldn't see her, strangely entranced with the way he sat in the tree and ate his apple, swinging his leg and surveying the world as if he liked it. His coloring, she realized, was very much like Jed's—the dark hair and the eyes, except that Jed was becoming florid already and stocky, ponderous, while this man was thin as a knife.

He arched an eyebrow at her, almost up to his hairline. She was suddenly aware she had been staring at him. She colored, and looked down.

"Will I do?" he asked.

"I'm afraid not," she said coolly, and then laughed at the sound of herself talking to a man in a tree. The anger suddenly rose and burst in her throat like a soap bubble, and was quite gone. In its place was a wild recklessness.

He saw the change in her face, and extended his hand to her again, leaning down. This time she took it, and put one slippered foot against the trunk of the tree. Anchoring himself with his back hand, he gave a quick hard tug on her arm, and she found herself seated neatly on the branch beside him, her skirt and dangling feet obscured from the ground by the surrounding branches. She crossed her ankles primly.

"That's more like it, don't you think?" he said approvingly. "Look around."

She did. Spread around her was the most marvelous scene, something she had never seen before, and yet familiar, like something between sleeping and waking. To the right, over a gentle rise, the sun was about to set, rinsing the sky with silver clouds. She thought she had never seen that shade of silver before, the clouds lying over each other like strips of beaten lead, gleaming dully. The scrub and the reddish dust, stained with bracken, stretched away as far as she could see on either side of the thicket.

To the left she could see the occasional flash of the creek bed that ran down to the trees. Straight ahead was the town, the buildings penciled in low square lines on the soft air, some of the windows filled with yellow light against the coming darkness.

She looked back towards the picnic. Through the screen of leaves the people looked as silly as ants, repacking the dishes and folding blankets. Through the still air came talk, and the sounds of the whispering trees. In the distance the church bells rang for the end of the evening. A chill ran over her skin, and she shuddered.

Hiram looked at the woman next to him. What eyes she had! As though a devil lived there, behind the green glass. Her lips were very red and her skin very white, lightly freckled along the collarbone. Her dress was decorous, cut square at the neck, rounded over her breasts. The skin that showed was delicate, pulled tight over the notched bone at her throat where the pulse beat. He could see a faint sheen of perspiration there, and powder. It was skin that looked as if it would bruise easily, and he found himself wanting to put his lips on it and make a red mark in the middle of that expanse of whiteness, to try his teeth against the edge of the bone. She felt him looking at her, and stirred.

She felt there was nothing holding her but the gossamer air on her skin. She looked at the town and the trees, and saw them all suddenly sewn up into a great jeweled net, strands sparkling from thing to thing, shining in the dimness.

She had always hated twilight, always gone from room to room turning on all the lamps and lighting candles for the pools of yellow light that would fight the melancholy of the day passing into darkness. The reflective air of the early evening frightened her. She had no gift for self-examination.

But now, tonight, she was not afraid of the loss of another day. She looked out over the land and stretched out her arms to it, laughing with delight.

The church bells rang again, to count the hour. The sound brought her back to herself. She looked up and found the young man's eyes fixed on her, an unsmiling intensity in his gaze.

"I must go," she said. "They mustn't find me here."

"They won't," he said. She believed him.

He jumped down lightly, then reached up and helped her down, neatly unhooking her skirt from a twig that caught it. She stood for a moment on the ground with his hands around her waist, caught in the blue of his eyes and the very faint aftershave smell of his skin. The air was soft. She was almost as tall as he was. She looked straight into his face and laughed, then broke his hold on her and picked up her skirts to run back to the picnic.

She looked back once to see him standing there, that same odd, questioning look on his face. Then she ran on, feeling her blood smooth and racing under her skin, her hands tingling. She joined the others and helped clear away the last remains of the picnic, keeping her face hidden. Not one of the Ladies came over to ask her where she had been. No one noted with disapproval her flushed face, or spotted the twig that had caught itself in the smooth pull of her hair, under her hat.

12. The Pike

Hiram watched her go. He had seen nothing like her since Nakomas Sorrel. He sat for a moment, thinking about Nakomas Sorrel. He thought of the fall of her black hair, the slant of her eyes, the notch in her chin. He remembered the pale curve of her bare feet, feeling an ache in his elbows that made him straighten out his arms. He pictured the Indian girl as he had last seen her, her skin pale and grey under its copper color, blood soaking straight from her knees to the floor, with the bundle in her arms.

He dreamed about it sometimes, watching Nakomas Sorrel, unable to rise, or move, to say a word as his mother went to do what must be done. He knew his mother looked at him differently now, a blank look, veiled with something he did not recognize.

He thought of Nakomas Sorrel, and Anise, and this new girl—the one with the roan-colored hair. Her hair, he thought, was the color of a horse he had when he was small, a pony with neat hooves and a black stripe running down the spine. This girl stirred things in him that Anise had never touched, although he had only known this girl for a few minutes.

He thought of Anise's upright ways, her fastidious bookishness. They suddenly seemed silly and pale. He had looked behind this girl's eyes and seen a creature that he knew, who went through life brushing the surface of things as he did, with no care for what went on underneath. He did not understand Anise's ceaseless prodding under the surfaces of things, her expectations of him, her rarefied fineness. Life for Hiram was immediate, something to be seized with the foot, the hand, something to be handled with motion and speed and grace.

Hiram was clever and shrewd but cared nothing for books. He only knew animal things, of instinct and balance. He could close a deal as gracefully as a cat. He read pulses, not words. Life sat on him lightly, as it sits lightly on all such creatures. He sensed that this girl was the same.

He was a man with pride, who kept things to himself. There was in his light touch a sort of showmanship, like the spieler of the medicine show—the created illusion of perfect escape. He practiced it until he could not tell it, himself, from the reality. Only his headaches showed the difference.

Hiram never talked about the migraines that came on him, creeping up around his neck and pressing against the sides of his face. No one ever saw him dosing himself with the bitter, pale packets of powder. He absented himself discreetly when he was ill, so that the only vision of him that people knew was rakish, upright, delicately and inflexibly balanced. Hiram was a man, and he knew what men were. The only poem he knew was by Rudyard Kipling, and part of it went:

> *If you can make one heap of all your winnings*
> *and risk it on one turn of pitch-and-toss,*
> *and lose, and start again at your beginnings,*
> *and never breathe a word about your loss . . .*
> *you'll be a Man, my son!*

Wester had made Hiram learn that poem by heart, and Hiram would teach it later to his daughters and his grandchildren. He would have taught it to his son, if he had one. The poem came to mean for Hiram the immaculate deception that pride demanded, the impossibility of admitting to a fault or a weakness, a failure or a debt. It was this poem that would lead him, in a way, to his destruction.

But in his youth Hiram had the stamina still, and the beauty to run the machine, to make it work with light and sound. His luck ran as lightly beside him as a dog.

He shook himself straight, raked his hands through his hair, put his hands in his pockets and went after the departing picnic. He was conscious of an odd, tight burning in the middle of his chest that had been there since the red-haired girl had thrown her arms open to the trees.

He went to church the next Sunday with Demeter and Fid. Demeter had heard promising things about young Reverend Net's preaching, and it had been her idea to come to the picnic. She was thinking of joining the congregation.

Hiram saw Francine sitting in the front row, her hands folded in her lap. Her bright hair was rolled on top of her head, and her dress was a dark sober blue, lying stiffly against her throat. He saw the dull gold of her wedding band gleaming against the dark blue. He hadn't noticed it before. He saw the space the others left around her, and her position in the pew, and knew that she was the preacher's wife.

And yet she had let him put his hands on her waist to swing her down from the tree, and had laughed while he watched, and spread out her arms. There had been a minute when she stood with her shoulders facing him, almost as tall as he was, and looked at him with her green eyes, something feral and wild behind them. There was a chink in her armor, no matter how straight she sat in the pew, or how firmly her hands were folded in her lap.

Francine had seen him walk in, the man from the tree, and she straightened her spine. Let him stare, and know who she was. The preacher's wife. Her minute of strangeness had passed, and she was herself again. She remembered the picnic, the hot swirls of green and bluish leaves, with a euphoria that left her dizzy and shaken. It would be her secret. Today she was the preacher's wife again, secure in her position. She lifted her chin.

After the service the stranger came over to her and smiled, introducing himself. She looked into his eyes calmly, and gave him her hand. Her palm was dry and cool.

"How do you do," she heard herself saying as she met his eyes. "So glad you enjoyed the service." She stood beside Jed, receiving thanks and fielding invitations, bending her head smoothly and smiling at the people who grasped her hands and asked her about renting tables at the bazaar.

Hiram left the church and wandered out into the sunlight, feeling vaguely cheated. She had removed herself from his reach. He could feel it. The splendid, tightly reined woman was closed to him, and he felt the pang, the wrongness of it.

He walked back to the house that he shared with Demeter, with the heat of the sun on his shoulder blades. He changed his coat and went out to get coldly, purposefully drunk. He drank all night, sitting in a dark bar with sawdust on the floor and sticky rings on the boards of the table. Men who came in left him alone, seeing his smooth tapered face set.

Hiram skipped work the next day, and the next. He stayed at the bar and drank, red-eyed. The bartender wiped the table around him, and silently refilled his glass when it was empty.

Hiram watched the light filter through the tilting whiskey in his hand, considering. He squinted at the amber liquid with one eye, and then the other. He thought about Fid. Fid had become submerged in Demeter. He was becoming a person strange to Hiram. This new person was different than the lanky, complaisant boy who had trailed Hiram since he could remember. Fid was strengthening and straightening, getting some starch to his spine, organizing his things. He smiled more often, and said things.

Demeter had been Hiram's twin and Fid his shadow, but now, as they swayed toward each other, he felt them moving away from him. There was an empty space where they had been. Hiram set the glass to his mouth with sudden decision and drank it down, his throat set against the burn, feeling the sweet tingle of it down to his belly.

After Hiram sobered up from his binge he was wilder, as if someone had set fire to the ends of his hair. His contract with Conoco ended, and he went into the trucking business, hauling concrete material—sand, gravel and cement—out to the places where bridges were being built. He owned two trucks, gravity dump trucks that held one square yard of material, with no cab and no windshield. There was a piece of canvas strapped on the gasoline tank, and Hiram sat there, driving the trucks forward over the rutted roads, gripping the steering wheel with white fingers.

On a hot, restless day, Hiram conceived the idea of crashing the two trucks together to create an enormous spectacle and bring the alarmed townsfolk running. He longed for speed and danger as he had once longed for the explosion of gunpowder and the rain of rocks during his powder monkey days.

He told Fid when Fid came to find him one evening at the saloon. Fid shifted when he saw the look in Hiram's eyes. He fought off an impending feeling of doom that made him scratch his head miserably.

The trucks were only wheels under a poorly constructed box, Fid pointed out, a spark waiting to ignite the gasoline tank which swayed and shifted under them.

Hiram said nothing. Fid looked at him, seeing that the line of muscle under Hiram's jaw was white with tension. He saw in Hiram's face a shadow of something lost, with a hard metallic edge. He knew that something had happened, something strange and subtle in which he had no part, and that Hiram didn't care, really, whether he lived or died. Fid sighed and scratched his head again and agreed to go along.

They planned the stunt for a Saturday night near the end of November. There would be plenty of people driving on the road, going to parties and coming home.

In the evening of that day they drank cupfuls of brown whiskey and left from the work yard, to avoid seeing Demeter standing on the porch, her hair coiled low over her ears and her hands in her white apron.

The trucks were cranky and started slowly in the cold air. They drove the trucks up over the crest of the hill side by side, the road unrolling in front of them like a shoulder bone, steep and baked white, shining faintly. They rolled down the long stretch, picking up speed in the rattling old vehicles, until Hiram felt the ground cutting him loose. He yelled happily, feeling his blood in his veins, free of the nagging feeling in the back of his head for the first time since he met the preacher's wife. Fid looked over at him, saw his eyes, dilated dark, and the skin stretched over his cheekbones. Fid tightened his own grip on the wheel.

They were going faster and faster, forcing the old trucks down the road, the ruts running under the wheels until Fid could feel all of the world turning to an absolute pull of unforgiving angles and vertices.

Hiram suddenly swerved and toppled into a ditch. Fid heard the tearing of the canvas as the truck rolled, and the squeal of metal. Then it was strangely silent as the truck lay upside down, wheels spinning slowly, the liquid gasoline underneath lambent and hungry for flame.

Fid braked his own truck and let it come to a stop, nosing it into the ditch with its front end pressed into Hiram's truck, as they had agreed. He got out to find Hiram. Dread had taken hold of him, and he moved slowly as if under water.

Hiram had been thrown clear, and lay on his back, his head tilted up and his eyes open, fixed on the sky. Fid dropped to his knees in the dust and lifted Hiram with one arm under his neck, looking frantically for dark spots on Hiram's starched shirt, streaked now with dirt. Hiram's long body was as yielding in his arms as a woman, and Fid lifted it up and buried his head against Hiram's shoulder, feeling a wild yearning unleashed in him, words that he had never spoken. Fid pressed his lips again and again to the white skin that showed through a long tear in Hiram's shirt, shaking with fear and shame.

After a minute Hiram stirred and freed himself with a gentle motion. "Look," he said. "Look up."

Above them the stars were wheeling in patterns like a net thrown on the sky, threaded with lead weights. It seemed to Fid, in the first great wash of his relief, that the stars were moving rapidly as he watched, swinging over their heads in vast arcs. As he knelt, still clutching Hiram's form convulsively in his arms, he felt the earth spinning madly, and the sway of the stars as if they might suck him up off the road with one breath and spit him out in the next. He was anchored only loosely to the surface of the earth. He reached down to the road with one hand as if to hold himself on it, to keep from drifting up.

He looked down into Hiram's eyes and saw the lights reflected there, double. Hiram was looking back at the overturned trucks, where a tongue of flame was licking out, festive and warm as a Christmas log. Hiram smiled.

"Leave me here," he said.

It was too close to the burning truck. Fid could smell the acrid smell of the charred canvas and melting rubber, and the gasoline. He moved to pull Hiram away, grasping him under the arms. Hiram broke away and got to his feet—he was quite unhurt—smiled at Fid, and hit him once, very hard, on the jaw. He caught Fid as he crumpled, and half pulled, half carried him to a patch of grass at a safe distance.

Then he went back and lay in the ditch where he had been. He could feel the heat of the fire now on his cheek, as it crackled and burned.

He closed his eyes and waited for the blast and the lift, the heat of the explosion. But it didn't come, and finally he opened his eyes and got up again, walking over to where the truck lay burning. He limped a little.

It was only a little fire that was burning the truck, he saw, mostly just the rotten canvas on top. All the excitement for nothing. He laughed at himself, standing in the middle of the road, and kicked dust over the flames to put them out.

Then he got into Fid's truck, which was still upright, and backed it up out of the ditch, back onto the road, the wheels screeching as they found purchase.

Cars had stopped and a crowd was beginning to form, peering curiously at the wreck.

Hiram drove the truck over next to Fid, who was beginning to stir groggily. He loaded Fid into the truck and drove away, leaving the group of motorists staring and pointing, watching the carcass of the burned truck lying still in the ditch.

That night Hiram lay awake with his arms folded behind his head, watching the sliding pattern of the branches outside the window. He thought of the preacher's wife in the tree. He could picture the exact shade of her hair, the roan color, like a rubbed penny. The hairs on her arms and her eyebrows were a lighter blond, almost white. He had seen eyes as hard as hers, but never in a woman.

He remembered the moment when she had stretched out her arms and laughed, for some reason that he didn't understand. She had spread her arms as if to take everything in, and hold it. And he had been part of that everything, at ease as he had never been. There was that sense of animal splendor about her that showed only through her teeth, pointed like the teeth of feral dogs. He knew her, knew the way she touched things.

Anise was gone, and only a vague shadow of her remained in his mind. He desired her, and yet she oppressed him, her rigidity stifled him. But her distance left him unbalanced, unfinished—he floated like something loose on the surface of the sea.

He got out of bed, too restless to be still. Outside, the shadows slid over each other. He dressed quickly and went downstairs, skipping the sixth step, which squeaked, and left a note for Demeter. It said, "Going out. I'm fine. See you soon. Love, Hiram." Fid would take care of Demeter, the business. Or maybe the business would die, fold of its own accord. That would be just as well. Hiram was sick of it. He was sick of everything.

He wanted to be free of the town. He had been in one place for too long. He went outside and started his car, feeling its welcoming air around him, stale and smelling of cigarettes and old leather. He slid the car out of the driveway, humming a toneless tune in his head, and took the car into the night.

He drove all night, hardly tired. At dawn he stopped at a roadhouse, pulling over the gravel with a skating sound, and paid a dollar for a room with grey sheets that smelled of mildew. He put his head down and fell asleep immediately, a soundless sleep that buried him. When he woke he breakfasted on black coffee and watery eggs, and got back into the car.

Hiram drove for three days, stopping only to eat or to sleep. The motion under the wheels was soothing to him, taking the edge off his nerves. He slept so little toward the end that he seemed to be sliding in and out of shadows as he drove, passing through borderlands where all the leaves were blue and spoke to him with strange voices, over the roof of the car. He swung the wheel like a rudder, singing to himself to stay awake.

On the afternoon of the fourth day Hiram saw in front of him on the road a man riding a palomino and leading a dark horse behind him, with a large bundle strapped on its back. The man was hatless, the sun shining on his bright white hair. He wore heavy silver jewelry with blue stones set into it. He had a strange look about him—an innocent, reckless air of the road. He tipped his head to the side, and whistled as he rode. Hiram slowed the car. The man turned around in his saddle, stopping his horse.

"How do," the man said, tipping his head to the side and looking at Hiram as if he had been expecting him. "You headed far?"

"Minnesota," said Hiram, because he had heard it somewhere and liked the sound of it.

"That's a fair piece," said the man, scratching under his chin. His voice was deep and throaty, burned-sounding. "Care to share a bite here before you go so far?"

Hiram realized that he had not, in fact, eaten since the night before. He was suddenly hungry. Water filled his mouth, and he nodded. The man laughed. His large eyes were brown and deep as a cow's, with something sad in them. The man guided his horses off the road onto a rutted track. Hiram followed with the car, bumping roughly until the track turned downward and crossed a small stream in a welter of mud.

It was cooler off the track, and dark with trees. Hiram stopped the car and got out, looking at the creek bed. He'd never get the car over it, or back. The man pulled up beside him, and tossed Hiram the reins of the packhorse.

"She's gentle," the man said, and let his own horse pick its way across the stream, hooves hitting the rocks like glass.

Hiram put his hands flat on the packhorse's back, feeling the coarse hair warmed by the sun. He jumped up, locking his arms straight, and swung one leg over in front of the pack. He felt the smell of the horse sink into his scratchy city clothes. He looked down at his car, sitting randomly in a welter of sticks and wet leaves, and he felt suddenly light and happy. He turned the horse and raced it up the hill, next to the man.

The man took no notice of him when Hiram pulled abreast, but pointed, when they reached the top of the hill, to a wooded cove that formed a gentle curve. The stream flashed nearby. There was a ring of stones around a blackened firepit.

"Camp," he said.

They rode to the place and Hiram saw to the horses, loosening the girths and wiping them down with handfuls of dry grass. Out of the corner of his eye he watched the man, who was pulling the large bundle off the packhorse and unrolling it. It was a package of long straight poles, and a huge piece of pure-white leather. As Hiram watched, the man bound the tops of the poles together at one end and set them upright, splaying the bottom ends, and swinging the leather deftly around them like a cape. In a few minutes it was a tepee, white as the rocks, with the trees around it. Hiram moved closer and touched the leather, wondering at its softness and the fineness of the stitches that seamed the hides together.

The man started a fire with wood he gathered quickly and efficiently, knocking a dry branch into pieces over his knee, and lit it with an elaborately engraved silver cigarette lighter he took from an inside pocket. Hiram noticed that the lighter was set with the same blue stones that the man wore on his fingers.

The man retrieved a dull metal coffeepot from the saddlebags, poured coffee and water into it, and set it on a rock in the firepit. This done, he turned to Hiram and smiled, his fingers spread wide.

"So where do you come from, that you would go all the way to Minnesota to get away?" he asked. His enunciation was curiously clear and distinct, with an odd rhythm to it. As he mixed sourdough starter from a tin with flour and water, and set it to cook, and cut long strips off a rasher of bacon to fry, Hiram told him.

He told the stranger things he hadn't thought of for a long time. He told about the Indian dance, about Nakomas Sorrel and the son who was never born. He told about Anise and the staged truck crash, of the strange look in his mother's eyes when she looked at him. He told of Fid and Demeter and his loss, and of the truck burning and the golden flame he dreamed of. The only thing he did not mention was the red-haired woman in the tree. He talked until his voice was hoarse, talked the sun down, until it began to get cold and he shivered a little in his shirt sleeves.

The man, who said his name was Jeffrey, handed him biscuits and bacon without comment. He watched as Hiram talked himself exhausted. When the moon had risen and Hiram fell silent, Jeffrey got up, brushed off the seat of his jeans and went into the tepee, where he had laid out the sleeping things. He took a red plaid blanket, smelling of horse, and tossed it to Hiram. Hiram rolled himself into it and fell asleep by the fire, feeling the heat recede from him as the fire died. The dark weighed down his head and filled it with emptiness so that he slept.

The next morning at sunrise he woke to the smell of black coffee, and sat up, tousled and dirty, to take the cup that Jeffrey handed him. Jeffrey was fresh and cheerful as though he had just bathed. His white hair shone in the sun. He cooked flapjacks over the fire, making perfectly round circles of golden brown in the dented skillet, sliding and flipping them with deft shakes of his wrist.

As he cooked, Jeffrey told Hiram of roads beyond this place, and even beyond that, roads that unfolded across the land from a black center like a web, old ways that spun out from wherever you stood, rippling under your feet like a red gullet in a swallow.

Jeffrey spoke of things that he had known, of ways a man could see through to the heart of things. He showed Hiram paintings he had made, canvases he kept rolled into his bags with his supplies. They were stormy grey-and-blue paintings of horses and men against the sky.

He told Hiram how he painted them from the center out, from one tiny dot of color, so that he might paint first the nostril of a horse, in the middle of the canvas, and then the nose in front of it, and the arched neck behind it, working outward as though running fire over invisible ink to make the painting show. It was like the roads, he said, the same way of standing at the center and feeling things wheeling out around you.

He told Hiram about consenting, and how the ancient Greeks in the temple would stroke down hard on the muzzle of the sacrificial stallion before cutting its throat, so that the horse would appear to nod, consenting to its own death. Consenting to your own death is the thing, he said. People fear death—they barricade the door with dressers like frightened children, and set the back of a chair under the doorknob, as if that would help. They bar the way with money and things, lovers and cars and danger, but death always comes through the door, in the end.

To embrace your death, volunteer for it, shoulder it—that's the thing, said Jeffrey, pouring another mug of coffee. That's the only way to live life without fear. No one can take from you what you offer up voluntarily. Your death walks with you always, just over your left shoulder, and that's the way it should be.

His words fell around Hiram like drops of water, with a pattern that he strained to see. And when he did see it for a minute, it drove to the middle of what he knew and split it open like a pomegranate. For one moment he knew that he could do with his life as he wished, if he would only take on himself the weight of his own body. He saw that he had weight and heft in the world, that he was drawing an indelible line with his life, a line that could not be erased.

And as Jeffrey talked the sun went down again. They had spent the whole day talking, carving bits of ham off the bone, wrapping it in bread, getting up to relieve themselves behind the trees. Hiram thought it was time to go. He stood and shook Jeffrey's hand, feeling as he did so a strange shiver run through him. His skin felt achy, and strange, and his vision wavered. Jeffrey held his hand for a long moment, the brown eyes very deep. Then he smiled and let go, with a slight pressure.

Hiram walked off down the hill towards his car, his hands in his pockets. He was very cold. As he walked, stumbling over loose rocks, he looked over his shoulder and saw a woman who looked like his sister, walking a little behind him. Her hair was in dark braids, plaited and tied smooth as Demeter had worn hers when she was young. Her face was hidden, and shadowy, but her skin seemed to give off a radiance that was smooth and hard, like a stone. She walked with a tread that matched his own, a weighty spring unlike a woman's. Bits of sage and brush bent as she passed, but her footsteps were silent. He stopped to wait for her, but as she came abreast of him she vanished as if she had turned a corner into the air, and taken a path that he could not see.

Hiram thought it might have been his own death that he had seen, walking to his left as Jeffrey had told him it would. He went on to his car, the deepening twilight reassuringly empty. He felt light, and giddy. He heard bells tolling in the distance. A dog howled somewhere, and he shivered.

He found his car waiting for him at the cut, the creek flowing darkly in front of it. He got in, rolled up the windows and locked the doors and fell asleep on the front seat. When he woke he sat up slowly, the mark of the armrest pressed into his cheek. His head swam, and when he looked into the mirror, his eyes looked dark and large, as if the pupils were spilling over into the blue. His throat felt odd and swollen, and his head ached.

He wondered if he had a fever, if the man and the woman he had seen were all a feverish dream, the man in the white leather tent, the girl walking behind him, expectation rising from her like the wind off a snowbank. He wondered how long he had been locked in the car. The air was stale and dull inside. He saw mud on his shoes—he had been out, then, in the forest, that much was true.

He turned the key in the ignition. To his relief, it started right off. He eased it over the muddy track back onto the road.

He drove for two more days. His tongue swelled in his head, until it seemed to take up the entire back of his throat. He crossed state lines, and officers in brown uniforms played their lights over him, suspicious of his pale face and wild, glittering eyes. But they searched the car and could find no reason to refuse his passage.

The days turned into nights and back into days, and he drove holding tightly to the wheel. The wheel was the only thing, it seemed, that stayed steady, as the world beyond the windshield dipped and poured in a tilted blur. Once he thought he saw a girl tending a flock of geese in a green field, so green that it was the color of poison, rippling and shining before him.

The heads of the geese were white, and Hiram stopped the car to lay his head in the goose girl's lap, for her cool hand to come down on his hot forehead. But when he staggered to the field there were no geese there, and no girl, but only white flowers, slick with pollen. He went back to the car and drove on.

He drove towards Minnesota, because he remembered Lee telling him about it, about a trip she had taken there once. She had told him of thick ice on the puddles, and blue sky over snow.

He said the word to himself, Minnesota, over and over, beating his hand in time against the steering wheel. It spoke to him of cold, of the depths of ice, the deep green of trees that would lie along his hot and swollen cheeks. He longed for the cold. The thought of the heat and dust of Texas was unbearable to him now. He wanted to lie still under a sheet of snow.

At moments he would blink his eyes and know that he was dangerously ill, that he must get help. Then the thought would slip mildly away and he would be sucked back into the vortex of the road, the wheels spinning under him, the road cast out before and behind him like the limbs of his own body.

By the time he reached Minnesota he had stopped eating altogether. He only drank water to cool his throat. He drove in the right direction with the concentration of a madman. He slept with his head pressed against the wheel when he slept at all, not bothering to lie down. Finally the air was cold around him, but his skin blazed and sang and filled the air with heat. He rolled down the window and swallowed great breaths of cold air that went into his lungs and pained him.

He drove straight until he reached the edge of a great frozen lake that stretched away into the distance as far as he could see. It was dotted with brown structures, small shingled houses with one side sheared away. Smoke rose from their tops.

The impetus driving him suddenly fell away, dropping him limp, and he sat staring at the lake, eyes half shut. He could not quite believe in this ice, this vast and crackling sea, like the white sand in his dreams.

A man came up to his window, stamping his feet and jingling in the cold. His face was sunk into a hood trimmed with grey fur. He looked into the car incuriously.

"Ice fishing, sir?" the man said.

Hiram nodded.

"That'll be fifty cents for the rental of an ice hut and harpoon from now until dark," the man said.

Hiram dug into his pockets and brought out some coins, gave them to the man. He was pleased to submit to someone else's will, now that his own had left him.

The man looked at him strangely—dressed for light weather, this one, no boots or warm clothes, a peculiar flushed look to his face. Still, there might be heavier clothes stashed in back. All kinds came to the ice lake, and it didn't do to ask questions.

He handed in through the window a harpoon with a handle four feet long, with three ugly hooked barbs on the end of the prongs.

"For the fish," the man said encouragingly when Hiram took it in his hand and looked at it blankly. The man wondered if this fellow was not quite right in the head. He moved slowly, stupidly, and his face looked swollen. Seemed harmless, though. "Your hut is number seventeen, third one along that line there—you can drive the car right out to it if you like, the ice is hard enough. Wood's stacked in the stove."

Hiram rolled the window up and drove slowly onto the ice. The man gestured after him, suddenly uneasy, then shrugged and went back into his hut to warm his feet over the grate.

Hiram let the car roll across the ice, feeling it move under his hands as if driving itself. The ice passed under the wheels silently, smoothly, with only a bump here and there. The strangest thing was the silence—the air was heavy with cold, muted so that he might have been on the surface of the moon.

He stopped the car at the hut numbered seventeen, and got out. He took with him, after a moment's hesitation, the strange trident. The man at the edge had been so insistent about it. His legs felt weak, as if they would hardly support his weight. Squinting his eyes against the white glare, he ducked his head to enter the little shack, straightening up once he was inside.

It smelled cool and musty inside, pleasantly dark with light coming in through the chinks in the walls. In one corner was a small wood stove, resting squatly on legs that raised it above the ice. At the other end of the rectangular hut was a rough hole chopped in the ice about three feet across, a thin skin of ice reformed over it since the last time it had been opened. An ice ax with a splintered handle lay near the hole. The floor of the hut was the same ice he had driven over, thick and glossily smooth, with ripples in it and a scarring of boot nails over the surface.

In the darkness of the hut, the light from under the ice blazed up at Hiram. It was like looking into a lighted aquarium. He fell to his knees. Waves of light from under the water passed over his face. Looking down towards the bottom, he saw a world of aquamarine and gold beneath him, fishes that swam and sank through underwater palms. He saw a landscape, deep and listing, filled with plants and animals sliding beneath his vision. He felt himself on the edge of mystery, hanging over a strange world. His vision began to blur, and the pounding in his temples grew worse. He rubbed his hand over his eyes to clear the mist.

He thought he could make out, far beneath him, the rising and falling of hills and mountains under the ice. Things crawled among them, ridden like horses. There was a white track that passed through the underwater countryside like a road. As he squinted at it he could make out a city, turreted with tiny castles and walks, pennants flying, an entire country below him. There was motion there, tiny figures moving along the roads. One of them caught his attention. It was rising, becoming larger and larger as he watched.

He blinked hard and saw a woman, a woman's body with the tail of a fish, winking silver in the dim light, swimming up towards him. Her torso was bare, perfectly white, with smoothly modeled breasts and pale arms. The tips of her nipples were dark and he thought her face was the face of the red-haired woman, the preacher's wife. She reached her arms to him, imploring.

As he squinted, trying to peer through the ripples of water that obscured his vision, he saw that she had Anise's face, the dark hair and the tender arch of skin below her brow. It was Anise, there under the water, and she was saying something to him, sadly, reaching up her arms, wound with pearls, and there were pearls in her hair.

He could see her lips moving, and the dread in her eyes, but no matter how he struggled he could not understand her, couldn't make out the words. It was like the day on the train platform, the day the train pulled away and her words were lost. It maddened him, that he couldn't understand, and he saw her drifting away, deeper and deeper, spinning down as if sucked into a deep water current.

He went wild with rage, that he couldn't hear her, didn't know what she was saying, and she was leaving, and he seized the ice ax and chopped at the ice, breaking through it. He took up the harpoon and stabbed down through the broken skin of the ice, stabbing through the broken shards, pushing the barbs towards her. She would not escape without telling him, not this time.

With all his strength he stabbed down. The ugly metal tines struck her, pierced into her white breast, and she raised surprised eyes to him, touching the dark blood that ran from her side. He stabbed down again, shuddering with horror, wanting only to finish it now, to make her stop looking at him. The tines pierced into her again, and lifted her, arching her back, her silver scales gleaming up towards the hole in the ice where he waited.

His breath was fast and he waited over the hole with his lips curled back over his teeth, drawing her up, pulling her. She drifted up towards him and then broke finally through the hole, gasping for breath, her eyes on him still surprised and round. And when he took her in his arms and forced the tine out of her breast, holding her and looking down at her, the silver light that shone from her skin began to die, leaving first the broad rainbow fin of her tail, and running in a sea of grey up her body until it entered her white skin, all becoming grey as lead. Finally the grey ran up into her face, so that the questioning look was frozen in her eyes, not understanding.

He pressed down on her eyes to close them, and take away the terrible question. And he held her cold, stiffening body to him and wept, tearing sounds that came up his spine as he sat there, rocking her body in his arms.

When the occupant of hut seventeen didn't check in after dark, the concessionaire called the sheriff. He was cautious about troublemakers, and remembered how odd the fellow had looked. Together the two men drove the sheriff's cruiser over the ice to the hut, and parked next to the Model T that was sitting there. They bent their heads and stepped inside the hut cautiously.

It was cold inside, and dark. The wood was still stacked inside the stove, which had not been lit.

The sheriff shone his torch around the dim interior, and his breath hissed in between his teeth. By the torch light, next to the ice hole, they saw a lightly dressed young man lying on the ice. He was tossing and twitching, his eyes swollen almost shut, muttering incoherently in the last stages of hypothermia and typhus. And clutched in the young man's arms was the slowly freezing body of a huge grey pike, one of the largest fish that the concessionaire had ever seen pulled from the lake in winter.

13. The Crucifix

A house burned down in Jed's parish, and he went to help rebuild it. Jed had given a particularly fine sermon the day of the fire, concerning the everlasting flames that awaited those who fell from grace, the searing, bone-charring heat in which sinners would dangle forever like spitted game. He was pleased with the sermon at the time. Later, in view of the disaster, he wondered if his choice of subject had been insensitive. Still, how could he have known?

The congregation turned out in force for the rebuilding, and it took on a festive air, like an old-fashioned barn raising. The Ladies brought picnic lunches, and the young girls crowded around to watch. The young men went about importantly and rolled their shirts back over their forearms, confidently wielding their hammers and saws. The work went quickly.

Jed was in good spirits, with his coat off, up among the men working hard. He felt that, in this moment, he was doing what the Lord had designed him to do: mixing his spiritual ministry with vigorous physical aid to his flock. His muscles stretched and bunched powerfully, hungry for the exercise. He sang with his robust baritone, leading the workers in hymns that made the work move quickly. It was almost, he thought, as if the Lord Himself were coming down to have a hand in the building.

Francine watched Jed from below. She saw him swinging his hammer wildly in time with his hymn singing, up near the top of the skeletal building, where the joists were loosely hung. He capered on top of the ladder, leading the builders on to greater feats, and she thought he looked foolish up there, his face ruddy with blood and good feeling.

As she thought it, she heard a crack, and someone yelled. The high slanted board propping up the ladder had come loose, and the ladder, with Jed on it, described a long graceful arc to the ground. He hit the ground with a crunch that reverberated to Francine's bones. She sat for a moment entirely still, frozen. She saw people running over to him, and heard women screaming.

She got up, dusted off her skirt and drifted over to him, almost as if her feet didn't touch the ground at all. She saw him lying on his stomach, his arm doubled under him. She watched his back and saw no movement.

The people around him fell silent, waiting for her.

"Roll him over," she ordered.

They rolled him over. His face was pale under its coating of tan. She noted with relief that he was breathing. But his arm, the hand that had been caught under him when he fell, was at a bad angle, unnatural. White bone showed through. And there was blood on his hand, so much of it that she wondered wildly where it could all have come from—surely there was not so much blood from a break? Then she saw the sharp-pointed end of the hammer he had been working with. It had driven up through the palm just in the center of his hand, where all the lines intersect.

"Pull that out," she said, pointing. One of the men reached out and, with a shudder, pulled the hammer from where it was embedded in Jed's hand.

Francine dropped to her knees and took Jed's head in her lap. She knew a little medicine from the farm, when she and her mother had taken baling needles to sew up the torn bags of cows who had been caught by the barbed wire. Concussion and internal bleeding were the problems, she thought. The hand could be taken care of later.

"Wake up, Jed," she said urgently. She slapped him lightly on his face. "Wake up."

His eyelids fluttered, and opened slowly.

"Francie?" he said. His eyes were confused, roving over the circle of heads bent over him.

"You fell," she said. "Watch my finger. Follow it with your eyes."

She ran her finger in front of him, and he followed it. His pupils were dilated normally, she saw. She made him move each part of his body in turn, except his injured arm. He was dizzy, but seemed to have no internal injuries.

"My arm?" he said. "Is it bad?"

"It's pretty bad," she said. She brushed the hair back from his forehead. "It's bad enough."

She looked up at the men around them. "Can you carry him to the house?" she said. "And then call the doctor. That hammer was dirty."

They carried him back to the house. He winced over the ruts, but kept his lips pressed firmly together. Francine walked beside him, holding his hand.

"Take him up the stairs, and put him on the bed," she said. "And someone please go for Dr. Harrison."

They sent a boy to run for the doctor. The men who had carried him in hovered around the door, nervous as cats.

"Go on home," she told them finally. "I'll call you if there's need."

They left silently, to join their wives, who had already gone home to begin baking the mountains of casseroles, the plates of cookies and the pies with thin crusts that they would bring to the house later, and heap on the table.

Francine stayed by Jed, cleaning his wounds as best she could with some hot water and clean rags. The broken arm was ugly, with the frayed end of the bone coming through the skin. Jed groaned whenever she had to shift him at all.

But it was his hand that worried her the most. She had seen the edge of the hammer, coated with rust and mud, and all that dirt was now deep inside the wound. He yelled so loudly when she tried to clean it that she had to leave it alone.

The door opened and the boy they had sent for the doctor came skidding into the room. He was out of breath, and feeling important.

"Doc says he can't come," the boy said. "He's attending Mrs. Wilding, and she's having twins, and he can't come now."

"For heaven's sake," said Francine. She stood up and wrapped a shawl around her shoulders and over her hair. "You stay here," she told the boy.

Walking quickly to the Wilding house she felt nothing but a vast impatience for the fools who surrounded her. Was there nothing that she didn't have to take care of herself? There was no one, no one at all for her to lean on. She was all alone. Underneath the impatience, she felt a growing sense of panic, and dread.

She opened the door to the Wilding house and went in without knocking. Up the white-painted stairs in front of her she could hear deep groans. Then there was silence.

She went up the stairs cautiously, and met Dr. Harrison coming out of the room at the top, wiping his hands on a towel. His face was drawn and weary. He brightened when he saw her.

"Mrs. Net," he greeted her. "I'm glad you're here. We're getting close now, and I'll need another pair of hands."

"I came about Jed, Doctor," she said. "He fell. His arm's broke, and his hand. You have to come, you have to come see him right away!"

He shook his head as if to clear it. "Oh, I'm sorry, it went clean out of my head. Francine, I can't come see Jed now. We've got twins turned backwards, three lives hanging on the line in there, and there's no way in the world I can leave her. You just dose Jed with some strong brandy, get those cuts clean and make him as comfortable as you can. He'll be fine. And I'll be there just as soon as I can, I promise you."

She turned away without waiting to hear more, and walked back to the house. Inside, she dismissed the boy, and went back to take her place by Jed. He was tossing slightly. His arm was hot to her touch, and the skin felt odd and flaccid. She picked up the rag and began bathing his face with it, automatically.

She sat by him all night, listening to Jed's muttering voice grow hoarse. The doctor finally came toward morning, his face white with fatigue. Jed was quiet. Francine wasn't sure if he was unconscious again, or just asleep.

"Get me clean rags," the doctor said to her brusquely, "and hold his head. Are you squeamish?"

She swallowed, and shook her head.

"Good, because there's no one here to tend to you if you faint. This is going to be bad. Are you ready?"

She nodded.

"All right, then," said the doctor, and he took hold of Jed's hand and gave a tremendous pull. Jed screamed, a deep sound ripped from him, and then fell back into unconsciousness. Francine looked at the bone in wonder, and saw that the arm was straight again, as it used to be.

The doctor splinted it neatly, and wrapped it with a plaster mixture that he mixed in one of her deep salad bowls. "That should hold," he said. "Now let's take a look at that hand."

He frowned as he peeled off her homemade bandage to look at the deep wound in Jed's palm. He poked at the flesh, but didn't say anything.

"Is it bad?" she said, unable to stand the silence.

The doctor nodded noncommittally. "There's some infection here. Keep it clean, and change the bandage often."

Francine looked over to see, and was shocked by the sight of Jed's hand, already swollen and turned an odd yellow color around the wound.

"It happened so fast," she said.

"It can," said the doctor grimly. "I'll be back later today."

Jed was quiet, so Francine saw the doctor to the door. He nodded to her, and left.

The doctor came every evening for the next few days. He looked at Jed, nodded over his arm and frowned over his hand. Francine thought that Jed wasn't healing as he should. His hand continued puffy and swollen, and the wound looked black.

Jed was mostly sunk into a restless sleep for two days. On the third day he woke up briefly, and asked for water. She gave it to him, holding his head so that he could drink comfortably.

"How am I doing?" he said, looking at her.

His attempt to smile pulled at her.

"Fine," she said, lying briskly. "The doctor says you're going to be just fine."

"What is it?" he said.

"Your palm," she said. "The hammer went into your palm." She felt a stab of fear when she said it.

"Like stigmata," he said, with that ghastly attempt at a smile. "You know, Francie"—his voice was very soft, and she bent her head near so that she could hear—"I was thinking that this must be the Lord's doing. I was feeling . . . I was in His hand that day, on the building. And then, the mark in my palm. Maybe this is a test. He's testing me."

His head rolled, and his eyes closed again. She let his head down gently onto the pillow.

Hogwash, she thought. If this is the work of the Lord, I want no part of Him. The Lord, indeed.

The doctor came and went, and the hours dragged for Francine. She sat by Jed and wiped his forehead, changed his horrible bandages. Each time, she saw that his hand was more swollen, turning dark shades of yellow and purple. The next morning, she saw a streak of red running up his arm. She watched it, appalled. In the space of twenty minutes the streak ran from his wrist to his elbow. She called the doctor. He came at once.

"It's gangrene, Francine," he said bluntly. He had learned respect for her during these last few days, and he appreciated that she did not faint or fall into hysterics. "I'll have to take his hand. We don't have time to get him to the hospital now. It's that or lose him altogether."

"Take it, then," she said, and her voice was steady.

She went into her room and took a bottle of smelling salts out of her dresser drawer. She had never used them. They were a present from her mother.

She took them into Jed's room, broke the seal and waved them under his nose. His eyelids flickered and lifted.

"You have gangrene," she said. "The doctor said he has to take the hand."

"If thy hand offend thee, cut it off," he whispered. "You're my good girl, Francine."

She looked down at him, and kissed him on the forehead. Then she went to tell the doctor that they were ready.

The doctor forced Francine to leave the room for the actual operation. She sat curled in a ball outside the door, her hands over her ears, but she could hear the scream, the silence, the sound of the saw rasping through bone. It was a sound she would remember.

The doctor called her in after it was over. The doctor was pale, but looked satisfied. He had pulled up the sheet under Jed's chin, and balled the bloody bandages in a corner. Jed was unconscious with morphine. The doctor patted Francine on the shoulder kindly.

"It's all in God's hands now," he said. "If the fever breaks by morning, we've caught the infection in time and he'll live. Give him these every few hours, for the pain." He left.

Francine sat in the chair, with her head dropped down onto her knees. In God's hands. The words rang in her ears. She saw a huge pair of hands, with dark hair on the knuckles, holding Jed, the fingers closing on him, squeezing tighter and tighter until she couldn't see Jed anymore. She sat up with a start. She had fallen asleep for a moment. She hadn't had a proper night's sleep in almost a week.

In God's hands. Suddenly her control snapped. She grabbed her wrap off the hook, and went out into the night. God's hands. She found herself running down the streets, her feet pounding on the pavement. A scream was building in the back of her throat. She could feel it there, like bile.

She pounded on the door of the first house that she came to. It was the Adlers'. Mrs. Adler was an officer for the Ladies Aid. Francine rested against the doorframe, her breath coming in sobs.

"Answer the door," she said under her breath. "Answer the door, you old cat."

The door flew open and Mrs. Adler was standing there in her housecoat, her hair filled with curlers.

"Why, Francine Net, whatever are you doing here at this hour?" she said, her voice rising at the end. "How is the reverend? Oh, I do hope that he isn't—"

"Come with me," Francine said curtly. She grabbed Mrs. Adler's elbow and pulled the astonished woman into the street, slippers and all. She ignored Mrs. Adler's objections and feeble struggles to free herself. Francine felt strength pouring through her veins like a wild tide.

She went from house to house of the Ladies Aid, holding Mrs. Adler in front of her like a hostage. At each house, she seized the Lady who answered the door and pulled her into the growing crowd of bewildered, sleep-frazzled women. They shuffled down the street like a herd of cattle, moving as if hypnotized by the bright beacon of Francine's hair underneath the streetlight. They complained in frightened voices as Francine dragged them along, striding through the deserted streets.

"I think she's lost her mind, that's what," said one woman to another beside her, under her breath. "The reverend's illness has just driven her stark out of her head. We must humor her, poor thing."

But the truth was that none of the Ladies could have left if they wanted to. Francine had fixated their wills, and they were drawn along in her wake like leaves, only protesting weakly.

Finally they saw that Francine was leading them to the church. She swung open the heavy wooden doors. A faint light of streetlamps and the moon came in through the windows, illuminating the whitewashed walls and the plain wooden pews. The large crucifix hung blankly over the altar.

Francine shepherded them all inside the church, and forced Mrs. Adler down onto her knees in the front pew.

"Go on!" She gestured angrily. "The rest of you, go on!"

They knelt at the pews, confused, wrapped in their house robes, their rumpled hair in long braids or covered with scarves.

"Now," said Francine. She lit the candles on the altar. She stood up straight and her shadow flickered, enormous, on the wall behind her. "Now pray! You're so holy," she said, spitting the words. "You have so much faith. So pray. Pray for Jed. You all say you love him so much. You talk about the Lord this and the Lord that, and the power of His Word and the Blood of His Lamb. Well, I seen real blood tonight, and I'm not seeing any more, you hear me? I got a child coming, and he needs a father. So you just pray in this church until I tell you to stop."

She went to stand like a sentry at the door. The women on their knees were silent.

"Pray," Francine commanded, and her words rang out through the church. One of the women began to pray timidly.

"Dear Lord," she said.

"Louder," said Francine.

And so they prayed, through the night. When one of the women tried to get up to creep through the door, she found Francine standing there in front of her, frowning, her red hair blazing in the dim light. "Like Lilith, for all the world," one of the women told her husband later. "I swear, Francine could have been devil spawn herself, for as crazy as she acted, and all of us frightened to death and not a thing we could do."

They prayed until the moon set and the stars went dim, their voices growing hoarse and exhausted. The candles guttered and went out. And when at last the sun began to shine weakly in the far corner of the sky, Francine released them. They straggled stiffly through the streets, bewildered, home.

Francine went home herself, her steps light through the dust of the early morning. She went up the stairs and into the bedroom where Jed lay, silently. He lay so still that for a moment her breath caught in her throat.

But then she put her hand on his forehead, and saw the pulse in his throat. His skin was cool, cool and normal, and he slept in a healthy, untroubled sleep.

"Oh, Jed," she said, and she lay down and put her head on the pillow beside his, and fell asleep.

And that's how Francine found faith.

14. Jezebels

When they pulled the young man from the ice hut and searched his pockets, they found only one dollar and thirty-nine cents in change, and a crumpled letter with a return address on it from Anise Frankell, of Austin, Texas. The sheriff took the young man to the pauper's hospital, and sent a telegram to the address on the letter. The telegram read: "Young man found Minnesota very ill stop identity unknown stop this address in pocket stop please advise message ends."

Big Mother surprised everyone. When the wire arrived, she read it and stuffed it into her apron pocket. She knew at once that it must be Hiram. Fid had been over almost every day, sick with worry, wondering if Anise had heard from Hiram. Fid thought that perhaps Hiram had gotten impatient with the separation, and had gone to New York to fetch Anise back himself.

Big Mother didn't tell Fid that Anise's letters never mentioned Hiram anymore, that these days she wrote only about a young soldier from West Point named Tommie. Big Mother simply said that as far as she knew, Hiram was not with Anise, and left it at that.

But this was different. Hiram was there, in Minnesota, ill and alone. Hiram had touched something in Big Mother, some long-buried romance and blood in her. He smiled at her and held her hand warmly, brought her flowers and was always polite in a way that made her frail old heart stir.

Anise might still be in New York, doing who knows what foolishness. But Anise was pledged to Hiram, and Hiram was, by virtue of the engagement, still family, and Big Mother would wither in hell before she left some member of her family sick with typhus in a state like Minnesota.

She wondered for a moment what he was doing in Minnesota. Then she dismissed the thought from her mind.

She stood up and wrapped her shawl more firmly around her shoulders.

"Cumin," she called. "Come here."

"Coming, Mama," Cumin called, and Big Mother heard her footsteps on the stair. Big Mother sighed, looking at Cumin as she came in. Cumin had still not captured any beaux, for all of their difficult and expensive move to Austin. She was too starched, and prissy, perhaps. And not adept at using those wiles that even Big Mother knew were necessary to get a man. Cumin was always competent and businesslike, forthright and getting things done. She had none of the helplessness that men liked.

It was hard to understand. Anise, now, she was just as upright as Cumin, maybe more so. But the boys flocked around Anise all the same. Perhaps it was her tiny bones. She looked like a little thing, even though Big Mother knew she had the iron of a drill sergeant inside her. Cumin was a little bigger, looked a little raw. Well, it couldn't be helped.

"Cumin, pack me a trunk, and one for yourself," Big Mother said with more decision than Cumin had heard from her in a long time. "We're going to Minnesota."

The train ride to Minnesota seemed very long. Cumin slept, her cheek on a handkerchief to protect it from the soot. Big Mother sat upright, swaying with the motion of the train. Big Joe was away when she left, and just as well. He would never have allowed her to travel across the country this way, two women alone. She had left the boardinghouse in Marjie's competent hands, but to go this far away, with no men around, made Big Mother's heart pound and her palms sweat. She delicately patted the perspiration from her upper lip with her handkerchief, the nice one with the lace border. She had never been outside Texas, never ridden a train in her entire life.

And yet she had known what to do. She had walked to the train station, up to the window, and ordered their tickets in a firm voice. She had known to send a wire to the sheriff who had notified them, to tell him they were coming. She had strapped herself into her stiffest undergarment, and tied her traveling hat down strongly over her ears. She was amazed at herself, at the unexpected wells of firmness she had held in all these years. It occurred to her that no one had ever really needed her before. Not the way that Hiram needed her now.

But the dark country running by the windows outside, the clicking of the rails and the constant swaying of the seats back and forth terrified her, despite her resolve. Why, any one of those men she had passed might come in this compartment at any minute. They might pull out a gun, or expose themselves, demand that she and Cumin give up their bags, or take her wedding ring. She turned the tiny diamond chip of her wedding ring inside, toward her palm, where it wouldn't show.

She took a firmer grip on the handle of the basket that she carried in her lap, filled with wine and beef and broth for the invalid. They wouldn't take the basket from her, not while there was breath in her body. They would have to kill her first, and throw her body out into the darkness. She stared fiercely out into the night, waiting.

When the train arrived at the station and ground to a halt, Big Mother and Cumin got out, bleary-eyed and exhausted. They hired a cab and went directly to the hospital where the sheriff told them that Hiram had been taken.

They paused outside the hospital apprehensively. The building loomed dirty yellow, with deep cracks running up through the walls. A stench of age came from it, and illness, and death.

They asked the nurse at the front desk to lead them to the young unidentified man with typhus. The nurse cracked her gum and looked up at them incuriously.

"You his people?" she said. "You come to pay his bill? He's got quite a bill run up. Down that hall and to the right, room thirty-four."

They walked down the hall, and their steps echoed. Big Mother was still clutching her basket, but her resolve ebbed under the greenish lights staring down from the ceiling. The hall seemed damp, with a strong smell of ammonia.

They went into room thirty-four. There were six beds in the room. Hiram was in the one by the corner. Cumin gasped when she saw him lying there. His eyes were closed, and sunken into his face, which was a waxy yellow color. He looked like a skull. She could only recognize him by the shock of black hair that grew in a widow's peak from his forehead. His lips were parched and cracked, bleeding at one corner. His sheets were soiled, and wrapped around him.

Cumin went up to him, and took his hand. "Hiram?" she said. "It's Cumin. From back home."

He opened his eyes and looked up at her without recognition. Then his eyes closed again.

"He's real sick, Mama," Cumin whispered fearfully. "I think he's going to die."

"Nonsense," said Big Mother briskly. "We haven't come all this way for him to die. Now I'm going to hold his head and feed him some broth, and you take these sheets and tell the nurses to boil them. This place is a disgrace."

Cumin took the soiled sheets in her arms and went back into the halls, to argue with the nurses about washing them. When she came back, victorious, with a load of fresh laundry in her arms, she saw Big Mother with Hiram's head tenderly cradled in her arm, spooning broth between his lips.

Cumin stopped involuntarily in the doorway, to watch. She felt almost that she shouldn't intrude. There was something so . . . fierce, almost, about the way Big Mother held Hiram's head, the way she looked down at him. It was a covetous, protective look. She had never looked that way at any of her own children, Cumin thought.

Cumin filled with bitterness, suddenly, at thought of the pale ghost of a woman she had protected all these years. Why, Cumin had practically had to raise all the younger children herself. After Little Baz died, Big Mother had just faded away into a corner, and the burden of loving and scolding had fallen on Cumin.

She had brushed and braided hair, checked homework and bandaged skinned knees. She had sat with her father, figuring out the finances, stretching the schooling funds so that each of the children could have a little bit of education, at least. And all the time Big Mother just wafted around the house, complaining about the cobwebs in the corners.

It had made Cumin a little hard, and shrewish before her time. No wonder she had never had time or inclination to catch a man. She had been worn out with raising children before she was more than a child herself.

And Big Mother had never thanked her. Not once.

Anise had been the youngest, the baby, and Cumin had cared for her most of all. She had protected Anise, so that she could be soft, and delicate, and pure. All the things that a man would want. And she had rubbed Anise's skin with creams, and brushed her hair a hundred times each night so that it would shine, and listened to her woes, and even finally convinced Big Joe to send Anise to New York, against his better judgment.

Anise had brought home Hiram, whom Cumin had loved from the first moment that she saw him. She loved his hair, and his tanned forearms with the sleeves so casually rolled up, and his dancing, laughing air. Cumin often sat in the room sewing, as chaperone, when he came in, and she loved him across the room as he bent carelessly over Anise. She loved him stolidly, and uncomplainingly. She never expected to have him for herself.

Then Anise went off to New York, and left Hiram. Cumin could tell from her letters Anise didn't love Hiram anymore. Anise loved this soldier, this Tommie. So Cumin had come to Minnesota with her mother, to rescue Hiram. She came because she was asked, and because she wanted to, and because Big Mother could no more stir without Cumin's sturdy uncomplaining shoulder to lean on than she could have flown to the moon.

And she came because there was a secret, unwatered place in her that still hoped, that thought perhaps there might be something for her, some time for her, now that Anise was gone. Surely Hiram knew that Anise wasn't coming back. He might even notice Cumin now, even if it was only with gratitude.

But now, standing in the doorway with a load of sheets in her arms and bitterness in her heart, she watched her mother bend over Hiram, and knew that her mother, even her own mother, loved Hiram more than Cumin would ever be loved by anyone.

Demeter sat by the table and twisted her fingers together, unseeing. On the table was a bowl of string beans that she had intended to snap in half. But sitting down, she had caught sight of her reflection in the polished tabletop, and it set her to thinking.

Demeter had to stay away from shiny surfaces. Even flowing water, or staring in the fire too long, could be a problem. She could see things in the flames, pictures and faces, sometimes even heard voices. Sometimes they would be of things that happened, and happened truly. Sometimes not. Sometimes she saw people that she knew, people in her family or from the town. Occasionally she saw strangers.

The fire told her sometimes of things that would happen, and sometimes of things that had already happened. But the images she saw weren't always nice. She saw lust, and fornication. She would see a man, sometimes, in the arms of a woman other than his wife. She had seen dark deeds in the water, things she didn't want to know.

Once she had even seen a man killed, and his body stuffed in a sack and thrown into the river. Later she had run into one of the killers on the street in Austin. She had started, and flushed, and hurried away.

It must be the work of the devil, she figured. She had read and read the Bible, and nowhere in it did it talk about the faithful seeing visions in the fire, or the water, or any shiny surface. Only witches, Jezebel and bad women, practiced witchcraft. Demeter secretly did penance for it all the time. She told no one.

But this day, when she sat down at the table to string the beans, she had made the mistake of staring too closely at the reflective tabletop. She had seen her brother Hiram, and he was stumbling down a hill away from a man with two horses and a white tepee. He looked ill, fevered, but she couldn't reach him in her seeing. All she could do was watch.

It seemed like Demeter spent half her life watching for Hiram in the surfaces of things. She remembered the day he had fallen and cut himself, the day he had shown her the sky, and how she had sat by him watching the blood seep onto the table and down onto the floor. He would have died that day if she hadn't been near him, she knew that. She didn't understand it, but she knew it to be true.

As long as her eyes were on him, he was safe. But now he had gone far from her view, so far that she couldn't even find him anymore in the fire. He was in a place she didn't know, a place that was all whites and blues. She wished that Fid would come back, so that she could stop staring at the surface of the table. He would surely think her crazy, if he came in and found her staring so intently at nothing.

Fid was a good man, Demeter knew that. When she thought of him she thought of hands on her hands, steadying her. When he was with her, she didn't fear the fire or the water so much. He had a goodness in him that made it impossible to be afraid. She still had the shell he had given her. She kept it in a special place, on a shelf. But she rarely took it down, because when she listened to the creamy curve of it she heard voices, telling her things that she didn't want to know.

Hiram's face came to her in a burst of light, Hiram staring into light entranced, stabbing at something she couldn't see. She moved to stop him, to halt him, and her motion broke up the picture, and made it disappear. She couldn't help him, or touch him. Not where he was now. She could only wait for him to come back.

He was so reckless, always dancing out away from her. And always before she had been able to find him, in the fire, and make it right for him. But he had grown to lean on her luck. She could feel it, with fear. He was pushing at the edges of his escape, like Houdini, binding himself tighter and tighter each time.

She had read of an escape Houdini had once attempted. He was chained and nailed into a coffin, then lowered into the ground, and covered with earth. The men around Houdini had waited for him to emerge. They waited long moments, until it suddenly seemed too long. Then they panicked, and dug him up. He was pale, bleeding from the eyes and the fingernails. He said the earth was too heavy for him to move.

That was what she feared for Hiram, that he would meet earth that was too heavy to move.

She had known where Hiram and Fid were going, the night with the trucks. She saw in her mind the fire in the truck. She had spoken to it, kept it small. She had seen it until Hiram kicked dust over it, and her vision was obscured.

It was the Devil plaguing Hiram that drove him to these things, she was sure. And yet it was the Devil that gave her the means to save him, to watch him. She couldn't understand it. But she sinned for Hiram's sake, sinned every day. She looked into the fire and into the water, into the mirror for him. She was bound to him, and damned.

She should pray more. Every day she knelt on the cold hearth, with the fire out, sometimes for hours, until her knees bore the imprint of the flagstones. But she was weak, and when the visions called to her, she would slide into a trance and watch, watch when she knew her eyes should be closed.

15. The Veil

Cumin and Big Mother nursed Hiram in the hospital, and they saved his life. It was fully two weeks before he recognized them, two weeks of changing damp and sweaty sheets, sponging his forehead, washing bedpans, and trying to persuade him to take sips of broth and wine.

Cumin sat by his bed, content to carry out her mother's orders and work on her own tatting. It was a large piece of lace, elaborately designed, with scallops around the edging. She would never have told anyone, and did not admit even to herself, what she was making. It grew under her hands rapidly, and when Hiram was awake he used to watch her hands flying through the fine threads with fascination.

He woke first on a cold, cloudy day. Big Mother was out of the room, helping with the noon meal. Cumin sat as always by Hiram's bed, rocking a little in her chair, with the lace growing in her hands.

It was some minutes before she felt herself being watched, and looked up in surprise to see Hiram's intensely blue eyes fixed on her face. She flushed, and put her hand up to her throat. She felt thick, and awkward, and the flush looked raw on her. She was beginning to have the look of an old maid.

Hiram's eyes were bluer than she had remembered. They were an icy blue, almost transparent in a way. She felt that if she stared at them, she could see through into the inside. But they were opaque, too—something blocked and frozen in them. It was as if the warm charm that spilled out of them was only for the observer, with no power to thaw the man behind.

He was weak, and disoriented, she could see. "It's Cumin, Hiram," she said gently. "You've been very ill."

"Cumin," he repeated. His voice was harsh from disuse. "And we are . . . ?"

"In a hospital," she said. "In Minnesota. You were ill here, and Big Mother and I came out to nurse you. How are you feeling now?"

"Odd," he said. "I had the strangest dream."

She came over to him and smoothed back the hair from his forehead. She had never dared to touch him before.

"Don't trouble yourself," she said. "Just rest now."

He closed his eyes and obediently fell back to sleep, his breathing even and regular. She stood where she was, marveling at her power over him. Hiram, who had always been so vital and energetic that he would only toss her a laughing word as he passed!

Now he was here in her power, dependent on her to feed him and give him water, to change his sheets and perform intimate offices for him, things that perhaps his mother never even did. She felt the surge of the strength that it gave her. It was the strength of women who wait. It was a dark, brooding strength, tender but possessive. It was strangely chaotic, and Cumin put her hand on her throat again and stood very still.

Big Mother came in, bustling. "How is he?" she said, coming over to lay a hand on his forehead.

"Better," said Cumin, amazed at her own daring. "He woke up. He said something to me."

"He woke up?" said Big Mother, not believing it. "And me out in the hall? What did he say?"

"He said that he had a strange dream," said Cumin.

"A strange dream? There he's been, at the door of death for two weeks, and he tells you he has a strange dream? Did you ask him how he felt? What's the matter with you?"

"He's obviously feeling better, Mother," Cumin said. She was beginning to enjoy herself. "Otherwise he wouldn't have woken up, would he?"

"Strange dream, indeed," Big Mother muttered. She shot a look at her daughter, and it was a strange look. There was jealousy in it, and a kind of rage. Cumin wondered later if there hadn't been some hatred there as well. "The next time he wakes, you call me."

"Perhaps he'll call for you himself, if he wants you," said Cumin. Big Mother shot her another of those looks, and left the room.

Big Joe had come home from his trip to find the house empty, Marjie out on a date, the dishes unwashed and the beds unmade. Clutter always made him nervous, and the unoccupied air of the house made him fear that some catastrophe had taken place while he was away. He paced the floors until Marjie came home, and he got the whole story out of her. She told him, reluctantly, of Cumin and Big Mother's trip, why they went and how.

Big Joe was angry, and felt that he couldn't admit it. After all, the women had done a good and charitable thing, had they not? Traveling across the country to nurse a sick man was hardly something that he could berate them for. And yet—it was his money they were traveling on, and his house they had left deserted and dirty, and all for the sake of that ne'er-do-well with whom Anise was obviously no longer in love! It didn't bear thinking about.

Big Joe's initial distrust of Hiram had grown into full-fledged dislike. The young man was uneducated, he was sure of it, despite Hiram's smooth talking and self-assured charm. His college credentials didn't stand up to any close scrutiny. Big Joe was none too sure that Hiram had even graduated from high school. And the thought of trusting his fragile daughter Anise, the bright one, the cultured one, the one who truly had a chance to make something of herself, to this libidinous building contractor with the wandering eye, depressed and enraged Big Joe.

He had tactfully held his tongue throughout the long years of their engagement, convinced that the unsuitability of the match would eventually become clear to Anise. And in fact, it seemed to have worked that way —she was gone, safely in New York in the arms of a cultured and intelligent young soldier, who would give her the life she deserved. He had blessed that soldier in his mind, and thankfully crossed Hiram off his list of private irritations.

But now it seemed that Hiram had enslaved the rest of his family, even in mortal illness. What was it about the boy, that the women were so mad for him? Big Mother herself seemed to become a girl again in his presence, giggling and blushing in a ridiculous fashion. And to think of her traipsing across the country, unescorted, infuriated Big Joe like an unreachable itch.

He said nothing in the letter he sent her, only ordered her and Cumin to return home immediately. But his resentment grew, and festered under his skin.

After another week, it was determined that Hiram was well enough to travel. Big Mother wired Big Joe for the money to pay Hiram's hospital bills, and was undaunted when he refused. She contacted the lawyer who handled the small bequest she had been left by her parents, and had him transfer a good sum of money into a private account. The lawyer was surprised, but willing—it was her money, after all.

Hiram objected when he found that she had paid his bills. "I can take care of them myself," he said, with all the dignity he could muster from his bed. Big Mother cut him short impatiently.

"It is a pleasure for me to be able to help you," she said, her eyes snapping. "And you will not deprive me of one of my few pleasures."

Hiram accepted. It seemed that he had very little choice. The transformation in Big Mother amazed him. He had woken from his fever to find her there, and Cumin, and had accepted it with the complaisance of the very ill. Big Mother seemed to be running things, and he was in no position to do other than to let her care for him. He had the light-headed and powerless euphoria of someone who had just escaped from death, and nothing seemed to matter much anymore.

When Hiram was well enough to travel, Big Mother determined to take him home to the boardinghouse. She did not consult Big Joe. She simply bought the tickets, and prepared for the journey. By the time that Big Joe returned from his next trip, Hiram was ensconced in invalid splendor on the living-room foldout couch, and Big Joe's house had been effectively turned into a sick ward. Big Joe wired Anise to come home immediately.

When Jed woke up to find that he had only one hand, he turned his face to the wall and didn't speak a word for two weeks. Francine worried for him. She had asked him to consent to the operation, after all, and he had given his permission. He had always been so strong before, so firm and set, that she hadn't anticipated any difficulty in his recovery. But the loss of his hand had wounded Jed in a way that she couldn't have foreseen, and didn't understand.

It wasn't just the phantom pain of the absent limb, although that was bad. There were nights when Jed woke up with pain coursing up his arm from his palm, which of course wasn't there. But that wasn't the worst.

The worst was the loss of his manhood. He was a cripple now. How could he be a man without a right hand? He had been a soldier of the Lord, strong, powerful. He had taken his physical might as a sign from God that he was meant to do the work of many men.

But now that God had taken away his might, had left him a weak and pathetic creature, a freak, someone at whom children would point on the street, how could it be that his mission was still blessed? How could he preach a whole dedication of the soul, when he was less than a whole man? How could he stand in front of his congregation and urge them on to feats of blessedness, when he would be so obviously a failed and partial thing? It seemed to him that God had turned away His face for Jed Net, and there was nothing for him but darkness.

Even the news that Francine gave him, that she was expecting a child, failed to pull him from his melancholy. A child! And who would teach it to hammer and pull, to throw a baseball and tie a tie, to do the things that a man must do? He couldn't be a father, not without a right hand. It was better if she would take the child and drown it in a sack. The child would thank her, in the end.

Francine had started to swell like a cat. This child was coming, welcome or not. Some things could not be halted. When she saw that she could not pry Jed from his melancholy by words, she took to bringing her books, or her knitting, into the room where he lay with his face steadfastly to the window. She rarely read or worked, just let the work sit idly in her lap, while she gazed at the wall, with a small rapt smile on her face and her hand resting lightly on her middle.

She was sorry for Jed, sorry as she could be. It was a terrible thing for a man to lose his right hand. But her mind was occupied now by the coming of the child, and she had little left to offer Jed except the calm of her presence. She merely waited by him, until the time that he should choose to speak.

The Ladies Aid Society brought food as offerings and laid them quietly on the doorstep, creeping away again without making a sound. When Francine met them in the street, drifting along like a ship under sail, they would bob nervously to her and wish the preacher well. The garden chores around the house were done, and odds and ends that

Francine had mentioned were needed appeared mysteriously in the mailbox.

She was no longer afraid of the Ladies, not since the night in the church. And they seemed to regard her now as something almost arcane, a charm from another place, that had nothing to do with the things of the world. She was still lonely. They did not treat her as one of them. But she was used to that by now.

She developed a taste for music. The Ladies Aid presented her with a phonograph and a stack of records, after she mentioned that she thought it might soothe the preacher to hear some music as he mended. Jed never listened, actually, to the music that she played.

But Francine played the phonograph all day long. She stroked the large heavy phonograph records in their jackets, and put them on to listen to the crackly silence in the beginning, before the music started. She knew nothing about the music she listened to, the great tradition behind the notes that she heard. But she knew that a certain melancholy in them calmed her. It was almost as if the child inside her wanted the sounds, and she played them again and again, for him.

Jed was sensible of her movements. He knew when she came and went, and knew that she sat in the room with him by the hour. It was no comfort to him. In the howling desert place where he was, every thought was a torment. All he could think of Francine was that perhaps God had punished him for lusting for his own wife, when his whole heart should have been given to the Lord. Perhaps he should never have married at all.

Although Jed was from the hearty Baptist tradition, which embraced preacher's families as enthusiastically as the preachers themselves, Jed had always had an aesthetic streak in him that was closer to the Catholic. He would never have admitted it, hardly knew it himself. But when he dreamed, it was of swinging censers and pure high-pitched choirboy voices, stained glass and shining gold. He felt somewhere inside himself that he was called to celibacy, and the demands of his great beefy body were a misery to him. He had married Francine to cool his longing for her. He thought they might live together sinlessly, like Mary and Joseph.

It hadn't worked that way. Her cool hands on him had only inflamed him. The more he possessed her, and the more he felt her soul elude him, the more he hungered for her. He had not been pure, not in mind or deed. And now he was less than a man. He was an invalid, everything he had ever secretly hidden or despised in the sickrooms that he visited. He had insulated himself from the sick, even as he prayed over them, blessed them and held their hands. They had been Other. And now he was of them, of their flesh.

When Anise came home, she walked in to find the house empty. No one had met her at the train station. The cabby followed her in, with his arms full of her bags.

"Hello," she called, "anyone home?"

She had changed, in her time in New York. She was sadder. She had that indefinable something that clung to her from the big city, a sophistication. Some of the bloom had brushed off, and some of the delicacy. She had looked into the face of things.

She paid the cabby and let the door slam closed behind her. Where could everyone be? She explored the house cautiously, feeling a stranger. Its smells and sounds closed around her with the stiffness of a cicada shell. She had expanded, and grown outside, with flamboyant wings. Now they were ground back into her sides, as the old things came up to surround her. She felt herself shrinking back into the way she had been—just the ticking of the clock in the hall, a dark brown cuckoo clock with wrought-iron pineapples hanging from chains, forced her down and back. The house was smaller and in more disarray than she remembered. With a shock she recognized Hiram's hat hung casually by the door, looking as if it belonged.

Big Joe had not explained much in her letter, only said that Hiram was ill and that she must come back immediately. She wondered what Hiram was doing here, if he was so sick.

She wandered around the room, touching things as if her eyes were in her hands. The heavy dark wainscotting on the walls, the rough brick and stone of the fireplace, the horrid pinks and blues of the china figures in the parlor. Big Mother's lavender scent hung lightly in the air, with the smell of dust.

She heard a noise in the foyer, and walked out to see Hiram coming in the door. He was laughing, and saying something to someone behind him.

He saw her and stopped short. He went pale, as the blood drained from his face. He was thinner than she remembered. He looked as if a hot fire had burned through him, and left him a husk. His skin was drawn more tightly to his bones, and the black peak of his hair stood out vividly against his skin.

He looked almost as if he were going to faint, she thought, although she had never seen him other than robustly masculine. But he seemed shocked. Was it possible that Big Joe had written her secretly, and not told anyone she was coming home?

He fell back a little, and she could see that it was Cumin with him. Cumin came in and stood looking somehow furtive, with her blocky hands hanging straight down by her side. She was dressed as Anise had never seen her, in a flowered dress that fell about her legs in soft folds. She wore a hat, too, with flowers on it that Anise thought looked vaguely ridiculous. Cumin's cheeks were flushed, and her hair done in an attractive style, up off her neck. She stood almost defiantly, looking at Anise.

"Hello, Hiram," Anise said, coming forward with her hand out. "I see that you're better now."

He took her hand and moved automatically forward to kiss her cheek. "I didn't know you were coming."

"Didn't you?" she said. She felt light, almost giddy. "Dad didn't tell you?"

"No," said Cumin, coming forward. "He didn't tell us."

Anise looked at her sister, arching an eyebrow slightly. The girlish dress was simply silly on Cumin. Her waist had thickened and her hands were red.

"Would you like some tea?" Cumin said, taking charge. "You must be exhausted." She swept past and into the kitchen, fighting despair. How could Anise come back, now, when everything was going so well? Big Joe must have called her back on purpose. He had always loved her best. Cumin had adored her father when she was little, adored him still. But it was always Anise he had taken on his trips, always Anise to whom he told stories, their heads together in the corner, reading books and laughing. Anise must always have the best of everything, and Cumin had helped give it to her.

And now, the one time that Cumin had tried to take something for herself, everything was against her. Anise would effortlessly disarrange what it had taken Cumin painful months to win. She had been so close— Hiram had put his hand on hers today, and leaned forward to look into her eyes, so that her heart raced and she was dizzy. They had walked around the park, slowly, out of respect for his convalescence, and he had told her stories of his adventures, bridges he had leaped over and cliffs where he ran horses. He was so light.

Cumin dreamed of Hiram at night, floating gently through where she plodded. The blood came up in her face roughly when she thought of him. She could not help but love him. She loved him dumbly, and devotedly, and until now had loved him without hope of his ever returning that love. But lately she really thought that he was thinking of her. Not in a romantic way, surely. But he needed someone like her, someone strong and disciplined, organized, to lay his table and cook his food—and bear his children. She would have done that for him, and never asked him questions about where he was when he was not with her. She would have been happy. It was more than she had ever asked.

And now Anise was here, looking so stylish and vaguely foreign, so thin! She had something to her now, something that had not been there before. She was so beautiful, and so composed, her mouth pressed together in a tight line. She didn't really love Hiram anymore. Cumin could tell that by the cool measuring way she had looked at him in the hall. But she would take him, because there was nothing else for her here.

Anise would scoop Hiram up as easily as she had taken jacks from the floor, in between bounces of the India-rubber ball, when they played the game in the hall as children. And Cumin would have to dress Anise for the wedding, would have to pin in her dark hair the veil that Cumin had made while Hiram was sick.

Cumin hadn't ever let herself know what that lace was for. But she saw now that it was a wedding veil. She had sewn all her hopes into it, her sorrows and her dreams. She had made it for herself, without knowing. And now it would have to be for Anise, as she should always have known that it would be.

Big Joe withdrew his promise of a large wedding for Hiram and Anise. The Depression had hit him hard, and the money was tight. That was the reason he gave, anyway. The truth was that the presence of Hiram in his home had choked him unbearably. His wife's obvious devotion to the boy, Cumin's unsettling adoration of him, and the fact that Hiram lay around like a sultan while Big Joe's family waited on him happily, all stuck in Big Joe's craw, and he would be damned if he would beggar himself for the fellow to marry his favorite daughter. Marry they might, but not on his nickel.

So they had a quiet wedding at home. Anise wore a dark brown suit, and Big Mother played the piano, calling up a remembered breath of skill into her old misshapen hands. Cumin stood over Anise and pinned on the veil, and tears ran slowly down her face like blood. She didn't make a sound, only wiped them away.

She lay the filmy stuff onto Anise's dark hair carefully, and pinned it down, and when she looked in the mirror to see if it was straight she saw that Anise, too, was crying. Before they went downstairs Cumin held Anise for a long moment, just as she had when Anise was a little girl, and Anise sobbed in her sister's arms as if her heart would break.

Then Anise straightened up, blew her nose, wiped her face, picked up the bunch of peach gladiolus that lay on the bed, checked her reflection briefly in the mirror, and went down the stairs, pale and composed, to marry Hiram Jameson.

16. The Throne

After Fid stood up with Hiram to see him safely married, Fid and Demeter got married themselves, in city hall. They told no one. The preacher's wife stood up to witness, and Demeter held a bouquet of sweet peas that Fid had gathered for her in the garden.

On her wedding night Demeter stared into the mirror to part her hair. She was going to braid it up as usual, but she decided at the last moment to wear it down her back. She shook it over her ears and it fell down heavily, almost to her knees. It was her one real beauty.

She looked at her eyes, wide and dilated in the mirror. Behind them she could see a reflection of trees, and water, a creek somewhere far in the distance. She could see Hiram, in a tree, and a strange woman with him, with red hair. Her eyes blurred and she saw Hiram in his wedding bed, with the white lace of the pillows around him, staring at the ceiling with his arms crossed while Anise wept, curled on her side. But Demeter shook her head and shut her eyes, breaking up the vision like a stone in a pond. Some things were better unseen.

The next day Fid and Demeter telegraphed their parents that they had been married and then bought train tickets and wheeled their bicycles together onto the freight compartment. They were going around the world. They hadn't told anyone their plans, because they figured that no one would believe them.

Hiram was dissolving his concrete-carrying business anyway, so Fid would soon be without a job. Hiram had become fascinated with the oil-drilling business, and was thinking of setting himself up as a wildcatter. He was planning on following the oil rush to Oklahoma, last anyone had heard.

Fid and Demeter took the train to the docks, where they bought tickets on a freight steamer bound for far places. The morning that they boarded the steamer was cool and grey, in early spring. They woke early in their cheap hotel room, and went down to the docks. Fid looked around, smelling the air eagerly. The big boats swayed and rolled restlessly, pulling at their moorings. He could smell pitch, and sea air. Demeter laughed and squeezed his hand, looking up into his face. They ran up the gangplank, lightly.

They sailed for years. If Demeter saw visions in the corner of her eye, if she stared too long at the polished surface of the metal plates bolted to the deck or watched the gleam from her plain gold wedding ring, she would shake her head and close her eyes. She couldn't help Hiram now. And she felt a kicking out, a pushing away from him, a turning away from her fate. Surely it was right that she have this time, only this time, to herself. Fid was happy, she knew. She could shake her hair down around her back, and look at him sideways, and make him laugh with joy. She was more than he had expected from life.

Demeter was happy, too. It was not a brilliant happiness, but a slow contentment that she felt. She was loved. The fever of the visions had passed for the moment, and she was free of her stewardship of Hiram. She played, as she had never played before. She had always been a serious child.

She and Fid were the only passengers on the boat. They lay on the deck for hours under the cold sky, wrapped in rough plaid blankets, watching the light moving and the sea gulls fighting for fish entrails that the cook dumped over the side.

Once the ship came to a tiny island in the Pacific, damp and smoldering with mosquitoes. They had been aboard for many weeks, and Demeter longed to walk on land. They asked to go ashore. The captain was agreeable, as he needed to restock his store of fresh water. The channel was too shallow for the freighter to dock, so a guide rowed Fid and Demeter in on a dinghy, and left them.

They were met at the dock by a group of excited natives, who had watched the boat putting in. The natives were willowy people with dark skin and bright eyes, dressed in bright colors. They had never been harmed, and so were friendly to foreigners who provided interest in the long mild days, and possibly things to trade.

Fid and Demeter were taken to meet the island king, who held court squatting under the shade of a large tree. The king invited them for coconut curry in his sand-floored palace. The curry was served by his youngest wife, who had delicate skin and large, slanted eyes.

Later the king served them a fermented beet-juice liquor. Fid and Demeter told him stories of telephones and cars, and shining swift machines that mince the earth and make the plants come up. In return the king told them stories of his ancestors, who came from a volcano.

Fid and Demeter asked him why he had no throne. It was customary, they said, in their part of the world, for a great ruler to sit high in state above his subjects. The king was intrigued by the idea, but said he had never heard of such a thing.

So Fid and Demeter determined to make him a throne. While the ship idled in the bay, trading pieces of ivory for fresh fruit and food supplies, they built the throne. It took them three full days, with the implements that he gave them, and dried pieces of wood that young men of the village pulled from the festering mass of the jungle.

When they were finished, they sat the throne in the shade of the tree, and the king sank down in it, sighing happily. The king's subjects gathered around, wondering, to touch the smooth joints, and the arms and legs of the throne where Fid had carved a sun, a moon and a Model T Ford.

Once Francine's pregnancy began to show, she swelled rapidly until she was big as a sheep. Her ankles thickened, and her cheeks, so that her green eyes peered out of her face like someone looking up out of a well.

But she didn't mind it, strangely—she was sunk into herself, as if under water. She slowed until she almost stopped moving at all. She would take her embroidery work to sit in the sun by the window, and dream, until her longing for the outdoors became more than she could bear.

So she would wander to the door and out into the yard before Jed knew to call her back. When he went to look for her, she would be sitting outside under a tree, leaning back against the bark, her eyes half closed. He could never understand what it was that she wanted outside—certainly it wasn't fitting that a woman in her condition should show herself. But he couldn't keep her in, short of barring the door from the outside, and that he would not do.

Jed had recovered from his accident, at least as far as it showed. He was working again, moving around the house and preparing sermons. But the ordeal had changed him. He was fiercer, and harsher, as if some underlying gentleness had been burned away in him. He had suffered the scourge, and under it his nerves were as fine and taut as barbed wire.

His sermons, which had once been gentle and filled with practical wisdom, and light, spoke increasingly of hellfire and the damnation that awaited all who would not repent. He was seized with his duty to the members of his congregation—he was convinced that through his time of testing, the Lord had chosen him to be a particular leader, and so he punished the people who were in his care. Whom the Lord loveth, so He chastiseth, Jed figured, and he must be the same.

There was a strange light in Jed's eyes as he wandered around the house, his maimed arm thrust into a pocket. He could not bear for it to be seen, so Francine sewed an extra pocket into all of his coats. He exhorted the congregation from the pulpit, his one arm hidden, the other waving in the air. He pointed, now, at the sinners. He knew their secrets, and whereas before he had been content to hint, to guide and lead, now he was impatient for the repentance. The wrath of the Lord was near, he felt— had he not felt it himself? The fiery breath was close, and those not prepared would be swept away.

He stared at Mr. Parkinson as he spoke of adultery; he shamed Mrs. Meadows by speaking of the slatternly housekeeper, and raised his brows sharply at Mr. Wildecott when he shouted about the thief who would steal in the night from his partners who trusted him. There began to be murmurings in the congregation against him.

If Francine had been at his side, she would have stopped him, perhaps. But she was sunk into her dreaming time, and didn't know what was happening. All she cared for was to sit under the tree, with her fingers digging into the dirt beside her, and the sun falling down on her to warm her belly.

It felt to Francine sometimes that she was dragging a piece of furniture around with her. Her body was so large, and unwieldy, and she had always before been agile on her feet. She stared up into the green of the trees for hours at a time, until the squirrels came very close and the birds sang above her in odd throaty stanzas.

She heard them sing again, in her sleep at night. When she closed her eyes she could see behind the lids the shifting green patterns of the leaves above her, the twisting shadows and gold, the blue that shone through. She longed to climb up into the tree, to be up among the lights that she saw, but her body was too heavy and earthbound. She would come into the house at supper with red dirt under her nails.

Jed had hired a girl to help while Francine was in her confinement. The hired girl was slatternly, and young, from a needy local family. Her name was Rebecca. While she was a poor hand at cooking or dusting, Rebecca had taken a shine to Francine's long fall of buttery hair, and liked nothing better than to brush it for her by the hour.

The lassitude of the house just suited Rebecca—Francine's dreamy immobility and Jed's absence meant that she had to do very little work to earn her board. She was not much younger than Francine, and the two became loose allies. They would sit together and watch the light pour through the dusty windows while Rebecca slowly pulled the brush through Francine's hair. Francine leaned her head back into Rebecca's hands, only her slender neck still showing the outline of who she had been.

Francine hardly spoke out loud anymore at all. She could feel the baby inside her, swimming like a fish inside the dark arch of her pelvic bone. She could almost feel, if she listened, the cells knitting together, the bones winding themselves into fingers, spiraling into nails, and ears. She thought she could hear the roar of the sea behind, and over it the thin music of order, as the child made itself. Francine had nothing to do with it, she felt. She was only the mountain around the cave, and inside the cave there was water, and something that with blind fingers was scrabbling together earth and stone, to make itself from nothing. It made her drowsy to think of it.

When the child's time came, Francine was alone, sitting under the tree. She felt the waters break and rush down around her ankles, wetting her dress. She thought for a moment that she was standing on the edge of a shore, the waves breaking around her feet. She seemed to smell salt water, and hear a rushing sound.

Then she dragged herself up to her feet, and went inside. She called for Rebecca, who came to sit, frightened, by her bedside. Francine would not have Jed called, or the doctor. She suddenly had a horror of someone standing over her and watching.

Francine felt herself spiraling into a small dark place, where she fit tightly against the edges of a shell. She had seen a shell like that once, a pink one with curved edges, and she descended now until she fit into the inside curve of that spiral, the soft edge winding against her and out, into the light.

She panted like a cat, and pulled on the rope that Rebecca tied to the bedposts. Francine marveled that her body seemed to know just what to do. She knew how to push, and when. She abandoned herself to the smooth, bloody slide of her body, letting the pain take her. She never screamed, only made hoarse grunting sounds, while Rebecca stood by and wrung her hands.

The baby was born easily, "quick as kittens," Rebecca said, and by the time Jed returned home with the doctor, horrified past bearing at the smell of blood in the room, it was all done. The doctor examined her in his matter-of-fact, kindly way, told her jokingly that it was disgraceful to suffer so little, and left her. The baby was healthy, wrapped in blankets and asleep. It was a boy. They named him William.

Jed was proud, but nonplussed. He held the baby in his arms and

looked down at it, waiting for all the things that he knew he should feel.
But he felt nothing, really, except a mild sort of pleasure at the baby's
completeness, and a revulsion from the bloody sheets that he had seen
Rebecca bundling out of the room.

He gave the baby back to Francine, who settled it to her breast
contentedly. Jed was confused by the change that had come to Francine in
the past months. There was a fever in her that had seemed banked, as she
sank into her flesh. She had become so heavy, so quickly, that he scarcely
recognized her. He had been much away from home, working with his
renewed zeal, and had not known what to make of her transformation, so
had said nothing. The smell of sweat and warm milk coming from her
disturbed him, and so he kissed her on the forehead gently and left her.
She scarcely noticed he was gone.

William was a good baby, uncomplicated, and grew quickly. He had
brown eyes and sprouted a crop of gold curls very early, so that people
loved to look at him on the street. Francine was absorbed in watching him,
so that the first two years of his life seemed to pass in a daze for her. She
scarcely knew that they were gone. She lived quietly, with the baby and
Rebecca as her only companions.

As William grew and began to toddle, Francine followed him around,
to keep him out of mischief. As she stirred into life again, she became
slimmer, and her face regained its angular contours, but her waist remained thickened. She didn't regret it, since the only time she looked in
the mirror was to see that her part was straight in the morning, after
Rebecca had brushed her hair and pinned it into a knot.

Francine was—not happy, for her idea of happiness was a brilliant,
lightening thing—but not restless, for the first time in her life. She felt as
if a thick, fleshy root bound her down into the ground. She missed the
feeling of the earth under her fingernails that she had when she was
pregnant, and so she took to working in the garden.

She dug, and planted, and pruned mindlessly in the warm sun. She
refused to wear gloves and only used tools when she had to, although
Rebecca bewailed the state of her hands. They grew firm, and callused,
with broken nails. Francine didn't care, although she had once been proud
of her white hands, and the smooth pink ovals of her fingernails.

When William was very small, Francine took him with her into the
garden, on a shaded pillow. When he grew older he was allowed to "help,"

and had his own patch to play in, and weeds to pull. Some of his earliest memories were like this, in the garden, looking up through the screen of his mother's bright red hair to the pink and cream of the roses.

Jed's hand lay heavily on his congregation. They talked of his change, and how different he was. His sermons were so extreme now, almost vulgar in their vehemence. There were rumors that Jed might have been driven mad by the accident, by the pain and the fever. There was even talk of possession, and exorcism. Men met angrily around kitchen tables, served coffee by sympathetic wives, and the adulterers and thieves were the angriest of all. Jed had flayed the skin from the church, and the bones showed.

They gathered, and they laid their plans. Jed was due to miss a Wednesday prayer for an important meeting with a church official. That afternoon the pillars of the congregation met, and with the ease of long planning, they voted Jed right out of the church.

When the deacon came nervously to inform him of what had been done while he was gone, Jed received him calmly. He was unbelieving. Not that he was shocked—he simply didn't believe it. The Lord had given him that church in a sacred trust, and no one short of the Lord was going to take it away. They hadn't the power. He said nothing, but showed up the next Sunday to preach as usual.

All the congregation was present, tense in their flounces and collars. The deacon, who had worked all week on his sermon notes, was just mounting the pulpit when Jed came in, casting his profile tall in shadow against the far wall. Jed walked very quietly up the aisle, and stood in front of the deacon, looking into his eyes for a long time. The deacon dropped his eyes finally, and went to the back of the church with hate in his face. Jed mounted the pulpit calmly, and stood staring around at the people with red-rimmed eyes. His face seemed hollowed out, somehow.

"Is it possible," he said, his voice rolling out over them, "can it be possible, that there are any of you here collected together who do not fear the wrath of the Lord? Let me tell you, my brethren, about the wrath of the Lord. Let me tell you of the tornado of flame, a hundred feet high, which will come sweeping down on you and touch you with the ashes of doom, if you do not repent and change your ways. Let me describe to you the charring, the smoking of the bones on the pyre of the Lord! There will be no return for the sinner who turns away his eyes. There will be no escape, for the anger of the Lord will sweep this town as clean as a storm, and what will be left will be only the bare smoky rubble of what used to be. You think that you can vote me from this church?" He leaned forward, and his eyes blazed out of his pale face.

"My brethren, I am here to warn you! I would be remiss in my duties if I allowed your fears, your weakness to dissuade me from my duties. My children, only the hand of God will remove me from my post, for I stand here as a sentry to the dangers of the night, which are even at this moment creeping forward in the shadows to claim you!"

The congregation sat motionless, transfixed by their guilt and the horror of Jed's pointing finger, which was swinging, preparing to level at them. No one noticed, in the back, the deacon leaving.

Francine had bathed herself and was giving William a bath when she heard the sound of footsteps below her, and thought she heard the door closing softly. It was never locked.

"Jed," she called out, "is that you?" It was early for him to come home.

William had provided an excuse for her to stay away from church, while he was so young, and she was grateful. The house on Sunday morning was quiet and filled with peace. While the night of Jed's illness had made a grudging believer of Francine, the violence of the sermons that Jed had been preaching lately disturbed her and made her stomach queasy.

She should speak to Jed about it, she thought. Really, she should. It couldn't be good for church attendance, harping at people that way, and after they had worked so hard getting new members, it seemed a shame to frighten them all away. Her political sense, long dormant, wakened and shook itself.

She should talk to him. Why hadn't she? He was so involved with God, he hardly had any sense about people. She had been in a long dream, it seemed, and hadn't lifted a finger to stop him on his way. Jed had been strange, increasingly strange, and she had done nothing. She resolved to sit down with him, the minute he came home. She would wash her hair and comb it out to dry, the way he liked, and put on a fresh dress, and make coffee. Rebecca could care for the baby. She had been too immersed in William. She owed her duty to Jed, too. She had forgotten.

But what was he doing home at such an hour? It was odd. She left the baby in the bathtub for a minute and walked to the edge of the stairs, squeezing water out of her hair in a knot.

"Jed?" she called. Rebecca was gone, it was her free day. "What are you doing home?"

She smelled something odd in the air, and heard a thing like paper crumpling. Her heart contracted, she could scarcely tell why. She wrapped her robe more tightly around her, wrapping it around up to her neck and yanking the sash into a knot. She went down the stairs, holding to the banister.

She heard the front door slam. She walked around the corner, slowly, to look into the kitchen. She saw the big black stove that crouched heavily in the corner. A sheet of flame sprang up in a line behind the burners, where the kerosene tank was. As she watched, the kerosene exploded, sending sheets of flame running up the curtains. They turned black as the flame ran over them.

She stood watching the flames. There was a heat, a sucking thing in the fire that drew her into it. She wanted almost to walk into the fire, to wrap it around her like a garment. The fire was coral-colored in its heart, with a smooth, rippling heat. It burned brightly, steadily, increasing itself until it stood in a wall of flame in front of her.

She stared into the heat of the fire, swaying, feeling her eyebrows singe. The warmth stroked her face. She could look through it, into it, and she thought that inside it she saw a strange kingdom, another place that was tinted amber and the color of cherries. It was like everything she knew, but different somehow, more real, like a place where the trees had leaves of silver and fruits that were rubies, sapphires and emeralds that you could eat.

She felt that she could stand in that place and fill her pockets with jewels, eat them until the juice ran down her chin, while the hiss of the fire licked her ear and told her true things. She felt on the edge of remembering things that she had just forgotten, as when she woke from a dream with a strain of music in her ears vanishing, and lay with her eyes closed, trying to hear that music again.

Then she breathed in a lungful of smoke, and the coughing woke her. The house was on fire, and William was upstairs. "William," she said, and ran up the stairs. He was still playing in the bathtub happily, and looked up at her to show her his boat. "Come on, now," she said, hiding her fear. "Come on outside with Mama now."

She wrapped him in a towel, and took a diaper from the bag, and ran down the stairs with him, holding his head fast to her breast. He squirmed, she was holding him too tight. She went to the closet, and tried to pull out an armful of her clothes, but she had carefully arranged the hangers so that every other hook faced the other way, and she couldn't get anything out. William was starting to cry, and she smelled smoke tingeing the air, she could feel the heat through the floor on her bare feet. She ran with him outside to the big tree in front, and put him down. She looked at the house—it was still cool on the outside, washed white. She couldn't believe, really, what was going on inside. Perhaps she had dreamed it. It couldn't be real.

Then she saw a wisp of smoke coming out. She put William down, firmly. "Stay here, Willie. Stay here now, Mama has to go back inside."

She ran towards the door, her heart thudding. She should call, she must call the fire department. She should get clothes, save—what should she save? Precious things, silver, photographs, some clothes for them, Jed's papers? The things in her life ran through her in a panicked stream, and she could not fish out what she needed. She should call, she must get to the phone.

"Marmar," she heard William call. She looked back and saw him toddling towards her unsteadily. "Marmar." He laughed and held out a stone that he had picked up.

"William," she said desperately, "you must stay here. Stay here now." She picked him up again and took him to the tree. "Stay here now." She was screaming at him, could feel the blood running in her ears. She started towards the door again, she saw the flames now through the windows, as if she were looking into a picture frame. William came after her, frightened now, clutching at the edge of her robe. He let out a wail of rage.

She tripped over him, and fell full length on the ground, and cried, beating her fists against the ground. "William, stay here!" But he would not stay, he was too frightened to be separated from her, he would follow her into the flames and she could not take him into that house.

She could only stand with him under the shade of the tree, wearing her robe, watching the house burn down. The bottom story burned first, the flames coming out to the edge of the house as they licked through the old dry wood. The beams charred, and buckled, the windows blew out in storms of glass, and the top floor slid slowly into the second like the melting of cake.

Calm with despair, she watched the burning in a strange silence. No one came, there was no one anywhere, and no sound but the crashing, the burning, the falling, the breaking of glass. William struggled in her arms and she let him down. He was getting very heavy. He stood still, entranced. Somewhere, far off, she could hear a bird singing.

When Jed came home from church, he found Francine in her robe and William wearing a diaper, standing silently under the tree, while the ruins of the house smoldered on in the warm afternoon.

17. The Wild Woman

Anise went casting for joy in her marriage with the resolution and rigor of a fisherman, set to stay motionless for long hours. She was adept in preparing the trimmings of happiness. She could do things, make up games, frost cakes, tell stories. She told herself stories of how happy she and Hiram were together. She authored her life with a masterful hand.

Hiram helped, because he was handsome, and charming, because he loved ladies and because there was a place in him where Anise fit, with all her fussy and prudish ways. Lee had stamped in him a place for a cool, pure woman.

Anise lay rigidly, looking at the ceiling, when he embraced her, but he expected little more. She would make him a good wife. They would present a joined front to the world, and have what companionship they could find in the hidden places.

Anise woke with a start and for a long minute didn't know where she was. It was her birthday, she remembered. She was alone here, in this strange new house. Hiram was away, on business, and no one in the whole world had remembered her birthday.

Their apartment was small, and ugly, despite her efforts. The afternoon sun cast into it with such short, hard shadows that she despaired. It seemed all antiseptic, fraught with black and white edges, and all the pretty things she put into it never blended in, only sat on top of the surface of the cold place, looking silly.

But this was foolishness, this was bad thinking! She mustn't let herself be sad. She must make herself be happy. She must appreciate all the things she had. She stared until her eyes blurred at a picture on the wall. It was an imported Swiss print of a bowl of golden flowers before an open window—pear blossoms.

She sat and stared at the pear blossoms, feeling a choking come up in her throat. She twisted her wedding ring on her finger. She hated it, with its tiny stunted diamond chips like cold lizard eyes winking up at her. She took out her journal and walked around the tiny place, slowly. She listed each thing that she had, each lamp, each etching, each bookend. There were rugs, and books, and flowerpots, and a funny Mexican man wrapped in his serape, sleeping with a cactus by his side.

But the candlesticks from New York agitated her and made her uneasy. It was wrong to think of Tommie now—she must not do it. She was married, and had given her promise, and that was forever. But it came into her head the time that Tommie had sat beside her, in the bleachers, with the sky blue behind his head, and his eyes looking down at her with such a warm light in them.

It was a lonely spring for Anise. Hiram was gone almost always. The air was raw, and wet, and she got so tired of mending her pocket handkerchiefs that she wished something would go wrong, so that she could fix it. She knew no one in Ville Platte, and the tiny apartment was soon set straight. She sat stiffly on the edge of the neatly made bed for hours, looking in front of her, twisting her long hands together.

She started reading the newspaper, for something to do. She would curl into the window box each morning with a cup of tea, and let the thin, cold sunlight wash over her while she read. The chill of the outside seeped through the panes into her skin.

She skimmed through the social columns—she had written them once, when she was a student, and considerably better than these, she thought with a certain pride—and flipped through the advertisements. She would write for the paper again, but Hiram didn't want his wife working. She thought of the days she had spent on the paper, running her fingers over the inky sheets. She lifted the newsprint to her face and sniffed it deeply. It comforted her. Something caught her eye. "Wild Woman Sighted," it said.

She read it. It seemed that there had been a wild woman at large in the country. The wild woman was first noticed with someone else—a boy, or man perhaps. Searchers had found two sets of tracks, and sweet potatoes missing from the fields. From the delicate size of the prints pressed into the loam, the guess had been that the two were Indians, or lost children. But what were they doing there, and where were their friends? The sleepy town was charmed, and intrigued.

The wild people caused no harm or mischief, but only stole corn, and chewed the cobs. Then a group of hunters had found a pile of leaves and twigs with a man's bones sticking out underneath. After that, the wild woman's prints were found alone. Her companion had died, of hunger perhaps, or had been caught in a trap, and she had dragged twigs and leaves to make his shroud.

Anise let the paper fall, sorry for the woman. The thought of the wild woman's tiny frame, bent over as she hurried to cover her companion's body against the light of the rising sky! It was too sad. Anise could see, almost, how the wild woman would look, her long hair trailing to the ground, her eyes ringed with white. Perhaps she was an unhappy gypsy, or a woman of good family, driven mad by a broken heart.

She read on. The wild woman continued to leave her traces in cornfields and the places where sweet potatoes grew. The narrow prints of her hands seemed to show that she was a frail thing. A gang of young men, their blood hot and stirred no doubt by the thought of a woman alone, unprotected by friends or family, had set a watch on a field that she frequently came to, and they had seen her! But she had leapt at their noise, slim as a deer, and ran away into the moonlit shadows. She had lingered only long enough for them to see that she was naked, and very slender.

That was the end of the story. Anise set it down with a sigh. Her pity and her imagination were stirred. What a horrible thing, that they couldn't just leave the woman alone, when she wasn't harming anyone. They would have to drag her into the light, drag her up into the daylight where her face would show dirty and desperate, when all the time she belonged in the friendly shadows of the night.

Anise watched the papers for more mention of the wild woman, but for a long time she could find nothing. The creature had been frightened, and would not come out. The farmers and hunters primed their rifles and hung them by the door. Their dogs were fearsome and alert, and there was no doubt that any marauder would be trapped and shot in short order.

Then there was another sighting. Anise read it with her breath short and her heart pounding. It seemed that the thing, whatever it was, had crept into an open house, stepped over the dogs that lay silent, and opened a cupboard containing a plate of butter, a loaf of bread and a pan of milk. The wild woman took half the butter, half the bread, and some of the milk in a pitcher.

When the loss was discovered the next day, the house was searched for theft. The gold watches, silverware and powder flasks were in plain view, and undisturbed. The only thing missing was a log chain, twelve feet long and weighing thirty pounds. The Negroes in the town began referring to the nighttime visitor as "the thing that comes."

Two weeks later the family of the house the thing had visited were startled to see outside their porch the missing pitcher, with the log chain coiled around it. But the odd thing was that the log chain had been polished until it shone the color of razors. No one had known that such base metal could be polished to such a gleam, or knew how it could be done. The bedazzled farmer hung the chain over the hearth, with a super-stitious awe, and used it no more.

Anise, too much alone, thought about the wild woman almost every hour now. She thought of her when she ate and when she drank water, wondering if the other one was thirsty. She thought of her at night, sliding into her own warm quilts, seeing the wild woman crouching in the forest, her thin haunches white in the moonlight, supporting her chin on her hand and looking into a pool, wrapped in her long hair against the cold. She could almost imagine the woman looking out to her with wide eyes, and holding out her hand. Anise would take her hand and they would go together into the forest, to live in a house of branches where the sun would filter through. They would eat the things that grew in hidden places.

The town of Ville Platte became more and more fascinated with the nocturnal visitor. They continued to write up suspected sightings in the paper. In the late winter the wild woman made a habit of stealing corn from one particular corncrib. The amount she took was so little, and the mischief she caused was so light, that the town's heart was moved towards her, and they wanted only to find and shelter her. Offers were made to give her home and family, if only she could be captured.

So they set a watch on the corncrib. One night the man on watch, who was sitting drowsing inside the crib with his hand on the door, was wakened by a steady rustling, and then a stillness. He knew it was the thing that comes, and he was seized with such horror at the thought of being shut up alone with it in the corncrib that he let out a yell, and the creature leapt up and vanished.

Of course, he was ridiculed in the paper as a buffoon and a coward for passing up an opportunity to help so needy a soul, but he insisted that the thing was a creature of the Devil, and that the town was well quit of seeing it. He himself left town shortly thereafter, and was never heard from again.

A farmer nearby had some hogs fattening in a pen. A bear had tried to steal one, and was set upon by the farmer's dogs, and killed after a squealing, bloody battle. The dogs were restless and alert, and eager to attack again.

And yet in the middle of this unrest, the wild woman crept into the pen and replaced one of the farmer's fine, fat hogs with a poor starved one from the forest. Anise imagined the creature cradling the pig in her arms like a dead infant, stepping over the sleeping dogs at midnight, her thighs glimmering in the pale light and her thin shoulders hunched under her burden.

The wild woman effected several more hog swaps of this nature, the only inconvenience being that sometimes the hog she supplied belonged to a neighbor. It was no use fattening up the original hog she brought from the woods—the servants were seized with a superstitious terror of the thing, and wouldn't have eaten it if they were starving.

Hunters found a camp they thought belonged to the wild woman, filled with stalks of sugarcane that had been cut and chewed. Obviously, the thing knew how to use a knife. They also found curious bits of twine made from the twisted outside bark of the cotton plant, and strange snares for small animals. There were no signs of fire or clothing, and only a bed of moss and leaves. They found a spoon, some table knives and a cup she had taken from a house. In one corner were some books, carefully kept dry, and a packet of letters of old date, with tender sentiments in them, addressed to a Miss Mackintosh. One of the books was a Bible. Could the woman read?

Anise's heart was wrung for her. She imagined the woman sucking her sugarcane, pawing through the packet of letters that had, perhaps, driven her mad, looking at them with eyes glittering through her long tangled hair. Anise wanted to go out to her. She felt a coming storm from the town, feared that they would harm the woman. Surely the woman could not remain lost, in the middle of such curiosity. They were combing the woods, flushing out her secrets.

The oddity now was too strong to resist. The townsfolk became organized; they made a plan. Hunters laid out boundaries, and split up the spaces into lanes. They patrolled the forest with whoops and dogs, beating their lariats against saddle horns and crying out, to find the thing that came in the night.

Men with ropes took positions along the edge of the prairie, with dogs running alongside them. Suddenly the dogs belled—it was a strange sound, of a game they had never hunted before. There was a rustling, and out of the brush burst the wild woman, running like an animal. She dashed under the nose of a startled hunter, who spurred his horse after her, swinging his rope.

He came within a rope's length of her several times, and it seemed impossible that she would escape. But his horse was so frightened of the strange creature that every time the hunter would urge it forward, the horse would shy to the side and spoil his cast. Finally he threw the rope anyway—it swung loose and missed. He got a good view of her—desperately thin, terrified eyes, with the long brown hair flying back as she ran. She was completely naked, and he felt horror and a rising lust. Oddest of all, he said to those who asked him later, her body was covered with short, fine, soft brown hair like an otter.

She ran into the woods and was lost. But she left behind her something that she had dropped, or flung away to help her escape—it was a wooden club, five feet long, polished to a high sheen by some unknown art.

Later that afternoon, when the exhilaration of the near-miss had worn off, and the hunters were tired and cross, the dogs came across another scent and went baying into the swamp. It was nothing but a black man in a tree—the dogs had perhaps come across his trail and gotten distracted. But when the hunters looked closer, they saw that the man was completely naked. When they ordered him to come down from the tree, he made no sign of obeying, but clung there silently. Finally he made a motion for them to go away.

They made as if to shoot at him, threatened him with their guns, but he didn't respond. Finally they climbed the tree and took him down by force. He trembled but said nothing. They looked at his hands and feet, and matched them to the prints in the loam—they were small and slender, just like the prints. A sailor who had been to the coast of Africa said that he knew of a tribe there that had such small hands and feet, a tribe that practiced such metal arts as the wild thing seemed to know.

Was this the so-called wild woman? No one knew for sure. They took the sad black man, silent still, to the jail and held him for a while. He languished in captivity, refusing all food. Finding that all of their attempts to clothe him, help him or get him to speak were a failure, they released him. He ran fleetly across the fields, and disappeared into the woods, leaving the sheriff and his men still standing puzzled behind at the door of the jail, rubbing their chins.

It was widely allowed that there had been no wild woman, that it was all a hoax, and finally the town grew slumberous and forgot.

But Anise kept her newspaper clippings of the wild woman, and believed in her. The wild woman was somewhere still in the woods, undiscovered, Anise thought, tearing with her white teeth into small raw creatures, and making her bed in banks of leaves at night. Anise left out plates of sugar sometimes for her, knowing that she liked sweet things. She longed for the wild woman, and wished her hope, and freedom, and envied her escape from the places of men.

Demeter and Fid came back from their trip around the world, tanned to an identical brown color and stained with salt. They had changed in other ways, too. Their family hardly knew them. It seemed that in their time on the ocean, looking out over the breakers, their colors had melted in the spray and mixed together, like watercolors painted on damp paper. They were blended into a thing that they hadn't been before, all of a piece. They were silent together, and easy, and the chatty home folks didn't know what to make of them.

They were too exotic for the tight dresses and gloves of the social set. They brought back gifts with them, huge carnival heads made out of papier-mâché and painted in garish colors, beads cut from human bone and rattles made of the seaweed that drifted onto the white beaches where they had been. Their gifts were received with confusion and some uneasiness, and put into the backs of closets.

Demeter came leading by the hand a little solemn girl, who had been born on board the ship. The girl's eyes were the color of sea foam. Her name was Bridget, and she was modeled to Demeter as closely as possible. The child told of Lee's blood. She had the spare look, and the upright nature. She would grow into that image, the older she got—she became a staunch Christian Scientist, pure and determined in the ways of the right.

But Demeter was carrying another child, too, one that hadn't been born yet. She had become pregnant with the child in Brazil, at a festival they had there where the Brazilians carried huge bobbing heads through the crowds, and dressed in silks and lace and danced till dawn, when they went home stumbling, stained with wine, eyes closing and withered flower petals caught in their hair.

Bridget had been tucked into her hotel bed, and the nurse was reading her a story. Demeter and Fid kissed her good night, and ventured out into the road downstairs.

Down the street they heard a rushing noise like thunder, saw lights flickering and bobbing, and heard music. It was a dancing, lilting tune that reminded Demeter of a carousel she had loved to ride when she was a child, but there was something sad in it too, and haunting. It was a procession they saw dancing towards them, lithe bodies under bright silks with animal heads on top, tossing torches, flinging bottles of wine so that the dark drops speckled the dust on the street like blood.

The revelers screamed, and sang, and danced as they came, winding streamers and ribbons around the lampposts. People watched from the windows, cheering and throwing down red rose petals to be trampled under the passing feet. Demeter and Fid stood and watched, bemused, and as the procession went by, hands reached out to grab them and they found themselves in the center of a sea of animal heads, dark and glossy, with smooth fur and flickering glass eyes.

Someone swung Demeter around and around, and she laughed and watched the sky as she let herself be swung, watching the stars dip and twirl unsteadily over her. She looked around and couldn't see Fid, but she felt wild and restless, and let herself slide into the stream of the people around her.

Someone put a sweet cake in her face, and she ate it; someone else handed her a flask of wine that tasted bitter and had strange, dark lees. She drank it down, and flung the bottle back over her shoulder, laughing.

Time passed strangely, warped and doubled. She danced in rings with faces of wolves and lions, gazed up at one bird with sharp, piercing eyes and a golden beak, and was lifted and thrown through a ring of tossing manes and wings. Someone juggled fire, and she watched entranced as the hot golden spikes of flames lifted and fell, lifted and fell under the sugared dark of the sky.

There was a sword swallower, and acrobats that bent themselves in half and touched their heads to their heels, and through it all Demeter could hear the music, piercing and sweet, making something rise up in her blood. She drank from the bottles that were pushed in her face, and wiped her mouth with her hands, and laughed, spinning around and around. Her hair came loose from its braided knot, and fell down around her face, half covering it.

She found herself dancing along in a crowd that seemed headed for the water. They had wound down the streets until the noise dimmed behind them, and two by two the revelers dropped away, disappearing into corners and courtyards. Demeter wasn't noticing because the sky seemed to have bled down into the water, which was slick with oil, and she became preoccupied with trying to straighten it back up again. But then it didn't seem to matter, and so she turned back to the dance, only to find that everyone had gone away except one figure, who stood looking at her through the eyes of a coyote, with rough reddish fur. It was a man, she could tell by the hand that he held out to her, strongly cut and sprinkled on the back with light red-gold hair.

She took his hand and they hopped unsteadily together down the rest of the street, covered with slick puddles and the remains of the last night's rain. In the distance the music sounded, very vague and far away.

The coyote-headed man led her into a boat that lay rocking by the shore. She ducked her head to follow him down below the deck, which was made out of a light wood. Underneath was a room covered in dark red velvet, with swags hung over the portholes, and everything trimmed in gold. There were marble things, and sparkling jewel colors in the edges of her eyes, and she couldn't tell if those things were real or only things she had dreamed.

The man drew her down onto a couch and pulled off the coyote head mask. Underneath it, she saw, his hair was the same reddish color as the fur on his mask, and his eyes were a bright, hard blue. He gave her some more sweet wine to drink, out of a glass that was cool to her hot cheek and cut from a single piece of green stone, with white marbling through it. She drank down the wine thirstily and held the cup up to the light, marveling at its thinness. The ocean sounded in her ears like thunder. The man took the glass from her hand, gently, and pushed her back onto the thick cushions behind her.

Sometime in the night Demeter woke with a cry. The man slept on beside her, his dark red hair streaked over his face, his head resting on his arm.

She sat up and looked around her, her heart beating fast and her palms wet. It wasn't the man, or that she was on the boat. These things were mortal sins, she knew, but she had many of these on her soul already, and so they were of no account.

But there was another thing, a thing she knew she was carrying now. She had felt the stirring of life inside her, too strong to be denied. In her dream she had looked down the long and complex roads that were the fortunes of the son she had conceived tonight, for a son it would be.

She went down the paths of the maze with mirrored walls that would be her son's life, the endless running choices and moments, each one branching from the other, constantly mutable. She could see through a mist on the mirrors the people and faces he would know, his memories and movements.

And she ran faster and faster, breathing harder and harder, beating against the walls of the mirrored maze like a moth, because no matter which turn she took, which path she chose, all the roads ended in a vision of grey metal and iron bars, the clanging closed that sounded in her ears, a ringing of desolation and the death of hope.

He would be punished for her, this child, and he would never escape.

She gathered her things together, quietly, in the half-light of the rocking boat, and stood for a moment looking at the man there. On the floor, staring up, were the glassy yellow eyes of the coyote mask where it lolled, half in shadow.

She went through the wet streets lightly, barefooted. Sometime during the night she had lost her shoes. At their hotel she found Bridget sleeping quietly in her crib, tucked up as the nurse had left her. Fid lay staring up at the ceiling with his arms behind his head, fully clothed, with mud on his boots. She didn't ask him where he had been that night, or what he had found. They never spoke of it again.

They went home the next day, knowing that the rambling time was over. Demeter had her second child at home. It was a son, and seemed strangely blighted from the first. He had jaundice that turned his skin a shade of yellow, and the first hairs that sparkled on his round skull were a glistening russet red.

18. The Dark Tide

Hiram started wildcatting for oil after his contracting business failed. He had traveled from site to site, his necktie pulled loose and hanging on the side, sweating through the hot, low-lying Louisiana air. The offices he visited were polite, but closed doors on him. There was no room, it seemed, for an up-and-coming young building contractor. He bid on three jobs, and came in second on all of them. Money was running out, and Anise's patient, pinch-mouthed economies ground on his nerves.

So he hired on as a roustabout on an oil rig, one of the thousand dotting the Louisiana skies. He stayed up on the crown of the rig, a hundred feet in the air, stacking drill pipe. Sometimes he ran in the hot sun stripped to the waist, burying seismometers in the burning earth— "hustling jugs," it was called.

He fell in love there—the great booming voice of the mud pumps, the cast of the greenish-yellow lights that flooded the flat plains around the derrick, chasing the night into day. He watched the heavy-headed drill stem forcing the huge bit twenty thousand feet into the earth, feeling the weight of the age under his feet, the dying creatures that so long ago had turned to wealth.

He loved the clanking of the steel on steel that sounded through the night, and the sexual thrust of the great spinning bit, chewing into the earth and turning up its secrets. The rotating pipe, smoothed by a column of heavy mud, lengthened as the bit went through hard rock, into the dark crevices deep below.

Hiram was there to tug and take the whole length of pipe apart when a bit had to be changed, and there to feed the pipe lovingly back into the earth. He unraveled the flashing of the "Christmas tree" lights, transcribing the red and green flashings into information that showed engine temperature and oil pressure, pump strength and strokes per minute, drilling speed, mud weight and gas and salt content. He collected, washed and analyzed the cutting samples, learned to tend to the running of the rig as gently as another might tend a child.

And he stood over the flat, dusty earth and felt the thrumming of the oil beneath him, encased in darkness, distant in time. The ground there cradled its secret, the black blood beating in his ears like a tempest. The earth was dry, for as far as he could see—but underneath the surface was an unlit sea, a crouching surf of living green oil that swayed and tilted with the earth's rotation, the oily drops flowing through the veins of the caverns beneath him like a pulse.

He studied the seismic maps and learned of the arching salt structures that might predict the sand that held oil. He smelled the wind, tasted the oil in it.

This was a new thing for him—he had always yearned away from the earth, wanted to be up and gone from it, moving over it as quickly as a car or a light horse could vault. Now he learned to kneel down, to smear his cheek with earth, and listen to the powerful rumbling below him.

He felt that he had a knack. He was sure that his luck, the luck that ran everywhere with him, would lead him to the oil. He would become a wildcatter.

Independent wildcatters were a particular breed of men in Texas, then and now. Proud, touchy, inveterate gamblers, they habitually staked their lives and livelihoods on the existence of an invisible well that few people credited and no one could prove.

The law existed mostly for wildcatters to circumvent. They were contemptuous of company men, who lay in the safe harbor of other people's money, making careful bets from behind a desk. A true wildcatter was never happier than when riding the edge of the lovely black wave, laying down the deed to his house and his wife's wedding ring on a loan shark's desk to raise the payment for the next well. The one he knew would come in, this time.

The fact remained that the big company generally won out over the independent wildcatter. Although wildcatters moved quickly, could cover more territory and had no one to consult with or slow them down, the companies had the vast reserves of money to sustain them through dry spells and losing streaks. Companies could afford the expensive leases, they could drill the deep wells. And the supply of oil was already dwindling. The earth was being sucked dry at an incredible rate. Most of the huge fields had already been discovered.

It was the job of the wildcatters to forage out in unlikely virgin territories and sink their drill bits into the rocky, sparse places that no one had ever dreamed would yield oil. It was their place to wrestle the new oil up, or die and break their families' hearts in trying. The odds against bringing in a new field, a paying one, were by that time one in fifty-five.

They were odds that my grandfather Hiram liked. He had a Southerner's love of a dying cause, a hatred of institutions, and an infallible belief in his own luck and strength. The oil he felt underneath the ground was like the blood in his own veins, its presence there and his ability to detect it as inevitable as his own magnetic charm. He would draw it up to the surface. It would call to him, draw down his eyes as water drew the dowser's stick. It was the ocean he had dreamed of, with its fragile, curling edge, so long ago.

Things were moving, and the world was new. It would make room for one more wildcatter, willing to stake everything. Hiram mortgaged everything he could get his hands on, sweet-talked the bankers who were his fellow Masons, complimented their wives and patted their children, and he raised a stake.

He got a partner, a man named Joejoe Simmons. Joejoe would keep the books and handle the paperwork. Together they opened an office in Louisiana, with clean painted walls and a cheap wood desk. They hired a geologist, a draftsman and a secretary, and had their names painted on the door in gold letters. "Jameson-Simmons Prospects," it said.

Hiram sat in the empty office at night with his feet up on his desk and his hands behind his head, idly watching the light from the hall come through the reversed golden letters. He dreamed of the black surf he would find, the boils of earth he would lance to bring the beautiful blood to the surface, the way the land would pour out its wealth for him, for him to keep always.

It was a sacred promise, he thought. The land had brought him this far, and it would provide for him. There would be wealth for his dreams, enough for everyone's dreams. He closed his eyes there, seeing the curves of the seismic patterns dancing behind his eyelids. It would be enough.

19. The Treasure Book

Anise had a child, a daughter named Amelia. The next year she had another girl, this one born with a halo of black curls. She called her Constance. Anise threw herself into motherhood as she had into literature. It was an anxious, bookish sort of motherhood. She joined a parents' study group, was elected president. She took careful notes on all the discussions, and sent away to *Parents* magazine for reduced rates for the group members.

She felt stiff, and awkward, holding the baby. She was always peering in Amelia's eyes, testing, seeing, looking for the responses she knew should be there from her reading. She took Amelia to a specialist, just to make sure.

"What is it that concerns you?" said the specialist.

"I don't know, nothing," said Anise. "I just want to make sure, just that she . . . I don't know."

The specialist kindly examined the baby. Normal, quite normal. He laughed when he saw that the baby had grabbed hold of her own hair, and would not let go, and was crying with pain. "All very normal," he said. "Call me if something changes."

Anise was alone with the children almost all the time Hiram was away. She was bewildered by his absences but had adapted to them. The strength that she knitted for herself served her well. It wasn't what she had expected, this life, but she took to it with fortitude. If she was stiff and stilted in her loving, she was, perhaps, not to be blamed. Never having had much warmth, she didn't know much about it.

Her religious life became stronger during this time as well. Her long, isolated days, crackling at the edges but hollow at their center, made her hungry for thoughts of God. These thoughts entered her life and permeated it. She read the Bible, and the Daily Word of Unity.

She became obsessed with the idea that negative thoughts cause negative events. She could control her destiny, she thought. And though she had come so far helpless in the palm of life, she determined to take her fate back from the faceless deity who made it, and redo it. She was at the same time supremely religious and completely heretical, in her refusal to surrender. God to Anise was a useful jinni, who could be bent with the proper application of thought and energy.

She began to make treasure books, cutting out pictures from magazines of health and money, of babies with shiny faces and straight teeth, of trees and lovely homes. All her wishes she cut from the pages of *Modern Housekeeping* and pasted them up. Then she would look through them each day, in the morning and again at night before she went to sleep. She prayed over each one, hanging her head down, forcing it with her will to become reality. Her dark hair hung against her cheek.

The muscles in her thin neck became rigid, from supporting the weight of things. She came almost to believe that if she stopped praying, if she stopped thinking and wishing, that the airplane would crash, that the machinery would burn and the girls would stop their breathing. The price she paid for her power was this—that she could never stop, never rest, or all the carefully woven elements of her life would fray and break.

And she guarded most carefully against the insidious darknesses that lived in the corners of her mind. Even here, living like a nun with her young children, those black thoughts prowled and she fought to subdue them. If she let them in, they would poison her life, and her girls' lives, and she couldn't allow it. She was ceaselessly vigilant.

It was about this time that she performed what she later referred to as the first miracle.

They were living in a tiny, ugly house. She hated it. In Ruston, Louisiana, the flats bred up only dingy tract homes. She created in her treasure book a tiny brick cottage, lovely, with roses climbing the walls and a view. Shining kitchen inside, delicate cream-colored walls, a bathroom with rose fixtures and pretty towels. This became her drive, her main thought. She fixed on it a thousand times a day, pushing from her mind despairing thoughts of the money, the knowledge that the war had shut down all building, the hopelessness of ever finding such a home.

She lay in bed at night, alone, listening to Amelia's soft breathing from her crib, alert for Constance's cries, and wandered through the rooms of her dream house in her mind. She saw herself, polished and laughing, serving cheese and crackers to visitors who would smile at her witty sayings, and drink raspberry-colored fruit punch from her matching glasses. She pictured the hall, with its carpet and plastic runner, the clean, flat stretch of the walls with their new paint smell, the kitchen in red and white with the faucet polished.

While she played games with Amelia during the day, took walks and tidied the small rooms, she saw the dream house. She told Amelia how it would be, and made up stories about the good times they would have there. She breathed it until it seemed real to her.

And one day she looked out of the small, smeared windowpane and saw that they were building a new house on the lot next door. She flung a thin sweater over her shoulder and ran out, unthinking, into the street to ask the workmen whose house it was.

It was a rental unit, they said. No one had taken it yet. No one knew why the war board had given permission for it to be built, when all building had been halted.

Anise went home lightly, singing. She swung Amelia around and hugged her, to the child's delight. She cooked hamburger and lima beans for dinner, and slept soundlessly that night with songs of praise on her lips.

The next day she baked a batch of oatmeal cookies, and took them over to the builders. They broke off work happily to come over and eat the cookies and talk to the pretty lady, slim in her housedress. No, the colors hadn't been picked yet. Nothing had been decided about the inside at all—only that the outside would be brick.

She visited them often, took them things, wandered out to admire the progress they were making. And it seemed perfectly natural, when the time came, that they should paint the bathroom rose, for she delicately suggested it, and wasn't a lady's taste better than these rough workmen's? They painted living-room walls an eggshell cream, and laid fluffy rust-colored carpet in the hall, with a plastic runner down the middle, without even knowing how it came about.

And Anise planted American Beauty roses along the walls, and wasn't even discouraged when they wilted and died in the hard Louisiana clay. She planted them again, working over them and breathing her breath into them, and when spring came around, they were living in the cottage. Anise shook hands with God and thanked Him for a job well done.

She spent much time, these days, trying not to wonder if Tommie had been on board the ships that had gone down in the war. She would never know. That was what hurt her the most, perhaps—that she had no right to know if he had slid from the deck into the cold waves, that she could not nurse him if he was wounded, kiss his eyes closed. She would never know. She adjusted herself to live with this, as she would have lived without a limb.

When the orders came that they were leaving Louisiana to move to a Texas town called Dalhart, where there was a new oil boom, she cried to leave the site of her first miracle. But she was inured by now to moving, to putting herself by, and to leaving the few friends she had made. So she

packed up the babies and their things uncomplainingly. Dalhart would be
a lovely town for them, she was sure. Hiram would do well in business
there. The girls would be happy. She would think positive. She would
learn to love it there. She would have to.

Anise had another baby girl in Dalhart, her third and last. She named
her Sarsaparilla, remembering her mother and the spices, and everyone
called the baby Sweet Sarsaparilla from the day she was born, mysteriously
ignoring the rule to shorten babies names. This is how Anise's girls were:

Amelia, the oldest, had light eyes and brown hair. She looked much
like Anise herself, but with a bloom that Anise never had. She was fiercely
loyal, with a stubborn streak in her that was hidden under the demure,
yielding ways of a lady. Anise leaned on her, took her for company and
made her an ally from the beginning.

Amelia was a charming, round-faced little girl, who took care of the
others and did the right thing, almost always. When Anise felt Amelia
growing away from her, she hobbled her by describing her as slow and
plodding, so that the little girl's natural brilliance was damped a little. She
grew into a graceful, deceptively delicate-looking woman, with a knack for
pleasing and framing those around her. She adored Hiram, with his coppery brilliance, but the clumsiness and fragility that her mother enforced
in her divided her from keeping up with Hiram's schemes and romps.

Constance was the second, the middle child. She had wicked black
eyes and black curls, photogenically pleasing and wild, with a rash thing in
her like Hiram himself. She was surefooted and balanced, and became
Hiram's pet, riding the horses with him and following after him.

Anise was fussy and rigid, Constance thought—she much preferred
her father's ways and swinging, light touch. She watched her parents and
saw that her mother labored through life, conscientiously, while her father
floated with brilliant color. She chose her father, wanting his magic. She
was decisive, and tough, and when she was a teenager swaggered like a boy
and wore leather chaps. She always wrestled with life, chewing off huge
bites and sometimes choking on them in her rashness. She grew to be an
immensely competent woman, with a wide pool of warmth in her, and
managing ways.

Sweet Sarsaparilla, the youngest, had floating blond hair and almond-shaped blue eyes that creased and disappeared, when she smiled, in a

heart-shaped face. She was innocent, and her touch was gentle. She was, perhaps, one of the few truly good people. What was in her was visible to the eye—loyal and trusting. Even when she was troubled, she was not turbulent, or dark. Life sat easily on her, with the care that it seldom takes of the pure. She had dyslexia, mixed her letters, so that learning came hard to her, and by the time it was discovered, felt herself not to be clever, and was marked by that. She pursued other things, pleasing talents. She had a generous grace that spread about her, an influence that was felt in its absence when she left a room.

Fatherhood descended on Hiram strangely. He felt it working in him, altering his pores and his dreams. He was shattered when he first held Amelia in his arms, saw her wrapping her hand around his finger. He felt it sink deeply into him. Even his dreams were changed.

He had been so light and unencumbered. It had hardly hurt him to leave Anise in one place and work in another. There were accommodating ladies everywhere, and he practiced his charm on them easily, without feeling it a betrayal. He was married to Anise, after all, and he didn't love any of the ladies, any of the married matrons who looked at him with long, jaded eyes with paint around them. He was neither stealing their virtue nor giving up his own—it was only that his high sex had to flow into some receiving pool. His long absences, and Anise's frosty embrace, set the pattern for him. But he never lingered too long in any one place, and thankfully washed the stale perfume from him when it was time to go home.

The arrival of the girls changed that. He became, in his own eyes, a patriarch, the leader of a family. He saw himself taking a tribe out into the wild places, parting the bushes on the hard ground. The cold memories of his own family, the distance, the long shadows, the afternoon that he lay bleeding on the table, while his mother was away—all these worked in him to make him hungry for the easy family that he wrapped around himself like a saddle blanket.

And more—these were women to adore him. From the time that he first taught Amelia to kiss his cheek, he felt the possibility of remaking himself in their eyes. He was all charm, all goodness, all warmth to them. What he saw in their looks was the man that he had always wanted to be, rinsed of all selfishness, all recklessness, all cruelty. Had he known this, he thought, he would have had children long ago.

Without knowing it, he became addicted to the lavish adoration that they gave him. It was pure, distilled, and he had nothing more to do to earn it than to practice his careless charms, to entertain them and show them their way in the world. He was born to be a father—it was, perhaps, one of his most successful roles. He played it with sincerity. Family became to him the center pole of the carousel, and around it the brightly painted horses of his life revolved.

Texans are strange animals—huge as giants and angry as children. You can read it in the histories, boiled back to a crazy gumshoe nationalism. The strangeness can be seen in the three stories we tell about our "war" for independence from Mexico.

The first tale is the fall of the Alamo. It occurred when one hundred and eighty-three men, most of whom had arrived in Texas only weeks before, stubbornly locked themselves in a mission against orders. They refused to admit a Mexican army of thousands, choosing instead to die to the last man.

Then we remember the men of Goliad, defeated prisoners of war who were marched into the road and shot like cattle by the crazy Mexican devil Santa Anna, a bugbear still invoked to frighten naughty Texas children.

And we recall the battle of San Jacinto, in which seven hundred and eighty-three dirty, sweaty, exhausted, untrained, bearded, braggart Texans beat a Mexican army twice their size in eighteen minutes. After their victory the Texans almost blew themselves up with a huge pile of explosive munitions because they refused to put out their pipes. Afterwards, of course, they saved the day by rushing into the blaze to put out the fires with their bare feet and blankets.

Then they tore off all the colorful green and red ribbons and epaulets from the Mexican soldiers, and gleefully stuck them on their own heads, saddled their ornery pack mules with the elaborately silvered Mexican riding saddles, and tied bows on them.

One soldier put two pairs of Mexican blinders on his mule—one over the eyes, where it belonged, and one pair over the poor animal's nostrils. Another soldier tricked out his mule with all the bright colors he could find but forgot to tighten the cinch of his saddle, and fell off the mule as it bolted across the camp. The captured Mexican soldiers howled with laughter.

What is there to do with such a people—passionate, brave, mad bullies? It is strange blood to carry, the blood of a place as big as a country, with its own President, who used his cuff button as a seal of state.

The proud touchiness is still there in my family, the dogged violence, the tall tales. Some of it is old Celtic gloom and color, from the Irish. We came from there in the 1600s. Those long-ago folk ancestors settled a plantation in the East, bred racing dogs and lovely, firm-shouldered daughters. They drank whiskey, laid bets, left their holdings to their eldest sons and whistled up the wind that carried them all the way across the country, to the huge pancake of Texas.

Texas legends are full of tales of buried treasure and lost silver mines —stories of men who stumble stupidly into a godforsaken wash of stone and scrub, and discover a cache of silver—maybe belonging to the famous Texas pirate Lafitte, maybe tossed out on the run by a posse of Mexican bandits. The man in the story always marks the cache and leaves, only to discover later that he can never find it again.

Treasures are easily gained and lost in Texas tales—dumped as excess baggage during flight, stuffed under a pile of boulders, hidden in a ditch with only the lonely white skull of a mule left as a marker. Troves are often traced out on maps by dying men, but almost never found—they linger like a silver rime of frost over all the bushes, just beneath the eye, barely over the next rise.

It may be because the land is so huge and featureless that a man might fear to put his soul down there and never find it again. Or maybe the legends were a kind of dowsing rod for the blacker cache that hung under every mound of shale.

The oil was our real treasure. Not as easy or clean or portable as the lost silver, it was just as poisonous to the men who wildcatted after it, who went mad to bet their homes and their families against the dark invisible tide under their feet. Better, perhaps, that they had never found it at all.

20. The Beasts

Big Joe went to the doctor for his regular yearly checkup, and the news was not good. He came home afterwards, put on his narrow wire-rimmed spectacles, and opened the desk where he kept all of his papers.

He had always been a thorough and conscientious man. His estate was in order, and his will was made. But there were a few things that remained to be done—just a few last things.

There was the disposition of the oil well. He had arranged it so that he and Big Mother shared it equally. She would be well taken care of after his death. The well was a steady producer. It had brought three thousand dollars per month for a long time, now. If oil prices went up it would be worth much more.

He took up his fine-pointed blue pen, the only type he used, and penned in quick incisive lines. He would leave his half of the oil well to his eight surviving children equally, a share to each. He tapped the edge of the pen against his chin, and sat, considering.

He thought of Hiram, the smooth-faced fellow. Big Joe had a feeling that Anise was unhappy there, but he was not one to interfere. She had made her decision, and now she must bide with it. But the thought of Hiram getting his hands on the oil income made Big Joe sit up straight, his spine rigid.

It would not happen, he was determined. If that fellow wanted to spend his time gallivanting around the country, leaving his wife and children alone at home and up to who knew what mischief when he was away, that was one thing. But to do it on Big Joe's money—that was something else again. Let the fellow drill his own well. He'd be getting none of the Frankell money.

Big Joe wrote further, concisely, clearly. The proceeds from the oil well would go to his children during their lifetime, and then, after their deaths, would pass to their children. "Life estate" was the legal term. His lawyer had coached him well. The spouses of his children would get nothing.

He put his pen down and stared into space, considering. Frank, his eldest son, would not be happy with this condition. Frank was a lawyer, and a man as punctilious, hidebound and correct as his father. Frank had no children—there was only his wife, Maundy, whom he adored.

Maundy was a delicate creature with pale cheeks and a knot of light brown curls. She was so delicate, in fact, that the doctor had said that having children might kill her, and so Frank had declared it out of the question, although Maundy had wanted to try. Frank had spent his entire life fencing Maundy off from the world, protecting her and showering her with unnecessary and recklessly expensive gifts. Their house was stuffed with things, pink satin lampshades with fringe and hundreds of the china figurines that she loved, so that she could hardly walk through the passage without knocking things over.

Frank would not be happy to hear that Maundy had been excluded from the inheritance. He might, in fact, be bitterly angry. Big Joe weighed the thought in his mind, carefully. Then, decisively, he wrote in the final phrases. Frank would just have to accept it. The prospect of Hiram Jameson wildcatting around with the money from Big Joe's well must be avoided at all costs. Frank was a good provider—let him provide for Maundy out of his own pocket.

Big Joe finished the papers, put them in an envelope and stamped them to send to his lawyer. He pushed the letter to the edge of the desk. He linked his arms back behind his head and put his boots up on the desk, staring out the window at the patch of brown sage he could see, trodden and fenced and dirty.

His mind drifted lazily, wandering back to those days when he had come on the train, awed and washed by the sweep of the land outside the windows. He thought of his old friend Diggory, and the day Diggory had stood with his head cocked and his arms spread, a strange smile on his face, rattlesnakes dripping from him like jewels.

Big Joe thought of the one white buffalo he had seen, and the way its tail switched, and the deep sad softness of its eyes. He had tried to read something in those eyes, and had failed. But now it came to him more clearly, and he sat up straight as he realized what it was. He would have to remember to tell Big Mother, he thought, as his arms and legs gradually emptied of feeling and a hollow darkness ran up his spine, creeping like a mist. She would never have guessed.

Big Mother took Big Joe's death very hard. They had argued, and been separated much, but they had been married for forty years and she hardly knew how to function without him, pushing against him and nagging him and tying his scarf tighter around his neck. His absence produced a vacuum in her life, and her mind began to leak into it.

She became more vague, and sometimes would leave for the store and wind up halfway to the post office, not knowing what she was doing there.

The silence in the house ground on Big Mother. She would start at things and think that Big Joe had come in, and would have to remind herself that he was dead. The constant irritation of not knowing where she was told on her nerves, and she became ornery.

She watered the plants in the garden by the hour. Once when her neighbor asked her to stop watering the pink roses so much, she turned the hose right on her neighbor's face. The woman had run into her house, wet-faced and shrieking, had telephoned Big Mother's oldest son Frank.

Frank had come out to the house and given Big Mother a talking-to, told her that she couldn't treat Mrs. Mitson that way, that Mrs. Mitson had always been good to her. But Big Mother chuckled and laughed and didn't give a damn. She had been so well behaved, all her life. Now she figured she was due to raise a little hell.

When Frank wouldn't leave her alone, but kept harping at her, Big Mother upset a pan of boiling sugar water on him that she was cooking for jam. He left in a hurry then, all right. He drove backwards all the way up the drive, his tires screeching. Big Mother watched him at the window and laughed all the way. Let him screech. Let them all screech.

But Frank came back the next day, with some papers to sign. He came every day, with papers to sign, until Big Mother was so sick of him she could hardly stand the sound of his neat, precise shoes scraping on the doormat, the exact way he rang the bell, three sharp rings that were always the same length. She knew what Frank was up to, all right. He wanted her to change her will.

Her will was exactly the same as Big Joe's, leaving her half of the oil well in equal shares to the eight children for their lifetimes, then to the grandchildren after their deaths. Nothing for the spouses.

And Frank wanted her to do something different now, so that his wife, Maundy, wouldn't be left out. Always on about his precious Maundy! Of course, it was driving Frank perfectly wild to think that if he died, poor Maundy would be left with no oil income at all. It kept him up nights, and made him itch as if with hives. Let him itch. Big Mother didn't care.

But he nagged and nagged at her until he wore her down. It began to seem not so important, after all. Would he hush up about the will if she only signed? He would, he said. So she agreed.

He wrote something up that he called a codicil, something to the effect that if a child of hers died without issue, then the oil money would go to that child's spouse.

Of course, everyone in the family knew exactly what Frank was doing, and why. Frank and Maundy were the only ones without children, of all Big Mother's family. But no one minded. Frank was the only boy in the family, and all his seven sisters just worshipped him. Anything he told them, they would do.

So Big Mother signed the papers that he waved in her face, and then settled back in the window to watch the street, the lace curtain pulled back a little to show her face. She had put some motor oil on the path, and thought the mailman might slip in it. She wanted to be there to see.

Frank left his mother's house feeling relieved and ashamed. What an old witch she had become! Really, she shouldn't be allowed to live alone. After she had turned the hose on the neighbor, there was no telling what she might do. She could easily set the entire house on fire. She should be put in a home, where she could be properly taken care of.

He patted his pocket comfortably, where the will was. Finally, she had signed it. He had been forced to grovel and harass her, but she had signed, and Maundy was safe, and protected. Now he had only to make sure of it. He didn't trust Big Mother anymore, not worth a damn. In her present unstable, malicious state, she was perfectly capable of turning around and undoing what she had done.

His foot hit a hidden dark patch of something slippery on the path and his feet shot out from under him. He fell onto the brick path so hard that he almost was knocked out. He would probably have whiplash. He had probably ruined his suit.

Wincing, he pulled himself up to a sitting position. He looked up to see his mother's face at the window, screaming with silent laughter. He couldn't hear her through the window, only see her. She had taken her plate out, and bare gums were exposed in her howls of mirth. With her grey hair wisping untidily around her face he thought she looked like a witch. He smiled unconvincingly at her as if sharing the joke. It set her off again into peals of laughter.

Furious and humiliated, Frank picked himself up, rubbing the sore spot on his hip where he had landed. There was something dark and sticky on the seat of his good suit pants. He straightened his jacket and walked off towards his charcoal-grey Cadillac, his ears burning with rage.

He was so close, now. If only he could make it until her death without saying something that would cause her to retract the concessions that he had won from her. The words were there on his tongue, all the things he wanted to say to her. They trembled inside his mouth like living things. But he swallowed them down and walked to the car, back erect.

She had always ignored him, always. He was the second-born son, after that monstrous Little Baz. He had been lost in a welter of girls, of petticoats and hair ribbons and the thick miasma of eight women in the house, hot female flesh drawing with the changes of the moon.

His sisters had always adored him and spoiled him, catered to him and deferred to him as the only boy. But he cared nothing for them. It was his mother that he had wanted. He had thought Big Mother wonderful, with her red hair and blue eyes. He used to creep up under the piano to listen to her sing when she played, her white freckled hands splayed out over the piano keys, her fragile voice soaring up. He had thought her like an angel. That time under the piano, watching her little booted foot working the pedals, was the closest he had ever gotten to her, really, the closest he had ever been to having her all for himself.

The rest of the time she was sweeping around the house in a barely contained frenzy, cooking, cleaning, collapsing in one of her melancholy spells when she could not bear noise and no one could disturb her.

She never loved him as he loved her. He knew that perfectly well. She had loved first Little Baz and then Anise. She had depended on Cumin and scolded Marjie and served Big Joe, and all the rest of the children had fallen through the cracks somehow. Including Frank. She had no time for the pale little boy with the ears that stuck out on the sides, who stammered a little. She had always brushed his clinging arms off her with ill-concealed annoyance, said that she was busy and why didn't he go bother his father.

But Big Joe had been busy, too. There was no place for a boy in his work. Frank noticed that there seemed to be plenty of time later for Anise, when she was born, time for Big Joe to take Anise out on road trips and tell her stories, teach her to read and bring her things home from distant towns.

And then Anise had married, and her husband was the same, taking all the attention for himself. Big Mother loved even Anise's husband more than she did Frank. Someone not even related to her! A smooth-faced rascal with quizzical blue eyes and a black widow's peak, obviously up to no good.

Big Mother would never listen to Frank when he tried to warn her about Hiram, and how he was trying to weasel into the family inheritance. She wouldn't tolerate an unfavorable word said in her presence about Hiram. And worst of all, Big Mother had never liked Frank's wife, Maundy. She had only turned a cold cheek to Maundy on their wedding day, never even properly welcomed her into the family, so that Maundy had cried on their wedding night, her poor head bent against Frank's arm.

Big Mother had never made the slightest effort to be fair, Frank thought, swinging the steering wheel of the Cadillac with sharp, angry jerks. She didn't even try. She just shamelessly indulged her favorites and left the rest to ruin. But it was Frank's turn, now. Now he was the lawyer, he was the strong one. He was grown-up, and he was in control. He was getting a little of his own back, now.

He had forced Big Mother to write Maundy into the will, and that was only the beginning. He was the executor of Big Mother's estate, and he would run it just the way he saw fit. Now that Frank was in charge, he thought, stomping on the gas pedal, everything was finally going to be perfectly, exactly fair.

By this time Lee and Wester were settled in Missouri, on a farm called Indian Bluff. Wester had worked his gentle engineering magic there. He strung fairy lights in the trees around the fishpond, invented a heater to keep the fish warm in winter and a washing machine, all run by the water power of the river. Lee rode her horses, and cleared the yard, and took occasional swipes at the dust in the house.

When Demeter and Fid came back from their trip they settled in Patience, Missouri, the town nearest Indian Bluff. They went there to be near Lee and Wester, although Lee and Wester no more needed assistance than a pill bug needs help rolling his ball of dirt.

But they settled there, and Fid opened a machine shop behind their frame house in town. He puttered there quietly, his long face solemn and his hands covered with black grease. His two children grew up there, dodging the bits of pipe and tubing hanging down, and making up games with the bright washers and wire that sat neatly in bins, gleaming like Aladdin's cave.

Demeter and Fid named their son G.A., short for God A'Mighty. Demeter thought it might help. The boy grew up next to his sister Bridget, lived the same and ate the same, played in the same dirt ruts and rode the same ponies. But never were there two children more different than Bridget and G.A. Demeter neither wondered over it nor broke her heart, for she had seen it coming from a long ways off.

Bridget was a girl of sparkling clarity. Things came easily to her, as they did to her mother. She was clever, quick, and obedient. Anything that she turned her hand to, she could do. Demeter taught her to do electricity and wiring and plumbing in the houses that Fid helped to build, to ride horses and jump fences and cook big hot meals with floury biscuits and veal in gravy.

G.A. spent much of his time away from the town, up at the farm. There he got underfoot until his grandmother shooed him outside, to play in the wide dirt yard, or fish in the fishpond with bent pins, and squiggling worms for bait.

He wandered in the green vastnesses of Indian Bluff, parting the bushes and swimming through the green waves of light as if they were water. He was much alone out there, but where the woods might have spoken to many a child of the growing and the living of things, to G.A. they spoke always of dissolution and decay, and endings.

He saw a baby bird thrown out of its nest by its parents, to break and die on the path. He came back each day to watch it bleach and fade into the rocks, its skin drying like leather. He saw a rabbit get killed and eaten by a fox, and watched as the fox pulled out a long intestine that glistened darkly against the light fur. He saw a snake wriggling out of the shale, slowly, to curve each way and then sink down, and a horde of bees come down and land on it, buzzing and raising up each time it twitched, and finally feeding on it entirely.

G.A.'s woods were full of rotting wood and bracken, broken into crumbling deposits, black slime mold that produced fungus as white as a dead man's toe. The motions of the creatures through the woods taught him that some preyed and some were preyed upon. The face of nature was laid bare to him, he thought, and he looked on the pitiless stone of that face. It shivered him to his soul.

The moments of sunlight among the shadow only seemed like brief things, to better illuminate the bleakness. Better, he thought, to be the parent birds than the baby, the fox than the rabbit, the bees than the snake.

Better to prey, and move quickly, than to be soft and fat and left behind. He began to practice small cruelties of his own—first on himself, sticking his fingers with sharp sticks and bits of stone, raising welts of blood with his father's razor, and then on the small creatures that came to his hand.

He was practicing to be a fox when he hit the squirrel with a rock and pinned it to the ground, and flayed the skin off it while the thing struggled, waving its little feet. He practiced to be the swarm of killer bees on the kitten he found, and Bridget never knew where it went.

Demeter suspected G.A. when Bridget's kitten turned up missing, but only sighed and wiped her palms on her apron, and turned her eyes away from the mirror that beckoned to her with its sliding, telling shadows. She didn't want to know. Some things were best unseen.

Something in Wester pushed him away from his grandson. He was horrified by the look in the boy's slit eyes. G.A. had reddish hair and a stocky frame, and one felt his eyes should be blue—but they were dark, dark as swamps. Wester knew that he should love his grandchildren equally, but didn't, and shied away from the boy when he came around.

His granddaughter Bridget, though, was another thing. Bridget just suited the old man—she was quiet, and tidy, and loved to sit with him and watch while he made his creations. She helped him string the lights around the fishpond, and admired his washing machine. The delicate up-tilt and the smooth skin on the insides of her wrists reminded Wester not of Demeter, but of Lee, as she had been as a girl, when he wooed her that hot June. He would look at Bridget and his eyes would mist over, and he would sigh.

Demeter mothered G.A. dutifully, but without any real warmth, and Fid ignored him almost entirely. Strangely, G.A.'s only advocate was Lee. They made an odd pair, the white-haired woman and the red-haired boy.

They didn't talk much when they were together, but G.A. was the only one Lee allowed around her when she was paying bills, tending the horses, or writing letters. She would fuss irritably if anyone else got underfoot, but didn't mind G.A. It was as if he was a neutral to her, neither acid nor basic. He didn't seem to want anything from her, only to hang about quietly in the background, and she didn't seem to give him any affection. But she let him stay near.

It was as if the dark that Lee had kept down so hard in herself had risen up in the boy, irrepressible as black oil bubbling from the ground, and Lee bowed to it. Together they were like one whole person, one half bleached bone and one half swamp loam. And though Lee dreamed uneasy dreams about the boy, and refused to pray for him, she allowed him to stay. They were often seen together, the stocky boy shadowing the wiry, upright woman, and the people of Patience wondered at the sight until they grew used to it, and then forgot.

21. Indian Bluff

Hiram and Anise took the girls to visit their grandparents at Indian Bluff almost every summer. Lee generally retired to the blue cool of her bedroom with a migraine when they came.

Anise annoyed Lee unbearably, although she wouldn't have known why. The truth was that they were too much alike—Anise was encased in a prissiness that Lee found stifling and repulsive.

And Lee felt that Anise made her redundant. Although Hiram had never really turned to Lee with his problems, she knew she had been the cool and moderating influence for him, an oasis of reserve. Now Anise took these duties over with a puritanical thoroughness that infuriated Lee. She would have died rather than admit that finally, long after her children were grown, she longed to be needed.

Instead, Lee's head swelled shut on her silence and she lay down to nurse her headache with a cool cloth dipped in vinegar on her forehead, and the shutters drawn.

The three Jameson girls met their cousins, G.A. and Bridget, for the first time in the summer of 1947. Bridget was a gentle, tidy girl, and allowed herself to be absorbed into their play. G.A. was separate and hung apart, wanting to be included but scowling furiously when the girls, nudged by Anise, invited him to join in.

Constance was fascinated by G.A., even young as she was. She felt his darkness as something wicked and direct that she longed to scratch. There was a straightness to G.A.'s violence that appealed to something in herself. Anise had carefully weeded the brutality in Constance, uprooted it and let Constance follow her tomboy ways, to air it, but there still lingered a touch of that heady chaos in Constance. She was drawn towards it with revulsion and a strange comprehension.

G.A. followed her one day, when they were going back from the pump house, carrying the milk and butter that Lee had sent them to fetch.

"Constance," he called out softly, "Constance, I've got my thing out. Right out of my pants. Don't you want to see it?"

Constance shuddered and kept walking. She did want to see it, something awful. But she knew she shouldn't, and the war in her between the good girl and the dark curiosity wore at her. She had the feeling it would be like picking a scab—a relief in the moment, but leaving a scar.

"No," she said reluctantly, "I don't think I better."

"Scared?" G.A. taunted her. "Are you scared of my thing? Scared it will get you?"

She could feel his presence behind her, rank and shadowy. "I ain't scared," she said, sticking out her lip. "I ain't scared of nothing."

"Then why don't you turn around and look?" said G.A. "Just for a second. I won't tell no one. If you won't, I'll always know that you're a chickeny chicken. Bawk! Bawk!"

He made chicken noises, and it was too much for her. She whirled around quickly, but kept her eyes squeezed shut. She peeked a little, at the last minute, and saw something that she thought might have been his thing, but wasn't sure. Then she turned around and ran, her pail banging heavily against her skinned knees, ran every step of the way back to the farmhouse until she was safe in front of the fire, with the room filled with warm lights and the safety of the grown-up people.

This is what Amelia remembers of that summer's trip to Indian Bluff: Hiram took her out one day to round up the cows that Wester and Lee ran on the spread. All she could see of the place around her, as they rode, were the hills and the trees, brooding. Hiram was riding Lee's great white stallion Traveller, and Amelia was on Dandy, the gentle old plow horse. Dandy wouldn't go, no matter how hard he was whipped, and Amelia's short legs barely came around the sides of the saddle.

Hiram got impatient, and wanted to go on ahead. "You stay here," he told Amelia, "and make sure the cows don't go up this hill."

He cantered on ahead to fetch the cows, and the mouth of the woods closed around him. Dandy jerked his head loose from the rein and leaned down to graze, and Amelia sat uncomfortably on his back. She was ner-

vous with horses. Their bigness, the crude hooves and the way they rolled
their eyes at her frightened her. But her father loved brave girls, and she
wanted to be with him, where he went. So she had mounted without
protest.

She waited, and waited, and the silence of the woods began to ring in
her ears. The dark green light, filtering through the trees and bouncing off
the ragged rocks, flickered in her eyes and seemed ominous. As far as she
could see, there were no people, nothing familiar, only the rough and
wrinkled face of the land around her, yawning into caverns as she
watched.

She remembered a story that her grandpa Wester had told her, when
he was left to sit alone with her one night and wanted her to be quiet. He
told her it was a true thing, but really he had gotten it from a much-loved
book of tales collected by Mr. J. Frank Dobie, a big old book that sat by
the fireplace.

Wester told her of a man and his family who had lived out in the
wilderness not far from Indian Bluff, by a river. There was a mother, and
a father, and a beautiful little girl, Wester said, just the same age as
Amelia.

And there was an old Indian, who lived on the other side of the river.
He was a sad Indian, who had a little girl of his own once, but she had
died. And he came to be friends with the white folks, and he would paddle
across the river to visit that little white girl, and take her doll figures that
he made from moccasin leather, dressed on top with real horsehair and
beads. And the parents let the old Indian take the little girl out with him
onto the river, where they would drift and catch fish, and the little girl
would trail her fingers in the silver ripples.

"No one knew why the parents let that old Indian take the little girl,"
Wester had said, shaking his head, "but that's what they did."

And always the Indian brought the little girl back safe and sound.

Then one day the Indian and the girl's pa got in a fight. Some said
the white man wanted the Indian to do some dirty work for him, and the
Indian refused. Some said the white man hit the Indian with a stick, and
some said with his fists. But there was a terrible fight, and the Indian went
away and didn't come back for a long time, swearing his revenge. And the
white people were sorry, since he used to bring them salted sides of beef,
and beads the color of the sky.

Then one day they saw the Indian coming back across the river again.

They watched him come, and they didn't know whether to be happy or sad. He came up to their house, and took the little girl child in his arms, and they saw her bright blond hair shining over his shoulder. He put her in the canoe and pushed off, and paddled till he got to the other side. Then he picked her up and walked to the top of a deadly high cliff.

The parents called for him to come down. The Indian had never gone this far away with the girl before.

But he only turned around and grinned a horrible grin to them, with all his teeth showing, and then he leapt from the top of that cliff with the girl child in his arms. He gave a yell, and the girl's blond hair streamed out behind them like the tail of a comet.

"Then there was nothing for the parents to do," Wester had said. "The girl and the Indian were both dead, drown-dead in the river. But they moved away, and ever afterwards this place has been called Indian Bluff. And if you look just over that bend in the river, you can see the very place, sure as I'm standing."

The story had frightened her quiet, all right. Amelia was sure that the rustlings she heard around her were the Indian, coming to take her across the river in his arms to the cliff. She could hear the wind whistling past her cheeks, falling down into the cold river, onto the sharp rocks. The river hissed and moaned nearby, and she could hear the wailing of that girl baby, wandering thin and lost in the forest.

The blood pounded in Amelia's ears, and she thought her heart would burst. She was afraid of G.A., and thought he might come and do something to her. Hiram had been gone so long, she knew he had gone away and left her. Maybe she had been so bad that he didn't want her anymore, and she would be left here forever.

"Daddy," she screamed, "Daddy, come back and get me. Please come back and get me. If you come back I'll never be bad again. I promise, Daddy. Please come back."

She sobbed and screamed herself into a fever, and when Hiram finally came back with the cows, pleased with himself and jaunty, he found her curled into a small hot ball on top of Dandy, shivering and tear-soaked, and quite unable to tell him what had happened.

Later, much later, when she was a grown woman with a child of her own, Amelia would discover that she had erased from her memory the feeling and image of her father, sparkling and brilliant, laughing, riding away from her that day in the sunshine, free of care.

Free of care had come to mean that he cared nothing for her, would just leave her there, and she could not bear it. He had been everything to her, everything! Just to be with him was happiness. And he didn't feel that way about her—he never did. Not once.

Her father's integrity wounded her, and she had no power to wound him back. She had tried everything to make him love her, and nothing worked. And so there came to be a small part of her, a very small, cold part of her that hated him, because she couldn't hold or hurt him.

Of course, Amelia could hurt him, and did later, almost to death, but he never told. That was the way Hiram was. So she never knew what she had done. She never let herself know. She bent her mind, in that way her mother had showed her, to just forget. The dark hand of forgetfulness reached gently up to her brain, and shadowed away the part that hurt, and she forgot . . .

My grandfather Hiram killed his mother this way: Lee and Wester came to visit the family in Dalhart only once. They were old and settled enough so that they hated to stir from Indian Bluff. Lee disliked the bustle of the town and loathed the thought of being trapped in Anise's house, where she would be forced to be nice all the day long, and have no place to escape with her headaches.

But it was a family duty, and must be done. Lee stroked Traveller in his stall, laying her head against his side, and gave him a double ration of grain and a handful of corn before they left for Dalhart. The hired man would care for him well enough, along with the other horses and the dogs and barn cats, while they were gone. But she hated to go.

She held Traveller's head in her hands, breathing in the sweet breath from his nostrils, and looking into the deep liquid brown of his eyes, with the S-shaped bits of light in them. She felt that he was trying to tell her something, that if only she could listen quietly enough, he would speak. His coat was rough now, and hoary. The years had passed over him as they had over her. It made her suddenly lonely, seeing the creaky way he shifted from foot to foot.

"We're old, you and I," she said, stroking his neck. "Those bastards, they made us old."

She had the sudden impulse to swing her leg up over him, jump the stable chain and gallop away, just leave and never come back. She could wander in the woods, and he could browse on the leaves. She would eat berries, and roots, trap small animals, or maybe only feast on sunlight until she was thin and withered, transparent so that the sun shone through her as through the veins of a leaf. Thin enough so that the breeze would lift her up into the sky, carry her away with all the dirty blood cooked out of her, pure and astringent on the air.

She remembered Nakomas Sorrel, the Indian girl who had walked so far with the blood down her legs. Where had she come from, that girl, and where had she gone? Lee felt that the girl had taken something of hers away when she left, something that she needed now and had forgotten how to find. If she could only remember—the Indian girl's eyes had been like Traveller's eyes, that night, trusting in their pain, knowing and wordless.

She could have wandered with that girl, in the woods. She should have gone with her, perhaps. But she had not held out a hand to stop her. She had not pulled her into the firelight, or fed her soup, or gone with her back into the cool shadows of the night. She wished she could find that girl now. That girl could have told her, perhaps, about G.A.—given her the answers to questions that she dreaded to ask.

Lee was not looking forward to taking the long trip with Wester in the pickup. On the farm she and Wester did very well. She could be alone with the horses and the dogs, mostly. But in the pickup, trapped into the metal rectangle, Wester's love came back to pluck at her, and she could not escape into the outdoors. There was something pathetic, something soft in his need for her that made her uneasy, guilty and edgy.

He wanted so much from her, and she had given him so little, really, all through the years. She had always thought that the passage of time might soften her, and that she would come to be a good wife to him. It had always been something on her list to do, when she had the time.

But age had only dried her skin closer to her bones, like jerky drying in the wind. She had less sap and blood to give Wester as time went on, instead of more. He seemed to understand, and had drifted into a half twilight of his own imagining, so that he looked out at her, kind and vague. If she appeared at the dinner table to spoon lima beans with butter and corn onto his plate, alongside of the ribs, he looked at her with quiet gratitude and seemed content. It was little enough for her to do.

The visit must be accomplished, however. She sighed, stroked Traveller once down his nose, hard, so that he nodded once in consent. Consent to what? she wondered briefly, then dusted off her hands on the seat of her trousers and went to get ready for the trip. She looked back long into the stables as she went, and felt a dark hollow place at her center, where her memories were.

The visit was as dreadful as she had feared. Anise was determinedly cheerful, and had made salmon patties and peach ice cream, both of which Lee detested. The little girls were noisy and pushed their paper dolls in her face. The house seemed too brightly lit and too warm. She could hardly breathe.

Hiram was jovial, but tense. Something was wrong between him and Anise, she could tell. Lee's face hurt with smiling and admiring the fussy way Anise had done the house. Heavens above! So many pieces of decorative junk, everywhere you looked. It was a wonder the woman could rest in her own mind, if she fussed up her head the way she did her home.

Lee's patience, never much tried, snapped suddenly. "Wester, it's time to go," she announced. Hiram looked surprised, and Anise hurt.

"But, Mother," Anise said, "you only just got here today. We were looking forward to having you with us five days, at least. And it's raining, and dark, and the roads are bad."

"Nonsense," said Lee briskly. "Nothing to it. Hiram can lead us out. Right, boy?" She looked across at Hiram, who was looking up at her with a strange, blank look on his face. For a moment she thought she saw candle flames etched in his eyes, doubled, and shook her head slightly to clear her vision.

"If you like," he said, getting to his feet slowly.

"So sorry," Lee said sideways to Anise, breezing through the room to put on her things. "It's just one of my headaches, you know, and much better for me to be at home through one of those. Ready, Wester?"

Wester was gathering his things, uncomplaining. Good man, Lee thought gratefully. Always there when you need him.

Anise was trailing them, fussy and anxious. "The roads . . . the damp . . ."

"Nonsense," Lee said again, shook hands with Anise mannishly, leaving her looking startled, and dodged out through the raindrops to the pickup, with deep relief.

Hiram started up his car, and drove ahead to show them the way. It was dark, and the way was slick. He drove faster, and then a little faster still. The headlights flashing on the turns fascinated him. He felt hypnotized. It had been so long since he felt something running through his veins, so long that he had been safe and secure. Forgetting himself, he forced the car through the night on the edge of the wet pavement. The trees flew by, and the raindrops divided sideways around him. He laughed out loud.

Behind him, Lee and Wester saw his pale lights flashing around the turns, moving away from them, with annoyance. If he lost them they would be wandering down these godforsaken lanes all night.

"Boy always did drive too fast," said Wester. He set his lips tightly together and pressed the pedal of the pickup closer to the floor. Lee put her hand out the open window, smelling the wet air, feeling how fast they were going, but said nothing.

They came to a traffic circle. Hiram passed another car, with careless skill, whipping away into the darkness. Wester saw an opening, just for a moment, and tried to pass the same car. The bumpers caught and ground into one another, mating metal with metal.

There was a shriek and a whirl of lights. When the darkness cleared, the other motorist was gone. Lee and Wester's pickup was upside down in the ditch, wheels spinning slowly.

Hiram looked in his rearview mirror and couldn't understand what he saw, for a long minute. Then he stopped his own car by the side of the road and went back. "Dear God," he said when he saw the underbelly of their truck, shining wetly through the dark. He started to run. He kicked the doors open and dragged them out.

Wester was only stunned and bruised. But Lee's hand had been trapped outside the door as the pickup rolled lazily over. Her long-boned hand with the oval nails was crushed into something dark. It glistened under the pale light. She walked holding it in front of her, staring as if it would go away. They took her to the hospital in Hiram's car, leaving the wreck where it lay.

In the hospital, the lights were bright and cast greenish shadows on their faces. They took Lee away, and Wester and Hiram sat in the waiting room silently, all night. Finally in the morning they were called into her room. She lay, washed and chastened, under the sheets. Her hair was the same white as the pillowcase. She looked odd to Hiram lying there, not swaggering in her boots.

She called him to the bedside. Wester stayed in the doorway. "I don't want to be here," she said. "It's against my convictions. I don't believe in doctors. Just pray for me, I'll be fine."

"Stay here, Mother," Hiram begged. "You have to stay here."

"They say I have to have another operation tomorrow."

"I know," he said, avoiding her eyes. "It's to save your hand."

"Phoo," she said, gesturing with her good hand. The other was hidden, down under the sheet. "They can't save that thing."

"Mother," he begged. She looked at him levelly with her grey eyes.

"I don't want to live now, son," she told him. "I don't want to live a cripple."

Hiram sat by his mother, keeping her there with his will. He never left the hospital, but wandered the halls, disheveled and unshaven. After three days, it seemed that she would get better. He left town for a day to take care of some business. While he was gone, Lee died, escaping as lightly as a butterfly. They buried her in the rain.

22. White Powder

After Lee died, Wester came to stay for a while with Hiram, Anise and the three girls. He stayed in Amelia's room. She moved in with her two younger sisters.

Wester became an old man, all at once. He changed the patterns of the household. He sat in the morning and waited for his breakfast. Voices were hushed around him. The house halted and slowed for his nap.

He could feel the balance tilting, sliding away from him into his son, his life pouring into his son's life. The ribbons of power slipped from his fingers. The family saw, and looked away.

Wester's ears stood out in flaps from his head, and his memory slackened gently, as if a wing had brushed over him. He remembered that once he had made marvelous inventions, lights, washing machines, had harnessed the river to warm the fish, but he no longer knew how it was done.

"I knew how," he would say, and his face was as frightened as a child's, pursed to suck something bitter. "It was easy."

He told stories again and again, so that the family showed listening smiles, their eyes sliding uncomfortably around the room. Sometimes at the end of a story he would repeat the beginning, and it sounded unfamiliar in his ear, like a foreign tongue.

Often he wandered from room to room looking for something forgotten, something infinitely precious that he had put down only for a moment, returning to discover its loss.

One day after Wester arrived, he was sitting on the toilet in the bathroom and found the electric heater was burning his skin. He couldn't reach it to turn it off, so he called to Constance to come in and do it for him.

She went in and turned the heater off, averting her face from the sight of his naked white knees, trousers around the ankles. She breathed the smell of his horrible old-man bowels. She ran out to her room and put her face into her pillow. Then she went and took Amelia's violin, and put it on the ground, and stomped on it until the strings twanged crazily and her foot came out the thin wood on the other side.

Amelia came in, and saw her standing there, the remains of the violin at her feet. She picked up Constance's favorite doll, the one with real human hair, and pulled its hair off. She thrust the ruined doll into Constance's face. Constance looked inside its skull, and saw the metal rods thrust into the rolling eyeballs like pokers. She screamed, and reached her fingernails towards Amelia's eyes. Amelia caught her arm.

"I don't want to be here," said Amelia, her hand locked deep into Constance's black hair. She jerked Constance's head back to look into her eyes. "I want my own room back. I hate you, and I hate living with you in your smelly old room. I want my own room back!"

Wester was walking down the stairs when he heard the racket. He stopped to listen to the screaming girl voices, pausing on the landing in his old carpet slippers. Then he turned and went back up the stairs, his breathing labored. He packed his valise carefully, laying in it the shirts that had become ragged in the collars since Lee died, the buttons rubbed off and the cuffs fraying. He put in his silver-backed brushes, and his spare spectacles, and the bandage for his knee.

Then he carried his valise down, and set it beside the door. He waited there all day for Hiram to drive him home.

Wester and Hiram arrived at the farm just after dawn. They had driven through the night in silence. Hiram swung the suitcase out of the back of the car, and carried it up the steps.

"You sure you want to do this, Dad?" he said. "I hate the thought of you being here alone."

Wester unlocked the door, fumbling with the key. The air inside rushed out to greet him. It smelled musty, like the drapes, and the grease that hadn't been cleaned from the kitchen. Lee's faint fragrance of cinnamon still lingered. He stood a minute, tasting his ghosts. Then he turned to look at his son.

"Why didn't you write your mother?" he said. "If you had written your mother like you should have done, she wouldn't have had to come out and see you. Why did you always drive too fast? What did you do with my best bottle of White Horse scotch?"

He stepped into the house and closed the door.

Hiram waited outside for a few minutes, and then started the car and drove back to Dalhart.

The next morning, Wester sat down at Lee's desk, pulled out a piece of her plain white stationery, and wrote a letter.

"My dear Hiram and Anise," he wrote. "You can tell Amelia that the indications are that she will not have to give up her room again to me for some time." He crossed out "for some time" and put in "till I get to be an old man."

"By that I don't mean that I won't visit you again soon, but I will sleep on the porch or maybe out in the yard. You can also tell her and Constance and Sarsaparilla that I'm looking forward to a wonderful time when they come up. Every day I think of something new that we will do, and I doubt if we will have time to get everything done . . ."

He felt tired, and didn't sign the letter, just pushed it into an envelope and stamped it for the postman.

The day after Wester wrote the letter, a housekeeper arrived at his door and rang the bell firmly. His son had hired her to come and care for him, she informed Wester. Wester accepted her presence without question. It had ceased to matter. She was a brisk, narrow-faced woman with a long nose, and she kept out of his way.

He spent his time upstairs in Lee's room. He slept in her bed, putting his head exactly in the hollow where hers had lain, breathing in the faint smell of cinnamon that still lingered there. He wandered through her study, touching her things, and sat behind the desk he had given her. He ran his hands over the smooth white sheets of paper that lay in stacks, ready to be covered with her careless, angular scrawl, in the colored inks she loved. He waited to dream of her, but the dream never came.

Two weeks later, as the housekeeper was frying his eggs, Wester died. He was sitting straight up at the breakfast table, wearing a white shirt and a tie, with his spectacles sliding to one side on his nose, smiling a little. They say he died of a broken heart.

G.A. just went wild after the death of his grandparents. No one took over their farm, and G.A. began to spend most of his time there. He wandered around the empty farmhouse, which made strange sounds, the shutters clanging and the paint peeling, the doors shutting suddenly on invisible breezes.

He hardly came home anymore, and he had gotten to be such a big boy that Demeter couldn't keep him. Even the threat of a lashing from Fid had no effect. G.A. would come in, scowling, to take some bread and hard-boiled eggs that Demeter had for him, and slouch out again.

Demeter didn't know where he was staying, but she suspected that he was up at the farm. A few times when the worry became too much for her, she got into the car and drove up to the farm, but never caught sight of him.

One day when she was at the farm, she got out of the car and walked into the woods surrounding the house. Not fifty feet into the brush she found a clearing that looked like a camp. There was a filthy scrap of red blanket, empty cans and bottles, and a greasy old magazine that she turned away from, with a shudder. She had seen bare skin and pointing breasts sprawled over the open pages. On the ground lay gnawed bones with pale pink scraps of flesh on them.

Looking closer, turning the bones over with her feet, Demeter saw that they were the bones of tiny birds and squirrels and some animals that she didn't recognize. The bones were absolutely white, with no charring of fire. She looked around the camp and didn't see any signs of fire at all. No cooking had been done here—those bones were raw. She closed her eyes for a moment, for her boy. Then she turned away heavily and got back into the car.

There was something she had not seen—hidden under a stone, and wrapped carefully in oilcloth to keep it dry, was a heavy blue-grey gun, an old-fashioned thing, loaded with bullets like dark stones in a mine.

Hiram's girls grew easily and well, under the shade of the hundred-year-old pecan tree. Amelia had a doll named Toodles. Sarsaparilla had Sassy Dog, a shaggy-faced thing that followed her faithfully. Constance rode horses and tagged after Hiram.

They lived in a summer kingdom, lovely and safe. They ran an old glossy black buggy to the top of a nearby hill, and rode it down with screams of laughter. They went for picnics carrying their faded Easter baskets, and made sandwiches out of bread and butter and sour clover. Once Amelia put poison oak in hers, and was ill.

They played in the sand, and grew brown. There was a hayloft nearby, and they jumped from it down into the hay, spreading sweatered arms like bright birds. At night there was dinner to be eaten outdoors on the porch, with moths rasping at the door.

Hiram built them a playhouse, white with blue shutters. He set legs into concrete to make a picnic table for under the trees, and designed a seesaw that was higher and swung more wildly than any in the neighborhood.

The neighbor children flocked around Hiram, admiring his cut, hard brightness and his fun. He played the headless horseman for them on Halloween, galloping his skittish black horse past their campfire, a cape tied over his head and a lighted jack-o'-lantern under one arm, sending them screaming. He sported with them lightheartedly, and Anise watched carefully from the door that he didn't go too far.

Hiram's transformation into a father had not really made him steadier—only given him more places to find adoring faces. He did things with the children Anise thought were reckless, charging them with things harder than their limbs could bear. Amelia shrank under the challenges, and learned under his tutelage to fail and fall short. Constance succeeded. Sarsaparilla tried, and laughed, seeing nothing wrong.

And always Anise was there to intercede, to remember birthdays and remind him of duties, so that no one ever knew the thought didn't come from Hiram himself. She cast a sheltering light over him, increasing his allure. She undergirded his rashness with her care, and made him safe— without her, he might have destroyed sooner.

The girls, too, became part of a plot to make Hiram seem the perfect man. They were accomplices, seeing him as he wanted to be seen. Things he did badly—risks he took or places he pushed too far—they looked away from, and forgot.

No one was more eager to protect Hiram from himself than the women around him. It made a pretty picture, the dashing man in the boots with his firm, upright wife and his sunny-faced girls. All heads turned towards Hiram, always. He was the sun around which they clustered, eager for his warmth. People called the family "Hiram's harem."

There were moments when his heedlessness caused pain. Once when Constance was in sixth grade, she wore a red turtleneck that clung tightly to her smooth, still-boyish body. She was preening in front of the son of Hiram's business partner, taking stolen sips of champagne and letting the light shine against her black hair, streaking it with bluish lights.

Hiram reached out and tweaked her nipple, which showed through the thin fabric. "Looks like someone's going to need a bra soon," he said loudly. The men around him laughed. Constance flushed and left for the other room, to choke herself with punch and scowl.

Then there were other times, like Sarsaparilla's dance. It was an important dance. She had a date with a wonderful boy, Frank Kennedy, the boy with the shining dark hair that she had been watching shyly from the back of the room in math class.

Sarsaparilla had been pushed, one day in class, and had dropped her books everywhere. Hot-faced, she bent to pick them up and found herself staring at a pair of brown shoes. Frank Kennedy was looking down at her, and smiling. Then he bent to pick up the books for her, and she scooped them back into her arms, hardly able to breathe.

"You going to the dance on Saturday?" he said.

She shook her head.

"Come with me?" he asked, and she nodded. He told her he and his mother would pick her up at seven, and went away to meet with the other boys, leaving Sarsaparilla to draw doodles of her party dress on the back of her notebooks and dream, so that her teachers spoke more sharply to her than usual.

On Saturday, Sarsaparilla insisted that Anise help her dress at ten o'clock in the morning, she was so afraid of being late. She had her blond hair brushed smooth into curls, and her dress was light white and blue, with flowers. She spun and spun in front of the mirror, and smiled so that her eyes almost disappeared into her cheeks. She wouldn't eat, and wouldn't sit down, for fear of crumpling her dress, and she waited that whole day, watching at the window and willing the sun to go down.

It went down, and the sky gathered lavender and started to go dark. At six she took possession of the door, and wouldn't let anyone near it. At six-thirty she was in such a fever of anticipation that she jumped at every sound, and opened the door at least five times before Anise persuaded her to go back and wait where she couldn't be seen. By seven o'clock she was rigid with nerves, and silent.

But seven-fifteen came, and seven-thirty, and finally seven forty-five, and there was no Frank. Sarsaparilla was white and silent. Anise ached for her, but there was no way of knowing what was behind her eyes, where all the light had gone out, and nothing to say.

At eight o'clock Hiram walked in. He had been watching from his office, with the door cracked. He had combed his hair, and put on a handsome blue suit and a tie.

He went up to Sarsaparilla, where she stood with her forehead pressed against the doorframe, and offered her his arm with such a funny flourish that she laughed in spite of herself. She looked down and saw that he was wearing his extra-special cowboy boots, the handsome white ostrich ones that were soft as feathers.

"May I have the privilege?" Hiram said, and she put her hand in the crook of his arm and walked out with him.

He drove her to the dance, talking to her like a grown-up lady, and earnestly requesting her opinion on a variety of subjects, so that she was busy thinking of answers to his questions.

And when they reached the dance, he parked and handed her out with such a gallant bow, and looked so handsome in his suit, that when they walked into the dance her chin was notched up. She looked at Frank Kennedy and his date, wearing pink, and could even smile.

Hiram danced with Sarsaparilla all evening beautifully, brought her cake and punch, held her gloves and twirled her around the floor saying funny things into her ears about the other people in her class, so that she laughed and laughed and almost forgot. The boys watched Sarsaparilla flying around in the arms of her father, the lights shining on her smooth hair, and her face smiling, and thought to themselves that the youngest Jameson girl was actually quite a piece after all, and should be considered.

A little later, Constance got permission to have a slumber party. It was considered a great event in the neighborhood, and the girls giggled and preened, and came in hordes over to the house, with their soft flushed faces and pleated clothes.

Hiram and Anise retired discreetly to the top of the house, and chaos reigned downstairs. The dark flickered around the grounds, and kids splashed in the pool and screamed, leaving puddles after them and playing the phonograph. The long glass windows stood open, and children ran in and out of the house.

At nine o'clock Anise came down to announce that all the boys had to leave, and supervised the girls crawling into their sleeping bags on the floor. Laughter and muted voices floated up to Hiram and Anise where they lay smiling. They listened quietly until Hiram heard the creaking of the french doors, darker voices and scraping boots. The boys were coming back in.

He went downstairs as he was, in his underwear. Direct disobedience infuriated him, and he had told Constance that no boys were allowed in the house after lights-out.

He heard voices, screamed whispers and the clatter of feet going out the french doors again, as he came into view. He went on down the stairs and out the doors, feeling the cool air against his skin.

The girls were huddled against the wall inside, he saw, with wide eyes. But outside, the gang of boys had turned and stopped at bay. They were only waiting for him to go back upstairs, when they would come in again. He could see the bristles of new mustaches on their upper lips, and smell their sweat. They were bulked with the first growth of muscle. There were twelve of them.

He came towards them in the darkness, the moonlight shimmering on his skin where it was pale, below his shirt collar. The boys snickered when they saw he was in his underwear.

"I think you'd better go on home, boys," he said. His voice was cool, and polite.

There was a surging in them. He could feel them becoming a mob, knitting all those hormones into a thing that would strike out with twenty arms and legs and slink home later, ashamed.

One of them stepped forward, pushed by his friends.

"You and who else going to make us?" he said, his voice rough and breaking a little. "Sir," he added, mockingly.

Hiram smiled. He had been home, and sleeping in his skin, for too long. He picked up a Coke bottle, easily, from the ground and broke it against a rock. The shatter rang out in the night. He held the broken bottle towards them. The light ran down the wicked edge, gleaming.

"I will," he said, still smiling. "Who's first? You?"

The boys considered him unsteadily for a moment, and withdrew. There was a long pause. Hiram watched them steadily, the bottle gripped loosely in his hand. One boy stepped back, and then another, and they paced back one bit at a time until they were far enough away, and then broke and ran through the trees, crashing down the garden. Hiram stood and considered them for a long moment, opening his hand to let the bottle fall to the ground. Then he turned and went back inside.

The girls were all silent, watching him. He nodded to them.

"Ladies," he said, and went up the stairs, his lean muscles moving easily under his smooth skin. More than one pair of eyes followed him all the way up the stairs, and more than one girl sighed.

Constance went to school on Monday hesitant and afraid that those boys would gang up against her and knock her books out of her arms in the hall.

But more than once that day, quietly and alone, boys came up to her, awkward, and said, "Your father's not bad, Constance," and one boy said with hungry eyes, "I wish I had a dad like that."

Constance had always known that her father was magic, because he never worried. He had this perfect buoyancy, a light touch.

She hid in his boot closet sometimes, crouched among the pointy toes and weighted heels, inhaling the faint scent of saddle soap. She tried to absorb his luck.

Once, years later, when she was looking for aspirin for a headache, she opened his medicine cabinet. She looked inside his black leather dop kit. Inside were syringes with long pale needles, and packets of white powder. When she touched them she felt soft clouds of white inside her head, like piles of shifting sand.

Later it was said that the packets contained painkillers for migraine. No one in the family had ever seen Sir ill with a migraine, and he had never mentioned it. Constance never asked him about it.

After he died she took a cardboard box and threw all the syringes away.

23. Oil in the Graveyard

Hiram's fascination with horses began to replace his feelings for cars. The things that he had loved in a car, the wheels spinning and the road thumping under them, the passage and the smooth hum of the lines as they went by, all faded in comparison to a horse.

It fit with something deep in his soul, the big animals with their ignorant grace. His quickness and physical coordination stood him in good stead with horses. He was balanced and poised, and had an instinctive understanding of the animals. He could weave atop a horse, controlling it with his knees and hands, and feel quiet. It brought him peace, and stilled the clamor for something, the blind wanting that made a hole in his life.

Hiram shopped around for a house in Dalhart that would accommo-
date horses, and found it. Hiram mortgaged himself to the hilt to afford
it, but didn't tell anyone. He was a graceful gambler, always. He would
have horses. There would be nothing to stop him.

So the barn was stocked with horses, and Hiram disappeared into
that world, the place of smooth, sliding haunches and sweet grain smells,
leather leads and saddle soap. Anise watched him drift further away from
her with barely restrained fury. Even on the rare occasions that he was
home now, he would be invisible in the barn.

Anise tolerated horses, but now they had taken her husband. She had
waited so patiently, for the time to come when he would not be so much
on the road, when they could be together and talk, and think, and be like
the couples she had pasted in her treasure book, fine-featured and loving,
their arms locked around each other. Now she began to know that time
would not come.

Worse, from her point of view, was the group of people with whom he
began to associate. He was a Mason, had joined early in their marriage,
and now discovered a branch of the Masons that performed Mounted
Patrol drills, on matching black horses. These men and their wives, with
whom Anise was necessarily thrown together every weekend, were folks
with creased faces and no fancy talk. They square-danced, raised sturdy
children and spoke to each other of thrush and hoof-and-mouth disease,
of girths and leads and ways to break a young horse. Anise wandered lost
among them, a smile painted on her face, thin and tight among their
ruddy, leathery folds.

It amazed her that this was the company that Hiram sought out, the
people with whom he was happy, the place where he was at home. These
people, kind and forthright as they were, were on the farthest star from
Anise. There was no one among them with whom she could discuss poetry
or books, no one who had been to New York, or who even cared that there
was a world outside rural Dalhart and the practice drills.

The possibility crossed Anise's mind that she had made a dreadful
mistake. The machinery of her life that she had set so carefully, the gears
that she had made to mesh, ground with sand in them.

When she was alone she had trouble breathing. Her world narrowed
like a thin hide wrapped around her, drying in the sun, a backwards chrys-
alis that gripped her, muffling her movements.

Her temper became uneven. She maintained herself with iron rule, snipping all the negative emotions from her speech, from her face and from her journals. But the anger festered and ran. She held herself rigid above the hatred, uncomplaining, until the weight of it became too great and she snapped, exploding.

She threw a heavy ceramic plate at Amelia once, and an entire carton of eggs, one at a time. She shattered wineglasses and left shards of them stuck in the walls. Once she hit Constance on the head with a frying pan.

The girls remembered Anise storming out the door with a suitcase. Once Hiram threw a gallon bottle of milk at her. Afterwards they found her in the kitchen, weeping and wiping up the milk blindly with a soaked rag that ran and left circles on the floor.

But mostly Anise believed in the power of the Lord to solve all problems, and to make her life work. She thought that the pain in her life was due to her own failings, and struggled to be more pure, to keep her temper, to be more loving and kind. She told Constance, "You must look for the good in everyone. Sometimes you have to look very hard," and she tried to do that, wandering through the thick-waisted, drunken people at the Patrol meetings and looking for the good.

It told on her. She aged rapidly, her delicacy shrinking down to a yellow rigidness. Her cool, austere air became a little dried, and haunted. She was wispy, paperish thin. Hiram turned from her in bed, and mostly slept with his back to her, his breathing falling evenly. She lay sometimes on her back, her hands in fists from the tension of the day that would not relax, her eyes closed and tears sliding from under her lids to her earlobes, where they made a wet spot on the pillow that dried by morning.

When she touched Hiram, he shrank from her. He felt, unreasoningly, that it was like being touched by an old kid glove, withered from being in the drawer.

Life, the hard beating of liquid under the skin, was outdoors for Hiram now, more and more. He fell with relief into the convivial life of the Patrol, the jokes, the motion, the horses. He blacked his horses with shoe polish and became one of the most enthusiastic members of the Mounted Patrol.

Constance loved the horses as well, and could do anything Hiram demanded of her on horseback. She learned to rope and ride the barrels, and Hiram watched her proudly, her young body erect and her dark curls floating in the breeze. "She's got a Jameson seat, that girl," he would say. Anise would just press her lips together, and say nothing.

Amelia had less luck. When she was nine, Hiram put her up on the back of a half-broken horse. She was proud to be taken out with him, afraid that he would leave her. She was soft, and secretly hated horses. She tried to keep up.

The horse set its teeth and threw her. She saw the blue of the sky and the white dazzle of the road wheeling, like the stars.

Hiram rode back to pick her up. He was handsome as a snake, and wore his hat tilted to one side. He made her swear to keep it secret, what had happened on the road.

She bit her tongue until blood ran and didn't tell. She lay on the hot nights with the sheet drawn to her, and watched her lungs trying to squeeze air from the cracks on the ceiling. Finally she fainted in the bathroom with her forehead pressed to the sink.

They took her to an angry doctor in a white coat. He pressed his lips together and found three broken vertebrae in her back. The fractures were inflamed by neglect.

The doctor layered her into a body cast with a trowel, like a brick-layer, and ran a wire from her head and feet, and twisted her on a spit in the hospital for six months.

When she came out of the hospital she wore a cast over her whole body. She had gone pale and patient. The cast stuck out in ridges, so that her flounced skirts didn't fit. She pulled a pair of Hiram's blue jeans over the cast, and stabbed them on with red thumbtacks, and went to school.

Hiram was the final master with horses. His ability became magical and legendary, part of him. His daughters thought he could do anything. He went to some pains to ensure that they continued to think so.

Once on a trail ride, Constance and Sarsaparilla sneaked up to Hiram's horse while Hiram lay dozing under his hat, and stole the girth off his saddle. They snorted with laughter behind their hands waiting for Hiram to wake up and try to get onto the saddle. They wanted to see him slide off the horse onto the ground.

Hiram woke up, rubbed his eyes and led his horse off, as if he suspected nothing. They didn't hear anything, although they listened carefully for the sound of his cursing as he fell. After a minute Hiram rode back into the clearing, sitting lazily on his saddle, which remained perfectly in place without the girth. Their eyes wide, the girls just got back onto their horses and followed him off. Hiram rode without a girth that entire day, never slipped and never mentioned that he missed it at all.

But it was Sundays that Hiram really came into his own. Sundays became carved into a family ritual. First Anise insisted that all of them attend church. After church there was a huge roast dinner, and a siesta. Then a horseback ride.

Hiram would wake early from his nap and go to the barn to saddle all five horses. He worked patiently. It took over an hour, and he worked alone until all the horses were gleaming, groomed and ready.

The girls and Anise emerged from the house and rode, whether they wanted to or not. No one had the nerve to refuse Hiram. He so seldom put himself out for other people that to refuse his gift of effort was unthinkable. They rode, with Hiram in front and leading the way.

He was close to perfectly happy at these times, with his entire family following behind him, each mounted, every piece of leather polished and every bit gleaming. Something moved in him then, deep under the rock of his soul, like a flow of oil, or the breeze.

Then they all went back to the house, and Hiram made cherry pies. He made them every Sunday, his hands still covered with sweat and leather soap and horsehair, kneading the dough expertly. Anise would nag herself almost to tears, trying to get him to wash his hands before he made the pies, but he laughed her off.

"That's the flavor," he said. "If I went and washed my hands, there'd be no flavor."

If she nagged him too hard, he would take the dough and bounce it off the ceiling against the dust and cobwebs. "If you don't like the way I make cherry pies, you don't have to have any," he would tell her. She would leave the room silent and humiliated.

The girls watched him with proud eyes, thinking him wonderful. Only their father could stand down their mother that way. Only their father didn't have to bother with washing his hands. He was above the germs that tormented Anise's dreams, above her viruses and fussy vitamins. He could do anything. He could make sweat and horsehair into delicious cherry pies. He said it gave them flavor, and it did.

After they moved to the new house, Hiram and Anise joined a new church in Dalhart. It had just been established not too long before, and was terrifically successful. The preacher who had started it was a one-handed, dark-haired man, with a heavy flush to his face and an impassioned way of preaching that Anise admired greatly. His name was Jed Net.

It was rumored that Reverend Net had been burned out of his last church, by churchgoers who squirmed under his too strict doctrine. But Anise couldn't see anything wrong with his doctrine. He was immensely charismatic, drew people around him like beans on a pole. He had a wife named Francine, a lovely tall woman with coppery hair of the most peculiar shade.

When Hiram and Anise walked into coffee hour after church the first day they had attended, Hiram brushed and handsome in a dark suit, his hand solicitously under Anise's elbow, Francine poured hot black coffee on her hand, completely missing the cup that she held. God's pajamas, she thought. Whatever was that one doing here?

She had never forgotten him, or that day in the tree. It stayed in her mind, mixed with blue and green colors and the memory of sparkling lines of jewels. She remembered how his eyes had bored down into her, so blue! Bluer than anything she had ever seen. And how she had felt so light with him, leaning into his arms around her, when he helped her down. It had a silvered quality in her memory, that day. It was like something that had happened to someone else. Yet she treasured it, took it out on silent days, when it rained. She hadn't thought about it much lately, not since the fire. There hadn't been time.

Jed had come home from church the day of the fire to find Francine wearing a bathrobe and holding William's hand in the yard, her neck as white and curved as a swan's. They stood in front of the burned ruins of the house, perfectly still, waiting for him to come and get them.

Francine had been afraid of Jed's anger, but he had been strangely quiet. He had loaded her and William, whose diaper needed changing, into the big old battered car and driven them to a friend's house to stay. Then he went out, that very day, and began to knock on the doors of rich men he knew, to raise money for a new church.

The fire had effected some kind of wild change in Jed, Francine knew that. She didn't know much else of what was going on inside his head. For once he had come to the fore, blown huge like a parade balloon. He had suddenly become an indomitable force in her life, and she could only bend and cling to the floorboards to keep from being blown away.

Francine realized that although her life so far had centered on Jed, like a ball swinging on a string, she had usually gotten things done for him, or even in spite of him. He had been young, with pure dreams. She had always been the shrewd, hardheaded one who met their challenges with a certain cynicism, covered under a sugary sweetness.

Now it was different. The covering had been burned from him. He was no longer innocent. The reins of the moment had met in him and crystallized, turned into metal anchor ropes. He moved with a new decision, and purpose.

The purpose confused her. Surely, after having been burned out of one church, he would be sane, would consider another career. Why, they could go back to her home and take over her father's farm. He was getting old, and would be glad of the help.

But Jed never once consulted Francine about their future. He was building a new church, it seemed. Things fell his way, and people did what he wanted, suddenly. It was odd. He was building this new church, just on the other side of town from the old one.

He borrowed money wildly, recklessly. He poured all of their meager savings into it, visited bank loan officers, wearing his white collar, and looking imposing, speaking with them quietly about the state of their souls, beaming at them an amazing warmth that poured from his frame like a lantern light. Cowed, charmed, bewildered, they gave Jed what he asked.

It would be the way he dreamed it, this new church. He found the perfect place for it, on the site of an old church that had burned. The tombstones still stood around it. He built his church big, and imposing, with a clean frame and white walls. He called it Red Rock, after the huge boulders that sat at the street's end, furred with wild bushes.

And he built a house for his family, attached to the back of the church. It had high ceilings, and was spacious. It was laid out impatiently, square with sharp corners and big rooms, since he didn't ask Francine. It was a man's house. Jed had just sketched out what he wanted on a napkin, and handed it to the architect over lunch.

Francine wandered the house with William, and felt bruised by the bluntness of its shape. She was bewildered by the changes, and seemed stunned. She smiled and nodded, and spoke encouragingly to Jed, but didn't really understand what was happening.

She didn't understand anything, in fact, until Hiram Jameson

walked through the door with his wife on his arm. In that moment everything seemed to slide into brilliant focus for Francine. She felt where she
was, with a start. That was when she had spilled the coffee.

Hiram had caught her glance at once, across the room filled with the
bustle of the young couples and their children. The people packed the
place with their slickers and umbrellas, putting drops of silver water down
on the floor like the mercury from a broken thermometer. There was still
some fresh sawdust that kept sifting down from the roof beams, and the
smell of new paint mixed with that of wet galoshes and coffee.

Hiram's eyes were drawn to Francine, the flaming hair behind the
coffee table. He smiled in recognition. She felt his glance and flushed,
spreading her hands instinctively over her waist, which had thickened after
William. She could feel, burning, the start of the double chin that she had
seen the other day in the mirror, the faint lines she imagined were beginning to scratch around her eyes. Even her hair, she thought, was fading,
fading. She felt as naked before him as if he had come into her room and
surprised her in front of the mirror, and it made her angry. She lifted her
chin.

He looked the same as ever, she saw, not without bitterness. She had
remembered him perfectly, even though she had seen him only twice. His
frame was lean, and angular, and the shade of his tie exactly matched his
eyes. He was tanned, and the slight touch of silver at his temples only
made him more handsome. He knew it, she could see, as he crossed the
room. He swam in his own charm like a warm bath.

She noted his wife, with interest. Tight, small woman with a pressed
mouth and a strained look. Whatever could the man be up to, to make
this woman so unhappy? And whatever could be wrong with her, to be
unhappy with such a beautiful animal of a husband leading her across the
room?

Hiram's young daughters followed him, lovely as three different colors of water. One dark, one brunet, one with blond hair, all dressed in
clothes that to Francine's discerning eye looked homemade, although
pretty. There was money trouble, then?

But she could see that he was proud of his girls, the way his eyes kept
going back to them. His wife spoke to him, and he bent his head down to
her politely, but didn't really listen. Francine could see that, from across
the room. She wondered that his wife would keep talking that way while

Hiram's mouth smiled but his eyes wandered across the room, assessing business opportunities and lovely ladies. Francine would never put up with that. She would have taken his jaw, and made him listen to her.

She realized with a start that they were coming towards her. Jed was bringing them. She composed herself, and poured cups of coffee for them, holding her hand out to greet them. Jed was introducing them. "In the oil business . . . these are the girls . . ."

She handed Hiram a cup of coffee and her hand did not shake. She met his eyes and was shocked at their blueness. She felt it all the way down to her feet, which were beginning to ache. He smiled at her, and his eyes said things that she had forgotten.

"We're so glad to have you at this church," she said evenly, smiling warmly at his wife. She had beautiful eyes, his wife—she must have been quite pretty, once, Francine thought pityingly. Poor thing. He must have led her a merry chase. "I hope we're going to be seeing a lot more of you all."

She must watch herself very carefully around this one, she thought, offering them the plate of sugar cookies. Very carefully, indeed.

Anise was pleased to be asked to serve on the church committee of Red Rock, and eventually to teach a Sunday-school class. Hiram was also asked to teach a Sunday-school class. He became more and more involved with the community, doing things with the Masons and for them, setting up service organizations. It was realized by those in charge that Hiram had a gift with young people, especially the boys. They would cluster around him, drawn as if by some peculiar smell that emanated from his tanned, tight skin.

Hiram was a man, the way boys dreamed of being a man. He had horses, he rode, he wore hats and winked, had the light touch of conversation and a charming grace. And there was something else to him, which always eluded definition. It was part of Hiram's makeup, his marrow. He never knew it until it was gone. It was just something deep inside him that drew people out, like the sugary sap out of a tree. He had the gift of making people love him. So Reverend Jed Net cultivated Hiram's presence in the church, rewarded him with tasks, slapped him on the back and called him a great guy.

Actually, Hiram and Jed had met and become friends in an odd sort of way, before Hiram and Anise ever started to attend Jed's church. The two men never told their wives how it happened.

It seemed that Hiram's daughter Constance and Jed's son William had gotten into a scrap at school. Constance had the best of it, pushing William into a mud puddle. But both children went home screaming, and the fathers met angrily in a deserted parking lot.

"If you weren't a one-handed man, I just might take a swing at you," Hiram had said.

"Don't let that stop you," Jed said, and fell on him with all the enthusiasm of his football days.

Startled, Hiram fought back, and was shocked at the quickness and weight of the other man. It seemed not to slow Jed down at all, that he had only one hand, and Hiram was hard put to defend himself.

They fought all through the afternoon. When it was almost evening, they were both staggering with weariness, and bleeding.

"I believe you are the toughest man I ever fought," Hiram finally admitted. "I don't know whether I can whip you or not."

Jed stood for a minute, sucking in breath painfully over his split lip. "That's just what I was thinking about you," he said.

So they fought a while longer and then called it a draw, and shook hands and were fast friends. They rode horses together, and Hiram sponsored Jed when he joined the Masons. When Hiram was quite sure of Jed's friendship, he asked Jed how he would feel about having an oil well drilled in the Red Rock graveyard.

Hiram had moved his family to Dalhart because he heard there was a boom there. He had arrived late, and prospectors had already bought up every inch of land they could find. All the private land had been sold, and most of the public land as well. There had even been a well drilled on the children's playground, beside the swing set.

The early finds in Dalhart had been tremendous. Dad Joiner, one of the most famous wildcatters of all, had sunk the first discovery well there, and it made him richer than a king.

It was all a game of chance. Dad Joiner's first well, for example, had been planned quite near the home of a Mrs. Daisy Bradford. She had threatened him with a broom and insisted that he move it further away, so that when the oil gushed it wouldn't ruin her washing on the clothes-line.

Dad Joiner obediently moved his site, and struck a huge gusher where Mrs. Bradford told him to drill. It was later established that his first choice of location would have brought in a dry duster well. Had he drilled there, he would have lost his entire stake, and the Dalhart field might never have been discovered at all.

Fortunes were gained and lost on such accidents. Wildcatting was such an uncertain prospect, and wildcatters themselves so superstitious, that charmers, doodlebugs and oil witches ran a booming business for many years.

There were different types of specialists in the oil-finding field. Doodlebugs held their divining rods over the land in question—usually baited with a bottle full of oil, suspended from a string. If the bottle rotated a certain way over the land, the doodlebug figured there was oil there. The more revolutions, the deeper the oil.

Then there were oil trompers—men who would sink to their ankles in dust over underground oil, while a normal man walking beside them would leave only footprints. Oil jumpers, on the other hand, screamed with pain and leapt up and down, as if someone were holding hot blades to their feet, when they rode trains over hidden oil.

Housewives dreamed of finding oil below their chicken coops, and were proved right by the drillers more times than not. Oil smellers sniffed the air for traces of gas. A sixteen-year-old boy from South Africa, born with a caul over his head, could spot oil because it gave him visions of black ridges. Diamonds were indicated by a blaze of heat, and underground water, he said, looked just like moonbeams.

Hiram first heard tell of oil tromping when he was out prospecting in the Dalhart fields one day, trying to find fresh land to drill. He struck up a conversation with the farmer who lived nearby. The farmer had thirteen dogs, and they rioted and bayed around his legs until Hiram could hardly hear what he was saying.

Hiram pointed out the leaning chimney on the farmhouse, and told the farmer that it ought to be straightened before it fell down. He had once been a building contractor, he told the farmer, and so knew his business.

The farmer explained patiently to him that the chimney wasn't really leaning—that it just seemed that way. There was so much gas pressure there that the normal processes of gravity were interfered with, the farmer said. Things that were level didn't look level, and things that were straight looked crooked.

Hiram asked the farmer how he knew about the gas pressure under the ground. The farmer explained that his brother was a genuine oil tromper. When his brother walked over the farm, the farmer said, he sank down twice as far as the farmer did.

Hiram snorted and excused himself, and moved on. He learned later to his dismay that the farmer's land had been drilled, and had brought in such a fortune that the farmer had become one of the richest men in the country.

The day that farmer's well came in, or so people said, he took his check to the bank. With some of the cash he bought a forty-dollar Stetson hat and creased it, just so. Then he went to the grocery store and bought eighty pounds of red meat, and five dollars' worth of bananas.

The red meat was for his thirteen hounds, he told the clerk. And as for himself, he had never yet gotten his fill of bananas. He was fixing to eat bananas that day until he felt like quitting.

The farmer threw meat to the dogs, who fell on it snapping and snarling. Then he took all the bananas and sat down on the bench in front of the store. He called over the neighborhood children to help him, and ate five or six bananas himself.

Then he got up, brushed himself off, went into the Cadillac showroom and purchased an enormous gold sedan. He loaded all his thirteen dogs into the car and drove around town, shouting to all the townsfolk that he would take anyone for a ride who could fit in among all the dogs.

After hearing that story, Hiram lost his faith in modern scientific methods. "To hell with geology," he would say. "Let's go dig an oil well."

"Not that I don't believe in geologists," he told Anise. "I'm such a fool that I always use one—pay him forty-five dollars a day to write papers and chip rocks. But when I'm ready to drill, I tie a tin can to a dog's tail and start the dog on a run across the prairie. And where the can comes off, that's where I drill."

Despite his high words and his optimism, Hiram never really hit it big. There has been much written of the wildly successful wildcatters, with names like Paul Getty, Dad Joiner, Tom Slick. Those men who tossed their fortunes on the rise and fall of a coin, and won, have their names inscribed today on fountains and in history books. Little attention is paid to the men who did not succeed so well.

Hiram drilled a few wells, and they brought in some income. But he was plagued with the poor luck of the mediocre—rigs that caught on fire, big deals that spit only salt water, land men that collected the checks and skipped town.

The biggest, most successful well that Hiram ever drilled was in the graveyard of Jed Net's church. All the other promising land in Dalhart had been drilled by the time Hiram arrived, and he figured the graveyard was the only place left to try.

Everyone was shocked, at first. The church board was horrified, despite Jed's support of the notion. They said it would be desecration, and that the church could not have made a valid lease "even if it had desire, for the donor of the cemetery had deeded it to the dead."

But the objectors were finally overwhelmed by those who dreamed of the money. So they drew up a special deed, speaking on behalf of the dead, allowing the drilling.

It was not an uncommon proposition in those days to dig wells in graveyards. It might have been because cemeteries were dug on raised ground, and ground was often raised over salt domes, which could hide oil. Or it might be that men were drawn to hide their bones, like dogs, over rich places.

Whichever was true, Hiram was sure there would be oil under the Red Rock cemetery. When no one was looking, one night late, he went to the graveyard alone and turned around three times, then tossed a silver dollar. He marked the place where it fell, just next to a white stone monument of an angel with a bent-down, brooding face. That was where they would drill.

Hiram signed up a driller named Handy, a local man, to do the initial digging and set the string of pipe. Handy did it, though he was a little disturbed by the dead sleeping so quietly just under his feet.

Handy's aunt was buried in that graveyard. He dreamed of her the night the digging started, her rumpled white hair on her unquiet head. He had uneasy visions of his aunt during his lunch breaks, tossing as the oil gushed underneath her, the butterfly bones of her ankles and her teeth knocked loose, shifting to the rhythms of the pounding rigs. He halted work with relief for the four or five days it would take for the cement to harden.

Some of the workers who were living in a tent nearby had watched Handy's discomfort. While he was gone, they rigged up a string of pipes leading from their tent to the cellar of the well. When Handy returned and started drilling, they began moaning softly through the pipe.

"Have mercy, O my God," they sighed. "Help me, Lord, I'm restless. O Lord, my God, have mercy, have mercy on me." They watched Handy from a distance and howled with smothered laughter as he grew more and more nervous, sweating and wiping his hands on his pants so that his grip wouldn't slip. After two hours he turned and walked off the drilling site without a word, and was never seen in that town again. Hiram had to hire another driller to bring in the well.

When the drilling was close to completion, Hiram went to shoot out the well, dropping charges of nitroglycerin down to jog the oil at the bottom into motion. Few prospectors did their own shooting—it was a dangerous business, and most shooters ended their life blown sky-high, with the mask of their face in one tree, and their mustache in another. Obituaries often remarked that "they didn't find enough pieces to fill a cigar box." But Hiram loved the danger of it. It reminded him of his powder monkey days.

In those times nitroglycerin was the most powerful explosive. An eight-pound blow or a sufficiently high temperature would set it off, so it couldn't be shipped by train. The ingredients had to be mixed locally, by a man who might or might not know what he was doing, and transported in a special car.

Hiram went to shoot the well in the Red Rock graveyard on a Saturday morning. The day was bright, and soft. He was in high spirits. Whistling, he suspended a six-foot-long can, like a stovepipe, over the well and filled it with nitroglycerin, being careful not to spill a drop—a single drop spilled on the derrick floor could cause a fatal accident.

Then he set the watch mechanism on the time bomb and lowered the shell gently, on a small cable. He did the same for a second shell, and then started on the third.

Just as Hiram was letting the third shell down, he felt the line slacken under his palms, and heard the gasoline engine speed up, with a deadly high whine like a mosquito. His hands went wet with dread. That sound was the nightmare of a shooter, a sound that was often the last he ever heard.

Hiram had never heard the sound before, but he knew it by the shrinking of his scrotum. He knew what was happening in that well, as surely as if it had been the dark, long canal of his own body. Those shells had hit an irregular pocket of gas, called a head, and they were now shooting back up the well at roughly thirty miles per hour, out of control.

The roughnecks heard the stutter and whine of the engine, dropped the tools they were holding and took off running away from the well as fast as they could run. It was unlikely, but possible, that they might survive if they could get far enough from the well before the shells hit the top of the derrick and exploded.

The gas was sending the shells up like feathers floating over a hot radiator. Hiram could hear them hissing. The odor was enough to knock a man down. He was about to turn and run, and follow the other workers, when he heard a sound from inside the church. It was the congregation, two hundred strong, launching with inspired vigor into the first verse of "Jesus, Lover of My Soul."

Hiram's vision slowed, and he seemed to see everything very clearly. His hands in front of him looked wrinkled and black, and old. He held them out in front of him, staring. Behind him the hymn echoed, and one voice soared out, very high.

Hiram turned back towards the well. He moved as though swimming under water. He went back to stand over the casing. His one chance was to catch the shells as they came out one at a time, disarm them and lay them on the ground before they exploded. He had never seen it done. He didn't know if it could be done. It seemed unlikely. He would have to catch the shells as they shot up between his legs, each one covered with water and oil, each slick as a trout and heavy as a small child.

He spread his legs on either side of the casing and waited until the gas pushed the first bucket of liquid nitroglycerin up. His blood roared in his ears. He forced himself to wait, wait until it was high enough. When it got up about waist high, he put his arms out gently, as if to a lover. He just reached out and hugged that shell to his body, picked it up and took it over to the corner of the derrick and set it down.

Sweat was pouring down his forehead so that he could hardly see. He had just started to wipe his face when he heard the hissing of the second shell. The roughnecks were watching him from a distance, silently.

The second shell emerged at a speed that would have shot it twenty or thirty feet in the air. Hiram grabbed it in both arms and gripped it with all his might. It was slick with oil, and he tore the fingernails off of both hands as he dug into it, but he held it. It was eight feet long, and weighed ninety pounds. He clasped it in his arms and eased it up out of the casing, slowly. He was still pulling the second one up when the blunt, evil snout of the third shell showed up over the edge of the casing.

There was no time to think, no time to breathe. Not breathing, he thought. Must breathe. Mustn't faint. He didn't know what else to do, so he put his foot on that third shell and held it down, while he gently let the second shell slide to the ground. Then he let the third shell bob to the surface like an egg in water, picked it up and carried it to the side, cradling it lover-like, in his arms.

When all three shells were laid on the ground, Hiram leapt to disconnect the time mechanisms, which were still ticking. He pulled the wires from each one and slumped to the ground in a near faint. Inside the church, the congregation went on with the hymn. The roughnecks wept.

The story of Hiram catching the three shells became a kind of legend around the oil camps. No one had ever seen a man with more grace and skill and flat-out luck, to catch three live shells and live.

But Hiram was embarrassed with the telling. He would never tell the truth about that day. He always told it like this, tipping his hat down over his eyes:

"It was a close call and no mistake. In the magazine I got some nitroglycerin on my boots. Later coming out I stamped my heel on a stone and the first thing I knew I was sailing up towards heaven. When I came back down I struck squarely on my other heel and went up a second time.

"I was up so high that I went right up through a cloud and made it rain in Arizona. I came down without much injury, except a bruised feeling that wore off in a week or two. You see, the nitroglycerin had stuck to my boot heels and when it hit a hard substance it went off quicker than Old Nick could singe a kiln-dried sinner. What'll you have, boys?"

24. Matty

Francine watched the rapid growth of Jed's church with an amazement that was tinged with disbelief. Jed was a big man, a bigger man than she had known. She had been impatient, before, with his holy foolishness. Now she was driven to a grudging respect, for he was creating a church with a size and a life bigger than any seen in Dalhart up until then.

Of course, the money from the graveyard oil well helped. Dalhart was a newly rich oil town, and Red Rock Church was a newly rich oil church. It became the place for smart Dalhart folk to worship. Couples brought their children—rich men drove their wives up to the door in shining Cadillacs, and carelessly dropped fat checks into the collection plates. The coats hung in the coat room were mink, and lined and feathered, even in the sultry Dalhart springs. And through it all Jed preached, his maimed arm stuck in one pocket, his other waving in the air as he pronounced and proclaimed.

His sermons were darker than they used to be—Francine could hear that, when she bent her head to listen closely, in a rare moment of reflection. They were not the sweet soliloquies that he had given as a young and innocent man. But neither were they the grinding, anger-filled things that they had been after his accident.

No, they were somewhere in the middle now—reverent, but touched with tragedy, God-fearing but not frightening, and joyful in some motion-filled way that flew quite over Francine's shrewd head. Jed had become a preacher, a real one. He had tempered down into something very fine, almost by accident. With their unerring nose for the latest thing of value, the newly well-to-do of Dalhart came flocking to Jed's church, to his picnics and his trail rides, turned out for his community prayer days and donated heavily to his charities.

Jed began to build quite a political base. With his charismatic looks and following, he was well worth courting as a grass-roots administrator, and not above taking up political causes that he felt were worthy. He worked hard—sometimes sixteen or seventeen hours a day. The invitations that he received to events in the community filled the silver filigreed basket that Francine bought him for that purpose, and overflowed onto the Italian marble mantel. Jed hired a secretary, an anemic-looking young man with dark hair, to help him keep up with his correspondence.

His energy seemed boundless. There was time for the Boys' Club, time for the opening of the Square-Dance Palace, time to visit the League of Women Voters and give a special prayer at the kickoff of football season. Francine saw very little of him. There was less time, apparently, for her and William.

But she had grown used to that, early on, and the glass skin that she had bred up in herself served her well. And she was in much demand as his empress consort. Together they cut the ribbon on the new town square fountain, and visited the orphanage. Francine amassed a wealth of lovely dresses suited for the events she attended, and jewelry, and other things. She spent much time hosting dinner parties in their large new home.

Francine privately loathed that house. It was as big, as square and as drafty as a barn, without any of the architectural details that she herself would have lavished on things. But Jed had built it before she had come awake again and taken hold of the reins of her realm.

Still, it was her comfort that he had given her a free hand with decorating. She bought things madly, now that there was money. She filled the house with belongings, tucking them into every corner and piling them onto every table. The fire had frightened her so badly, with its clean loss of everything that she had, that she didn't feel safe unless she was surrounded by things, any sort of things, the more expensive the better, more things than she could ever need or use. She would walk through the house, trailing her fingers over all the valuables that she owned, and feel some sort of cold peace inside her fevered chest.

She bowed her head and looked properly holy when Jed gave the invocation, filled her days with volunteer work for good causes, and bore the eyes of the community on her every day, all the time.

It was different than their early days in that first church, where the

Ladies Aid had owned them. Then she had been young and bullied. But she realized now that there had been a patronizing indulgence in their ownership, that those Ladies had actually been fond of her, had tried to treat her nicely, to be kind and make her feel at home, if only she had looked up to notice it. But she had been too young, too panicked and too resentful, too determined to succeed at her impossible tasks to appreciate or even notice their awkward, well-meant overtures.

Now that she was with a different class of people, she sometimes missed the old church's homey possessiveness and frank, occasional malice. The people she was with now, the newly rich folk, spoke to her with sugared tongues but raked her over with their eyes, expertly sizing up and pricing her clothes.

With the rush of oil into Dalhart had come an instant, ready-made high society. They were in the big leagues now, she and Jed. There was even less margin for error now than there had been before—less tolerance and no room for mistakes. Francine had to be bright, and gay, and glittering, but not too much—friendly and cordial, but never flirtatious; gracious and warm, but never smarmy; poised and cool, but never haughty.

There were eyes following her when she entered and left a room, checking to see if she accepted an occasional cocktail, and how fast she drank it, and if she took another. If she ever spoke to an unmarried gentleman she could be sure that there were eyebrows lifted and ears cocked. Finally she hardly ever spoke to unmarried ones at all, except from the safe haven of a group.

And still, no one ever told her anything. She felt sometimes that she lived in a glass bubble suspended above the rest of the world, to which floated occasional bits and snippets of the truth. No one would tell her what was going on, save in the most blanched and boiled way. She was assumed to be too pure to be interested in gossip, and besides, no one wanted to run the risk of bad stories getting back to Jed. Jed was worshipped and adored—his good opinion was everything.

So Francine grew very adept at reading behind the lines, guessing at things and blowing up the tiny snippets she heard into full-bore stories, often more lurid than the actual events.

Francine had only one real friend, a woman named Matty Westy. She had recently joined the church with her uncouth cattle baron husband, Shinola, named for the barroom brawls of his youth. Matty was a raw-boned, lanky woman with hair as red as Francine's own—although

Francine's hair had that strange pink, coppery tint while Matty's was just a frank, plug-ugly red.

Matty was warm, and sophisticated, and languid, and delighted in saying shocking things. She smoked a cigarette in a holder, and wore blue jeans and men's shirts, in an era when women dressed like sugar angels on a cake. She cursed like a sailor, rode like a jockey and raised a flock of animals with indifferent, expert care and a hard hand—beautiful red Labrador dogs and sleek racehorses. She and Shinola had never had children, and Matty's figure was like a boy's still, long-legged and slim-hipped.

Matty Westy was too clever and witty for anyone to notice that she wasn't beautiful. And although she appeared not to give a damn for anyone's opinion, she was in fact shrewd enough to know exactly how far she could push the tight, tiny society of the Dalhart rich. She amused them with her apparently bawdy ways and outrageous sayings, and they loved to exclaim over her parties, but she took a great deal of care that no breath of actual scandal was ever attached to her name.

Matty worked long and skillfully in front of her mirror to restrain the pure sexuality that smoked from her like musk from a skunk. She was determined to win her way into the inner circle of Red Rock Church, and she had decided that making friends with Francine was the way to do that. She was cautious. She knew that although Francine was drawn to her easy ways, she would be shocked past bearing if she knew the truth of Matty's flagrant carnality and her frequent, easy affairs.

Matty and Shinola Westy were as wealthy as anyone in the congregation, and they won Jed's heart by donating an exquisite new baptismal font, made out of green marble shipped all the way from Spain. After breaking the ice with this initial gambit, Matty cultivated Francine and Jed carefully, inviting them to handpicked parties of the best people at casual, brawling hamburger dinners in the Westys' acres of back yards, or on horseback rides. Jed was often tied up, so Francine generally came alone.

Francine was fascinated by Matty, and a little afraid of her. So locked into herself, Francine had gone underground and generally got her way with careful manipulation, winning flies in the time-honored honeyed way of Texas ladies. But Matty got her way with a combination of brazen demands and laughing dismissal of objections that Francine found bewitching.

The two women spent much time together. Matty made herself available to help at the frequent dinners Francine gave, and ran errands with her, shopped and compared china patterns, clipped out recipes and chatted on the phone. Francine came to depend on Matty's salty, wry company, and almost without noticing it, began to feel a lessening in her loneliness.

Matty gave her a cheerful running commentary on the scandals in the congregation, and so Francine felt more a part of things. Matty advised Francine on her marriage and took her shopping for lingerie, rejecting Francine's first demure choices and thrusting at her the wildest concoctions of red and black lace. Matty waited propped up against the wall outside the dressing room, smoking a cigarette, while Francine wrestled with the odd straps and bows, and laughed when Francine tried to back out of it, and wouldn't let her leave without personally paying for five or six of the exotic garments.

It was altogether a bright thing in Francine's life—she felt herself beginning to let down her guard. She even came close—not quite, but almost—to telling Matty about the time in the tree with Hiram Jameson. She hadn't done anything really wrong, of course, but she had kept the secret as faithfully as if she had. Now she was tempted to tell for the first time, but something kept her from it.

She and Jed had established an appropriate, friendly rapport with the Jamesons as soon as they had appeared at church. Jed seemed to have taken a particular liking to Hiram, a development that both pleased Francine and made her strangely uneasy. They invited the Jamesons to their large dinner parties, and sometimes rode with them on congregation trail rides. But Francine and Hiram were never alone together, nor was she very intimate with Anise. She took pains to keep it that way.

But Matty was different, Matty was a friend. Francine had never really had a woman friend of her own before. It was a new thing for her, and she unbent very slowly.

Trying to draw Francine out was a business that Matty found tedious. Francine had very little to say—she was so guarded, Matty thought she must even say polite things in her sleep. But there was an undercurrent of malice in Francine that Matty sensed, with her unerring intuition for such things, a streak of acquisitiveness and hidden wildness, and she set herself out to expose these things in Francine's nature, and bring them to the surface to crack Francine's careful armor.

Matty might have succeeded, too, if she hadn't been distracted by the

arrival in the congregation of Hiram and Anise Jameson, and their three
girls.

Matty was at Francine's elbow one day, helping her serve black coffee
at the coffee hour after the service, when she first spotted Hiram.

"Francine," she purred into Francine's ear, "who is that absolutely
divine creature that just walked in, with the little tight dark woman on his
arm? Don't tell me that he's been here long. I would have seen him."

Francine flushed, but kept pouring steadily. "That's Hiram Jameson
and his wife, Anise. They're lovely, they've just joined the church."

"You must introduce me," Matty said, and steered her away from the
coffee table so firmly that Francine felt helpless to resist. She found herself in the awkward position of making introductions that she suddenly
wanted very much not to make, although she didn't know why.

Matty was making her nervous, and Francine chatted and stammered
in an absurd way. It wasn't that she didn't trust Matty around men,
around a man like Hiram. Not at all. It was just that Matty had looked so
—predatory—when she was gazing at Hiram across the room. There had
been an amber feline glaze in Matty's eyes that Francine had never seen
before. Francine had been actually frightened of her, for a minute.

But her worries subsided when Matty, looking terribly chic in her
black close-fitting trousers and a matching bolero jacket, attached herself
firmly to Anise's side, with hardly a "How-de-do" to Hiram and a pat on
the head for the girls.

Francine went back to the coffee table, feeling oddly empty and displaced. She could see Matty's flaming head across the room, bent over
confidingly towards Anise, and she could see Anise relaxing and smiling,
gesturing and speaking with more vitality than Francine had ever seen or
elicited.

Francine felt a stab of guilt. She should have paid more attention to
Anise, she knew that. Anise was new, and needed friends. But somehow
talking to Anise made her feel so odd. Now it looked as though Matty was
taking care of that. Francine tried to be grateful, and dismiss it from her
mind.

But Matty's new infatuation with Anise Jameson was more than a
passing thing, apparently. Each week the two women became closer, and
better friends. They arranged to be on church committees together, and
collaborated on decorating the church for Easter with a collection of stunning arrangements that everyone agreed were the most gorgeous ever.

Each week Francine heard them making plans for family outings and rides, barbecues and picnics that soon became so regular that they only had to set the time and place. It became assumed that the Jamesons and the Westys would sit in adjoining pews, and drive home together in one set of cars or another after the service.

Francine rarely saw Matty anymore—Matty always seemed terribly busy, these days. She smiled and nodded when she met Francine, and insisted that they absolutely had to sit down for a chat this minute, it had just been a coon's age since they visited, but the visit never quite came off. Francine sank herself back into church affairs, and planned a huge dinner party in the most glittering style, which was much admired.

But she rarely went into the cream-and-rose-colored parlor where she used to sit when Matty came to call, smoking a cigarette in her long holder, telling shocking stories in her raspy voice, with her head thrown back and her long legs sprawled over the couch.

And the altar cloth that Francine and Matty had started to make together, drawn with charcoal patterns on the fine linen stuff, sat in a drawer and yellowed, and finally a mouse chewed a nest in it, and had a litter of young there. Francine could sometimes hear their tiny feet rustling through the walls, as she lay alone in her bed, watching the shadows pass over the walls from the whispering cars outside.

25. Ball Lightning

When Fid thought that G.A. had stayed out in the bush at Indian Bluff long enough, he went and fetched him home. Fid walked into the camp that Demeter had described to him, kicked aside the empty cans and chewed bones, and took hold of G.A.'s arm, where he lay on the blanket with his smeared magazine in front of him.

G.A. looked up, surprised, and growled at his father like an animal. It seemed almost that he had lost the proper use of his voice. Fid glowered down at him from his thin, dark height.

"Come with me, boy," he said. "Your mother has cried over you long enough."

He took him by the elbow, and jerked him to his feet. G.A. followed him to the car, sullenly, but he went.

When Fid led him into the kitchen at home, Demeter was standing at the kitchen sink, looking out the window, twisting up her hands in her apron. When she saw them come in, she went towards G.A. impulsively to kiss him, but drew back because of the smell.

"Wash up," she said, pointing to the stairs. "Up there."

G.A. hesitated. "Do it," his father said, and gave him a push. G.A. climbed the stairs slowly. Fid sat down at the table and lay his hands out in front of him, studying each wrinkle and hair and fold with the grease etched into it.

"He's got to go back to school," he said, "and try to be a normal boy. If he don't, then he can leave, and not come back."

Demeter bent her head to her husband's pronouncement. It was seldom enough that he spoke on anything. When he did, it was graven like stone.

She went back to wash the dishes in the sink, automatically, the tears running down her cheeks and into the dishwater. Fid knew, although her shoulders didn't shake. He came to stand close behind her, and put a hand on each shoulder. They stood there for a long time together, perfectly silent.

G.A. went back to school. He was big for his age, and puberty had pummeled him, so that the thunder ran hard through his blood. It made his skin greasy and gave him muscle swellings and the beginnings of hair long before other children his age. He fit awkwardly into the small wood-and-metal desks that the students had to sit in. He was slow at his lessons, and had missed much school, so that the teacher made him say his lessons with the younger children.

The brighter students feared the big, blocky boy who looked at them with such hate. When they discovered that he couldn't even read, they taunted him as they would have baited a caged bear. With the eyes of the teacher on him, he was helpless to do more than growl at them.

His one comfort was knowing that he carried, pressed close to his belly and cool down the front of his pants, his gun, the heavy thing of blue-grey metal that he had found stuck in a drawer among his grand-mother's things. He had never seen Lee shoot a gun, or known that she had one. But he felt sure that she would want him to have this one, to remember her by.

Two things kept him from leaving the school, where he was so misera-ble, to go back into the woods where he belonged. One was the ships. His father, in a rare moment, had told G.A. that he had been conceived on a boat, a big one like the ones in the books. Fid had a picture of such a boat still, which had hung over his bed before he married G.A.'s mother.

Fid had showed the picture to G.A., and explained what all the differ-ent parts of the boat were called. He revealed the way that all the pieces worked together to help the boat wallow through the water, buffeted by the waves. It was amazing to G.A. that anything so heavy as a metal boat could float, that it would not sink like a rock, or like the small animals he weighted with stones and sank to the bottom of the Indian Bluff fishpond.

It seemed a miracle that the rules were suspended to allow these boats to float. For G.A., boats were a break in the dreadful and inevitable cruelty of nature's laws, like a break of blue in a sky of storm clouds. He leapt towards it, with all the joy he owned.

Also, it was one of the few things G.A.'s father had ever taught him about, or spoken of with any enthusiasm. That moment they had been together, when Fid had told him about the boats, was a moment that G.A. hugged to himself with secret delight. He took it out, to turn it over, and taste it, whenever the day was particularly dark.

So model boats reminded him, and he delighted in them. He was amazingly deft with his big hands, and could put together rigging and paint tiny flags with precision. He was happy when he was building his models, and if the teacher had let him build them all the time he was in school, he would have stayed without complaint.

The teacher, a faded, fussy woman who once had been idealistic, had felt a stirring of sympathy for the boy. She was touched by the way that his clouded, angry mind seemed to clear when he held the tiny spars in his hand, and varnished the small decks. She showed him the few books that they had on boats in the wretched library, and let him stay late after school to study and pore over them.

The teacher promised G.A. that if he would learn to read, he could spell out the stories about boats for himself. It was this prospect that kept him coming back day after day, wrapping his long legs around the chair and biting his pencils, breathing harshly and frowning as he puzzled over the letters that refused to stay put in his head, ignoring the jeers of his tormentors. His advances were few, and hard earned.

The other thing that kept G.A. coming back to school was Mary Frank Masterson. She was the tiniest, most delicate little blond girl in the world, and G.A. had managed to position himself, by dint of growling and many threatening stares, directly behind her, where he could stare at the shiny gold of her hair, and the thin curve of her neck as she bent over her books.

Mary Frank was from a poor-white family, one of nine children. Her parents worked long shifts at the cotton mill and brought home barely enough money to feed and clothe their squalling brood. The boys in the family were glowering and ugly, the girls painted and loud.

But Mary Frank flourished in the midst of all the dirt and confusion of her home like a perfect pale lily, creeping out of a slag heap. Her skin was white and thin, almost transparent, and her eyes were shy and blue. She had a fragile boy's body, with an absolutely flat chest. There were brown warts on her white hands, and so she was ashamed of them, and hid them. Her blond hair was fine and cottony, and floated above her shoulders like the halo of a retiring angel. Her clothes were faded hand-me-downs, too big and washed until their colors were indistinguishable.

Sometimes people in town would give her family a charity box, and Mary Frank would come to school in dresses that were purple and yellow, too short, and she would be silent with shame and sit in the back with her head down and her legs tucked under the chair.

In one of those boxes had been a shabby old pair of roller skates. Mary Frank had watched them revealed with hungry eyes, as the lid of the box was laid back, but she held her mouth shut and said nothing. To ask for them was to open herself up for torment.

But her favorite brother had looked down and seen her big eyes, and tossed the skates to her in a moment of careless kindness, cuffing down the protesters with hammy fists.

The skates became her chariot. She could leave all of the bitter noise and foul smells behind when she whipped down a hill on them, with the clean air in her face, crouching low. She often wore bandages on her scratched and scabby knees, from the times she fell.

Mary Frank's eyes were widely spaced, tilted slightly in her thin face, and peculiarly innocent. Her mouth was the delicate color of a pink prim-rose. And she could sing like a nightingale, a high, pure soprano that soared up above the tuneless voices of the other children like a silver fish.

She was altogether the most beautiful thing that G.A. had ever seen, and he hungered for her with a single-minded fever. When he dreamed at night, threshing in his hot bed, he dreamed of Mary Frank Masterson's head on top of a body like those of the women he saw in his magazines, with their voluptuous, pouting breasts like pigeons and the pink curves of their flanks. In his dreams she enticed him, whispered to him and beck-oned him with wet lips, and he woke strained and exhausted each morning from having wrestled with his dream woman each night.

Anise found her best joy in being a mother. She was fiercely protective, ruthlessly productive, and melted herself into her daughters' lives without a thought.

She picked out clothes for them, stuffed them with vitamins and constantly monitored the divine balance of their lives by the glossy pic-tures that she cut out and continued to paste in her numerous treasure books. She prayed for them and scolded, struggling to indoctrinate them in the ways of healthful eating and exercise.

Anise's partnership with God had gathered strength over the years. Her feeling was that God had pretty much the same opinion of things that she did. As Anise's feeling of responsibility for running the world widened, she began to take Civil Defense classes, and to apply her prayer techniques to the Communist crisis in Cuba. She became enmeshed in a worldwide network of prayer, so that she could summon up extra help on a moment's notice, if one of the girls had an important paper coming up, or needed a date for the prom.

Once when Constance rebelled and refused to study for a crucial algebra test, Anise told her that she had an evil spirit in her like the ones that Christ used to cast out, and made Constance pray with her that the evil spirit would leave in time for Constance to pass her test.

Constance was the constant headache and heartache of her worrisome mother. Beautiful, heedless and athletic, Constance rode as the sweetheart of the sheriff's posse in a glittering white cowboy outfit Anise made with much love, and a little apprehension. Constance moved so quickly and was so vastly devoted to Hiram that most of the care she needed was perfunctory, matters of clothes and food and transportation to the many parties of which she was reigning belle, with her raffish good looks and high spirits.

Sweet Sarsaparilla was the last daughter, the one left at home after the other two had gone to college. She felt sometimes that she had been cheated, that her mother had been drained of her best time and attentions before she had been born. It was true—Anise had given the largest part of her heart to Amelia, and worried the most over Constance, so Sarsaparilla was left with the sticky end of the sweet bag.

But Sarsaparilla was a graceful child, and survived her turbulent teenage years with no worse damage than a stock of beautifully handmade dresses, a thorough indoctrination in religious practices and a truckload of child-rearing advice, which she later put to good use with her own two boys.

It was to Amelia that Anise gave her heart, and from whom she reaped her deepest elation. She hardly distinguished the girl as separate from herself, but thought of her more as an extra hand or foot, which she sent into the world joyously equipped to enjoy the experiences Anise herself had missed.

Anise bought Amelia's shoes for her, designed her raincoats and settled the details of her wedding with no more thought of invasion of privacy than murder. Anise told Amelia that it was her eldest daughter that made her life rewarding.

It never occurred to Anise that making her life rewarding was a heavy business for a young girl. Amelia never thought to complain.

Amelia's response to her mother's possession of her life was to yield gracefully and succeed marvelously. She was universally acknowledged as beautiful, clever and staunchly virginal. One of her schoolmates said, "There's something about Amelia Jameson that's just so perfect it drives you crazy."

Amelia was nominated for sweetheart in college and voted one of Texas Tech's most outstanding students. She won scholarships and started clubs, took a master's degree and eventually became Dean of Women. They were all accomplishments that vanished later under Amelia's vast unassuming modesty, so that she came from her victorious field assured that she had accomplished almost nothing.

It was Anise who hungrily absorbed all the sweetness of Amelia's triumphs, and there was little left over for Amelia herself.

Jed sat in his office, going through stacks of papers. His office was a handsome one, paneled with mahogany, its floor covered with a rich, dark green carpet in which he sank almost up to his ankles. It irritated him.

He cared little for such things himself, but Francine had insisted on outfitting the office for him in something that she called "fittin' style," which apparently included burgundy leather chairs so deep that he had to struggle out of them, and a gold-tipped pair of steer horns that hung on the wall.

They were rich now, richer than he had ever expected they would be. The well that Hiram Jameson had drilled for them in the church graveyard had blown in at 300,000 barrels a day. It was enough to furnish money for all of Jed's charities, give chunks to the politicians he liked, support the church in fine style and allow him, Francine and the children to do pretty much anything they damn well pleased.

Hiram hadn't gotten much out of the well, though. It was a shame, Jed thought. Hiram had worked so hard getting the well through, and then everyone had gotten rich off of it except him. Apparently he had overextended himself getting backing for the well, promising away so many pieces of the pie that there was little left over when the well actually came in. Jed felt bad about it, but what could he do?

Jed could have kept all the money himself. The well was on his land, as was the church, which had turned out almost accidentally to be a self-supporting, politically powerful institution all by itself. But he plowed a large part of the oil money into good works, feeling that it was only fitting.

You couldn't tell, he reflected, you just couldn't tell how someone would be about money until he had it. Jed was proud that he himself had turned out to be remarkably levelheaded about it. The eye-popping, mouth-stretching amounts of cash that came with oil and made most people mad, had passed over Jed and left him relatively cool and un-touched.

Oh, he had bought some things for Francine. She had picked out gaudy, loud baubles that surprised him with their size. She favored dia-monds, and packed them onto her hands, huge ones that sparkled and poured lights from their facets like cut ice. She wore them on her neck and wrists and fingers, with vehemence, as if she had been hungry. It had made him wonder if she had felt deprived, all those years in the ugly house with other people's cast-off things. It had never really occurred to him before.

And she had filled the house uncomfortably full. There was a passion in her for ownership that he thought strange. She seemed driven to pile things around her, to have something to hold on to. It was as if she thought she could bar the door to her age and her increasing waistline, if she only surrounded herself with beautiful things, shining teaks and mahoganies and silks, china and crystal, flaming colors and delicate tex-tures that left Jed quite unimpressed. He was not a sensual man.

But she didn't gush over the objects, or even seem particularly pleased about having them. She bought them with the absent focus and determination of a man piling sandbags into a breach, to stop the flood-ing.

But not even Francine could turn time backwards, with all her massages and facials. Jed laughed gently to himself at the thought. Age was touching his wife at last, though she had fought it valiantly for so long. Her bright coppery hair was fading a bit; her waist was coarse and there was flesh under her jaw and around her eyes. Her outline entirely was softening, fleshing out.

She looked shockingly like a matron, clutching her handbag, so that it surprised him when he saw her across a room. She still carried her body well, the wide shoulders and awkward hands, and there was still a chic in the way that the expensive clothes sat on her body. But she was no longer the stunning girl, or the striking woman, that she had been. She was—not old, but older. Getting on.

Still, weren't they all? Jed stared down at his paunch, crossed with the handsome, well-tailored dark blue suit. Another of Francine's purchases. His own football bulk had run to fat, but he was still a huge and imposing figure of a man, his neck thick as a bull's in his hand-monogrammed shirts.

He did like these shirts, now—the finespun cotton was light and silky as a cobweb, and he found himself appreciating things like that as he got older. Once it would not have occurred to him. He rubbed the stump of his right arm idly, where it ached. It ached more these days, especially when it was about to storm.

When he looked in the mirror to shave he saw that his hair was as dark and smooth as ever—no grey in it anywhere. But his face was flushed and ruddy with all the years of good living, could hardly be contained inside his collar. They had not left him untouched, the years. His doctor said he should eat less steak, more green things. But he never could seem to remember things like that, always too busy, and when he was hungry he just ate whatever was laid in front of him.

Francine was trying to get him to cut down on salt, too. It all seemed a little ridiculous, somehow—that a little white sprinkling could make a difference one way or the other. But he tolerated her looking after him— even appreciated it, in fact.

They had come to their peace, Francine and Jed. She had long ago stopped clawing at him, given up the hungry kind of seeking that he had surprised in her eyes from time to time early on, before William was born. Maybe William had settled her down. He rarely saw Francine or the boy, truth be told. There were just too many things to be done, to keep Red Rock going, and despite his army of administrators it seemed that every-thing had to have his one-handed stamp on it, or it would falter and fail.

He hardly had time for anything anymore, if he stopped to think about it. Even his God. Of course, he spent all his days in the service of the Lord, doing the Lord's work. Surely that made it right. But the ringing, the clear and constant brilliance, the feeling of the Lord's hand always on him, behind his head, pushing him forward—no, that feeling he had lost some time ago, and not noticed until it was gone.

There was no longer time for the long hours that he had once spent in prayer, feeling privileged and close to the source, peering over the edge of the pit that flowed with the endless lava of salvation, pure and white, like the cream of liquid gold.

He got up and went to stand at the window, his stump concealed in his coat pocket. He felt suddenly empty, and bereft. He looked out over the rig, pumping up and down regularly. He wondered if the inhabitants of the graveyard minded much, the oil being sucked out from underneath their bones, gleaming in the dimness like sea urchins, their blood old and black.

Come to think of it, the oil was like old blood too. The blood and bones of the sea creatures that had swum sideways there before they were petrified into salt domes, smashed by the earth into the gummy black stew men prized so highly. It was an odd business, living off the earth's black blood, sucked up through old bones. It made Jed feel a little uneasy.

Restlessly, he ran his hand through his hair. His breathing seemed short, and labored. His feeling of loss grew stronger as he watched the arm of the rig mindlessly pumping, up and down, like a monstrous feeding animal.

He wondered how it was that he had drifted so far, that he had been abandoned by the passionate fever for the Lord that had possessed him. The fever had caused him to build up these walls, to contain it. And in the building, the spirit had slipped away, and left only these walls standing empty. Where had it all gone? He had hardly noticed.

Outside, there was fixing to be a terrible storm. The sky was dark, a greenish grey, the trees breathing uneasily in the half-light. There was a restless waiting in the air. It suited his mood, and he opened the window, pulling open the large french doors. He stood in the wash of the pale green air, breathing deeply. He loved Texas storms—there was something deep about them, the weather raging over the absolutely flat plain of dirt, in and out of the houses so randomly imposed on the land.

It occurred to him with a strange feeling of relief that, in itself, a storm was neither good nor bad. It was simply irreducible, a thing of huge and awesome power, too large to fight, too large to do anything but just fall to your knees in wonder. A tornado alone on an uninhabited plain was just itself, a glowering jinni, eating the wind.

But bring human beings into the landscape, now, and that changed everything. It was only as the wild, the untamable things of nature hit men that they became nibbled down into good or evil. If a tornado took a house where there was a baby sleeping, and ate it up, then that tornado would be called an evil freak of nature. But if there had been no house in the way, why, no one would blame the tornado at all.

It seemed unfair, and Jed suddenly found himself wishing that there were no houses on the horizon, that there were no papers or oil wells, that the huge, fragile sweep of the brown land would be scrubbed of all the houses, all the dirt and the fussy gardens, all the roads and filth and broken bottles that men left behind them. He wished it would be turned back to the gods of wind and sky that birthed it. He felt dirty, being part of that wave of debris, and longed to be washed away into the dust, the vast and impenetrable ocean of land.

The storm was whipping up outside, more and more mad. He knew he should close the french doors, but didn't move. He saw lightning flares around outside, out of his view, and he wondered idly if there would be more fires tonight. The dry Texas storms were a fury for fires, just flogging over the dry dust and scourging things drier and drier, burning things that were already parched as hay.

He saw movement out of the corner of his eye, just outside the doors, and turned to see what it was. It was a ball of fire.

The ball of fire floated towards Jed, perfectly round, as big across as his waist. He blinked, thinking he was seeing things, but it was still there when he opened his eyes. It came drifting at him out of the half-light, and he wondered dazedly where it had come from—he hadn't seen any lightning strike. It sailed towards him quite steadily, and he automatically ducked his head as it came through the french doors and into the room. The hairs on the back of his neck rose, as he felt the heat of the thing.

It wafted on through the room, absurdly slow. He watched it, hypnotized. It went over towards the wall, and grazed delicately against the telephone mounted there. The bell rang, and the receiver danced on its hook.

Then it bounced away from the wall and came towards Jed again. It moved with the unearthly grace of a waltz. Jed gazed into its heart as it came.

He saw the white-hot core of it, with the outer flames fanning into red. The pure, drowning loveliness of it struck him blind. It seemed that everything he had missed, everything that he had once known and forgotten, everything that had ever broken his heart or made him shiver with awe to be alive, was there in the melting splendor of this floating ball of fire.

And he felt redeemed. He heard a matchlessly tender voice just behind him, calling his name. The presence that had shrunk from his life came back to claim him, and he cried out and sank to his knees in front of it, ecstatic in his surrender.

He spread out his arms, and threw back his head to look into the heart of it, and as it descended on him, he cried out again as it ran into his veins. His body jolted, shuddered and jolted forward again. All of his hairs rose together and singed in one great moment. The blood leapt out of his veins, eager for greater things, and he pitched forward, his skin blackened, and smiling.

26. Ashes

G.A. took to following Mary Frank Masterson home from school. He would lie in wait, shrouded by the berry vines that scratched red lines in his arms, at a particular place by the road. Mary Frank always stayed after school to get extra help from the teacher. The kindly teacher had seen an early promise in Mary Frank's scrawls, and thought the child had the soul of a poet. She put out her poor timid hand to do what she could to salvage Mary Frank from her family.

At exactly quarter past three each school day, Mary Frank would come soaring around a certain point in the road on her skates, crouched low, with the ragged edge of her dress fluttering. If his position was just right, G.A. could catch a soul-searing glimpse of what lay underneath, covered with thin grey panties.

At those moments he thought that he had never seen anything more beautiful than Mary Frank. Her thin, clear skin flushed, her arms outspread, she did not know that anyone watched. She flew for those few moments that she was alone, coming down the hill. She loved the speed, and the road rose up to bow to her, and give her the things it had hidden. Her thin shoulder blades were the stumps of wings, and the hissing, alternately frying sounds of her skates against the pavement were the only thing, it seemed, that held her bird-boned body from leaving for the sky.

G.A. watched and worshipped silently. She was all he knew of the air. He himself was rooted, buried in the bog of his dark imaginings, a thing of the earth. He only watched her.

Then he began leaving her presents. They were small things—a piece of stick, with lichen growing on it just so, or a rock that had glistened in the sun. He laid them carefully on her doorstep at night, and crept back into the forest so that he would not be seen.

But his gifts never reached their mistress. The heavy-footed men of her family, her father and brothers, would fling open the door every morning before anyone else was up, drinking their black coffee, and kick the "trash" that they found off the doorstep. They would look around, with heavy scowls, wondering who was littering their step. So G.A. thought he would have to make himself known.

He caught a mouse in one of his traps. It was a delicate little thing, with the softest pale grey fur, and a pink nose and tiny feet. It had been all night in the trap, trying to chew itself out. G.A. held it in his hand, feeling a little bit of sorrow for the first time, over a creature's coming death. But the mouse must die—if it squeaked, he thought, Mary Frank might be frightened, and displeased. Or what if it bit her? So he closed his thumb down over the tiny thing, and broke its neck.

He put it in a box that he asked his mother for, with a ribbon that he tied himself. He worked over the bow for a long time, until it was a little dirty and ragged from his great, soiled hands. But it was important that he do every bit of it himself, and so he persevered, sweating and swearing under his breath, until it was done.

He carried it shyly hidden in his lunch, and waited all day impatiently for school to be through. At the appointed time he crept into the bushes, rigid with excitement. He waited and waited, and thought perhaps that she wasn't coming at all.

But she came around the corner, stooped and soaring, with the breathless flush to her face. For a moment he sat still under the bushes, thinking that he had no right to disturb such a silvery thing with his own presence. But impatience got the better of him—he bolted from his hiding place and ran into the road, suddenly afraid that she would pass him by, and he would never be seen at all.

The sight of the big, awkward boy bursting out of the bushes frightened Mary Frank, and she went down in a tumble of thin knees and elbows. He ran to help her up, and she shrank away from him, staring. Looking down, he saw that he had a little of the mouse blood on his shirt.

"Look," he said, "I brought you something."

She looked up the road, to see if there was someone coming to save her. The road was empty both ways, and the woods were silent. They were completely alone. Her heart was beating so hard that she thought surely he must see it. She forced a smile to her face, to calm him. She mustn't excite him, she knew.

He was holding out a box to her, with a strange, intense look on his face. She had seen G.A. in school, of course, the oversized boy with the nasty scowl, working his lessons with the little children. He was dirty often as not, and word around the classroom was that he was insane, as well as stupid. But she had never seen just this look on his face before. She wondered if he had gone completely mad.

"Go on," he said, pushing the box at her roughly. "Go on, open it."

Shrinking from his touch, she took the box from his hands. He thrilled to see her hands hovering over the bow that he had made and pulled so tight. Her hands were as beautiful as the rest of her, thin-boned and almost transparent, marred only by the brown warts sprinkled on them like freckles. They seemed to flutter helplessly over the bow now, like butterflies afraid to come to rest.

"Here," he said, unable to wait anymore. He grabbed the box back, ripped off the ribbon and pulled off the lid, to expose the mouse curled like a fetus. "Here!" He shoved it back in her face.

Mary Frank Masterson gazed into the box and put her head back to scream. The screams rang out of her soprano throat like glistening silver, peal after peal, lighting the woods and hanging on the trees like icicles.

The start he had given her, the lonely ring of the woods and the tiny broken body of the mouse shocked her into hysterics, and she could not seem to stop screaming. Her eyes were wide and ringed with white, and her screams rang piercing and clear through the air until G.A. backed away, confused, backed away further and further until he was running, his breath sobbing in his chest, crashing into the woods and covering his ears to shield them from the sound of those screams.

Matty Westy had been Anise's best friend for as long as she could remember. Nine years, if Anise stopped to count, not that she would ever have time to. Amelia was in college now, and Constance with her, and that necessitated a constant stream of vitamins shipped in the mail, letters and long-distance prayers and arrangements to be made for their visits home, with money tighter than ever.

Sarsaparilla was still at home, pouting and sullen over her momentary lack of boyfriends. And Hiram was in financial trouble, as always—he wouldn't tell Anise much, but what he did let slip made her wonder what they were running on. She thought that there were things she didn't understand about their situation, things that didn't all fit together.

Hiram still left town every week to go see to some wildcat oil deal in Fort Leavenworth, Kansas, as he had for years. He left on Monday, and came back Thursday morning, regular as clockwork. All of her nagging and persuasions couldn't get him to work closer to home. He would just pat her hand and tell her not to worry, that wildcatters traveled, and that was that.

But they were on the brink of ruin almost all the time, she could tell. She knew it especially when Hiram came home with a migraine, his normally handsome face drawn and his jovial way strained. She researched in all the nutrition books to find vitamin supplements to cure him, prayed over him and diagnosed him as having low blood sugar, so that she was constantly forcing small snack packs of nuts and raisins on him. She suspected he tossed them as soon as he got away from the house, but he always said they helped.

Hiram had been in partnership for many years now with a man that everyone said was a bad businessman. It seemed to be common knowledge now that Joejoe Simmons was terribly unreliable, and she only wondered why no one had spoken up when Hiram first went into partnership with

Joejoe. In all the years, Anise had wondered why they never seemed to get ahead. Now it was clear that Joejoe had been fixing the books and skimming the profits for years. But Hiram appeared unable to do anything about it.

In fact, there was something surfacing in Hiram lately that Anise liked the look of less and less. She had bent to him, built her life around him because he seemed enormously strong-willed, so that he could wrap the world around him like a yo-yo on a string. She had thought it would be exciting to be near the center of all that white-hot heat, all the activity. She was proud of his charm, and his handsomeness, the way that fellows would move in from other states just to be his neighbors.

But now she was beginning to notice, as Joejoe sank into bankruptcy hopelessly, blubbering, keeping Hiram strapped by him like a harpoon in the side of a dying whale, that Hiram was unable to move on his own. He talked about going on alone, he made grand plans. But she saw, without wanting to see it, that nothing was ever done.

The suspicion grew as she resisted it, beaching slowly in her mind like a foundering corpse. Hiram could not make up his mind. He was simply incapable of making big decisions. Once someone had made a decision for him, he would move heaven and earth to carry it out—but he would never do it on his own.

And his inability to act was hidden under such a marvelous screen of firmness and decision, charisma, motion and vivid charm, that no one had ever suspected. Who could accuse such a splendidly cut jawline of irresolution? And she herself had fronted for him, she realized. Her absolute determination, the perpetual motion and manipulation of the world around her that caused a friend to remark, "Being with Anise is like being on the wrong end of a cattle prod"—all that had covered for Hiram's weakness. She had camouflaged his weakness so well that not even she had seen it. Not for all these years.

It left a taste in her mouth like unswallowed aspirin. She worked harder. Parties, youth entertainments at the high school, square dances, trail rides, charities—she organized, and motivated, and frantically bull-horned people into giving money and doing good.

Her one place of rest in all the furor was Matty Westy. Matty said Anise worked too hard. And Matty was always available—at least, almost always—with her cool, vinegary wit and running commentary on the ridiculous. She had a delicious perspective, Matty did, and being with her made

Anise feel almost like a young girl again in New York, where they had sat in their rooms with their hair up in curl papers, waiting for the world to discover them.

Anise's girls had grown up with Matty—called her "Aunt Matty," in fact. Matty laughed at them and nursed them through their early heartaches. She had a wry, offhand way about her that charmed the girls, and they borrowed her clothes and raided her refrigerator almost as casually as they did their own.

Anise had surprised a strange, hungry look on Matty's face sometimes, when Matty looked at the three girls. At such times her eyes would take on an odd, amber glaze. Matty never seemed so happy, or so relaxed, as when she was in a knot of screaming teenagers. She delighted in loaning them money and jewelry and solving their troubles.

Anise had asked her, once, why she had never had children of her own. Matty had stubbed out her cigarette with an impatient movement.

"Honestly, Anise, don't you think I would have if I could have?"

"You can't?" Anise said stupidly.

"Not me—the cattle baron there." Matty jerked her head in the direction of Shinola, who was wielding the hamburger spatula with drunken glee outside at the barbecue, giving loud directions to other picnickers. "Shinola's completely impotent, the idiot. Has been for years."

"Isn't there anything you can do?" Anise asked.

"We've tried, scads of things, of course. Even went to a special doctor in France. You should have heard Shinola roar! But no, nothing . . ." And Anise caught an odd look on Matty's face, something she had never seen there before. It was sad, and even a little frightened.

Nowadays Shinola was generally swollen with drink. His dullness multiplied by the number of whiskey sours he swallowed during the long, hot afternoons.

Matty talked to Anise that day about divorcing Shinola. She spoke of it with a peculiar cool detachment, smoking her cigarette in the holder, her long legs curled up under her on the couch. Anise was shocked at her casual tone.

"Matty, whatever can you mean?" she had said. "You know Shinola adores you. Your relationship may not be"—she dropped her eyes, finding it hard to say—"fulfilling, exactly, but he's a good provider, and you know each other. That's worth a lot, at our time of life. And he would do anything for you."

Matty shifted, and did not meet Anise's eyes. She blew smoke up towards the ceiling. "Oh, I know all that rot," she said. "But Shinola just bores me to pieces. And I've been bored for so long now, I think I deserve a change. Don't you, really?"

"No, I certainly do not," said Anise. "I don't believe in divorce. And I didn't think you did, either. What's come over you?"

Matty got up restlessly, stretched like a cat and wandered over to the window, pushing aside the drape. Then she looked at a picture hanging on the wall—an enlarged photo of Hiram breaking a horse outside in the arena, whipping it round and round in a circle on a long lead.

"That's a lovely photo," she said. "Hiram should never do anything but just break horses, all day long. He's so ornamental."

Anise looked up briefly, and shuddered. She hated it when Hiram took horses into the ring—the hooves flew so wildly, he could easily get kicked and break a leg. He had insisted on hanging the photo there.

Matty roamed over to the piano, picked up a picture of the three girls, and looked at it. "What a handsome family. Such beautiful girls you have," she said. "Three perfect different shades of girl—one dark, one blond and one just in between." Something in her voice made Anise look up, and she surprised that strange, bleak look on her face again, a look that made Matty's bones look peaked and sharp.

"Isn't Amelia home on vacation?" Matty said. "Bring her over. I'm perishing for a look at her new haircut."

"I'll tell her," said Anise. "Are you taking something to the Wednesday potluck?"

"That's tomorrow, isn't it?" Matty said, putting the picture back down. "Yes, I'm taking creamed broccoli. Come by for me around three?"

"Yes," said Anise, "I will."

It always amazed Anise that Matty never seemed to have anything to do. Although she raised countless horses, always had foals in the stable and brood mares wandering on the lawn right up to the front door, sticking their noses hopefully into the windows in search of a sugar lump, an enormous garden and at least three golden retrievers at any one time, she never seemed to be rushed or hurried. Matty just lounged around in her languid way and flicked the crop that she carried tucked into her boot at any of the creatures she thought needed it. Anise envied her, for her cool repose and spotless house, and all the extra money she always had.

"Look, Anise," Matty said, getting to her feet abruptly. "The fact is,

I've already booted Shinola out onto his arse. He's not living there any-more. So when you come by, just let yourself in, will you? I may be in the back and not hear the door, and I've given all the help the week off."

Startled, Anise just nodded. Matty hugged her briefly, hard, and left.

When Anise went to Matty's door the next day just before three, she looked around at the immaculately manicured lawns, admiring them as always. Matty had marvelous gardens, filled with exotic blooms, some of which Anise had never seen anywhere else. But the place felt strangely empty to her, without any of the tumbled teenage clutter that Anise was used to.

She knocked on the door, which boomed loudly, then remembered and went in. She couldn't see or hear anyone. "Matty?" she called, look-ing around.

She went on into the kitchen, which was green and white, big enough to roller-skate in, with shiny fixtures and imported Italian tiles on the walls. She saw a note on the table, and picked it up to read it.

"Darling," it said. "Have had to rush away before the broccoli was done, can't make it to the potluck after all. Won't you be a doll and take it along? I'll call you Thursday. M."

Anise picked up the note and put it in her pocket, and checked the broccoli in the oven. It was almost cooked, but not quite brown enough on top, so she left it in for a few more minutes, and wandered around the kitchen. She felt a little timid but strangely exhilarated. It was lovely to be in someone else's home, all alone. She had never been in the house when Matty wasn't home.

She was drawn out of the kitchen and into the long, cool breezeway, smelling of the oil soap on the polished floor, and up the pale-blue-carpeted stairway into the upstairs. She told herself that Matty wouldn't mind, but felt mildly guilty, anyway. She wandered down the long halls, admiring the sparse elegance of the place.

It was a look that Anise coveted but could never quite bring off. Her own house always seemed fussy and overfull, packed with the girls' things and who knows what all, belonging to children from the neighborhood. She had always dreamed of having a house like this, pale rose and cream, blue silk and, on one floor, pure-white carpet! She could hardly believe the extravagance. It was every bit a woman's house, though—Shinola's print hadn't been placed on the house in a single room, except one with a twin bed that had a leather chair with a pile of *American Sportsman* magazines beside it, and a gun rack.

She felt a little sorry for Shinola, suddenly—he had always been boisterous and cheerful, a generous, if none too bright, member of their foursome. She had had no idea that Matty was so unhappy in her marriage. It had gone along for years with no change. Why had she suddenly tossed Shinola out now? She pictured Shinola, drunk and unhappy, in some hotel or men's club in the city, probably wondering to himself what he had done this time. It was true that he adored Matty, although she mostly ignored him, and kicked him around like one of the dogs.

Feeling daring, Anise went down the hall and peeked into Matty's bedroom. She wondered suddenly why she had never been in it before, in all the years of their friendship—somehow all of their socializing had been at Anise and Hiram's house, with the children around, or downstairs at Matty's in front of the big stone fireplace.

Matty's bedroom was large, with windows all down one side, streaming with light. It was done in sea foam green, with pale peach pillows, and lacy curtains. All the furniture was a wan blond wood. Anise loved it. She went in, looking admiringly at the modern prints on the wall. She wondered if she and Hiram could scrape together some cash for improvements —maybe she could do something like this in the spare bedroom, after all the girls were gone.

Then she saw something odd on the dresser, and she went over and picked it up. It was a picture of Hiram, a large glossy one in a frame. Anise had never seen this particular photo before. She was struck with the cruel, sensual set of his mouth in the picture. He looked like a stranger, someone she didn't recognize.

She stared at it for a long time, as if she didn't know what it was. Then she put it very carefully back on the dresser, exactly where it had been.

She went downstairs and out to her car, closing Matty's door behind her. She drove home, pulled up into the carport and got out, leaving the car running. She went inside her own house, feeling its dark comfort close around her. She picked up the phone and called the airport.

"Yes, can you tell me what time the regular flight gets in from Fort Leavenworth, Kansas, on Thursday morning?" she said when a male voice came on the line.

"A moment, please, I'll check," the voice said, and went away. "Here we go," it said after a minute. "Sorry, ma'am, there's no regular flight that comes in from Fort Leavenworth, Kansas, on Thursday mornings."

"I see," said Anise. "Hasn't it ever come in on Thursdays?"

"No, ma'am," said the voice. "Not in the years I've been working here. We only run one flight from Fort Leavenworth per week, and it always comes in Wednesday afternoons, about four. If you hurry, you can make it. It's due in about twenty minutes."

"Thank you so much," she said, and put the phone down.

Anise stood at the bottom of the stairs and called up to Amelia.

"Yes, Mother?" Amelia called back.

"Will you come down here for a minute?" Anise said. "I need you."

Amelia came down, looking bright-eyed. When she saw Anise's face she faltered for a minute. "What's wrong?"

"Come with me, please," said Anise. "Do you have a sweater?"

"I don't need one," said Amelia, looking frightened.

"Get a sweater," said Anise automatically. "It's damp outside."

Amelia did, and they got in the car together and drove off.

"Where are we going?" said Amelia.

"To the airport," Anise said.

When they got to the airport, they pulled into the short-term waiting area, back from the door.

"What are we doing here?" said Amelia. "Look," she said, pointing. "Isn't that Matty's car?"

Matty's celery-green Cadillac sat in the sun, shining like a fish.

"Yes," said Anise. "Now hush."

They sat and waited. Amelia thought that she might be sick. Her stomach was feeling odd, and her feet seemed very small and far away.

After a few minutes, they saw Hiram come out carrying his small suitcase. He walked jauntily down the line of cars and got into the passenger seat of Matty's Cadillac. The car started instantly, its engine working in a deep throaty purr, and pulled away from the curb and into traffic.

Anise and Amelia followed the green Cadillac across town. Anise drove perfectly steadily, her knuckles white on the wheel. The Cadillac pulled up in front of the Westy house, and Hiram and Matty got out. They went up the driveway, and Hiram pulled a key off of his key ring and unlocked the door. They went in and shut it behind them.

Amelia and Anise sat in the car for a long time. Anise put her head back against the seat, as if her head were too heavy to hold up.

"Mother?" said Amelia. She was feeling very queasy. "I think I'm going to be sick."

"Go in those bushes over there," Anise said, and pointed.

"No, never mind," said Amelia. They sat there a few minutes longer.

"Go get your father and tell him to come home," said Anise.

Amelia shrank back. "Mother, please," she said.

"Go on," Anise said ruthlessly. "You just go on up there."

"I can't," Amelia said.

"You just go on," Anise said, and folded her arms. She stared straight ahead, into the glare of the windshield.

Amelia walked up the walk, forcing her legs forward as if she were walking under water. The walk stretched out in front of her, and looked rippled. She thought she might faint. She had never fainted before, and was mildly curious about what would happen if she did. She finally reached the door and knocked on it, hearing the knock boom out hollowly.

After a long pause Hiram answered the door, laughing at something. Amelia could hear Matty's voice in the other room. She couldn't make out what Matty was saying. She looked down, and saw that Hiram's feet were bare. Her eyes felt heavy, and she could not drag them away from his feet. She stared at them, fascinated. His toes were long and crooked, like fingers, and there was a brief shadowing of dark hair on the second knuckle of his toes. There was a red corn on his left foot, by his little toe.

The laughter went slowly out of Hiram's face as he stood looking at Amelia, although his mouth stayed in a laugh shape for a long time, as if frozen there. Amelia heard Matty's voice, impatient, questioning.

"Mother says you should come home now," Amelia said. Her voice sounded strange to her, and she cleared her throat and tried again. "Mother says come on home."

"All right," Hiram said. He looked down at his feet, seeming surprised to see that they belonged to him.

Amelia turned to get back into the car. Hiram closed the Westys' door behind her. He closed it slowly, gently, as if it were made of glass and he was afraid of breaking it. The sound of its closing, the click and the latch, rang in Amelia's head like the time when she had wet her finger and run it around the pure, round lip of a crystal glass, just before it broke and cut her.

Anise dreamed that night that she was walking across a plain, where the air was charged and livid, draped over the brushes of sage and the dust like bars of gold. She could feel a storm coming, and as she walked she felt the first drops begin to fall, making a round wet mark in the dust on her arm.

She could see the horizon in front of her, clear into the distance, and then she saw a single rider on a black horse. He came over the edge, swimming in her eyes through the heat.

She blinked to clear them. She looked again, and heard music, dread and clear, around her. It seemed to be coming from the dirt under her feet. The rider rode on towards her, and she could hear in the air the clanking of a metal buckle on his saddle, and the creak of wet leather.

She knew that it was her husband coming to claim her, except that his face was dark, his hat pulled down to hide it, and she knew that she had to hurry. She started to run. But the dirt sucked at her feet, so that she felt she was swimming through mud, and all the strength she could muster barely pulled her arms through the approaching storm.

He flickered in the sulphur light, muzzily fading in front of her eyes, and the closer she came to him, the further he seemed to recede, until at last she could hardly see him at all. Then he rose up in front of her suddenly, quite close, so that she could smell the horse's wet skin and the faint, sweet smell of grain.

She cried out, because behind him she could see a thundercloud massing that shone around him like a dark halo. The rain was falling faster, falling in patterns on the brush that wrapped around her legs as she ran forward. She brought the back of her forearm up and wiped the wet hair from her brow, where it was streaming.

She saw the cloud again, very close now, with silver thunder poking out its sides like a dog in a bag. She saw that there was nothing on the plain, nothing at all, for the lightning to strike but the man.

And as the water ran in trickles, gathering to rushes that wound down the gullies, she threw herself forward and tried to scream as the lightning cracked out of the sky into the rose-gold light. She heard the roll of the thunder. The tip of the silver finger reached down and touched the man, riding against the sky. She screamed again as there was a popping sound, and a light that lit the awful plain.

The figure on the horse stopped, frozen, and she ran on, moving easily now with light feet, counting the beats of her heart, until she was

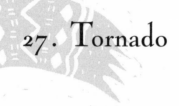

standing next to the horse and the rider. She reached out one finger to lay it on the knee of the man who sat, his face still in shadow.

But when she touched him he began to crumble, to break into ashes with sharp sides. His face slid into itself, horribly. One side of his shoulder drifted down, and then the other, dissolving in a wreath onto the body of the horse, which toppled also into ash.

The ashes slid and fell as softly as sand, breaking into smaller and smaller pieces until they were only dust, catching the rivulets of water. Anise held her face in her hands and stood under the angry light, the rain falling fast around her. She looked at the ashes pooled at her feet and saw that they were exactly the color of the roses she had burned once in the fireplace when she was a girl, to see what would happen.

27. Tornado

G.A. ran and ran in the forest, with the sound of Mary Frank's screams still in his ears. He shook his head, trying to clear the ringing sound away, and to lose the sight of her face, horrified past bearing.

He ran for a long time, until he stumbled onto a camp of carnival workers, who were preparing to move into town the next day and set up their show. A burly man stood up and caught him by the elbow as he stumbled past on the fringes of camp. Someone was cooking in a large pot over an open fire. It smelled good.

"Hold it, boy. Where you going?" the man said. "You running from the law?"

G.A. eyed him warily, and said nothing. His chest heaved up and down. He knuckled from his eyes the few tears that the wind had stung there. He tried to wrench his elbow out of the man's grasp, and was surprised when the man's arm stayed on him, easily as anything. The man grinned at him, harder this time, lifting up his lips to show teeth filed to points.

"Want it like that, do you?" he said. "Don't waste your time. I don't care if you're running from twenty coppers. But we need an extra hand here, and you seem to have come along at a good time, see?"

G.A. did not see, nor did he care, but he found himself soon enough seated with a bowl of the stew in his lap, and a dented tin spoon. The stew was surprisingly tasty, with large chunks of meat floating in it, and fat.

The carnival workers watched him eat, exchanging glances. The boy was dirty, and looked not quite right in the head, but it was true that they needed an extra hand. The best roustabout had broken his leg only that morning, and lay sodden with whiskey and groaning in his tent. They needed a full complement of five men to mount the five-sided tent properly, and peg it down, or it would take them twice as long to set up and fold, and that would cost them money. The boss would be furious.

The man who had caught G.A.'s arm sat down beside him, and when he had finished eating, offered him a job and a place to sleep, no questions asked. So G.A. joined the carnival, and traveled with them.

He was never anything but a roustabout, in a dirty, brightly colored coat, who helped put up the tents and pulled them down, but he grew an impressive mustache. Eventually he made a specialty out of erecting the Ferris wheel, with its gaudy, flimsy spokes. People appreciated his strength here, instead of laughing at him. And although they said strange things just out of his hearing that he never understood, they were kind to him in an idle sort of way.

The performers in the carnival were a different sort of creature than the roustabouts, who chewed tobacco. The performers were fragile and many-jointed, and they wore bright clothes, and lay about idly until show time. The women were painted and wore feathers in their hair, and bleached their curls white with a strong-smelling bottle. They wore skimpy bikinis made of sparkling gold strings. Their job, as far as G.A. could make out, was to writhe languidly in front of the crowds and draw the men back to the special show afterwards.

Backstage before the shows, and between towns, the women lay on the jostling beds of their cars and scratched their armpits, yawned, cracked and ate pistachio nuts. And though they never let G.A. touch them, they were content enough to let him watch them as they dressed, drawing on the soft bright skins of their costumes like a flock of lazy birds. He would watch them, pressed against the window of their cars in an agony of lust, and they would preen towards him, thrusting out their white breasts at him and laughing.

G.A. never wrote back to Demeter or Fid to tell them where he had gone. He couldn't write well enough to make a letter himself, and he was too shy to ask for help.

Demeter watched for him sometimes in her glass, and knew that he wasn't dead, although she thought his soul was probably in mortal danger. Fid became grimly silent on the subject, and gave G.A. up for lost with an equal mixture of regret and relief. The boy was grown, anyway, and if he wasn't dead, Fid figured that he was probably up to something that didn't bear examination. It was time for him to make his own way.

G.A. never forgot Mary Frank Masterson, for all the women he saw, and all the time that he was away. He kept his gun with him. He would look at it on his dresser, wicked and blue in the light, and promise it solemnly that both of them would go home someday. This time she would welcome them. There would be no more screaming, no more of that dreadful flashing look in her eyes. This time, she would be glad to see them. They would bide their time, and then go home.

It was a good twelve years before the carnival made its way back to the town of Patience.

This is how Hiram killed his wife:

For a long time after she woke up, Anise thought that she would die. Not that she would lay hands on herself, but her body just refused to do anything. She wasn't even hungry. She lay in bed, all day sometimes, and looked idly out the window towards where the birds were nesting, in the early-spring air.

She had the strangest feeling, as if something inside her were ruptured and leaking slowly. She felt it sliding out of her, and felt anemic. She tried sometimes to lift up her legs and arms, but they fell back down again. Her hands, which had always been so busy and filled with such a number of things, lay idle on the sheets, curled up towards the ceiling. She couldn't sleep, just lay watching the patterns of light change on the ceiling, as she had done long ago, when she was a girl.

She couldn't understand what had happened to her. In some ways it was the most natural thing in the world—scads of women had unfaithful husbands. She knew that.

It was something else—it was that the loom on which she had raveled up her life was nothing, broken to pieces on the floor. Everything she had thought, everything she had believed! For nine years, half her marriage. For nine years her best friend had taken her own husband, and she had never known, never suspected. Anise tasted herself as the fool, and it was bitter.

The sacrifices she had made, the compromises. They all came back to her now, with jeering, haunting faces, sharp like glass. She had paid everything, everything she had, for a lie. It was too high a price.

And it wasn't that she didn't forgive Hiram. She believed that she did forgive him. She thought it, she wished it. It was for him that she had done everything, hidden his false faces from the world, written birthday cards in his name, so that no one would ever suspect his heedlessness, shored him up with prayer and vitamins, knit him up so that he would appear whole to the world.

It could not be Hiram. Because she knew him, knew his large beauty, like an animal, and she knew that if he kicked her and damaged her, it was only because he was so vital, he didn't see. You couldn't expect a man like that to watch for the niggling concerns of everyone else.

No, it was Matty Westy on whom her hatred fixed, and burned. She saw the evil face of Matty now, the whore, the seducer, the liar. The woman had lied to her and won, won! For nine years. And all for the purpose of taking her husband away.

She knew it all now, knew why Matty had released her hold on Shinola, and gambled everything on gaining Hiram. But Matty had failed. She, Anise, would see to that. She would never give up her husband, never be cheated out of what was her due by a redheaded devil spawn who smoked cigarettes and walked with the same lazy indulgence as Hiram himself. It would never happen.

Anise lay on her bitter bed, and her cancer was born. She didn't know it at the time, didn't find it until years later. But it nested next to her heart, under her left breast. It spawned in the place where her blindness and her love fought with her pain. It was made out of betrayal, and denial, and rage. Because she could not speak her poison, it stayed inside her veins. She would die of it, without surrender.

When she died, many years later, she died of her stubbornness, of her religion, of her betrayal. But most of all, she died of Hiram. She believed this in the end, when she pointed her yellow finger at my grandfather and spoke these words: "He did this to me. He killed me." And the family was shocked, and silent, for in some part of ourselves, each struggling to be blind, we knew it to be true.

Lying on her bed, Anise decreed that the family should cut off all contact with the Westys. She did not explain why. Constance, rebellious and fond of Matty, rode on over to the Westys' anyway, with her new boyfriend in tow. Matty received her cordially, covering her surprise.

Matty had made a serious mistake, one that she should have been far too clever to make. She had actually fallen in love with Hiram. It was difficult not to. She had deceived herself into thinking that he would leave Anise and the girls for her, and so she had gone ahead with divorce proceedings against Shinola, with her faith held in her hand.

When Anise had commanded Hiram to return home and he had done it, leaving his shoes behind and walking the several miles home on the hot pavement, it had taken Matty off guard. For one of the few times in her life, she had been shocked. She hadn't spoken to him as he left, expecting him to return. But he hadn't returned. He hadn't called. He simply excised himself from her life with the same insolent ease that he had allowed himself to be seduced by her, those nine long years ago.

Matty had gambled and lost, and she felt the acid of it sharpening her tongue. She canceled her divorce papers, and sent for Shinola to come home. He did, without asking questions. Matty put the picture of Hiram deep in her dresser drawer, and mourned him till she died.

When Constance went home, and defiantly told her mother that she had been to see Matty, Anise raised herself from her bed and screamed for the first time since her silence, the cords in her neck humming like piano wires. She seized a water glass that was by her bedside and threw it at Constance. Constance ducked, and the glass hit the wall and broke, leaving a five-cornered wet stain and a large shard of glass, stuck in the wall.

"You will never see her again, never!" hissed Anise. "Do you understand me?"

"But, Mother, why?" said Constance, shaken.

Anise sat up and adjusted her pillows. "Do you want to know why? Do you really? I'll tell you then, since you insist. That woman tried to steal my husband. She tried to take my husband from me. She tried to take my husband from me." Her voice began as a harsh whisper and ended shrill, and she fell back onto her pillows, her head tossing back and forth.

Constance held her down on the pillow, and forced a drink of water through her clenched teeth, and sat by her stroking her hand until Anise had calmed, and fallen back to sleep.

Privately Constance understood what Hiram had done, and why. Constance was of the pragmatic bent of mind. Mother's frigid ways would drive anyone out of the house, she thought. Constance was just surprised at her father's choice. She thought he could have done ever so much better than Matty Westy.

When Demeter was sixty years old she learned a new trick. It was to ride home on her bicycle balancing a full load of groceries on the handlebars. Not bad for an old lady, she thought.

She rode home through the woods on an afternoon when the air was a strange color. A greenish grey, it was, and she thought there might be a bad storm. She pedaled energetically over the ruts in the dirt road, loving the clean rush of the air against her face, and the brooding feel of the sky.

She liked storms, always had. Storms in the Batch when she was a child had been comforting. The family had gathered on the screened sleeping porch to watch the crashing of the lightning, and the scudding sway of the few trees that grew around the house. The progress of the storm across the broad, flat plains could be marked by the gold grass bending in front of the wind as it went by.

She had felt closer to her family there, during those storms, than she ever had before or since. They came vividly before her eyes now, as she rode—Lee, grim and white-haired, Wester, kind and vague, Hiram, his face smooth as a snake. He had been so handsome, even as a boy. She remembered the flat blue bowl of the sky the day he had touched her on the hill, the nape of his neck fragile and pale.

Something had happened to him back then, she thought, something strange. She thought it had to do with the Indian woman who had come that night, so long ago. Hiram had never mentioned it, of course. None of them had. She herself had pushed the thought deep into the recesses of her furthest mind. But it rose up in her sometimes, the dreamlike stillness of that night. She felt guilty by her birth, by family. A wrong had been done, and she thought it might not easily be forgiven.

She could have done something, could have gotten up. She could have arrayed herself against the formidable eyes of her brother and her father, and gone to help that girl. The girl had around her a torn nimbus of suffering. Demeter could see that. But she had sat numbly, and done nothing.

She had seen the girl again after that, often. She had seen her in pools of water and puddles, and in fires late at night. She had seen her growing, her face changing and settling, finally aging, the flesh around her face falling, the black of her hair penciling in with ash.

Of course, that was right. That girl would age as Demeter herself was aging, as Hiram was aging. He was still handsome, with his white hair and creased brown skin. He had weathered into a new kind of beauty, different than that of his youth. But he was virile, hard and lovely as leather. In the times that Demeter had seen the girl reflected dimly in her dreams, the girl had carried something in her arms. And she had stretched out her free hand to Demeter, asking something, or giving it. Demeter did not know what it was that she wanted, but she had woken from many a restless dream, that girl's outstretched hand beneath her lids.

Something had taken place that night. Her family had turned with one face away from a gentle shadow. They had refused something, and lost something else, and never even known what it was. The thought of it filled Demeter with apprehension. She was accountable. They all were, all the ones who had sat in that room and watched the girl turn and go back into the dark night.

Demeter hit a hard rut in the road and it almost jolted her from the seat. She reached out her hand to steady the groceries that rode in front of her, and noticed that the bag was starting to tear on the side. She would have to hurry home, to beat the bag before it ripped entirely. What would she do if it ripped? She smiled to imagine herself marooned in the woods by a torn bag of groceries, kneeling in a welter of tins and brightly colored papers.

The sky was uneasy and pale, rolling over itself like a wave. Far in the distance, as she topped the rise and began the last coast towards home, she could see the solid black bank of clouds. Dipping down from it in greasy fingers, she saw three even points.

Tornadoes, they were. Any plains girl could spot a tornado in her sleep. She estimated the size and advance of the fingers, and even as she thought it, she smelled the wind of them in her teeth, a raw, vegetative smell. They had been elsewhere, then, doing damage and rooting things up. And now they hovered, waiting to dip down again and paint their dirty dishwater grey across the sky and down into the town.

The wind blew harder, almost blew her over. There were particles of dust in it now, and small sticks. She squinted her eyes and pushed harder at the pedals. She passed a small dog who was headed for home, pressed almost flat by the wind. A door banged shut, and she heard shutters flapping as she passed a house.

She turned onto her road, and looked down at the end of it, where her house was, and the machine shop. The sky was green as glass. She had never seen it such an odd color. The storm broke around her with abrupt fury, the wind howling in her ears like a whipped child. She bent over the handlebars and put all of her efforts into making it up the street and into her house, her heart racing. She was too old for this, really she was.

When she looked up she could see the tip of what must be one of the dark black storm fingers poised nearby. It looked different from just underneath, she noted. The central point of it was round, with the funnel billowing up above like rings in a pond.

She reached the house and dropped the bicycle with a breath of relief, leaving it where it lay. She headed for the storm door underneath the house, carrying the groceries in her arms, kicking at the storm trap to open it. She staggered under the sudden gusts. The wind had ripped the shutters open and the house was filling up with dust, she could see, but there was no time to secure it. Demeter was luckier than anyone she knew, and practically without fear, but she feared the storms. She hadn't seen this one coming. A lucky thing she had insisted that Fid put in this storm cellar.

The trapdoor banged shut behind her, leaving it suddenly silent, and dark. She smelled potatoes, and earth around her. It was cool. The dust of her footsteps made her sneeze. She remembered where the candles were and headed towards the shelf cautiously in the dark, still carrying the groceries. She put them down and felt along the shelf, her fingertips light as eyes. She didn't want to disturb a spider, or a rat.

She found the candles, and the matches, and struck one with relief. The thin flare lit up the tiny room, the cans piled on the side and the bottled water. Fid was such an orderly, methodical soul. He hadn't wanted to build this shelter at all, but when she had asked him, he had dug it out with his own hands and furnished it as thoroughly as could be. She could even see a can opener and a radio with a spare battery, stowed neatly in its own narrow box. What a good soul he was, and a kind man. He was in the city today, buying parts for the machine shop.

Outside, the wind raged and spat, and she hunkered down in a corner, wrapping her arms around her knees. She hadn't gotten creaky in the joints yet, thank the Lord. Her legs were still as thin and smooth as a girl's, though a little shabby around the ankles. It would have been nice to have a blanket here, but her body heat warmed the small earthen space, and the candle flame made it seem almost homey. She must remember to tell Fid that they had forgotten a blanket, she thought drowsily, letting her head fall back against the rough wall. He hadn't thought of everything after all.

She slept, and in her sleep she heard a huge grinding and a tearing, a screaming as if nails were being pulled from joists. Things ripped, and cracked, and there was a monstrous scraping in her dream, as if a bilious raccoon had raked its claws across a rock. There was a big stone like that, a white one with mica flecks in it, at the farm, she thought. She wondered vaguely how the farmhouse was weathering the storm.

The thought of the storm startled her out of her doze, and she scrambled to her feet, almost banging her head on the low earth ceiling. Fine camper she was, falling asleep in a closed space with a lighted candle. She could have burned herself to bits, and never known it. The candle had drowned itself in a pool of grease, and the wick was quite cool. She wondered how long she had been asleep.

She put her ear against the door and listened. It was very still outside. There was no noise at all, not even a bird song. When she could still her breathing she heard a choked guttering sound, like water running up from the ground.

She opened the trap a little, cautiously, and blinked at the daylight over her head. The air seemed scrubbed clean and almost reflective with golden light, particles floating in the air. She could see something strange in the large tree just outside the driveway, something white. She squinted and looked closer. It was a sink.

She shook her head and looked again. She had never seen anything so odd in her life as that sink sitting in that tree. It perched there perfectly contentedly, almost smugly, trailing a mess of copper pipes under it like the plumage of some alien bird. She swung the trap all the way open and climbed out, sneezing.

The yard seemed almost the same, although all the flowers had been mowed flat by the wind as if smacked by a huge hand. Her bicycle rested against the fence, which was missing a whole section.

But when she turned to look at the house, she saw that it was gone entirely. The back of the shop was there, only half of it, sitting in the pale gold light, bits of tubing still gleaming out just as they had been left. There was nothing where the house had been, though, nothing at all, except the foundation and a welter of rubble and boards.

Astonished, she walked out to it. She felt like a traveler on the moon, a visitor to some far-distant place that was almost like the one she knew, and yet vastly different. To just go, just like that! The entire house. It was very strange.

To her surprise, she felt a sudden lightening in her, as if her bones had been jointed with copper pincers, and only just now released. Something welled up in her, a bright tide. She waded into the rubble as if it were a surf, kicking her way through it. She recognized a pan from the kitchen, and a wad of steel wool. She kicked it into the air, and it flew about a foot.

She stretched out her arms in the middle of the mess, and shouted into the silence. Then she laughed out loud. The laughter came out of her, peal after peal, her face flushing with it and burning. She was free, free at last! She hadn't known, she had never guessed, how imprisoned she had been by that house until the moment she had seen that it was gone.

She wanted to sing, and holler, and catch hold of the lowest branch of that tree and shinny up it as she had when she was a girl, skinning her knees and her palms until she sat swaying in the very top nest of it, looking down on everything below. She wanted to sit up there next to the sink, and scream with laughter.

She didn't, though. Instead she sifted through the rubble and salvaged a few things. She found a potted plant, miraculously untouched and standing erect, not even a leaf broken. She found a pincushion and a teakettle, and she went back and picked up the steel wool that she had kicked. She made a bundle of the things and wrapped them in a piece of curtain that she found, and lashed them with the belt of her dress. She went and picked up her bicycle, and wheeled it back towards her pile. The frame had been bent a little, and it wobbled, but she could still ride it.

She balanced the pile on the front of the bicycle, and swung her leg up over the seat. She paused a moment, and looked back at the sunken concrete pit and the standing fireplace that had been her house, and she felt the laughter in her like a white bird, stretching out its wings and its long, pale neck.

Looking up at the plume of disturbed dust that still smoked in the air, just over the trees, she thought she could see the narrow soul of her mother drifting unseeing, released from its mooring at last. She blew her mother a silent kiss, and saw Lee scowl and turn her face away into the brightness of the sky.

Demeter had done her duty for so long, so long! She had come to this tiny no-account town and had swallowed her rage, her fury, her impatience, to be here near Wester and Lee. And they hadn't needed her a bit. They had never asked her for help, never asked her for a thing. But here she had been, the whole time. Good Demeter, the dutiful daughter. Even after they died, she had stayed on for them.

And all the time she had been holding Lee here, with her own wishes. She thought she had stayed here for Lee's sake, but really, she had kept Lee here for herself, here in the tiny dingy town of Patience, and in the moldering floorboards of the farmhouse, deserted now and rapidly falling to ruin. She had just never known. Never even suspected.

Demeter's burden shifted, and broke, and ran from her like water. She had never guessed until this moment how much she hated the town of Patience, the pinched, suspicious looks of her neighbors and the shabby general store. She shook her head with awe, the silence on her like a balm.

She lifted herself up onto the seat of the bicycle, and pushed down on one pedal and then the other, slowly at first, getting the feel of her awkward bundle, and then faster, coasting down the hill away from the ruin. She rode hard for the neighbor's house, to wash her face and get a drink of water and call Fid in town, to tell him that they had to build a new house.

28. Dallas

Francine was surprised at how well she continued to function during the days after Jed's death in the spring of 1972. She would look at her hands sometimes, staring at them as if the ugly, standing veins and the few darkening spots were unfamiliar to her, but amazed and grateful that they kept on doing what they did so well. She seemed to be in the grip of some unrelenting calm that kept her in. She longed for it to break.

During the day she manned the church as the floods of people poured in with their flowers and fruit and useless offerings of food. She had no idea that Jed had such a wide impact on the community.

Oh, the church had been big, and active, had become rich, but she had somehow never translated all those faces into people who would consider themselves bereaved, who would actually show up at her house with swollen eyes. Sometimes she would lock herself in the house at night and rock in her favorite rocker with her feet sticking straight out in front of her, rocking violently, and laugh until she cried.

She looked into herself for the mad pool of passion that she felt should be unleashed. She had seen the pictures of women from poor countries, shrouded to their eyes in rough black veiling, bent on their knees and wailing with a shrill, inhuman call. Keening, they called it. She had tried it a few times, alone, feeling foolish. Her voice wouldn't do that, it seemed. The registers that she commanded seemed thin and sharp, not the full-bodied wail of grief that they still knew in lands without supermarkets.

She took up knitting, to keep her hands busy. She heard that it was good to take up a hobby at such a time. She loathed knitting—it seemed fussy and grandmotherly, which she couldn't abide. But people seemed very comforted, when they came to succor the grieving widow, to find her knitting. It seemed such a normal thing to do.

William was away at college, but he came back, of course. She let him perform his awkward ministrations and tried to feel comforted, but actually wished him back at school, wearing his handsome lineman's uniform and doing whatever it was that he did on the football team.

He was a large boy—he had a blond curly crop of hair, and beamed with such bland goodwill that it was hard to refuse him anything. He had a corn-fed kind of good looks, and tanned easily in the summer. She had heard that the girls were quite wild about him.

But she could not trace in the blunt features of his face the thin-faced little boy that had fascinated her so, whom she had watched for hours, like a jewel turning in the light. That little boy had died somewhere along the way, leaving this beefy, well-meaning lunk that got underfoot. It seemed a double crime to her, a double loss.

Then there were questions to answer about the manner of Jed's passing. People had heard things, of course. They were too well mannered to say anything in her presence, but she could hear the buzz of speculation begin the minute she turned her back or left the room: ". . . and they found him . . . quite blackened . . . perfectly healthy, no one knows . . . and the windows open!" She only smiled and passed by, a ship under sail.

The doctor had told her that Jed died of a heart attack, something caused by a mysterious electrical shock. They had checked all the circuits of the room, but had not been able to find any loose wires capable of delivering the jolt that had apparently killed Jed.

The doctor was puzzled about the exact cause of death, but had assured Francine that it was not self-inflicted. There was nothing to indicate that Jed had taken his own life, and that relieved her. It would have nagged at her, had she thought that he was that unhappy, without her guessing.

It was quite sudden, of course. But Jed had been rigorous about keeping his papers in order, and she and William had been quite well provided for. Almost ridiculously well, in fact. It had been a shock when the executor of the will had informed her that she was wealthy enough to be required to pay a quarter of a million dollars in income tax several times a year. That was really quite wealthy.

She smiled a little when she thought of it, wondering how it would have sounded to the long-ago girl with the green cat eyes, who had ripped off her absurd lavender dress and stared at her naked body to figure her chances of escape. She didn't know what that girl would have thought about all this money. The girl seemed very distant, like another person that Francine had known once.

She remembered how her blood had beat so hotly in her veins then, how she had seen Jed and determined to use him for her escape, quite cold-bloodedly. How foolish she had been! And how young. She had chosen better for herself than she had known. Jed had been a good husband, considering.

She missed him quite a lot sometimes. It took her by surprise. She had felt very self-sufficient, but she hadn't counted on all the habits, all the ways that they had grown together like two trees, wrapping around so that the bark grew closed over them.

She missed odd, small things about him—the way that he cut up his fried eggs, greedily soaking up all the yellow with his toast, the way his eyes squinted shut at the edges when he smiled, the ritual way that he stood in front of the mirror and slapped his cheeks with aftershave, quite sharply, first the left one and then the right.

He had hummed a particular breathy tune while he shaved in the morning, counting up in his head all of his appointments for the day. She found herself humming that tune over and over as she worked around the house.

Then there was the matter of the church. It had been root and branch of Jed's being, born out of his body as much as William had been out of hers. Francine was at a loss to know what to do with it.

She appeared to be the only one thinking about it. The congregation seemed perfectly content to go on with the church as the center of all the community events, and herself as reigning dowager, with no one actually giving sermons. It shouldn't go on like that, she knew, but she wasn't sure what needed to be done. She promised herself that she would think about it later, when there weren't so many people around who needed comforting.

As it turned out, the decision was made without her. The parish of Dalhart, who had nominal control of the church, chose this time to make their presence felt. They selected a young preacher, a nervous man just out of seminary, to accede to Jed's throne and inherit his kingdom.

The young preacher's name was Joshua Threaby. He came to call on

Francine, shook her hand limply, and drank his tea with three lumps of sugar. He had a nasty habit of rolling his eyes up into his head to express a point. She thought him silly, and a little pathetic.

The congregation was outraged that the church powers would think to fob this effeminate, pale-skinned thing off on them. They had known the touch of a powerful master, and smelled fear like horses. This young preacher would get nowhere with them. He was a stranger, practically a foreigner. They turned their backs on Reverend Threaby, and refused to go to his sermons, and kept congregating at Francine's house, which was of course built into the back of the church. It was very disquieting to the young minister to hear distant peals of laughter through the halls from the house as he exhorted the almost empty pews in the church.

Finally he called on Francine again and pleaded with her. Another two weeks of vacant pews and he would lose his standing, perhaps lose the whole church post. It was his one big opportunity. She had to help him. He looked at her with his large eyes, which showed white all around the edges, and his nose grew pink and quivered, like a rabbit's. He rolled his eyes up into his head, and seemed about to weep.

"You must help me," he said. "For the community. They won't stay here forever, you know. They'll all go other places, start attending other sermons, and then everything Reverend Net worked for will be lost."

He had a point, she conceded. Jed had built Red Rock as an empire, and had always cherished the hope that someday William would give up his dream of professional football and come back to take over the church.

But now Francine could see perfectly well that William hadn't the slightest interest in going into church work. So it was true that if no one took the reins, the Red Rock congregation would break up and be lost. And that, she was sure, would pain Jed greatly. If he was anywhere close enough to care, which she tended to doubt.

"What is it that you want me to do?" she said. "I can't force them to attend your services, you know."

It turned out that Reverend Threaby had a plan. He explained it eagerly. What he had in mind was a sort of baroque processional, a visible sign of the passing of the power to show the community that she supported his reign. He was convinced that if they saw her walking with him across the churchyard that Jed had built, then everyone would accept him. Francine had her doubts, but she agreed to do it.

The day that was chosen for the processional walk was in early June, a hot day. The entire congregation had turned out to watch, promptly at noon. The sun was directly up in the sky, and the dry dust burned. Pinning on her hat in the hallway, Francine could hear cicadas whirring in the low grass, and people shifting from foot to foot outside, occasionally shushing whining children.

This was really a very odd thing to do, she thought, as she checked herself over once more in the mirror. But she had dressed carefully. She looked pretty smart for an old lady, in a cleverly tailored dress and a very flattering hat, just the shade of green that she favored to bring out her eyes. She felt very old, though really she was only a few years past fifty. She had brought out her most magnificent jewels to wear. The old queen, walking to the gallows! she had thought wildly, and loaded her fingers with rings.

She took a few of them off now, and laid them on the hall table. No point in looking ridiculous. Reverend Threaby was waiting for her by the door, looking pale and damp as a frog in the heat. He kept twisting his neck and loosening his collar in a gesture that she found particularly annoying.

"All right," she said, holding out her hand to him and smiling her best smile. "Let's go."

He settled her hand on his arm and smiled tremulously back, as they stepped through the door.

The memory of that walk stayed with Francine a very long time. She never forgot it. It was the strangest feeling, to be walking past all these people, faces that she knew, nodding and smiling to them, bending her neck just the right amount. She had done it for so many years, it was really her best talent. They watched her, nodding back unsmiling, and she thought she saw tears in the eyes of many that she knew.

They walked slowly, in accordance with what she figured was the dignity owed to an old matron like herself. The walk seemed endless, and the red dust puffed up and onto her gold satin shoes. She could feel the rocks of the path through the thin soles. The sun beat down on her shoulders, and still the walk went on, past the rows and rows of solemn and smiling faces.

She felt the past crowding up around her, all the faces of her past, spinning to surround her and gawk at her with gaping mouths, bone heads with bare eyes and hair falling to the ground. They were laughing, and the laughter was her own, like the night when she had seen her face in a dream, floating in front of darkness with bloody feathers, howling the loss of her youth and beauty.

She flagged for a minute, before that old pain, and then something in her straightened her back, firmed her knees. She wasn't beaten yet. No, sir! Not by a long shot. There were years in her yet, and if she wasn't what she had been, still she was here. That was more than some could say. That counted for something. She would just have to do the best she could with what she had.

She looked up to see Reverend Threaby looking down at her, concerned. He had felt her falter. Just beyond his head she could see the welcome shady hole of the church, and just in time. Someone stepped out to hand her a bouquet of flowers. They were lovely, vivid scarlet foxfire.

She smiled up at Threaby, and buried her nose in the flowers. "I think I'll give you the house along with the church," she said. "I've got a hankering to see a real city."

And that was how Francine came to take over Dallas.

29. Big Talkers Do Big Business

Shortly after Anise got up out of her bed of despair, a man knocked at the door.

She was in the kitchen when she heard the knock, and wiped her hands on her apron as she crossed the living room. She opened the door and saw, almost without surprise, that it was Tommie McCovey from West Point.

He had hardened as he aged, the youthful cut of his features fined down to planes, the skin burnt tight to his bones. His eyes were the same, brown as pools. She compared the golden flecks in his eyes to her memories, and was proud that she had remembered them so perfectly. His eyes rested on her, rueful and with something else in them that she didn't recognize.

The thing she saw in his eyes was shock. Tommie had come to see her, but hadn't expected what he found. Anise was so much changed, all of her fragility charred into rigid lines, and endurance. She looked in great pain. He thought she must have been ill.

He had his hat in his hand, and wore civilian clothes, but the habit of military dress was stamped on him. Her eyes, involuntarily, went to his left hand. He wore no wedding ring.

"May I come in?" he said, smiling.

She opened the door, automatically stepping aside.

"How are you?" he said.

She was acutely conscious suddenly of how she must look to him, the fallen skin under her jaw, her yellowed complexion, the shapeless fit of her flowered print dress. She smoothed her hair back, and caught his eyes on her.

"Fine," she said. "Just fine. Can I get you some coffee? Come and sit down." She turned to lead him into the kitchen. He followed her, watching the jerky path of her movement. She was all angles now, the delicacy he remembered turned prominent and hard. The freshness was gone, and in its place had grown a ruthlessness, the look of a survivor. Anise had turned into a woman who got things done.

They went into the blue-and-white-tiled kitchen and she snapped on the light to dispel the late-afternoon dimness. Her hands reached out for the coffee things and began putting them together automatically. He watched her.

"Hiram is out of town and the girls are at a party," she said bravely. "Amelia is in college. I got married, Tommie. I have three girls . . ."

The weight of the years fell hopelessly between them. He closed his eyes briefly to see her as he had seen her the day they met, her face laughing, her dark hair with snow in it, mired in snow to her knees. She had been twenty-five, no more, so alive, her bones slender as a bird in flight.

He crossed the kitchen and took her hands away from the coffee things, held them. Her hands were icy in his.

"Anise, I'm sorry to burst in on you like this without warning. I know it must be a terrible shock. But I was in the neighborhood, and heard that you were here. I couldn't call—I was afraid you wouldn't see me. And I have to know. After all this time, I can't be easy until I know."

He paused for a minute. "I want you to tell me the truth, and then I'll go away and never bother you again. Why didn't you ever answer my letter?"

She was looking at him endlessly, poised tense with dread.

"What letter?" she said. Her voice was toneless.

"The letter I sent asking you to marry me," he said, and he smiled down at her. "You might at least have written me back."

She sighed, and it was as if something heavy went out of her, leaving her hollow. She turned and looked out the window.

"Oh, Tommie," she said. "I never got it."

They stood silently in the kitchen. Outside a light rain began to fall.

He kept watching her eyes. The girl she had been came up in them just for a moment, floating to the surface like a fish baited to the hook. She handed him a cup of coffee.

"I never got it," she said again. "I waited and waited, but it never came."

They sat down at the kitchen table. She kept her hands in her lap.

"You married?" she said.

He nodded. "She died five years ago. Leukemia."

"I'm sorry," she said inadequately, and fell silent. Her eyes shifted to his face. She traced it hungrily, adding the new lines in it to her memory. "Children?"

"One son. A soldier, like his dad," he said. She saw his pride. "West Point this year."

"After you left," she said, leaning forward, "we went to West Point, and watched the wrestling, and they sang the Alma Mater. I thought of you."

He moved uncomfortably in his chair. "Do you have anything instead of coffee?" he said. "I've got this damned ulcer."

"Of course," she said, and got up to pour him some milk, grateful to be busy. She set it in front of him gently. He drank it down, feeling his muscles unclench.

"Thanks," he said.

There was a long silence. "Well, I'd better go," he said, and moved as if to stand up. He felt restless in this tidy kitchen with its straight lines. The years of living in hotels after his wife's death had removed the marks of domesticity from him.

She stood too, unwilling for him to go.

"Just was in town, I had heard you ended up here," he said. "I just thought I'd see, you know. About the letter."

She nodded, her eyes very wide. She came around the table to him. Almost, he kissed her. He smoothed his hand over her dark hair awkwardly, and held her to his chest for one minute, wanting to comfort her. He breathed in the faint smell of vanilla and cloves that he remembered.

He kissed the top of her head briefly, and closed his eyes.

"So long," he said, and went out blindly, bareheaded, into the rain.

Constance and Amelia both married, each to smooth-faced boys, normal boys who they thought might rescue them from the charming, exhausting eccentricities of their own family. Hiram walked both girls down the aisle, and whispered in the ear of each one that she didn't have to go through with it, that it wasn't too late.

Each boy was overshadowed by Hiram—Hiram saw to that. He would do one-handed push-ups when the boys came over, and challenge them to wild riding contests that they would always lose.

But they admired him. Everyone did.

Constance had children, a boy and a girl.

My mother, Amelia, married a man who seemed perfectly normal. For that matter, my mother seemed perfectly normal when she married him. They were both young, healthy, attractive examples of Texas stock, charmers of their peers and doers of the right. They looked well together— my father, Drake Deleon, blond, blue-eyed and firm; my mother, Amelia, gentle, dark-haired and dark-eyed. They had each been voted favorites in their high school and college classes. It was like a marriage of Mr. and Miss Congeniality, Texas style.

They moved into a tiny house and refinished it, filled it with antiques and painted their bedroom dark blue and white. My mother gave birth to

me nine months to the day after the honeymoon ended, and I was as
normal and pink-faced as everything else about their life.

It was only later that their strangeness began to erupt, the strangeness that would drive them out of Texas, to Washington and finally to
California, mythic places of which the relatives back home had heard only
strange rumors. Alone, my mother and father each upheld the status quo.
But together, they combined to fuel each other as rebels, as radicals and
artists, until their Texas folk hardly knew them.

I believe the central fact of my father's life, as of my grandmother
Anise's, was that he was born in Amarillo. The cracked and bleeding face
of that dry land shaped him as definitively as it did Anise, and in much the
same way. There was an unformed hunger in him for things he could not
find in the blowing dust. The land did not swallow him, but spat him out,
and everything he did, he did to escape its monstrous maw, the bleakness
of its spread, the flat, unlovely souls of its inhabitants.

Something touched him that passed his relatives by. He sat huddled
in the basement of the ranch house, and read books and planned his
escape. He starved for beauty, and it became a punished fever in him.

My father's father was a drunkard, and a playboy. His name was
Mance. Mance came from a family that was rigorous and dark in its
Methodism. Mance's father, Granddaddy Davis Deleon, was a fearsome
preacher, his face as long and black as his surcoat. Granddaddy Davis
abhorred drinking, dancing, dicing and levity of all sorts. He whipped and
starved his children into submission, and they lived as he lived—all except
Mance.

Mance was handsome, light-fingered and light-footed, and not to be
broken. He drank in the direction of his father, swallowing his father's
face at the bottom of every bottle. Mance played golf and gambled on his
golf games. He spent his days at the country club, drinking rum punches
and shooting dizzily at the golf tees until his eyes failed him, and he fell
down to sleep where he lay.

Granddaddy Davis cursed his eldest son, with the practiced rigor of
one used to cutting off an offending limb. Mance would go to hell, it was
decreed, for his gaming ways. And with him would go his family—Mance's
wife, his daughter and his son. It was regrettable, but there it was. The
entire family was damned.

My father grew up in the shadow of this curse, and never knew
anything outside its murk. He was accustomed to the pity of the other

family members, the way they would look at his father, and whisper. He cursed them back, as soon as he was old enough. But something of the old awe had taken root in him, and flowered in a grim nightshade.

He believed that he was cursed and would go to hell with his father, at the very same time that he dismissed it as angry nonsense. He sucked in Mance, and Granddaddy Davis, too, and the two men continued their bitter feud in his mind long after they were both dead and buried. The result of their living bones inside him was that Drake could never rebel without punishment, or conform without resentment. He shot from end to end, from black to white, from side to side, and could never view the world from the middle. He knew two voices, and neither of them was his own.

Mance never touched his son except to beat him. He saved his bright and burnished charm for the ladies in the clubhouse, and for his bridge partners. He gave his son only the back of his hand and the buckle end of his belt.

Drake's earliest memory was being whipped around in a circle at the end of that belt, as his father held him by one hand and lashed him with the other. He was four years old. He remembered his mother screaming, "You'll kill him. You'll kill him."

Drake remembered being seven years old, and watching Mance fall asleep drunk at the country club. He remembered dragging his father out to the pickup truck, slowly, by one arm, one heave at a time. He remembered loading his father into the back of the truck, and putting the key into the ignition. He didn't know how to drive, but he had watched. He was an observant little boy. He crept along the road, reaching down with his feet for the pedals. Each time he saw a car coming he pulled off the road, not knowing what to do, sweating and weeping with rage and fear. These are the memories he kept of his childhood.

When Drake turned nine, he looked carefully at his father and decided that all Mance loved was golf. So Drake took an old golf club and went out by the garage, which loomed up in the middle of the flat red plain. He took a bucket of old balls, and began to hit them against the door of the garage. When he had gone through the entire bucket, he filled it up and hit them again. He drove balls that night until after the sun went down. When he looked at his hands, he saw that they were bleeding.

He did the same the next night, and the next. He did it every night, until his aim was true and his eye knew all the ways that the ball would turn. Then he went out on the golf course, and began to play golf. He poured his anger into it, his grief, and his fear. When he was seventeen, Drake became state golf champion of Texas. He was the youngest man ever to win that trophy, and with it came a scholarship to college.

But Mance never played golf with his son, not once. Drake watched his father load his golf clubs into the pickup truck every day and drive away, and never once did the older man turn and hold out his hand to his son.

The day that Mance died, when Drake was twenty-one, Drake put away his golf clubs in the closet, and never took them out again.

He emerged from his childhood smooth-faced and golden, with an infinite capacity for deception and for presenting to the world the face he thought it wanted to see. He had a deep distrust of men, all men, and his vision of sex was a dirty and stained thing.

There were other things that had happened to him before he escaped Amarillo, darker things. He never spoke of them. They lingered in him, and festered, and blackened his view of the world.

For protection, as he grew older, he armored his slender body in a case of large muscle. It was as if he had inflated himself from the inside, so that no one could see. And the thing that he cradled so closely and invisibly was a strange thing, a thing that no one in his hometown could ever hope to understand.

Drake's soul was not raw and bloody like the beefsteak manhood of the boys who grew around him. It was a delicate and white thing, a wasp-waisted figure with a pale painted face and mournful eyes. It beckoned to him and whispered of the things of the East, the refined and rarefied dances of a people unimaginably far from Amarillo.

The Orient fascinated and drew him, as the thing most distant from the things he knew. And the soul dancer in him grew, and exerted its force, until at last it was strong enough to pull him away from the dearth of his childhood, and make him forget.

He became a lawyer after Mance died, as that seemed the expected thing to do. He hated it, and ate too much, and was fat for a while. He taught business law, and went to school, and acquired a Ph.D. in international relations. School was a marvelous place to him—his mind was quick and agile, and the strumming sounds of the ideas he heard quickened his blood, and gave him the tools he needed to escape.

The voice of Granddaddy Davis in him drove him to the law, with its linear, stacked clarity and rigid discipline. But the voice of Mance in him made him loathe the law, and kick it over. Drake didn't practice law for long.

By the early years of his marriage, Drake's rebellion was beginning to show. He grew a beard, in explicit defiance of the unspoken Dallas law that only hippies and no-goods wore beards. He moved his young family away, to Washington, where the tidal pulls of the old ways were far away.

He taught himself opera, and art. The romantic in him swelled until it was huge, and grandiose. Every grappling hook that he could set to pull himself away from the tepid plains of Amarillo he used, but he never escaped. Never quite. The bleakness of the place he had left stayed with him as a constant fear, a void in his soul, and he battled it as he would have a vigilant enemy.

Drake's vision of the world was dark, alternating with a searing loveliness. He wept over snowstorms, and protected his family from the complex morass of the world. His stance was defensive, always. He fought his way through things, not trusting that anything would be given him. Everything he had he earned, he scratched out of rock with his hands. When easy gifts were offered, he did not see them. He was an exuberant man, a passionate man. He was a frightened man.

The Oriental in his soul prodded him, and he bought a roll of rice paper, and a book on Japanese painting. He laid the roll of paper down on his living-room table, and gave it a push, so that it rolled wildly across the table and down across the floor. He made ink with an ink stone, and dipped his brush in it, and began to paint.

He sold his first painting for a hundred dollars, and determined to be an artist. He gave up his law career, and rented a studio, and painted wildly. A few years later, Amelia quit her counseling job and became an artist as well. They struggled, and worked in relative obscurity, but they made the rent. They rolled in colors and visions, and the rich patterns of things.

The Texas family heard reports of them, and wondered at their strangeness. Constance had married a man who sold automotive fixtures and made a lot of money. They moved into a flat Dallas home, huge and filled with things. Sweet Sarsaparilla, too, lived in a house with many rooms, and drove a Cadillac. Money was the foundation, for Constance and Sarsaparilla. It was what they judged by, and they were curious and lost when they watched Amelia and Drake living in a tiny apartment, driving a tiny car, scraping a living from the paintings they could sell.

But Amelia and Drake were wealthy in style. I grew up in a world that was bounded on the edges with my parents, inventive and laughing. Their studio was a marvel for a child, filled with paints and clay and beads. There was time for the things that needed doing. Living well was the best revenge, my father decided, and we lived extremely well on what we had.

He taught me opera, and to appreciate wine, to hunger for exotic, foreign parts, to wander through a museum with an educated eye, to see the delicate, somber way of things. I was held in wonder, and in riches.

Drake paid a price for his loves. Although the gambler in him was pleased at his rebellious lifestyle, the inside minister beat him with a rod of iron for the loss of security. There is nothing to fall back on, the voice of his grandfather said inside his ears. No one will catch you when you fall. And Drake had grown in the Texas way, where the mark of a man was the money he made. His art was his joy, and his curse. He never forgave it for not making him rich.

But the three of us became the perfect family that Drake had determined he would build, weeping in the basement, long ago. We were molded into one thing, and we had one opinion, one style, one belief. Sunk into a gossamer world of paintings, and sculptures, to the fine-drawn sounds of the romantic composers, we were richer than anyone we knew.

I met my grandfather when I was two. It was Easter. The light coated the trees like liquid. We were going on a horseback Easter egg hunt and picnic, at the site out in the country where my grandparents planned to build their new house outside Dallas. Everyone in the family was there, along with my grandparents' good friends Mr. and Mrs. Mosely.

My grandfather was at his very best for these large family gatherings. Flushed with the wealth of his own loins, he sparkled and entertained. He was daring and enchanting. He lived for these times. With the carefully trained eyes of the family reflecting back to him what he wanted to see, it was the triumphant finish of his dreams.

We rode to the picnic grounds, and everyone climbed off their horses. I was being led on a pony. I felt the horse, smelled the sharp scent of his skin, felt the rocking swell between my legs. I refused to get down. My hands locked on the leather lead.

The adults threatened and cajoled, insisted that I would get no eggs. My grandfather noticed me, and smiled.

"Let her stay," he said. I worshipped him from that minute.

The picnic blankets were spread, and the hampers of food were opened. Fried chicken, and round warm tomatoes, makings for sandwiches, fruit salad, cake, juice, whiskey for the men. The practiced white hands of the women lifted things out, spread them, filled empty plates, removed rinds. Everyone ate until they were full, then lay back on the blanket, staring up at the sky or out at the vista that my grandparents would see when the house was built.

My grandfather was restless and a little tinted with the whiskey. Nothing exciting enough to satisfy him was happening. He got up and slipped away over the corner of the hill, where the workmen had left their things. The family watched him go lazily, but said nothing.

They heard a buzzing, and then a roaring. Everyone sat up, not knowing what to expect. Suddenly my grandfather appeared over the brow of the hill riding a huge mowing tractor, its cutting blade flashing wickedly. He had the speed stick in his hand and he was pushing it forward, too far forward, too quickly. He came towards them, grinning and waving his hat and whooping, the tractor jostling him up and down over the blades. Everyone watched him come, motionless, as if he had sucked all the movement from the place into that tractor.

Drake watched him come, too fast, and thought: He's going to kill someone. He made a grab for me, still sitting on the horse, and pulled me down into his arms. I shrieked in protest.

Hiram came on, still with the tractor stick jammed all the way forward. Someone screamed. He ran the blades over a piece of tree stump that was lying in the way, and the razor edges chopped the hard wood into bits and spewed them into the air.

Drake watched them coming, heard a deadly hum in the air like mosquitoes. They were rotating, each piece of wood moving at incredible speed, and they soared, strangely graceful, towards the people on the blanket. Drake pressed my head down into his chest.

Everything had slowed to the speed of a dream, and he watched silently as one of the pieces of wood spun closer and closer to Mr. Mosely, who had turned and was looking at his wife, who had let out the shriek.

She was white, her hands pressed to her mouth as she watched the piece of wood flying at her husband. Hiram had drawn level with the picnickers on the tractor and was now moving by them, still grinning. The pieces of wood still floated in his wake.

The chunk nearest Mr. Mosely flew into his temple with a loud cracking sound. He slumped immediately to the ground, a strange puzzled look still on his face. Mrs. Mosely leapt to her feet, and ran to him, dropping down to huddle over his body. She screamed again.

"Pete! My God!"

The spell broke, and everyone moved. They gathered around Mr. Mosely and felt for a pulse. He lay very still, a small trickle of blood running from his temple to the ground.

Amelia ran after her father, who was still riding the tractor like a bronco, whooping and waving the hat. She ran after him through the high grasses that caught at her knees and scratched her, gold cicadas leaping up out of her way.

"Look what you've done," she shouted at him, over and over. "Look what you've done."

It was a sober party that loaded Mr. Mosely's body onto the horses and took him back, as quickly as they dared, to the cars and to the hospital. He was still breathing, but unconscious, and his eyes were dilated strangely. Mrs. Mosely sat beside him in the ambulance. She had been slapped out of her hysterics, and now huddled with her knees close to her chest, holding his cold hand.

Hiram went home, bewildered that everyone was so angry at him. It had been an accident, surely they knew that.

Mr. Mosely stayed in the hospital, locked in a coma, for a week. After that he woke, and shook his head as if trying to rid it of a weight of water. He had no hearing on one side, the side where the chunk of wood had hit him. When he tried to explain it to his wife, he was shocked at the sound of his voice—it came out slurred and slow, as if he were drunk.

Mr. Mosely never recovered his hearing, or his power of clear speech. He died just over a year later. Mrs. Mosely never visited my grandparents again.

After that time I belonged to my grandfather, and I called him Sir. I carried the memory of him wherever I went. I waited for summers, when I would be with him.

He met me at the airport when I arrived each year, standing at the arrival gate under the greenish lights. He was tall and thin, with a hat, his long legs tipped with eel-skin boots.

He had fifty pairs of boots in his closet, one made of purest-white ostrich skin, soft as cotton. He wore a diamond Mason's ring on his third finger, and a leather jacket that smelled of hay and horse's sweat.

At the house, I wanted to ride the horses. I had been waiting for a year. The grown-ups laughed and told me it was too late, but Sir took me down to the barn in the half-twilight. I could hear the cicadas.

In the barn the horses were moving in their stalls, huge shapes banging against the boards. Their breathing was loud in the darkness.

"Mitzi's been waiting for you to come back," he told me, stroking her neck. "She told me so this morning." He lifted me onto the wide, warm back. Mitzi snorted and shied, flaring her nostrils at the shadows in the barn.

My grandfather suddenly smacked the horse's rump loudly with the flat of his hand. The horse bolted, skidding around the barnyard. She broke for the gate. She hit the chest-high chain across the barn at a gallop and lifted heavily over it, landing awkwardly on the other side and pounding on down the darkened road.

I held on to her neck, dodging the tree branches that whipped down at my eyes. I could hear the faint echoes of Sir's laughter fading behind me in the barn.

He gave me gifts silently, like a lover. He gave me spurs in a box, wrapped in white tissue. They were silver arcs, with a star that spun.

He gave me a cowboy belt, hand-tooled with my name in raised letters. We went to the leather shop, where the tanned skins of whole cows hung in racks along the walls. I sniffed the air and rubbed my hands across all the sheets of leather while he talked business with Roy, who did the leatherwork. After a while they called me over.

"Which one you like, punkin?" Sir asked. He showed me tooling patterns, flowers and leaves carved into the rich dark stuff. I chose one.

Roy measured my waist, and together we picked the skin for the belt, and the color of the stain. It was weeks until it was done.

The belt arrived looking unfinished, like a headless snake. It had no buckle. Sir pulled something out of his pocket that flashed silver and blue in the sun. He fixed it onto the belt—a round buckle of silver and mother-of-pearl, inlaid with tiny squares. He watched as I laced it around my waist.

I wore it until the day I wandered into his dressing room and found a loose buckle on the counter. It was a dull grey metal oval that said "Big Talkers Do Big Business." He came in and found me weighing it in my hand. "Do you like it?" he said. "You wear it."

He gave me earrings for my birthday—tiny gold flowers with centers cut from a lump of coal. They were chips off the first piece of coal he dug from a coal mine he owned once. The coal mine went bankrupt.

The earrings are still in my jewelry box. They are tarnished, almost rusty. The day he gave them to me they looked like gold.

When we rode horses together I wore an old hat of his that was too big, and while I was riding fast through the scrub it fell off. He turned his horse and raced back to the hat, leaning out of his saddle and scooping it off the ground, whooping, never slowing down.

He rode back to me slowly, examining the hat. He pulled out his pocketknife and cut the leather thongs from my saddle, threading them into the hat to make bonnet strings. I wore my hat tilted, like his.

Whenever I was at Sir's house I stayed in the blue room. It was painted and carpeted all powder blue with a dark four-poster bed, a match-ing dresser with old-fashioned mirror and lace doilies, hatpins and tor-toiseshell combs and sepia photographs of some wasp-waisted ancestress with Gibson girl hair.

I smuggled scrawny barn kittens up to the blue room in a cardboard box, and played with them under the bed. Hanging over the bed was a picture of a cupid in a dark wood frame, pointing his arrow downward and simpering. It was given to some unfortunate young male ancestor by his mother on his eighteenth birthday, or so the story went. I always secretly thought he might have preferred a baseball.

There were photographs in the blue room that I loved. They were of my grandparents, in some unforgivably distant past. In one photo Sir and my grandmother are walking down the street. She has her hand tucked into the crook of his arm, and a book clasped against her side, like a schoolmarm. She is wearing a dark suit with a lace fichu, and a hat cocked over one eyebrow.

She is not beautiful, but her eyes are large and the brows delicate, the mouth pressed too thinly for grace. She has a delicate, practical, frigid face; she looks trim under the dark suit. Sir is dapper in a tilted straw hat with a band, a grey suit, a barbershop tie and a carnation in his lapel. They are rounding the corner of an official-looking building.

In another picture, my favorite, Sir leans confidently against a log, resplendent in a white suit and carefully knotted tie. He is almost obscenely young. He looks like a movie star. His face is sharp and watchful, his eyes shadowed. He does not smile.

When I stayed with Sir I swam in the slightly musty, tinted air of the blue room as though in a strange sea, waking up with a start. I hurried to scramble into clothes and boots and spurs like his, a cold, early-morning excitement in my stomach to think that I was really, truly there, after a grueling year of waiting. There was never time to waste. I hoarded my moments there jealously. We ate breakfast together—always raisin bran and toast with peanut butter.

My grandmother compulsively burned the toast. The house always smelled of burned toast and she was forever scraping the black bits off into the trash can. The smell of burned toast still puts me back in her kitchen. Sir, of course, never burned the toast.

He loved to carve wood, and do things with his hands. I remember him stringing a coconut shell with rubber bands to make a ukulele for me. He always carved the dates when the entire family was together on a post in the living room, and he marked my height there as I grew. Once he carved me an owl out of cedar. It was smooth, and fit into my hand.

The hours that were not spent with the horses in the barn or dogging my grandfather's steps, I spent flat on my stomach in the dim light of the dusty balcony, reading until I had a crick in my neck. I turned the thick yellowing pages of the old books carelessly, sometimes punching a hole in them with my fingernail.

From the balcony I could look down on the flat rust-colored tiles of the living room that made spurs ring out loud when you walked over them booted. The living room was built with thick hoary beams from the barn at Indian Bluff, where Sir's parents had once lived. There was a huge stone fireplace with its curved hearth, big enough for everyone to sit on and open presents at Christmas.

I loved all the parts of the house—Sir's office with the green carpet and shining dark desk, the laundry room with peeling red linoleum, the blue bathroom with the slow-flushing toilet, my grandparents' bedroom with the television that swiveled in the wall to face two rooms. There was Sir's dressing room, so full of his scent, with his fifty pairs of boots in the closet, big mirrored sliding doors and belt buckles all over the counter.

There was the kitchen, where my grandmother was always cutting up fruit salad; the porch with the creaking swing that smelled of summer, and peach ice cream; the tiny rock fishpond Sir had built, where my cousins and I swam in our underwear when we were very small. There was the dining room with the big sideboard, where the family gathered when they were all together, and Sir's big leather chair by the window, where he would rock back and put his boots up to talk on the phone, the big diamond ring on his finger glinting in the light.

Even the huge knocker on the door, almost too heavy to lift, sent out a hollow boom when you dropped it that spoke to me of lustrous, long summer days.

One morning when I was twelve, I woke at Sir's house and went downstairs. The family room was quiet, and the door to my grandparents' bedroom was open. I knocked and went in.

He stepped out from his closet, stripped to his underwear. I froze. He smiled at me, asked me a question, stretched. He had always been beautiful.

I could see what he couldn't. The crumpling of the skin, the hairless, sunken chest, the bony shoulders. His skin gave off a slightly medicinal smell. There was a line where the sun had stopped across his neck and shoulders, exposed.

I went into the pale blue bathroom and vomited with fear. He had always promised me that he would live forever.

30. The Sign of Distress

Anise went to visit Amelia in Washington, where she lived with her husband and daughter. She called Amelia into her room, the guest room, and took off her shirt. Her shoulders were bowed and fragile, the veins blue.

"I have this lump," she said, and took Amelia's hand to the place, under her arm. "I've had it for the longest time. I prayed and prayed, but it won't go away."

The cancer had taken hold of Anise's body, and the doctors recommended immediate surgery. They thought the lymph glands might be involved. Poison spread through the beating channels of Anise's veins, white cells multiplying like mosquito larvae in her blood.

She refused the operation. "God will provide," she said. She started a rigorous and heartbreaking campaign of vitamins, of organic food, of faith healers and the laying on of hands. She studied laugh therapy and the benefits of vitamin C. She sometimes only drank the juice of carrots, and sometimes beets.

Hiram only withdrew further at the news. In the dark of one night, she turned to him, tossing restlessly with the growing discomfort. "You did this to me," she said. He believed her. The horror drove him out of the house.

Demeter and Fid built their new house on a plot of land right next to Hiram and Anise's, outside Dallas. The land was shrouded with bushes, and stunted oaks, and it suited Demeter perfectly.

She felt a deep contentment there, raising up the beams with Fid.

They did all of the work themselves, levering the huge timbers into position and standing them upright with pulleys. They studied brickwork and
the construction of dry wall, and how to lay carpet. Demeter took a class
in stained glass, and filled the upper windows with rich constructions that
refracted back the sunlight in colored shards—amber and cerise, pink and
magenta and pale lime green.

She ran the wires through her hands like living things, joining them
together so that the breath of electricity could pass through. Fid handled
the copper fixtures and the plumbing. They bought chandeliers and set
track lights deep into the ceiling, so that the light would be rich and heavy
below.

Every day the house lifted itself up, and grew. Fid drove into town
and came back with the pickup full of bricks and buckets of sand for
concrete. They laid the fireplace with the native red stone, and when it was
finished cooked hot dogs in it, crouched in the half-constructed shelter
and listening to a dog howl somewhere, far away.

People said they were crazy, two old folks in their seventies building a
house with their own hands. Something would fall on them, people said,
and crush them, or they would break a hip. It would take years to finish,
and who knew if they would be alive to see the last shingle put in place?

Demeter answered those objections by putting the roof on early, and
shingling it first thing. She sat happily on top of the pitched roof, strad-
dling the long line of it, breathing the smell of pitch and cedar, nailing in
the shakes with her tiny hammer. She could see so far from there, out over
the stunted woods and the rolling pastures, past the creek and out into
another place, where G.A. rode with the carnival and pulled the gemmed
teeth of the Ferris wheel erect every night.

She feared what she saw in him, even from a distance. She could read
heart fires with her eyes closed, and his was dark, and large. She had
released a beast on the land, one who lived out all the things she had
hidden away in herself.

Lee had known it, about the boy. Demeter had watched her mother
with her son, and had seen Lee submit to something for the first time. Lee
had bent her head and taken on the darkness she had refused that night,
so long ago, when the Indian woman had come to the door and been
turned away. Demeter had never seen her mother surrender to anything at
all, anything but that.

The tornado, and watching her mother's likeness soar up into the storm-tossed air, had put Demeter at peace with the thing. What happened, would happen. But she still feared the raw bluntness of her son in the world. Although she had held upright a rule for him to grow by, he had grown some other way. And he held her blood in him, her veins like a zipper that he could slide easily, parting her into two halves. He menaced whomever he touched.

She would pay the price for him, she thought. But when she looked into the fire these days it was still, and silent, and told her nothing but the dropping of an occasional ash on the hearth. The twilight was blue-purple, and empty. It was a great irony, she reflected, that once she was old enough and wicked enough to seek the visions of her own accord, they refused to come.

She picked up her hammer again and looked over toward Hiram's house, where Anise sickened daily. There was some poison in that place, something that Demeter could not leach out. She had held up Hiram above the things that imperiled him for all these years, smoothing the places that held danger, reaching out with her shadowy hands into the visions she saw, to make it safe for him. But now there was brewing something beyond her strength, and it bred without her consent. She was growing old. They all were.

In the spring of 1977, Big Mother finally began to fail. She was ninety-nine years old, crazy as a coot and mean as a chunk of flint. Sometimes she would drum her fingers on the coverlet, close her eyes and croon hymns in her thin, cracked voice, thinking she was once more the girl she had been, the church organist with high-piled red hair and skin transparent as glass.

She cursed and screamed and ran nurses out of the house, so she lived on her own for a long time, until they caught her crossing the street with the intent to beat up her neighbor, who she believed had stolen her wheelbarrow. Finally the family moved her into an apartment not far from Anise and Hiram, with an extremely well-paid round-the-clock companion.

On her hundredth birthday Big Mother's children dutifully gathered around her for a huge celebration. They were all there, not a face missing —each child except Cumin had married, once and once only. The Frankells were an amazingly regular family. There were no divorces, no adoptions. Anise was ill, but all the other children were fit and active, though they were all in their seventies or eighties. The clan drew up around Big Mother's wheelchair, and had a banner painted. It said, "Happy Birthday—100 Years and Going Strong."

They wore ridiculous paper hats and passed around plates of ice cream, and tried to ignore Big Mother when she cursed the help and deliberately upset her punch cup in Maundy's lap.

When they lit the candles on the cake, and sang "Happy Birthday" over Big Mother's complaints, she realized that something was going on.

"What's happening?" she said irritably, pulling at Frank's sleeve.

"It's a birthday party, Mother," he said, loudly, for her failing hearing.

"Whose party?" she said.

"Why, yours, Mother," he said. He kissed her cheek. "Happy birthday."

"Well, how old am I?" she said, looking anxious.

"You are one hundred years old today," he said, and everyone blew their party horns.

"Rats," she said, and subsided into cranky silence, refusing to speak another word to anyone for the duration of the celebration. She died quietly in her sleep the next day.

After her death Frank was jubilant. It had been so long since she had been the lovely and graceful woman of his memory that he could hardly find it in him to grieve for her. He had waited so long, and been so patient, and she had abused him, every step of the way. He would get things straightened out now, all right. His Maundy would be taken care of so well that she would never want for anything.

But Big Mother's will, directing that Maundy would inherit a full share of the oil-well proceeds if Frank died first, was not enough. There were problems with the codicil he had written up, it seemed. The lawyer he had taken it to had shaken his head, and told him that whoever had drawn it up should give Frank his money back. "Not worth the paper it was written on" had been his exact words.

Those words stung Frank, loomed up in front of him every morning in the shaving mirror. Of course, he hadn't told that lawyer that he had written the codicil himself. There was no call for that. But he knew it, and the shame burned him. Seemed as if he just couldn't do anything right.

But he'd be damned if the rest of the family would find out. They all thought he was marvelous, and they'd go right on thinking that. He would see to it. It should never come out that the codicil was badly written, and failed to protect Maundy. No one would ever know, because he would cover it with another agreement. He locked himself in his study and worked on it every evening after dinner, far into the night.

This new agreement, called the '77 agreement, stipulated that all the grandchildren—Anise's children, and Marjie's, and all the rest—would deed their part of the well back to their parents, in fee simple. That meant that the parents would have full control of it, could leave it to whomever they chose. Frank hit the typewriter keys hard, making the letters come out black and clear.

That would settle Big Joe. Frank ground his teeth, thinking of his father determining the way the entire family should live generations after he was gone. He had ruled with an iron fist, that man, and he was still running Frank now, years after his death.

How did Big Joe have the right to determine that the well should pass to Big Joe's children, and then to their children, with never a thought for people like Maundy, who might be left out entirely? The will deserved to be broken. It should be broken, and it would. Frank was almost eighty years old, now. He had waited an entire lifetime to be his own man. He feared that it was too late.

He wrote up the agreement, and sent a copy of it around, explaining to everyone in the family that it was a good and necessary thing. Something to do with the oil company, he told them. Just sign it, and then the older generation will make a verbal promise to leave it to their children anyway, although there would be nothing on paper saying that they must. Who else would parents leave it to, after all, besides their children? And this was Texas, where a man's word was his bond. No reason to doubt anyone's integrity. We're all family here.

Anise called her three daughters to her sickbed, when the paper came around. She showed it to them. "Don't do this," she said, her voice unexpectedly clear, and bleak. "If you do this, you will be signing away your birthright. This well is yours, from your grandparents."

They thought she was ill, and frightened. They comforted her, and looked over the papers. It all seemed in order—and of course there was the

verbal promise, that the well would come to them in good time. To refuse
the man in the family, when he cited business reasons for such a thing,
was unthinkable. It would have been rude, it might have implied that they
wanted the well for themselves, that they needed the money. Trained to
ever-graceful submission, it never occurred to Anise's girls to refuse to
sign the '77 agreement.

Everyone signed, complacently. Anise turned her face to the wall on
the day of the signing, and refused to talk to anyone, but no one thought
much of it. After all, Frank was the clever one, and had been running the
financial affairs of the family for such a long time. He was a lawyer, and
these things were his business. It all sounded perfectly acceptable, and no
one thought twice.

Except Drake. He was a lawyer himself, and something in the language of that agreement troubled him. Still, it was none of his affair, he
told himself firmly. This was a Frankell family matter, and he was only a
grandson-in-law. It was nothing to do with him, really. With some effort,
he dismissed it from his mind.

Hiram found it more difficult to forget the matter. The stalwart refusal
of any of his own wells to hit pay dirt, the continued elusive dance of the
sands and the salt domes, the waves of black oil that undulated just out of
the reach of his vision, infuriated him and kept him awake nights, restless,
with the bitter copper taste of failure in his mouth.

In his buoyant way, Hiram had made up a story to tell the girls when
they were small, to explain why they weren't as rich as everybody else in
Dalhart. He told it for Sarsaparilla at first, but all the girls came to love it.
They demanded to hear it again and again. He told it this way:

"Well, punkin, it's like this. Your old dad's in the business of drilling
down into the ground, to find precious things. So one time I went to
Kalamazoo, to drill for essence of peppermint. The big boss told me to
expect peppermint at a depth of nine thousand feet. And if I didn't hit
peppermint, he told me to drill right on down and hit bay rum at twelve
thousand feet.

"So, I set up my rig, and spudded in and we were drilling good. Then
I met the Admirable, Estimable, Respectable, Notable, Worthy Commander and Juju Bouncer of Kalamazoo, and he invited me over for
breakfast. When I got back to the rig, I found my crew of roughnecks

sitting around just too sick and fat and lazy to move. And what do you think had happened?"

The girls always knew the answer, and they shouted it out.

"That's right," Hiram would say. "They had struck buttermilk, and they drank it all up. Well, soon came another invitation from that Admirable, Estimable, Respectable, Notable, Worthy Commander and Juju Bouncer of Kalamazoo, for me to go to lunch at his house, and so I went and told the men to stay at work and not drink any more buttermilk.

"But when I came back they had hit a well of champagne, and they were raising so much Cain I could hear them whooping off seven miles at sea. After that, I never could get them sober enough to work, so I got disgusted and went back to the Juju Bouncer's house for dinner.

"And when I came back again, I fired all the men. I cabled home for a new rig and a new crew and spudded in at a new location. I pulled up the tools one day when I was down fifteen hundred feet and found them covered with something white. Well, I thought it was more buttermilk, but then I tasted it, and what do you think it was?"

"Sweet cream!" the girls would yell.

"That's right. It was the sweetest cream you ever tasted. And I got to wondering if those heathens in Kalamazoo had ever had ice cream like the peach ice cream we make right here. So I spent all my money and bought machines, and sugar, and ice, and peaches, and had it all sent to the well of sweet cream to make ice cream. But when I got back, what do you think had happened?"

The girls were silent here, because it was a sad and somber thing.

"All that cream had soured," Hiram went on, "and so I couldn't make any ice cream after all. And that, punkin, is why we're not as rich as everybody else in Dalhart."

It was just a story he had made up, but when he thought about it, it had the ring of truth. Things had soured on him, somehow, just like a huge cache of sweet cream gone bad. Nothing that he did seemed to come off, and he floundered in a pit of debt.

It wasn't something he could reveal to anyone—his private code forbade it. "If you can make one heap of all your winnings, and risk it on one turn of pitch-and-toss, and lose, and start again at your beginnings, and never breathe a word about your loss . . ." A man didn't complain, or moan about his debts. Or even mind them, really.

The code of the wildcatter said that if you weren't in debt, it was because you weren't aggressive enough. There was no room for the timid or faint of heart in the oil fields, and it was generally agreed that there was no shame in being down on your luck one season, as long as you bounced up to ride high the next.

Hiram had seen a fellow wildcatter walk into a bank for a loan and get his sleeve caught by a banker, who insisted that the wildcatter pay off his existing loan. The oilman told the banker to go to hell.

"I haven't come here to pay you back your goddamn money, I've come to get some more!" the man roared, and the banker gave it to him. "I must be the richest of the two of us," that man later told Hiram. "I owe more than you do."

Oilmen were stubbornly self-interested and unashamed of their big losses. They never apologized or expressed a regret. To do so would have jinxed the soaring look of their luck, and his luck was the only thing any independent oilman ever had going for him.

Even with the invention of seismic devices, wildcatting remained a hit-or-miss proposition, and the blithe assurance that he was on his way to the big strike, the ability to bluff, was what saved many a wildcatter from the hole and gave others the faith to extend his loans. Appearance mattered. If you ever gave on that you were cursed, you were finished.

So Hiram floated by necessity above the rough wake of his business failures, keeping his boots polished and his hats sharply creased. He gambled with the assurance of a Texas man that his covenant with God would give him what he wanted, when he wanted it. It never occurred to him that he would fail.

But he was getting on now, and it seemed that he had made money for everyone but himself. The thought of the Frankell well, already established and producing nearly a million dollars a month, occurred to him in its full potential for the first time. He had known of its existence, but was always screened from it by the knowledge that the well would bypass him altogether, if Anise died first, and go straight to the girls.

But this '77 agreement, now—this was a horse of another color. This raised the possibility in his mind of having that well, and all the things he might do with it. He could get his rigs out of hock, and put them back to work. He could pay off the house, and buy some more horses. To be solvent, to operate on something more than paper and promises—to have something to back up his carefully groomed infallibility, so that he could stop paying the price with his migraines—well, that was something to get into a man's dreams.

Of course, it was impossible, since the '77 agreement would give the oil share only to surviving spouses who didn't have "issue," as the lawyers called it. And that left him right out, because he had issue. Three of them.

Count on Frank to make it all right for himself and his precious Maundy, and leave everyone else out in the cold, Hiram thought with disgust. He didn't get along with Frank, never had. Frank was too fussy by half, and Hiram resented the feeling he often had that Frank was talking down to him.

So Hiram wouldn't be getting anything out of the '77 agreement. But the thought had been planted, and he thirsted for that well. He wondered if there might be another way . . .

He went to see Ford Hatterly. Ford, aside from being a fellow member of the Black Horse Mounted Patrol and one of Hiram's best friends, was also the family lawyer. They understood each other. More, they were Masons together, and that bond was one that overcame other loyalties.

Hiram's father had been a Mason, and his grandfather, and he had heard tell of a story that his grandfather's house had been right in the path of Sherman, during the Civil War. His grandfather, who had come home from the front only after his leg had been lost, had herded all the women and children outside to face down the army.

The army halted, looking down from their sweating horses with contempt at the band of ragged folk. The captain raised his arm to give the command to burn the house. Two soldiers sat ready, torches lit.

But then Hiram's grandfather had stepped forward and given the Masonic sign of distress. There was a long pause, and a long silence. And then the captain of the Yankee troop gave back the answering Masonic sign of acknowledgment, and he turned and ordered his troops away. They rode off into the night, leaving the house untouched and the family weeping with relief. And that was the power of the Masons.

So Hiram went to see Ford, and they sat in Ford's pleasant leather-lined study, and talked, and sipped good whiskey.

After they had visited a while, Hiram let Ford in on what he had been thinking, and why. Hiram wondered if there was any way to get to that well, around all this issue nonsense. His own girls, he was sure, would want him to have the money. They were all well married, to good men, and he knew they wouldn't begrudge him a last fling in his old age.

They talked around the issue, and talked of other things—the success of the last mounted horse drill, and their chances of winning the state finals.

Then Ford steepled his fingers and touched them to his upper lip. "You know," he said. "You know I'm supposed to come on over to your house next month to write down Anise's will."

Hiram did know this. "Well," said Ford, "how about if you ask Anise to handle it in her will, giving control to you? Seems like if Big Mother could break old Big Joe's will by adding in a codicil, and this whole inheritance pattern is weakened by this '77 agreement, then we might get away with Anise leaving complete control to you."

That was a possibility, acknowledged Hiram, but there was a problem. He didn't say it out loud to Ford, but Ford knew. Anise didn't trust Hiram worth a damn. Not anymore. And she was quite as likely to go on fencing Hiram around with restrictions in her will as she had done during her life.

Hiram itched at the thought of it. It made him maverick, the thought of going on being controlled by this woman for years and years, until his own death. He had paid a price to father this family, had given up a lot of good times. Lord knows, Anise hadn't been any picnic in the loving area. And that he would go on paying, and serving out the terms of her mealymouthed wishes, that he would never be free of it, not until he died—it whipped him into a frenzy.

Lawlessness was a practiced state for Hiram, almost a holy thing. He had never yet seen a sign barring access to a road that hadn't compelled him to drive on it, never seen a woman forbidden him that he hadn't taken, never heard someone say something couldn't be done that he hadn't gone out and done, and devil take the hindmost.

He had never been much concerned with the law except to evade and foil it, to test his cleverness against the system. That was why he kept two sets of books—one for the IRS and one for his own personal information.

It wasn't the spirit of the law that enraged him so much as the letter of it. To be prevented from doing what he wanted by a bunch of words that had been written by lawyers he had never met—it was like being hungry and tied up with thousands of tiny threads, two feet away from a delicious meal and not able to reach it. It just didn't make any sense. And it wasn't in him to sit back and let his life be legislated by this woman as she lay dying.

"There might be another way," said Ford slowly. He explained the difference to Hiram between "fee simple" and "life estate." Fee simple meant it was yours to do with as you pleased, to spend or sell or leave it to whoever caught your fancy. Life estate meant that you had the use of it as long as you lived, but then it would go to some predetermined person.

In this case, Ford was pretty sure that Anise meant to follow the letter of Big Joe's will and leave that well to Hiram in life estate for his use, with the remainder to go to his daughters when he died. That meant pretty poor fun for Hiram—he couldn't sell it, couldn't wheel or deal with it, couldn't use it to bluff for his deals or use it as collateral for another loan, which he desperately needed. If he married again, he couldn't give it to his new wife. His hands would be tied.

But, said Ford. But . . . if they worked some language into Anise's will that was ambiguous, that might cause some doubt as to what she had meant, that might leave a little shoehorn to Hiram to wangle that well for himself, in fee simple.

All they would have to do would be to establish reasonable doubt in the court's mind as to what exactly Anise had meant, and Ford was sure the court would side with Hiram. But would there be any trouble with the girls? Ford was a little concerned about them—he was a close family friend, and had watched them grow up, really more like an uncle than anything else.

The girls wouldn't give any trouble, Hiram assured him. They were good girls, and loyal, and they would want Hiram to have the well. It was only the fool legal things that were in the way.

Just to insure it, Ford suggested, they would draw up a paper for all three girls to sign, to be sent around after Anise's death. It would simply say that each girl agreed to give her interest in the well to Hiram in fee simple, and then all the legal details would be taken care of.

Hiram agreed that it sounded like a good way to do business, complete and tidy. He clinked his glass to Ford's, and they drank to the well, and to freedom. Hiram went home that night and slept soundly for the first time in months, feeling the end of his troubles coming, so near now. He slept even through Anise's moans, and never woke up once.

31. The Wagon Sail

Anise's skull became as fragile as a bird's. She still believed that she would win, that she could vanquish the forces of negative thought that had made the cells flatten inside her, twisting together like the fingers of Little Baz's hand. She thought of Little Baz often during this time. The cancer mortified her flesh like a passion.

When she was very ill, Hiram announced that he would go on a trail ride. "You can't do this, Daddy," Constance told him. "You can't leave Mother here alone, this sick."

So he didn't go. He stayed, and resented it bitterly. The smells of the sickroom horrified him. The specter who had been his wife, the shriveled thing with the skeleton face lying moaning in the bed, repulsed him. He had no abstractions, no comforting concepts to take him through his duty. He had always been a man to reach out and seize what he wanted, to gamble on what he could get. He was not a nursemaid or a poodle, to sit by her bed.

Anise's rage at him grew daily. It was the final betrayal. He would not help her cut up the fruits and vegetables for her juices, and she was too weak to do it alone. She was forced to abandon the diet that she thought might have saved her. She saw his revulsion when he looked at her. She writhed in a stew of rage and despair and frustration.

They spoke of getting a divorce. Amelia looked down at her mother, pinned flat to the pillows by the weight of her own bones, and thought that everyone had gone mad.

"You're going to get a divorce, now?" she said. "Mother, you're ill. You can't get a divorce now."

"It may be my last chance," Anise said bitterly.

Hiram ran from himself, and struggled. He pinned himself in the last place that he knew. He went into the stable to talk with King, his beautiful black horse, gifted and gentle. Hiram rode King sometimes with only a thread for a rein, and walked him backwards down the stairs.

Hiram put both his hands flat onto King's back, and stood there for a while, with his weight braced against the horse. He felt King's ribs move softly with breath.

"If it were you sick, boy, I would never leave the stable," he said. He said it low, so that no one would hear. "Why can't I do it for my wife?"

King turned around to look at him, pressing with his nose, and whickered softly in his ear. Hiram wrestled himself, and made a decision. He would do it. He would come forward and shoulder the weight that he had been evading for years, maybe for his whole life. It was late for him to come to the art of husbandry, but he would try. He would try.

He was as good as his word. Anise had no night nurse, and so Hiram became her nurse. He sat up with her all night, every night, and worked the next day with his eyes half closed. He bent his will, in the end, to making her laugh, and cared for her gently. He was never more gentle than when he slid the point of the needle into her arm, with its relief of pain. He always measured carefully, and his hand never shook.

Anise's liver stopped working, and the doctors said that now she would surely die. Her bones had become a rack to stretch her skin. She was yellow.

While she was on her deathbed, her sister Cumin came to visit. Anise ordered the door locked, and refused to allow Cumin into the room. The family was embarrassed. They stood against the wall, looking away.

My grandmother chanted this phrase: "Every day in every way, I am getting better and better," over and over, loudly, so that her sister could hear her.

Cumin stood outside the door for a long time. She aligned the toes of her pumps, brown alligator skin with a fine sheen. They matched her bag, which had a gold clasp. She lined up her shoes so that the toes were exactly even. She waited, watching her toes. There were fine beads of moisture on her upper lip, showing through the pale pink powder.

Inside the room, my grandmother continued to chant. Her voice was growing hoarse, and rough. Finally Cumin lifted her alligator bag, straightened her collar and went away.

My grandmother Anise was stoned on morphine at this time. The morphine, and the exhaustion of her coming death, made her say strange things. They rushed and bubbled from her wasted frame with the force of long silence. She drew crystal paths in the air with her fingertips. She told truths at last, a sly, wrinkled sibyl in a pink bedgown.

She sat upright in a rollout cot tucked into the corner of the dining room. She refused at the end to be in the bedroom, where she had lain next to my grandfather for so many years. She was fragile and bald. I tucked a sprig of lilac behind one ear.

"Listen," she hissed. "I will tell you something very important. Write this down. Are you writing?"

I said that I was.

"Write this down," she insisted. She winked at me. "The most important thing to him is . . . Are you writing? The most important thing in the world to him is . . . his horse."

Then she laughed loudly, and fell back on her pillows.

My aunt Constance painted her toenails as my grandmother died. My grandmother's death took many months, and there were things to be done.

My grandmother looked at Constance for one moment during those months with great love, her dark eyes gleaming in the withered monkey face.

Constance packed another wad of cotton between her toes, and painted Coral Obsession onto the toenail of her big toe with three firm strokes: middle, left, right. She was preparing for her sister's wedding. From a wild tomboy, Constance had become the one who held upright the standard of the family. She was the rock around which the breakers struck, and subsided. She dreamed of climbing a mountain and screaming into the wind at the top.

She felt my grandmother's eyes on her face, and blushed. She screwed the cap back on the nail-polish bottle. My grandmother continued to look at her steadily, with sudden knowledge that spilled down her thin cheeks in tracks.

Constance shifted under the silence. She asked, "How you doing, sweetie?" and tucked in the bedsheets. She would later remember this. My grandmother did not often look on her daughters silently with great love.

My other aunt, Sweet Sarsaparilla, brought her young man Teddy McKinley to my grandmother's bedside. They were going to be married. Teddy had ginger-colored hair and a kind look. He sat down next to my grandmother and took her hand. It was cold. He said, "Mother, we're going to be married. What do you think of that?"

Anise looked at him and said, "Well, you know, Teddy, we've never much liked you."

There was a long silence. Sarsaparilla and Teddy went away to plan their wedding. My grandmother decided that she would live until then. Although the doctor said it was impossible for her to live without a functioning liver, she did it.

The wedding was in Constance's house. Constance filled the house with flowers the color of apricots. My cousin Rachel and I were bridesmaids. Our dresses were long, made out of shiny, clinging fabric that matched the flowers. We did our hair up in buns like the grown-up ladies, all in the same mirror.

Sarsaparilla came down through Constance's living room on my grandfather's arm. She wore a wide-brimmed white hat and a dress like the blooms on a cherry tree. My grandfather wore his cowboy hat, tilted down a little and to the side.

He leaned down and whispered in her ear, "It's not too late. You can still back out of this." Sarsaparilla went on, smiling.

My grandmother was propped on a couch, with a bank of apricot-colored flowers behind her. They had painted her face with rouge. She moved her hands restlessly in her lap. The light shone in her eyes, with their dilated pupils.

Sarsaparilla and Teddy lit candles the color of apricots. They said their vows and exchanged rings. They gave the mother of the bride and the mother of the groom each a white rose. They were married.

Anise failed quickly after the wedding. They called Amelia in Washington, and she came.

Hiram had, impossibly, begun to hurt himself. He had always been immune from pain and damage, although he did the most outrageous things. But whether it was hidden guilt that lashed at him, or whether Anise's constant prayers for him had provided protection that slipped when she became too ill to pray, the fact was that while Anise lay yellow and suffering on the rollout cot, Hiram injured himself again and again.

It started with the horses. He was riding King when the horse unaccountably slipped and fell, trapping Hiram's leg against the horse's side as

he went down. The leg had been broken, and the hip badly damaged.
Hiram was in a certain amount of pain ever after that.

He was unused to the betrayal of his body. It had always served him
so beautifully, with thoughtless grace. He didn't know how to be careful. It
was not a skill he had ever learned, and he could not learn it now. He
didn't even know that he was reckless, never having been any other way.
He was simply horrified when things began to go wrong, and he could not
hold back the slipping tide.

Then a horse reared in the barn, with Hiram on his back, and struck
Hiram's head against the barn rafters. He fell with a mild concussion, and
reinjured his leg.

In the last part of Anise's illness, he was shopping in the Safeway,
looking for some fruit that would tempt her to eat. Her system was turning in on itself like a snake, consuming itself, so that anything she ate
would make her scream with pain. But food she must have—it was not in
him to let her starve, although sometimes it seemed that it would be
kinder.

Hiram wandered the aisles under the greenish lights. He felt dazed,
as if he wasn't in his proper body. He didn't really know his way around
the grocery store. He had never had to shop—there had always been someone else to do it. First Lee, then Demeter, then Anise. Now there was no
one else to do it, and so Hiram went to do it. But it was strange to him.

He went up and down the aisles, staring. The garish colors of the
papers and packages on the shelves swam in front of his eyes, jabbering at
him like mindless things. He rubbed his forehead and tried to concentrate.
Someone banged his hip with their shopping cart, and he winced.

He wanted to escape from this place, with its long slick floors and
bright lights. But at home there was only the smell of the sickroom and
Anise, moaning and twisting on her bed in torment, trying to find a
comfortable place in the hot, rumpled sheets.

So many times he had been tempted to overfill the syringe and slide
it into her poor protruding veins, and let her be silent at last. She begged
him to do it, caught at him with her fragile hands, begged him to make the
pain stop. But he was powerless in front of the illness that worried her like
a dog. He had caused it, she said. Perhaps he should end it. So many
times, no one had been there but him. He could have done it, a hundred
times.

But something kept him from it, something always stopped him. Even when she begged him. Even when she looked up at him with vague and dimmed eyes and refused her food with matchless cunning, thinking that she would escape that way.

He had measured the narcotics carefully, exactly. He had searched for food to bring her, to tempt her into eating, even when he was no longer sure why he was doing it. Something drove him to keep her alive, even when in the late hours of his exhaustion and frustration he was tempted to pick up a pillow and lay it down over her face, gently, to stop her moans. He hadn't done it. Maybe he should have.

Now, under the surreal gleam of the Safeway lights, he was no longer sure of anything. Maybe when he went back she would be gone. Maybe she had never been at all, and he could awaken with relief. Or maybe when he went back she would be lying there in the dark, alone, her skeletal fingers reaching out and begging him to help her, help her. That seemed the most likely.

Wandering near the produce section, looking for coconuts that he could split for the milk inside—the only thing she could drink, and keep in her stomach—he slipped and fell. There was a pool of water along the floor that he had not seen. His feet went out from under him and he fell forward, hard, his head meeting the floor with a jarring crunch. He lay there, for a minute, wanting just to stay still. Next to his eyes he saw a pool of blood slowly forming on the ground.

He heard a commotion and saw feet next to his eyes, anxious voices. "Are you all right, sir?" said a young voice. He tried to say that he was, but his throat was filled with blood, and he couldn't say anything. They picked him up and took him in the back of the store, to a dark cold room that smelled of soap and ham hocks, and bandaged his nose roughly. It wouldn't stop bleeding.

Someone sat with him back there until the bleeding stopped and he felt that he could stand again. He sat dully, humiliated. He had never fallen in his memory, not like that. Not on his face. And his memory told him that he had not tried to save himself, hadn't even put out his hands to break his fall. He had just fallen, as heavy and unresisting as a tree.

When he looked in the mirror he was shocked at the way he looked. The white of the bandage across his nose stood out sharply against the flesh of both his eyes, which were beginning to swell and purple alarm-ingly. He hadn't looked this bad since that night he had fought the boy who had made a remark about Anise, the night he met her, so many ages ago. It seemed fitting, somehow.

He got up and staggered out into the night, searching for his pickup truck. When he found it he got in and sat for a long time in front of the wheel, waiting for the pounding in his chest to subside. He felt exhausted, as if his heart were pumping water through his veins instead of blood. He drove home, slowly.

When he picked Amelia up from the airport the next day, she was shocked to see the way he looked, with the bandage and his two black eyes. She had never seen him injured before. She was more horrified to hear that he had slipped at the Safeway. Hiram! At the Safeway! It was wrong, somehow, it was terribly wrong to think of him there, shopping, like any common person. And for him to fall there, to slip, to lay humiliated and bleeding, with curious housewives looking on. It shook her to her very foundations.

The lion had been felled. She was so used to him, his power, his invincibility like a charm that she had hung from and resisted all her life, that she could not bear to see him sunken. It came to her suddenly, the irresistible turning, the passage of time, the irreparable counting off of the beads. They were failing, her parents, the strong ones, who had always kept the world spun out clearly between their two hands. The balance was sliding her way to vest in her, with a clanging, closing permanence that terrified her.

She put her arms around his waist and hid her head against him, begging him in her mind to be all right again, to make it all the way it had been. Surely if she could shore him with her faith, her belief, if she could go on showing herself weak, and him unbreakable, it would all go right again. If he could see himself strong in the mirror of her eyes, then he could go on sheltering her from the horror that she felt creeping up around the edges of her vision.

But he looked back at her blankly, out of his swollen face, over the white bandage, his shoulders stooped. She saw something new in his eyes, something she had never seen there before. She puzzled over it, looking up at him. He lowered his eyes under her gaze, and she was suddenly appalled to name what she saw there. It was fear.

The night before Amelia was due to go back home, Anise was lying on her bed tossing with pain. She got up carefully, to use the bathroom. She was as angry at her body as anything. That it should betray her now, embarrass her in front of Hiram, was more than she could bear.

She had always backed herself with hard work, with discipline, determination. She had never had Hiram's charm, but she had tried to hold everything together. Now she couldn't hold anything together, not even her own body. She wondered what Matty Westy's body looked like. She wondered if Hiram longed for it now and compared it with her own, now that her own was covered with bedsores and the bones broke through the skin.

She had spent so much time, and so much effort. So much business, and for what? On her death certificate it would say "housewife." She had never done the things she wanted to do. Not any of them. She had never even finished a book. All the years, held together with gristle and ground teeth, and her husband only nursed her because he feared the scorn of his children. And she didn't want to leave her girls. She didn't want to go. She wouldn't. She wasn't ready. Nothing was done, nothing completed.

She had put so much faith in the belief that God was teaching her, was preparing her, was leading her in the ways. She had known that it would all get better, that she would not fall. Now when she closed her eyes to pray she could summon no words. There were no words left for God, now that He had gone and left her in her own private hell that smelled of medicine and the pool of her sweat. She loathed the detention camp of her broken body, and yet she would not leave it. She wouldn't give God the satisfaction. Or Hiram.

She pulled herself up and reached for her walker. It was one of her few remaining prides, that she could still get herself to the bathroom. The bedpan was a humiliation that she had fought, and avoided.

When she got up, something in her broke. Pain flooded through the holes in her bones, exquisite, eternal, crumpling her bowels and flowing up her gorge to her throat, filling her mouth with screams. She hung there, half out of bed and half hanging on to the walker, screaming and screaming, endlessly, the bloody waste flowing from her body, out of her control.

Hiram came running in from one way, and Amelia from the other. Wordlessly, he caught her in his arms and she continued to scream, her eyes locked up in her head. He thought confusedly that someone had been torturing her, her bald head and emaciated body, the stinking flow of her bowels.

Amelia went running into the kitchen in search of a large pan. They had no bedpan. She found one, and brought it back. Hiram held Anise in his arms tenderly and balanced her over the pan. After the flow of her bowels had stopped, and her screams muted to cries of fear and pain, he walked her around the room. She was so light now, she weighed almost nothing. He walked her around and sang to her softly as she wept, just as he had walked Amelia when she was a baby, sobbing with the comfortless mystery of her birth.

The next day my grandmother Anise died. As she died she dreamed that she was crouched in the red wagon with Little Baz, the sail lifted against the sky, scudding over the plains towards home. She felt the rushing motion, and flung her arms out. Little Baz put up his hand to feel the wind in the sail. "Hold on, Little Baz," she called, and she laughed to see the land sliding away from her on either side, faster and faster. "Don't you fall. Hold on, Little Baz, hold on."

32. Diamonds

Francine had a marvelous time in Dallas. She moved into an apartment in a high rise, and furnished it like a nest, wound with lovely things. It had a view, and she could look out over the whole city, practically hold it cupped in her hand. It gave her a sense of power she had never had before. She woke in the mornings and showered and decked herself in her best clothes every day, soft sheaths of silk and wool, carefully lined and cut to her figure. She wore her jewels, too. She put her hair up on her head, and had it tinted back to its original bright copper color. She lined her eyes with smoky colors, and darkened her lashes.

With her every movement she could feel the lack of eyes on her, measuring, judging, weighing eyes. She spun through her days with a marvelous lightness, like candy.

She sprang onto the Dallas scene like a set of Christmas lights. She entertained and took friends to plays, and sponsored charity events. Her hand dipped into the rich purse she had been given, and came out dripping with cash. She never had to think of her money, or nurse it. It seemed that Jed had left her so much that it took care of itself, breeding in the cold metal vaults where it lay.

She had an investment counselor, and a tax accountant, and some other very friendly gentlemen who seemed to ask for nothing more out of life than to see to her accounts. But Francine decided to take an interest in her affairs, and learn the ropes herself. The bankers were a little dismayed. They were accustomed to running the affairs of widowed ladies with a free hand.

But Francine smiled up into their faces so graciously, and leaned her weight on them, and confessed her absolute helplessness with figures, so

that even while she was absorbing the knowledge of their trade, they continued to think her charmingly dependent about the whole subject.

She learned tax law, and inheritance law, and oil law too—just in
case. She studied investment and banking, and all the processes involved
with stocks and bonds and capital preservation funds. Her shrewd mind
grasped all these things, and wrestled them into place.

She was brilliant financially, actually. Her pragmatic bent and dis-
creet paranoia, her insistence on saving things away, and her mania for
surrounding herself with things that would keep her safe, forever safe from
the grinding dirt that had reduced her mother to a weeping shadow—these
things made her a wizard with figures. If she had the chance earlier in her
life, she could perhaps have become a stockbroker, or an investment counselor, herself.

But everyone had always done everything for her. And by the time
she came to her fortune, she was long past wanting to handle other people's money. She would just handle her own now, judiciously and well.
And she would stack those bundles of dollars so high across the door that
nothing could come through to trouble her. Not ever.

She began to take control of her investments, and to direct her
bankers where things should go. Although they objected in the beginning,
her orders were veiled so skillfully as suggestions, and phrased so charmingly, that no one noticed she was actually running the whole show until
much later. And when they realized that the choices she had made were
actually paying off, they whispered among themselves that she had kind of
a charmed luck. They would even secretly invest money of their own,
where she had put hers. It always paid off for them.

Francine penetrated the rigorously tight social scene of Dallas with
hardly any effort. Her money was oil money, and had come from the
church, so the taint of newness was removed. Even in Dallas, Jed's name
had come to be known, and so she had the balance of sympathy on her
side.

But even more to her advantage was her cultivated manner of being
absolutely unobtrusive while she got her way. Not for nothing had she
spent so many years under the vicious scrutiny of women determined to
pick out her failings. She had an unerring political sense, and knew how to
maneuver.

Her special gifts were charming information out of people, and avoiding inquiries that anyone might make of her. If anyone asked a direct question, she would retreat into helpless vagueness, and tell them that she just didn't remember, didn't have any idea. And if they persisted, she would become very hurt, and make her mouth soft and her eyes round. It was an unbeatable combination, and it took her far.

She made powerful friends, wealthy friends. And the businessmen that she charmed into her pocket increased her wealth, and her feeling of security. Surely, no one could hurt her or drag her back, with these powerful people around her! Surely, now she was safe.

A certain prominent Dallas gentleman who owned many of the politicians in town fell into the habit of giving Francine a new Cadillac from his dealership every year. They made a ritual of it, had lunch and then drifted into his showroom, so that she might pick out the color she most liked. Their relationship was platonic, mostly—the gentleman just liked to sit in her lavishly padded apartment of an evening, and sip her outstandingly fine liquor, and talk business with her.

He enjoyed her eagerness to learn, and her gentle allure. He found much pleasure in instructing her innocence about the financial scene. She deftly concealed from him the fact that she could have bought and sold him several times over, and was delighted to accept his gifts.

Besides the new car every year, he gave her diamonds sometimes, and sometimes loaned her ten thousand dollars, instructed her how to invest it, and then allowed her to pay him back out of her winnings. She occasionally hosted at his dinner parties when his wife was out of town, smoothing the path of the conversation with her impeccable chat, and pouring the wine with her soft white hands. It was an amicable arrangement all around.

But Francine was far too clever to plant all of her cacti in one row. There were other businessmen, too, other friends whom she amused and entertained, and relied on completely in her helplessness. They gave her jewels sometimes, and sometimes her own box at sporting events, things for her apartments, fabulous trinkets that she set around on the polished mahogany surfaces.

They advised her and protected her investments, and loaded her with as many gifts as she would accept. And she accepted almost all—except engagement rings. She turned down some marvelous diamonds, for the simple reason that she had been married before, and roped to the wagon of someone else's pleasure. She wouldn't give up her freedom so easily, not this time.

And then, too, the thought of Jed lingered in her mind. Although she no longer missed him with the abrupt stab of new loss, she still felt a certain loyalty to him. With all his failings, he had been a fine figure of a man, a strong husband and a leader in the community. The men who offered themselves up to her now simply didn't measure up to his memory. And the businessman who was her particular friend would be displeased if she married. He had hinted that the yearly cars would stop, and the investment gifts, and even the jewels.

So she remained unmoved by her suitors' pleas, but dismissed them so warmly, pleading her mourning and her inability to love again so gently and kindly that they remained more loyal than ever, and pressed presents on her to excuse their presumption.

When she heard that Anise Frankell had died, she went to the memorial service as a matter of course. She dressed in black, and sat near the back. She saw Matty Westy there, waving her over, but ignored her. She was shocked at the gall of Matty to come here, at a time like this.

Francine had heard, of course, of Matty's affair with Hiram. Such things had a way of being passed discreetly around the closed shell of the Dallas upper crust. She had heard, also, that the news almost killed Anise, who, of course, had been among the last to know. Matty had been quite vocal about the affair to her several "confidantes," including her reasons for divorcing Shinola and her expectations that Hiram would marry her.

Francine had terminated all dealings with Matty out of respect for Anise, the minute she had heard. She didn't tell Anise anything, just counted on the network to pass her the news that Matty Westy was no longer received at Francine's house. Francine thought it was the least she could do.

But too late to save Anise. Francine pulled her veil more closely around her face and allowed herself a moment of private grief that she had never really been a close friend to Anise. She had stayed distant from her for some reason, all those years, and allowed Anise to be hornswoggled by Matty, without ever voicing her own suspicions of Matty's lack of good faith.

Of course, any interference on her part probably wouldn't have done a lick of good. By all accounts Anise had been an extraordinarily loyal soul, and anyone passing her the news of an affair between her husband and her best friend would probably have been treated to the sharp side of her tongue. Something like that was best left alone.

Still, Francine wished that she had tried, and felt a sharp stab of loss. They were all getting so old! Anise had been sixty-eight years old when she died, Francine had heard. And she herself was nearly . . . but it wouldn't do to think about that.

She looked around to see Hiram, but couldn't spot him anywhere. She hadn't seen anything of Hiram since she left Dalhart for Dallas, and he and Anise had moved out into the country. There was a slight distur-bance up front, she saw, where Anise's daughters were talking to the minister. He was nodding and looking up in the air, exasperated.

The preacher came to the altar and raised his hands for silence. "Friends," he began, "before we begin, I should tell you that Hiram couldn't be with us today. He is taking Anise's ashes somewhere to rest, his daughters tell me. It's as she would have wanted it, I'm sure."

There was a confused buzz in the congregation that settled into si-lence for the eulogy.

"Loving Anise was something like being at the wrong end of a cattle prod," the minister began. There was a ripple of fond laughter. "And how we will miss her with us, ever prodding us to do the right."

Two days later Francine took over a huge basket of peach gladioli to Hiram's house. He was sitting in a pool of sunlight by the table when Constance, his middle daughter, let her in. He barely looked up to nod when she came in and laid the flowers on the table.

He seemed bewildered, confused, quite unlike the man she had always seen him to be. She had never seen this side of him, this soft side that looked so hurt, as if the world had done him a dirty trick. It rearranged all her thinking.

She squeezed his hand and kissed him on the cheek, and he looked at her with dogged, red-rimmed eyes. He didn't know who she was, she could swear to it. He looked exhausted, just defeated. So she squeezed his hand again, gave her best wishes to the girls and went away, wishing there was something she could do.

She couldn't have known that the sight of the flowers she left upset him as nothing had since the night Anise had screamed without stopping. He left the room and refused to come into it again until the flowers had been carried away, and the window opened to clear the room of their scent. Peach gladioli were the flowers that Anise had carried down the stairs, white-faced and calm, on the day of their wedding.

After Anise died there was the problem of what to do with her remains. She had been cremated, by her own request, and her ashes resided in a handsome brass urn, to be displayed at the memorial service.

Hiram took the ashes home with him from the funeral parlor, strapping them into the seat belt next to him in the pickup, and set the urn up on the dresser when he got home.

He walked around that night feeling the presence of the urn in the room watching him. He slept uneasily, and kept waking to check if it was still there. It always was.

The next morning he left the room with relief and went to eat raisin bran and skim milk and peanut butter toast for breakfast. Automatically he reached for the vitamin bottle. Anise had always insisted. Then he paused, and put the bottle back. There was no one in the world who could make him take vitamins anymore if he didn't want to. He squared his chest and went to sit down at the table, in the sunshine, to puzzle out what to do about her ashes.

Long ago, when he had first taken her to his parents' farm as a young bride, she had made him promise they would both be buried there. He had thought it an odd request at the time, even been charmed by the strangeness of his frail new wife. Thoughts of death were alien to him. But she had insisted, so strongly that it stayed in his mind. She had even picked out a spot, and marked it. So he figured he should take her remains there.

He finished his breakfast and washed up the dishes, aware of an uncomfortable hollow feeling in his chest. The room seemed very empty, with her sickbed cleared away, and all the bottles of pills gone. It looked as if no one had lived there for years. The familiar things in the room, the chairs, the table, the television, seemed stale and weary. He opened the window, to clear out the last of the sickroom odors.

He felt oddly expectant, as if Anise would come around the corner at any moment, demanding to know if he had taken his pills. She had always been in charge—surely a thing like death wouldn't slow her down. It would be just an inconvenience for her, a brief indisposition that she would figure her way around.

He walked through the house slowly, as a stranger might. The rust tiles in the living room echoed hollowly under his feet, and the sunlight poured in through the big plate-glass window with a pale gold radiance that was almost white. The rug had been rolled back where the housekeeper had been scrubbing the floor. The fireplace sat still, the ashes cold in the grate.

Hiram picked up a photograph of the five of them—he, Anise, Constance, Amelia and Sweet Sarsaparilla. A professional photographer had come to the house to make it, and there had been much flurry among the girls as to what they should wear. The two younger girls had taken Amelia in hand and put makeup on her, more than she usually wore. She came out, shyly, and asked him how she looked. He had remarked that her eyelashes looked all gummed up. He remembered that she had looked hurt.

Actually she had looked pretty, but he hadn't been able to say that. He wished he had, now. It would have been a little thing to do. He had always had that problem with Amelia, going off and leaving her when she needed him, saying the wrong thing at the wrong time, or not saying anything at all.

She had always been so different from him, so delicate and bright. Her mind was like Anise's, he could see that from the beginning. Constance was like him, all fire and go, physical and immediate. Sarsaparilla was sweetness. But Amelia loved books, and words and ideas. The path to her was complex, and she had always baffled him.

Amelia had made him a father, and she was particularly dear to him. But he could never quite find the way to tell her. It always came out wrong, and twisted. He would see Anise in Amelia's eyes, pulled tight and pained by his distance. But he didn't know how to go closer. Sometimes she would say something to him that he didn't understand, and he would have to turn and walk away, frightened at his own inability.

Now he felt regret, as if all the girls had died with Anise. It seemed that there had not just been one death, but the death of an entire family.

When Anise's hand slipped away, it took with it the mask that she had held over his face for so long. She had molded him, to make him look as she had wanted him to. Now he took a deep breath of freedom, feeling his features rearranging themselves as they had once been, as they should have been all along.

He remembered riding down a road at night, the pedal of the car pressed flat to the floor and his mouth set in a scowl, leaning on the horn over and over. He thought that he had never felt so alive as that night, never felt the painful edges of his blood against his veins so clearly, never seen such colors in the black and white of evening.

He thought of Nakomas Sorrel, as he had not done for a long time. He wondered if she would have been different, if she would have lain there fighting the cancer with fury until she became a thing to frighten children. He wondered if she would have called for morphine, and sobbed with fear and rage. He thought not. Her choice would have had more dignity, somehow, more silvery lines.

And he allowed himself to wonder, at last, about the child that might have been born. A son, she had said. He hadn't known, then, that it would have been his only son.

He imagined his son as he might have been, tall and straight, with black eyes and black hair and a widow's peak, set just in the middle of his white forehead. His eyes would have been slanted, like hers. His hands and feet would have been large, like a young wolf. He might have run that way too, straight and slim, eating up the miles.

Hiram imagined the first fuzz of adolescence on the young man's jaw, the breaking voice, the challenging call of the young stag. It struck him suddenly, the price he had paid. He had yearned with dread for his son his entire life, and had never known it. His son had come to the door when Hiram was young, and Hiram had sent him away. Now that Hiram was old, it was too late to call his son back.

Hiram went into the bedroom and picked up the urn of ashes, walked out the door and left it unlocked, got into his pickup and started the motor. Today was the day of Anise's memorial service. He was due to be there at noon. All of the friends and family would be there. He heard a voice in his head, telling him that he must go. Must go. Must go. It chattered in his head with the cow-prod whine of Anise, telling him what to do again.

He shook his head and put the truck into gear. No one would tell him what to do anymore. He still felt the ringing feeling of unattachment, that the cord binding him had come loose. It made him a little dizzy. He felt the air on his face.

There was no one to command him, no one to tell that he was going, no one who would expect him to arrive, or worry if he never got there at all.

They might wonder where he was, when he didn't come to the memorial service. Let them wonder. He was alone now, as he had been. Like a boy. He slid back, slowly, diving among the submerged rocks of his memory, to where he had been long ago. Before the grief and the darkness had set in, before the divisions, when he had only known the straight edge of speed, and the flat blue bowl of the sky.

He put the pickup in gear and drove as he used to drive, the wind in his hair, chewing a straw that he found and humming to himself a strange tune that he remembered from long ago.

It was nearly dark the next day when Hiram arrived at the farm. He pulled up and got out slowly, carrying the urn. The place looked different than he had remembered. It was tumbled down now, with piles of gold weeds blown against the doorways. The walls sagged and the woodwork peeled, breathing out the faint smell of age in the warm sunlight. Somewhere a hinge creaked.

He walked around the side of the farmhouse, and then off into the brush. The path that he remembered was gone. He whistled to hear himself in the gathering twilight, and kicked the leaves and creepers out of his way.

The spot that Anise had picked so long ago was on top of a rise, he remembered, marked by two trees that had grown around each other. Anise had said that she hoped they would become like those trees, grown together, so that one bark covered both trees. Hiram thought of it and shuddered. It seemed to him entirely too likely that she had gotten her wish.

He went on, crashing and stumbling through the brambles. The vines caught at him, and something tore a gash in his shirt sleeve, cutting his arm. The air was rapidly cooling as the sun went down, and the night noises were beginning to sound somewhere out of the reach of his footsteps. He stumbled once and almost dropped the urn, thinking ruefully what a fool he would look, down on his knees trying to separate his wife's ashes from the dirt and rocks on the ground.

It seemed to him vaguely horrible, to think of Anise's broken body turned into ashes. But in another way it seemed clean and distant, a purifying thing. All the evil smells and erupting wetnesses were gone into the flame, charred down to a pure sifting of dust. Dust was clean. He thought it not a bad way to end up.

He remembered the gasoline flames he had courted once, when he was very young. It had seemed a wonderful wish then, to climb into the peaked gold flames. Sometimes he still wondered.

He climbed a rise that appeared in front of him. He was beginning to run out of breath, and the dark was closing in fast. Somewhere a toad croaked loudly, and it seemed to be just under his foot. With a start he moved forward, and heard another rustling just behind him.

He whirled to see what it was, and strained his eyes through the soft dimness. He couldn't see anything. Still, it had left him uneasy. Get on with it, he told himself, and get back to the pickup, with its bright lights and radio. He would stop somewhere on the way home for a cup of black coffee, and a hamburger, and maybe a piece of pie. Pecan pie.

He set his face forward again and trudged up the hill. A bramble snapped back and caught him across the cheek, leaving a scratch. A blackbird trilled in the bushes ahead. He slapped at mosquitoes, and listened for the running of the creek that he remembered had run not far from the place. He heard nothing.

He struggled up the rise and stood for a moment on the top, catching his breath. He looked for the two intertwined trees but couldn't see anything. He must be on the wrong rise. A burr had worked its way down into his boot and he put the urn down for a minute to get it out, taking off his boot and shaking it upside down, standing foolishly on one foot in the middle of the wilderness. For the first time he wondered if there was anything larger than mosquitoes in these woods.

He listened carefully and thought he could hear a whooping sound, like a large bird, in the distance. It grated on his nerves. He jammed his foot back in his boot and picked up the urn, walking faster now. He was beginning to lose his temper, and his patience. Something breathed coolly down his neck.

Hearing a rustling behind him to the right, and then to the left, he lengthened his strides and then broke into an awkward jog. There was a loud shrilling sound just underneath his feet. Panic rose in him. He was in a straight run now, crashing through brambles. The branches caught at his face with wicked fingers, tearing at him until he felt the blood run down. He cradled the urn to him with one arm and ran blindly with the other arm up in front of his face, his breath hissing in his throat.

The woods closed in around him, a black yawning mouth stretching to swallow him. He was seeing moving shapes out of the corner of each eye now, things that wailed and gibbered and followed him, wringing their hands. He could see the gable of the farmhouse rising beyond the trees and it seemed a horror, a sleeping place for things with no names. His heart expanded in his chest until he could hardly breathe.

"For God's sake, get me out of here," he said with a gasp. His chest hurt him and he leaned over, pressing it with one hand. The woods grew still, with a listening quiet.

"This is crazy," he said, out loud again, calming himself like a horse. It was good to hear a voice, even his own. He could feel the hair in his ears standing straight up, pricking for a noise. "Ridiculous. Who's ever going to know?"

He upended the urn there, just where he stood, and watched the fine dust puff up and coat the plant that grew there. Then he turned and fled back to the truck, shoved the key into the ignition with shaking hands and drove away, leaving Indian Bluff behind him. By dawn he was back across the border into Texas, full of pecan pie and doing eighty miles an hour.

Amelia was alarmed at the way Hiram looked when he came back from his trip to the farm, where he had left Anise's ashes. He was grey and routed. From the moment of his return, it had seemed as if something vital had been sapped out of his frame. He sat around the house, beaten. Amelia feared for his life.

She came into the room one evening, when he was sitting in front of the fire, staring into the flames. His hands were idle. They hung limply in his lap. She felt a stab of fear again. She must interest him in something —he must have something to do, or he would just sit here by the fire and die.

"Daddy," she said gently, sitting down next to him. "Why don't you take a trip? Why don't you use the money from the oil well, and go away somewhere?"

It took him a long time before he answered. He looked at her strangely, she thought. It was a queer, testing look.

"Maybe the Frankells wouldn't like it," he said. "They didn't want me to have that money."

Something rose up to Amelia's lips that she checked before it was spoken. "What about me, Daddy?" she almost said. "Why don't you ask how I would feel? It's my well by Big Joe's will. The well is mine."

But she didn't say anything. She wanted for him to wake up, wanted to revive him.

"What do you care what the Frankells think?" she said, forcing a cheerful tone. "You've never cared a bit what they think. You take that money and have a good time."

Hiram shifted and stirred in his chair, and she thought with relief that she had reached him.

"I might do that," he said, turning back to look at the fire again. "I just might do that."

When it came time for Anise's will to be read in Ford Hatterly's office, Constance asked her father if he wanted her to come along. He told her no.

Constance knew the depth of the toll Anise's death had taken on Hiram. She herself had been there at the sickbed, had nursed Anise loyally and driven the long miles from home to Anise's house every day without complaint.

She had paid a price for it, too—her husband, Arnold, berated her, and told Constance that her place was with her own young family, with him and their two children. He felt that her loyalty was divided, and that it must be something strange that would compel a woman to spend all that time by the bedside of her dying mother. He learned better, later, when his own mother sickened and died.

But for the time of Anise's illness, Constance had fought him. She had fought herself, too, the dragging exhaustion of cooking and caring for her own children, of the long drives, of sitting the endless hours by her mother listening to her harsh breathing and her occasional moans of pain.

Constance had never been close to her mother. She had been a creature of Hiram's, always, from the very start. He had her loyalty and her heart, and although she knew Anise was good, and upright, she felt her mother's coldness. Anise had always showed her love by doing things, by doing the right things. She had instructed Constance well in the ways of creating ambiance and atmosphere, of making celebrations and decorating shelves.

But Hiram had always had the magnetism that Anise lacked, and Constance wanted his way. She loved the way he seemed to skim over the surface of life easily. She wanted that ease for herself, and it divided her from her mother.

So she understood when Hiram had his affair—what man would not have, if faced with the choice of a frozen statue in his arms or a real, flesh-and-blood woman? The streak of amoral pragmatism in Hiram came out in Constance, as well, although Anise tried her best to temper it with church and talk of the good.

That streak was there in all three of the girls, covered with purity and right purpose of spirit. But it existed within them all the same, like a hidden vein of purple dye. There was an immediacy to their wants and needs, an ability to inflict pain and an insistence that they get what they want, regardless of the consequences. It was in their blood, and cropped out in startling places.

G.A. had it, too. In G.A. it was as if that dark and hidden vein had taken on human form. It ruled him entirely, and seemed horrifying to the more civilized branches of the family. But Constance understood him, for the directness of his action called to the same thing inside her. She had heard that he had a gun, and that he had pointed it at people who stood in the way of what he wanted. It made sense to her in a way that all the preaching of her mother had not.

When Anise died, Constance was exhausted, and sorrowful, and bleached white as bone from the witnessing of so much suffering. There was a hole, a space where the pulling and prodding of Anise used to be. But she could survive the loss. Anise had not taken Constance's heart with her when she died.

So the extremity of Hiram's grief and the height of his brokenness was a surprise to Constance. She thought he would feel as she did, the pain mixed with relief. When she offered to go with him to Ford's office for the reading of the will, it was to comfort him and also to lend the presence of someone who felt with him.

But Hiram turned down her offer of company because there was something else operating in him that even Constance didn't recognize. It was guilt.

Hiram was entirely unused to feeling guilt. It roiled in him very low, and usually he did not recognize it at all. It drove his motions, sometimes—it had driven him home, after Anise had found him with Matty. But it was not a clear-voiced thing, only a silent rumbling in his blood. And this silent rumbling now told him that he would rather not have any of the girls present when Anise's will was read.

It wasn't that they would object to the ambiguous language that Ford had written in. Probably none of them even knew enough about the law to recognize what they were hearing, or what it meant. The difference between fee simple and life estate was an esoteric thing, a legal matter.

And if they did recognize it, he told himself, they wouldn't mind. Hadn't Amelia given her permission for him to take the well? Hadn't she told him to enjoy himself, to have a good time? There couldn't have been anything more clear than her instructions. She had spoken just as he knew she would. No surprises there.

Still, there was a small, hard kernel of unease deep in Hiram. And so he went to Ford's office alone.

Ford offered him a cigar, snapping open a handsome inlaid wooden box to show Hiram a selection. Hiram picked one and bit the end off it, with satisfaction. He didn't normally smoke anymore, but a good cigar was not to be passed up. Ford lit it for him, with a heavy silver lighter.

"How you holding up, Hiram?" Ford asked with sympathy.

"Oh, you know," said Hiram, stretching out his legs. "Fine. I'm fine."

Ford knew him well enough not to ask further, and discreetly dropped his eyes down to the papers in front of him on the desk. Neither man mentioned the last matter they had discussed.

"Well, I guess we should get down to it," Ford said. "You ready?"

"Shoot," Hiram said, and leaned back in his chair and pulled his hat down over his eyes.

He listened silently as Ford read, but the anger in him mounted. He ceased feeling guilty for the little language change he had instituted—Lord above, the woman had thought of everything! She had fenced him in as thoroughly with that will as a bull to be cut, laying out the way he must keep books and pay taxes, stipulating that he might have the income during his lifetime to maintain him "not in excess of his prior standard." What did she think he was going to do, go and gamble it all away in Vegas? Live the high life on the puny little stipend she had left him?

But it was all there, all right, just as Ford had warned him. She had left him everything in life estate only, to be passed over to the daughters after he had finished up his measly, constrained, "not in excess" existence. Hiram set his teeth, feeling the shackles come down on him. She would go on controlling him forever, out of the grave or in it. He would never escape her.

Ford had been clever with the language he had worked in, almost so that no one would notice. In fact, Hiram wasn't sure that he would have noticed if he hadn't been watching for it. The will said that although Hiram had the money only for his lifetime, he also had the complete power to "manage, control, dispose of, pledge mortgage, lease, sell and convey" anything he damn well pleased, with the ability to "vest in any purchaser the absolute fee simple title."

Now that was tidy, Hiram reflected. Because, of course, if he could sell the property and give the buyer fee simple title, then he must logically have fee simple title himself. Made perfect sense, and no one in the world would argue about it.

Ford finished reading out the will. Hiram gathered his legs together and stood up, shook hands with Ford, exchanged a last few words. They stood by the door for a minute, silent. Then Ford said, "You still want to send around that document—the one to the girls, giving you fee simple?"

"Sure," said Hiram. "Do it. And as for this will, Ford—I think it would probably be easier for the girls if we just kept the actual copies of the will between you and me. No reason to clutter up their heads with this legal stuff. They got any questions, they can ask one of us."

"Sure, Hiram," said Ford. "I'll draw up that document and bring it by on Monday."

"Thanks," said Hiram. "You coming to the drill on Friday?"

"Sure," said Ford. "See you there."

So it was done. Hiram sent around a document to each of his daughters to sign. The document made reference to the estate of Anise Frankell Jameson, which was left "in fee simple to her surviving husband."

On the second page it also said the girls "admit that Hiram Jameson is entitled to succeed in fee simple to the interest of Anise Frankell Jameson in that certain oil well" and finished by stating that for the sum of ten dollars, the undersigned "release any and all claim they might have to that well now or in the future, of whatsoever kind and whatsoever nature."

Hiram enclosed a cover letter, explaining that this was just some legal business, and would the girls please sign and send back the forms by return mail.

Amelia got her copy on a Saturday afternoon, and was just sitting down to sign it when Drake came in. When she told him what she was doing, something uneasy stirred in the back of his mind.

"Let me see that for a minute," he said.

She gave it to him, and went into the kitchen to start lunch.

Drake skimmed the papers with a professional eye, and stopped with a jolt. He read the sentence again, more slowly this time. Sure enough, it said "fee simple" there. Now why would it say "fee simple," when everyone knew Anise had willed things to Hiram in life estate?

"Honey, come in here a minute," he called, and Amelia came in. She sat down, wiping her hands on a towel.

"What is it?" she said.

He read the document to her, and explained the difference between the two phrases. She sat, silent, feeling a little sick. Surely it was a mistake. Surely it was.

Amelia and Drake looked down at the paper, sitting squarely aligned, white in the middle of the dark wood table. It seemed vaguely sinister to Amelia, and she had a rushing feeling, as if all the things in her memory were jolting forward at a terrific speed. "Stay back," she wanted to tell them. "Stay back." She gripped one hand tightly with another.

"I'm sure it's a mistake," she said, keeping her voice level. "I'll just call him and ask him what he meant. He probably doesn't know the difference."

"Probably not," said Drake. But he eyed the paper again, and when he went to put it away, he slid it into a brand-new manila folder. With a red pen he marked across the top: "Frankell Family Estate—Legal Papers."

Drake took the precaution of phoning Constance and Sarsaparilla, and warning them not to sign the papers or send them back until the "fee simple" matter had been cleared up. At Constance's house he reached her husband, Arnold, and explained the whole thing to him.

Arnold understood perfectly. Drake found it a strange relief to talk to another man, another son-in-law and outsider in the Frankell family, who might be willing to entertain suspicions of Hiram's motives. Amelia was so completely hornswoggled by her father that she couldn't talk rationally about the whole thing. She just insisted hysterically that it must be a mistake, and that she wouldn't listen to a word against her father.

Arnold agreed with Drake's view of the situation, and admitted that it made him a little uncomfortable, as well.

"I'll tell you something else, Drake," Arnold said, shielding the phone with his hand and glancing up unconsciously to see if Constance was around. "Hiram has been signing Anise's name to the checks that Texoil is sending, and cashing them. They don't know she's dead."

Drake was struck dumb by this news. At the death of a recipient of oil dividends, those checks were supposed to be tucked neatly away into an escrow fund, until the will was probated and all the inheritance details straightened out. If what Arnold was saying was true, Hiram was guilty at least of forgery and impeding due process, and possibly theft. What could the man be thinking?

Drake was a lawyer. He played strictly by the rules and abided by the laws, and the thought of Hiram wending his lightsome way through the morass of red tape by committing a forgery or two made his blood begin to heat. His sense of fair play was outraged.

And then there was something else, something older and darker, that rose with fear and trembling, and wore a familiar face, in an unlit shed. It came with the memory of smothered moans, and blood, and the smell of rust. Fathers were not to be trusted. Not his father. Not Amelia's father. Not anyone.

"I didn't know that," Drake said, and his voice was tight. "Are you sure?"

"Sure as shooting," Arnold told him. "My father has contacts at Texoil. You know my dad?"

Drake did. Arnold's father was named Travis Daw, and he and Arnold were as alike as two men could be. Arnold worked in Travis' firm, and Arnold's son would work there too, when he was old enough. Arnold and Travis were tied with a direct umbilical cord—what one of them thought, the other thought as well.

"Sure, I know your dad," said Drake.

"Well, my dad thinks somebody ought to notify Texoil about Anise's death. Said he was thinking about doing it himself," said Arnold.

"I understand," Drake said. "Thanks for telling me. I'll be in touch."

Hiram was dismayed when he got the letter from Amelia asking what he meant by the fee simple document he had sent around. She had sent a businesslike letter, brief and to the point, and Hiram would bet his back teeth that Amelia hadn't written it. It had the crisp imprint of Drake's voice in it. Hiram was shocked upright by being at the business end of something that smelled like a lawyer.

The seed of discomfort that had been in him rose and hardened, and became anger. He was angry that his daughter would sign her name to a letter written by her husband, with that accusing tone. Drake wasn't concerned in this, anyhow. He had no business putting himself where he didn't belong.

It seemed that Drake had stolen Amelia's loyalty—stolen it to the point that she would do anything Drake said. That was gratitude for you. Raise up a child and then watch her turn on you.

Hiram had misgivings from the start when Amelia had decided to marry Drake, clean-shaven and personable as he was. He was a lawyer, and Hiram had never trusted lawyers. It seemed to him that good intentions and a handshake should be good enough for anyone trustworthy, and a lawyer's insistence that they get everything on paper just proved that they weren't to be trusted. Besides which, this put him in a cursed uncomfortable position.

He called Ford Hatterly, and read Drake's letter to him. There was a long silence on the other end of the phone. Ford said, "Damn, Hiram, you said the girls wouldn't mind."

"They don't," Hiram said. "It's just that damn lawyer that Amelia married."

"Well, pull back, for God's sake," said Ford. "We don't want a mess on our hands."

Hiram called all three girls and told them to never mind the thing he had sent around. He hadn't quite gotten everything straight. But there was nothing to worry about, it was all just legal Texoil things, oil stuff, and they shouldn't be concerned. He joshed them and joked, and they all went back to forgetfulness.

Except Drake. The thing that had startled him awake stayed in his mind, and he began to think back through all of the strange things that had happened, the strange documents sent around, the bizarre paper that Frank had made all the children and grandchildren sign. There was something here that he didn't understand, and he wanted to get to the bottom of it.

He was protective of Amelia's inheritance, not only because it was hers and she was entitled to it, but because they needed that money.

Drake's paintings were large, strange and luminous, and spoke vividly of another world, slightly above and behind this one. They poured out of him in magnificent bursts, and floated in his dreams. All the craving for beauty from his starved time poured from his fingertips into those paintings, and shone suspended there like jewels. People who knew would gaze captivated into the depths of those paintings, and read the strange symbols in them, and dig up the money to buy one and take it home.

But those people were rare. Far more common were the housewives with wealthy husbands who complained that the painting didn't match their sofa. Drake wore himself weary taking the paintings up and down on pastel walls, where women would squint at them and refuse them, because of the carpet.

So the sales came infrequently, and meantime there was food to buy and rent to pay and his daughter, who needed clothes and clarinet lessons and new bathing suits, and who would have to go to college. Drake lay awake nights and stared at the ceiling in dread, trying to figure how it would all be done, wondering which painting hanging on his studio walls would sell and pay the next month's rent. There was nothing in reserve, no savings. Only Drake's sweat and essence kept his family on the tightrope, away from the void that loomed under him, the horrible emptiness he could feel chewing at his bones.

That inheritance would someday mean that his wife and child could be safe, and secure. His daughter would go to a good school, and Amelia would have the trip to Italy that she longed for. Meantime, he cringed with shame when his daughter came home and told of a coat she had seen, a coat of honey-colored fur, with a gold hood. She talked of it only as something beautiful she had seen, with no hope of owning it.

Drake took the money he had been saving for paints, and drove to the store and bought the coat, and put it in the closet. Just before she went to bed he asked her to describe it again, and listened to her story of how the fur hood went around her face, how it was a princess coat. He went to the closet and pulled it out.

"Was it like this?" he asked, and was well rewarded by her face.

She slept with the coat that night, and Drake stayed up with his ledger book, trying to find the places to trim back. He went over them again and again, over and over, until the sun came up and Amelia found him there asleep on the table, his head on his arm over the accounts. She gently pulled the book out from under him and led him to bed, where he dreamed of coats and paints and the dreadful emptiness that hunted his family through a murky enchanted wood.

33. The Ladies' Heels

The next time that Francine saw Hiram was in a hardware store, several months later. One of her well-concealed talents was a gift for handiwork around the house. Although she would have died rather than let anyone see her taking apart pipes or handling a wrench with anything approaching confidence, she secretly enjoyed putting on her overalls and blunting her nails against the inner working of the sink or bathtub. It was a secret that she paid her manicurist well to conceal.

She loved to wander inside the hardware store, running her fingers through the brightly colored bins of nuts and bolts, gleaming and neat in their places, the huge bins of chain and rope, the wealth of light bulbs and cans of spray paint. It gave her a feeling of comfort and security, the vast masses of things in the world that were named and numbered, that she could buy if she chose. The order of it calmed her.

She was looking for a 5/16-inch screw when she came around the corner and saw Hiram Jameson standing there, one hand in his pocket and the other idly handling a piece of copper tubing. He was saying something to a salesgirl, and Francine could see by the way that the girl was blushing and ducking her head that he was laying on the charm. He must be recovered, then.

She moved closer to hear the tail end of the conversation, and the girl's eyes flicked up to her guiltily. Hiram followed her eyes and turned around, almost bumping into her.

"Well, hello there," he said to Francine. "Thank you very much, Marcie," he said over his shoulder to the girl, dismissing her. "You've been a big help." She left, smiling back over her shoulder.

He turned his attention to Francine. His eyes were clear again, she saw, clear and as bright blue as they had been. But there was still a crack in him, right through to the core. He had been shivered to his core, and the fault remained. He had lost the impeccable glossy hardness that he had once had. Why, he must have really loved Anise, Francine thought, pityingly. I wonder if he knew.

"What a pleasant surprise, to meet a pretty little gal like you in a place like this," he said, smiling down at her. "I must have done something good today."

She shuddered a little under the unleashed force of his magnetism, and was surprised at herself. It wasn't as if she was a schoolgirl, after all. She had seen quite a bit of the world. But only one other time had she ever had his full attention trained on her like this, all to herself. It occurred to her with a shock that they were both single now, that there was nothing standing between them, nothing at all. The thought alarmed her, and she began to back down the aisle, her composure slipping.

"It's lovely to see you, too," she said. "I'm glad to see you're up and around again—you're looking well, so much better than the last time I saw you." She stopped, embarrassed, and could have bitten out her tongue. A fine thing, to remind him of that, now.

But it didn't seem to bother him too much. He sobered, but the light stayed in his eyes. "That's right now, you came by the house with those flowers," he said. "It was awful good of you."

There was an awkward silence, and then they both spoke at the same time. She blushed and insisted that he go ahead.

"I was wondering if I could thank you by taking you on a horseback ride," he said gravely, his voice a little mocking. "I've got the best-looking horses in town, and they would surely be honored to meet a lady to match."

"Well," she temporized, "I don't know. I'll just have to look at my schedule and see. I have so many of these silly fund-raising things to do, you just have no idea how unreasonable . . ."

She stopped because he was standing very close to her, and it was making her knees feel a little strange.

"Say you'll come," he said, very softly. "I could use a lovely lady friend, right now."

"I'll come," she heard herself say. "I'll be there."

He released her hand and set a date and gave her directions to his place, out in the country, and she paid for her things in a daze and left, not realizing until she got to her car that she had forgotten the thing she came to the store to get.

She swore softly, under her breath. How had she gotten into this? The last thing she needed right now was a bereaved widower, who would be a sponge to suck up every last bit of time and attention she had. There was no room for something like that in her life now. She was far too busy.

She looked up in the mirror to check her hair, and was angry at how old she looked, how puffy and aged. She would have to do her hair again, the roots were showing. And she began to rummage quickly through her closet in her mind, imagining what in the world she could possibly wear to do something so ridiculous as horseback riding.

Hiram went home floating several feet above the ground. It was odd. It was queer. It was a feeling he hadn't felt in—well, many years. Leave it at that.

He glanced up into the mirror of the pickup, taking off his hat and sliding it into the special rack he had installed on the ceiling of the truck, just the right size for a Stetson. He ran a hand over his hair, and looked experimentally at his teeth. His hair was all silver and grey now, but his teeth were pretty good. Like a sturdy horse. He was holding up all right, aside from his hip, and an occasional shortness of breath.

He drove home and hummed, because he felt like humming. When he got there he walked around the grounds restlessly, feeling a surging in his boots that ran right up through his body. He stopped to look at the petunia bed, which had become draggled and neglected since Anise's death. He decided that he would have someone come in and tidy it up. Maybe Constance would do it. She liked to garden.

Whistling, he went upstairs to take another shower, and went for a long ride by himself. King was in a good mood, feisty and wanting to go. He let the horse have his head as they crossed over the Thousand Acres, loping gently over the rise of the hill so that he could see all the rust and gold ground, scattered with rough bushes and gopher holes.

Hiram felt his heart strain and expand, as if it would burst, and he stopped King on the very top of the rise, looking out over it. He felt a feeling, a strange feeling. It was like something he might feel in church, except that he wasn't really a churchgoing man.

The land flooded up through King and into Hiram, up his legs, through his sore hip and up his chest, out into his arms so that he wanted to fling them out, embracing the sky, and the sorry hard ground. He didn't, though. He sat motionless on the horse, letting that joyful feeling run through him, and then he went to the arena and galloped King around and around, pushing him, riding without hands, swooping around using only his balance and his knees to tell the horse where to go.

King paced through his drills perfectly, his dark eyes wide with understanding. Hiram rode him home and wiped him down and curried him for a long time, picking up each hoof to check it for stones, rubbing King's coat until it gleamed with red lights. Then he turned the magnificent horse out into the pasture and watched him walk sedately away, the wind ruffling the short mane, the horse's hips swaying like a woman's. Hiram rubbed his hands together and went to make himself a cheese and walnut and pickle relish sandwich for dinner.

He had suggested a sunset ride to Francine, and so she came over on the agreed day the next week, looking cool and easy in her jeans and the soft pink shirt that she wore. He watched the way it stole around her throat, like the petals of a flower.

He was uneasy, his charm having failed him for a moment as he helped her out of the car. They were both very jovial and bright, talking a little too loudly. A couple of times they said things at the same time and then had to stop, and laugh. He felt a fine strain over him, as if there were a net around him that was being pulled tight. He wanted so much for it to go well.

They rode quietly in the sunset, still at last, and stood on the top of the rise where he had ridden before. She looked out over the plain, dry and filled with gorse, and understood his feeling for the land. It filled her with peace, and with pity, and with something else that she couldn't quite put a name to. He reached out and held her hand, as they sat there, the horses blowing gently and shifting from side to side, and watched the darkness come.

Later, at the house, as he fixed them drinks, the unease descended on him again. Damn, he was so old. The years had crept around him as softly as spiders, spinning him into a crust that only hardened suddenly, when he tried to move. So many years were gone by, and what did he have to offer her now, now that his youth was gone? There would be no children, no growing old together, maybe not many years. He was seventy. What did he have left?

But he longed towards her, sitting on the couch in the dim room with her head turned towards him expectantly. She, too, had aged, and he wanted to stretch out his hand to keep that from her. The flaming beauty she had, the unspoken breath of sex that had moved with her when she moved, had banked now into a comfortable and padded charm. But charm she had, and her hair in this light was as bright as it had been. In daylight it showed the dye, and sometimes the roots.

But he loved her for the vanity that had kept her at the mirror, fighting the passage of time with her hairbrush and her dye bottle. It was a valiant stand that she took. They had wasted so much time, the two of them. Surely there was no one who would begrudge them the little that they had left.

He went back and sat down next to her on the couch, handed her the drink. She set it down and turned back to look at him, her hand coming up to trace across his jawline. It was faded now, the skin hanging down from it, but she could see behind it the hard bright line that she remembered, the young man she had known. And the man he was, grizzled and tanned and tamed a little, made her blood race brightly in her veins. His body was lean and sat on him with the ease of long practice, a blue jean jacket worn with seasons into a lovely thing.

"I'm too old to pretend, Hiram," she said, and she leaned forward to kiss him, and it was just as she had imagined that it might be, all those many years ago.

It was the beginning of a sweet time for both of them—their last time, and their best. Francine drove out to the house almost every day, and they rode together, and she took Hiram into the city for lunches and plays. He didn't have any money to spare, she figured that out immediately. So the high-flung life she had been leading, the long dinners at five-star restaurants and black-tie appearances at the symphony and opera, had to be curtailed. It wasn't his thing, anyway. He was more comfortable at home, in his riding clothes, and she loved him for it.

He worked hard to make their time amusing, on the budget that he could afford. He was too proud to use her money, and so they pooled what they had, and played with that. It made him ashamed, that he couldn't give her what she wanted. She told him that she only wanted to be with him, and didn't care for the other things. But she saw that he felt it, and didn't know how to ease his shame.

Sometimes she was crafty, and plotted to pay for their dinners for his birthday, or special occasions. One of these times they went to a very posh place, where the valet took their cars. Standing at the entrance afterwards, they watched as all of the cars rolled out, shining—the Cadillacs and the Rolls-Royces, the Mercedeses and the Lincolns. Then came Hiram's dark blue pickup. He had washed it, but it looked strange sitting there with all the others.

He cringed a little as they got in. He leaned over and kissed her cheek. "Ain't you glad to have a man with a sexy blue pickup, instead of all those stuck-up kind of cars?" he said, and she told him she was. But he was silent all the way home.

He told Francine things that he had never told anyone. Anise had held him away, with her preaching ways, and the girls had been too young, and his men friends had too much at stake in competition with him. He had never really had a confidante, his whole life. But he could talk to Francine. She came to him after the storm, and he had been tempered by what happened, and softened a little.

He confessed his debts to her. Over a million dollars that he owed, and no way to pay it off without more capital, to put things in motion. The house had been mortgaged twice, and the revenue from Anise's estate was limited, and his hands were tied. Really, he had only his social security, and a few small investments. He told her lightly, but she heard the bitterness.

The businessman had stopped giving her a new car every year, as she had known he would. She didn't regret it. But Hiram wanted to give her the things she had given up for his sake. He longed to hang her with jewels, diamonds the size of walnuts, shining silks and fast motorcars, with leather insides.

He had never wanted to give Anise gifts like this. He felt, looking back, that she had extracted things from him with the thin milk of duty. He had always been hard put to remember her birthday. Or anyone's birthday, for that matter.

But now he looked at Francine and the things welled up in him that he wanted for her. He wanted to make her safe, and secure, to tower over her and keep her from the storm. It galled him ceaselessly that it was her money that was their safety. He could not refuse it when she offered to pay off his million-dollar debt, but it left him beholden to her, and that was the most shaming thing of all. He determined that he had to get his hands on some money, whether he had to beg it or steal it. There must be a way.

He asked her to marry him knowing that he hadn't anything to give her, or leave her, and that it would be insane for her to legally link her millions to his estate, shoddy and makeshift as it was. But he had to ask her. And she said yes, laying her head on his arm so gently that he had to look up at the ceiling and clear his throat.

They were married on a sunny afternoon in June, in a tiny wooden church on top of a hill. The parking lot for the church was at the bottom of the hill, with only a gravel road connecting them. Francine drew the owner of the church aside, and explained to him that she was worried about the ladies in her party climbing the hill, that the road would ruin their heels.

Such was her charm, and her helplessness, that the owner begged her to allow him to have the road paved, at his own expense. She graciously agreed. It cost him ten thousand dollars.

So the road was paved, and the ladies climbed lightly in their bright dresses and shoes dyed to match. The whole of Red Rock Church turned out, and Reverend Threaby presided, rolling up his eyes in his head and speaking out the words in a timorous voice.

Reverend Threaby had become an accepted and popular preacher at Red Rock, although he never achieved the standing that Jed had. It struck Francine, with a moment's strangeness, that Jed's successor should be presiding over her second marriage. But she dismissed it. She was happy today, happy as she hadn't been in years. Her dress was a very light peach-

colored satin, and floated around her as she had once dreamed that a dancing dress would do.

Hiram wore a dark suit, and a white shirt, and his beautiful polished boots. He was so handsome, so lean and angular, with his silver temples showing under his hat, that she was amazed. She carried a bouquet of white roses, and cried during the ceremony, and turned her face up to his at the end with a full heart, as his wife.

34. Poker

Francine faced her three made-to-order, grown daughters with mixed feelings. They were lovely girls, all. She had watched them growing up, seen them married and knew them a little, from a distance. Now they were family, and it was all different.

She listened to Hiram talk about Amelia, so far away. He felt Amelia turning away from him, and listening to her lawyer husband. There was a good deal of awkwardness that had to do with Anise's will, apparently. Francine didn't listen too closely, because it seemed indelicate.

And anyway, she had many other things on her mind—settling into the new house, redecorating it in a way that would suit both Hiram and herself. He was attached to its frumpy, square furniture, but wanted her to have her way in everything. She settled finally on something that she thought a nice balance, knocked out a few walls and opened up the kitchen, but kept most of the things and the feel of the place. There was a horrid old laundry room, with red linoleum tiles, that she pulled out, and a blue bedroom upstairs filled with Anise's old things that she wanted cleared up.

She invited the girls to come and get the things that they wanted of Anise's, wanting to tread very gingerly on that ground. The girls had mostly been very kind and welcoming, for Hiram's sake, but it hadn't been that long since Anise's death, and she could understand that they might be feeling a little delicate about the whole thing. She made her overtures to them warm and gracious, but not pushy. She was so happy that she could afford to wait.

They came and collected the things they wanted. Amelia was in Washington, of course, and couldn't come, so she didn't get anything. The other girls packed some things for her into a box that they thought she might want. But the only things Amelia really wanted, Anise's wedding ring and a set of fruit knives, were lost somewhere in the shuffle.

Truth was, after the girls had gone through and picked out their part, Francine figured that the rest of it was hers, to do with as she pleased. She moved some of it to her son William's house, in Houston, and stored it in his attic. Some of it she sold, and some of it she kept. When the girls would come to her later, asking where this or that heirloom had gone, she couldn't be bothered to hunt it up. And anyway, she figured that if they wanted it, they should have taken it when she offered. Now it was hers. It added to the things that she kept from Jed's house, all the things that surrounded her and made her feel safe. Hiram had little else to leave her—she thought she was entitled.

"Where are the family paintings?" they asked her. "Where is the silver? The books?"

"I forget," she would say absently. "I just can't remember." And it honestly seemed to her that she had as much right to those things as the girls, though they had been in the Frankell family for generations. She was bewildered when the girls asked for the things with such emotion, saying that they wanted their family heirlooms back. Wasn't she part of the family now too?

Meantime she and Hiram wore matching cowboy shirts, and rode, and went to all the Masons' activities. Francine sank herself into the business of being a wife as she hadn't ever really been before, and hugged all of its restrictions gladly. The very ordinariness of staying home and making dinner, going outside and striking the dinner bell to ring Hiram in from the paddock, seemed marvelous to her, after all the years of eating out. But Hiram still worried, and fretted over the money.

For the moment, Texoil didn't know of Anise's death. He had seen to that, by signing the checks and cashing them when they came in. It seemed to make sense to Hiram—Anise would want him to have the money to live on, and her signature on the checks was really just a technicality. After all, their property was mostly joint property, and their checking accounts had been joined, and he was her executor.

Besides, he was aware that the minute he stopped signing the checks and told Texoil that Anise was dead, control of that well would pass to his daughters, and the checks would be sent to them. In the '77 agreement they had said they would give him the proceeds of the well, even granted him control of it. But still, the checks would come to them first. They would be giving him money, doling it out to him. The thought of living on his daughters' charity was galling.

He fretted over it like a dog with a burr. Then one day Francine saw him come in from collecting the mail with a strange look on his face.

Odd things were happening with Anise's family, the Frankells. He had told Francine a little, about Big Joe and Big Mother's will, and the '77 agreement. Though she found most of it unpleasant and technical, she listened sympathetically.

Now it seemed that Drake, Amelia's husband, had found a huge and nasty loophole in the '77 agreement that everyone had signed. Apparently, by reversing the normal inheritance process, by children deeding the oil well back to their parents, the family stood to pay millions of dollars in inheritance taxes to the government. No one had foreseen this complication, of course.

It seemed to Francine that Anise's brother Frank must have been a pretty poor lawyer, not to predict this hitch in the process. But Hiram had explained to her that Frank was crazy to protect his wife, Maundy, and so had perhaps overlooked some of the fine print of the business. He could understand that position himself lately, he told her, kissing her cheek.

But in any case, the fact remained that unless the family did something, quickly, to reverse that disastrous contract, they would all stand liable to pay millions of dollars that none of them had. The only thing to do, Drake had suggested after consulting with another lawyer, was for everyone to sign another piece of paper agreeing that it had all been a ghastly mistake, and that they wanted to rescind the '77 agreement.

If everyone signed, the agreement would simply cease to exist. But it had to be unanimous. If even one person refused to sign, then the whole thing would go to court. Everyone would be liable to pay the taxes, and everything would be a dreadful mess. Of course, everyone would sign.

But Hiram was standing there thinking, holding the paper in his hand. It occurred to him that this might be an opportunity, a chance for him to bluff himself into some much-needed cash.

He reasoned it this way: It wasn't really his daughters that were keeping him from the oil well—it was just that lawyer Drake. Whereas Hiram was sure that, alone, Amelia would have signed that well over to him in fee simple immediately, Drake had gotten in the way and turned her thinking around.

Drake played a man's game, a lawyer's game. All right, thought Hiram, two of us can play at that. Supposing we imagine this whole thing as a giant poker game. Now you've got control of something I want—that oil well.

And thanks to this latest development, I have something you want. You want my signature to rescind that agreement. But if the agreement is rescinded, I lose what control over the well I have. It's only fair that I should be compensated for my loss. So let's deal. I'll give you my signature if you give me the oil well. Simple as that.

He was like an old war horse stirred to action again by the thought of a deal, wheeling and bargaining, his wits against the next man's. This was his art, the place he truly excelled. He had always had a wonderful poker face. And if he could win an inheritance for his new bride by using his wits, all the better.

He went downstairs and drafted a letter, whistling. "I will sign the rescission," the letter read, "if you will sign the oil well over to me."

So the battle was joined.

When Hiram's letter reached Drake and Amelia, what she mostly felt was disbelief. It was beyond her capacity to believe that her father would treat her this way—would use her affection for him as a bargaining chip. Surely it wasn't true.

But there was another, older, darker part of herself that believed it immediately. It was this part that had seen, in bits and pieces, his defections over the years. She remembered being left at Indian Bluff; she remembered lying on the hard-packed road, dizzy with pain. Part of her knew that, indeed, this was exactly the kind of thing he was likely to do.

But her mind pushed it back. All of Anise's training rushed to the fore, and covered over with a foaming wash all of Amelia's dark suspicions. She rejected them, and put them into the darkest hole, the deepest place, where she would never find them. They would come back at night, sometimes, and she would cry softly in her sleep.

Relations between Drake and Amelia began to become strained. It was perfectly obvious to Drake what was going on, and he was consumed with impatience because Amelia refused to recognize it. His legacy from Granddaddy Davis was one of scrupulous fairness, a vision of estates divided as neatly as squares of chocolate, each in the right hand at the right time. Once he had gathered that Hiram meant to pursue no such course, he was certain that Hiram was capable of anything.

Drake wondered at the want of family feeling that Hiram showed. He, himself, had been bamboozled by the man. He thought of the time he had walked with Hiram, how Hiram had laid his arm along Drake's shoulder, and talked with him. Drake had expanded gratefully under the gaze of a generous man. Like everyone else, he had breathed in Hiram's charm and bent towards him. Hiram was different, he thought, than his own father, and he considered himself doubly blessed to be marrying into a family that had such a father, such a weathered pillar of family cohesion.

Now his anger had in it the force of betrayed love. It was an old song that sang through Drake's voice now, a thing that he had brought with him through his dry, dark childhood. But there was new pain too, and the frustration of being ignored.

Because Amelia was ignoring him, as much as was humanly possible. As the only child, I well remember the tension of the house in those days, drawn and coating the place like milk curdling in a pan. There was glass in the air, acid etching, long silences, slamming doors.

I remember once I was in the living room, with my homework spread out on our dark wood table, when I heard shouting upstairs, in the bathroom. Then my father, Drake, came walking resolutely into the room. A moment later my mother came running after him, naked and wet from her bath, her skin shining palely against the shutters. Her hair was tousled and her eyes were red. The dark splotch of her pubic hair shocked me, and I looked away.

She threw herself down at my father's feet and put her arms around his knees. Her arms were white against the leather of his boots.

"Please stop talking about it," she sobbed. "Please just leave me alone. Leave me alone."

But he didn't leave her alone. He couldn't. He had been taught to abhor injustice in all its forms, and the injustice of Hiram holding the entire Frankell family for ransom, threatening to make them pay millions of dollars for his own personal gain, rose in him. It began to invade his dreams at night, and made his days unquiet.

The story of the destruction of the family is in some ways the story of Amelia's coming of age. Sheltered always, lovely, graceful, she had existed in an arbor of other people's wishes and expectations for her. She had been stamped with the mold of the Southern lady, and acquiescence was her way.

To oppose her father was an unthinkable thing. He should have what he wanted, and if it was at her expense—well, no matter. That was the way it had always been. She had spent her life showing her father what he wanted to see, in her eyes. There was no one more protective of Hiram's state of mind than Amelia. She protected him most of all from the embarrassing notion of his own selfishness, the pure strain of his narcissistic gaze.

Now there was another powerful man—her husband—on the opposing side, insisting that she stand up for her rights. Their rights. And those of their daughter. She felt herself like a tarred rope, pulled by two raging antagonists. It had never occurred to her that she had any rights in herself.

But in the struggle something began to rise up in her, out of the sleepless nights and the weeping dinners. It was the voice of neither her husband nor her father. It had long, bright wings, a beak that was sharp and cruel. It stirred, restlessly. It was herself, and she had never seen it.

It suggested that perhaps her father was wrong to do as he was doing. Perhaps he should be opposed, in his gaming drive to take what he wanted. But not in the way that Drake wanted. Hiram shouldn't be destroyed. Just stopped. Someone should stand up to him. She had no thought of it being her, not at first.

Finally she began to think of it. Added to Drake's overblown persuasions were her own secret memories of desertion and injury, of a father acting not like a father. There was grief at the bottom, under all the piles of shining goodness, black grief and betrayal, and even hatred. She never named its name, or even knew it was there. Her wounds slept.

To know that she had loved Hiram, that he had been everything to her—and then to see that she had always failed his tests, that he never loved her back with the same intensity—gave her a banked and hidden rage. Always her weapons had been too blunt to reach him, too muffled by his indifference. But now she had been dealt a hand in the card game. She stood equal to him at last, in her potential for destruction.

He might manipulate her for gain, sell her love for a share in the oil well. But finally she had something that he wanted. She held the integrity of the family in her hand.

From the day that Hiram had held Amelia in his arms and her presence had made him a father, he looked to her for that sound of himself. It was instinctive, largely hidden. He enjoyed Constance more, he coddled Sarsaparilla. But Amelia had made him a father. And she could unmake him.

The knowledge was the more dangerous for its hiding place. Even Amelia didn't know her hatred and her rage. She couldn't have guessed. Anise had made her blind and deaf to herself, so that she swung her weapons like a hooded knight. They were sharper than she knew.

When Hiram received Drake and Amelia's refusal of his first offer, to give him the entire oil well in exchange for his signature, he was not surprised. It had been a bid, only an opening move. He expected to bargain down, and bargain down he did, offering seventy-five percent for himself, twenty-five percent to be divided among the three girls. It seemed fair.

What angered him was the increasingly personal and agitated tone of Amelia's letters. She wrote him asking if he didn't think of her as a daughter anymore, asking why he was treating her like a business associate, why he was bargaining with her over something that was hers to begin with.

Just like a woman to drag personal matters into a business equation, he thought. He sat down to explain. "If I had the prospect of an oil well in my hand, I wouldn't give it to my business partner," he wrote. "Why would I give it away to my daughters?"

The gaming instinct in him prevailed, and rode over everything. Anise had protected him too long and possibly too well. He had never had to worry about the mechanics of being the father or head of the family. She had always produced cards for him to sign and cakes for him to cut, throwing a magician's cape over him to hide the holes that glared now in the light.

It simply never occurred to Hiram that he might be injuring his daughters by treating them the same as he might treat a business opponent. It was all a fair fight, and nothing really to do with how much they loved one another.

When the letters failed, and all the phone calls produced only confusion, Drake and Amelia went to visit Hiram.

Hiram met them at the airport. Everyone was terribly civil, in the time-honored tradition of the family. Although Amelia had prepared herself in the tiny airplane bathroom, combed her hair and put on lipstick so that he would see her as a woman, and a player in her own right, something in her twisted at the sight of him standing there.

They drove home, making polite chat. Francine welcomed them, and Amelia and Drake settled their bags upstairs. Drake pointedly went for a walk. They had agreed that Amelia should do the talking, to keep matters from escalating.

Hiram invited Amelia down to his office. He showed her to the chair, and asked her what she would like to drink. He seemed to understand her, Amelia thought, exultant. He was treating her as a grown woman, and not a child to be shuffled out of the way.

Amelia had long since gathered her courage for this moment, but it almost slipped out of her grasp again. She stared out the window at the hitching chain that swung outside against the long oval of the driveway. The chain was as thick around as her waist, and studded with rust. The cicadas shrilled gently in the yard.

"It's this way, Daddy," she said. "You're living on seventeen hundred dollars a month. So are we. The difference is that there are three of us, and there's only one of you. Or two of you. I take it that Francine has her own income. Anyway, we're looking at sending our daughter to college. I know you want that for her, too. But it's going to be expensive."

She paused, and took another sip of the drink, feeling the bite of the scotch on her tongue. She went on, with a breath, "And so I need that money. I need my share of the oil money. When we signed the '77 agreement, that well was producing three hundred dollars a month. Now it's producing nine thousand dollars. You can't possibly need all of that yourself."

Hiram got up and walked to the window, looking out.

"We signed the well back to Mother in the agreement knowing that she would give it to you. It was ours, and we did that because we loved you."

"You didn't give anything," Hiram said. He was still looking out the window. "Your mother left me that well, fee simple, in the will."

"But we gave it back to her, Daddy," Amelia said. "Don't you see that? If we hadn't signed the agreement, it just would have come to us. We wouldn't have had to do a thing. But we wanted you to be taken care of."

She paused to take another breath. "Well, now you've been taken care of. That well is producing more money than any one man could use, and I need some of it."

"That seems reasonable," Hiram said, slowly, turning back from the window. "I think we can work something out."

They talked, that day, long and thoughtfully. Options were discussed. Hiram admitted the possibility of selling some of the land Anise had left him, and living on the proceeds. The next morning Amelia woke joyfully with the words of a song running in her head, again and again: "The dragon doesn't live here anymore."

Amelia had broken a taboo. It was that women never, ever ask for anything they want—especially not money. But once Amelia had achieved it, Constance and Sarsaparilla weren't far behind. When she called her sisters and told them the news, their minds began to work. If Amelia could have her share of the oil money now, they reasoned, why couldn't they have theirs as well?

Faced with the prospect of losing all the income from the well, Hiram retreated. In the next few days he stopped talking about selling the land, and began to insist again that the well was his, that he failed to see any reason to give it up. His conversations with Amelia were full of red herrings, conversational blind turns that would take her off the point and leave her confused and gasping. She was never able to understand what was in his mind, and he kept it that way. Drake began to get angry again. Amelia felt betrayed.

The whole family gathered, treating Drake and Amelia's occasion as a reunion. As was custom, Hiram carved the date of the gathering into the oaken post in the living room. Everyone gathered for a huge dinner of roast beef, mashed potatoes and brandied peaches, the bottled ones that Hiram called "drunk peaches."

Midway through dinner, Hiram announced that there was a cherry pie in the refrigerator, but that he wasn't giving any to anyone else. Everyone laughed, slightly strained. Drake seethed. It was this attitude, he thought, that was causing all the trouble. Hiram just did whatever the hell he wanted, was as selfish as one could conceive of, and everyone laughed and thought he was clever for it.

Before dinner was over, Drake excused himself and went to the kitchen. He opened the refrigerator and saw the pie there, with its laced pastry crust and cherries red as blood. He took it out and began to eat it with a fork, quickly. He shoveled the crusts into his mouth, feeling the mass of the pie growing in his stomach like a fetus. The juice dripped onto the floor in sticky spots. He thought with satisfaction of the literary metaphor it made: "If you don't share your cherry pie, you will lose your cherry pie."

When it was done, he went into the dining room and announced that he had eaten the cherry pie. All of it. Everyone stared at him, appalled. Hiram got up and left the room. No one spoke to Drake for the next several days. He lived as a pariah in the house, unrepentant.

No one in the family ever forgave him for that cherry pie. They remembered it long after the more complex memories of legalistic slights had vanished. Hiram was particularly embittered. It only confirmed his feeling that Drake was an unfeeling thief.

The rest of the family were beginning to understand the enormity of what Hiram was trying to do, and unrest was working through their ranks like yeast. Even Hiram's most loyal ally, Constance, began to think that it was time something was done to stop him.

Hiram went with Constance to a football game, in which her son was playing. They sat in the bleachers under a clear sky, with a hint of breeze. It was beginning to get hot.

"Daddy, you know, Amelia and Drake are starting to get really angry about this whole thing," she told him.

"I know," he said, lazily, shifting his feet to cross them one over the other. "I'm going to have to do something about that, one of these days."

"We're all thinking about getting a lawyer," she told him.

He looked her straight in the face. "Punkin, you do just what you need to do. You've got to take care of yourself."

Constance had inherited Hiram's love of a fair fight. To her this was permission to fight him, and still to love him. He was the lodestar for her existence, and she would no more have thought of cutting away from him than she would have chewed off her own arm. She had more to lose, if she lost him, than Amelia—and fewer grudges. His favor had always descended on her warmly.

The rift was taking its own toll on Constance. Her husband, Arnold, was squarely in Drake's court, and thought that what Hiram was doing was monstrous. Arnold's own father, Travis, was a law-and-order sort, whose goal in life was to build up his empire so that his children might inherit it intact. It was totally foreign to Travis' way of thinking that a father might struggle to take an oil well from his children so that he could spend it himself.

One day Travis picked up the phone and called his friends at Texoil, to advise them that Anise Frankell was dead, and that Hiram had been signing her checks. The checks stopped coming to Hiram at once, and began to accumulate in an escrow fund. Travis never told anyone what he had done, not even his son Arnold. Hiram was furious when he discovered that Texoil had been notified. Privately he was sure that Drake had told them.

Drake and Arnold became allies, and Arnold plagued Constance to stand up to her father and fight for her inheritance. She finally agreed, after many weary battles that sapped and nearly killed their tenderness. But she determined that she would do it her way, and that she would have a father to come back to when it was all over.

Before long, however, Constance and Sarsaparilla found a point of division between themselves and Amelia and Drake. There seemed to be operating in Amelia an impulse to push away from the family, a deep and abiding bitterness that had more than the oil well at its root. Hurt, Constance wondered sometimes if Amelia even wanted to be her sister anymore. Sometimes it seemed that she didn't.

Constance wondered if Drake was jealous of Amelia's strong family ties, and was trying to pull her away, to have her all for himself. Certainly

Drake's position was more unyielding, more punishing than Constance's own position. Constance merely wanted what was coming to her. Drake seemed to be out for revenge. Constance felt it was necessary to show Hiram that she and Sarsaparilla didn't feel the same bitterness as Drake and Amelia. In her opinion, Drake and Amelia had simply gone too far.

So Constance and Sarsaparilla got their own lawyer.

Drake was bitter at the defection of the other two daughters. He thought that perhaps they were using Amelia as a stalking horse, running her out to fight their difficult battles for them, and then following behind to pick up the loot.

He told Amelia that they weren't truly her sisters, that true sisters would never betray her and leave her exposed in the middle of the battlefield. He told her the story of her betrayal so often that she began to believe it.

Constance and Sarsaparilla nursed their own hurts, and bewilderment that Amelia seemed so greedy, so angry, so unyielding. For the two younger daughters the bonds of family were sacred, and unbreakable. Amelia would always be their sister, and Hiram always their father, no matter what atrocities either of them might commit. Constance packed a box of precious things for Amelia, and hid it in her attic, to wait for the time when Amelia might want to come home.

35. The Letter

It was about this time, the year I turned fourteen, that I went to visit my grandfather. Communications had been strained and difficult, and I had yearned for him with the frustration of parted lovers. We wrote letters to each other, and never mentioned all the trouble. When he invited me to come down, I was mad to go. My parents wrestled with their collective consciences, and decided that they couldn't keep me from him. So they paid for my plane ticket, and I flew down alone.

He met me, as he always had. I almost wept to see him there after so long, so dear and so familiar, wearing his battered leather jacket and his hat down over his eyes. There was something in him that breathed of horses and sunlight, even in the stilted fluorescence of the airport.

I ran straight to him, burying my head in his shoulder. He put his arm around me and we walked out to his pickup. I inhaled the particular scent that he carried with him, and thought fiercely that I would kill anyone who tried to keep me from him. I was perfectly happy here, in the battered pickup with the radio on the floor and wisps of hay floating, gold in the air.

I don't remember what we talked about. We never talked much. He told me of the horses, of the new tricks that he had taught King. He had a pony for me, he said, my own pony. She was red, with a black mane, and he promised that I would have the breaking and naming of her.

We ate raisin bran and peanut butter toast together each morning, and I waited impatiently for him while he did business, and he would be free to ride with me during the long, hot afternoons. I spent hours in the barn, combing wisps of straw and horsehair into dolls, stacking horseshoes and discovering bent horseshoe nails like the treasure of the lost conquistadors.

The sun was fierce and the grass all burnt into long, broken hay, with cockleburs everywhere, and tiny frogs. The water bubbled into the cool horse tank, green with moss, and I would spend hours there, staring down at my reflection. I went in among the horses in their stalls and lay along their backs, breathing in the smell of the hides and warm hair, listening to the breathing.

I caught and rode my pony, whom I named Penny. She was a vicious little mount with a hard mouth and a wicked temper. I thought she was marvelous, and when she bucked I didn't even know it. I never thought of falling off; only wondered why her head was going up and down so strangely.

Sir watched me ride and showed me off to his friends. "She's got the Jameson seat," he would tell them, and rest his hand on my hand, and I would gleam with pride.

I woke early each morning and went to sleep reluctantly each night, prying my fingers from the day with difficulty. I remember the smells most of all, as if my pores were soaking in the things that would have to last me forever.

Did I know that this summer would be the last? Who can say? But I hoarded it as a miser might, and impressed each thing on my memory so clearly that I have them still. It is little enough.

One day my grandfather called me into his office. He had a phone, on his dark wood desk, and a bent metal round thing, with threaded edges. I picked it up and asked him what it was.

"That's my age teller," he said. "If someone knows what it is, I know how old they are."

"But what is it, really?" I said. He picked it up and handled it thoughtfully. "It's the radiator cap from an old, old Model T Ford," he said. "It melted one day during a picnic, a very long time ago."

He set it down. "Come and sit here, punkin, and let's talk," he said. I settled into the hard wood chair by the window.

"Now, how much do you know about this whole legal thing that's going on in the family?"

"Not much," I said. It was true, I didn't know much, except that my mother was crying and my parents were fighting all the time. They had been careful to keep me out of it, knowing how I felt about my grandfather.

"Well, I think you should know about it, don't you?" he said. "You're getting pretty big, practically a grown-up."

I nodded.

"So, it's like this, punkin," he said. "Your grandmother left me some money. And your mother thinks that she should have some of it. There's a lot of other complicated things that you wouldn't understand. But that's the main point. Does that make sense to you?"

I nodded again, uncertainly.

"Now, I know your mother needs money. But I think of it this way: She and your father decided to be artists. Right? And artists don't make much money." He looked at me, and I allowed that this was so. Certainly I knew how precarious our living was.

"So," he went on, "I figure that if they want to be artists, they should. But they shouldn't ask anyone else for money. After all, it's their choice. If they wanted money, your father could have gone on being a lawyer."

It all came perfectly clear to me. My father and mother were whining for money from my grandfather, when the lifestyle they had chosen failed to support them. I felt ashamed. How could they do such a thing? And to my grandfather, of all people, who would be tormented by his own generosity. Certainly they should abide by the decision they had made. It was the only right thing to do.

"Do you think you understand this any better, now?" my grandfather said. I told him that I did. I didn't say much about it then, or later.

I saved the brunt of my scorn for my parents, when I returned home. I remember sitting in the back seat of our Toyota, watching the backs of their heads and seething with hate for them, for their cowardly, irresponsible ways. I wished I could stay with my grandfather forever, to hold him up against the trouble that my parents had made for him. Failing that, I did his work for him as well as I could, presenting to my parents his arguments as well as I could remember them.

My father was furious when he found that Sir had brought me into the argument. He explained things as well as he could to me, and then refused to talk about it anymore. Secretly he decided that I would not be allowed to see my grandfather again, since Hiram seemed determined to use me as a weapon in the war.

I gladly left the disagreements to the adults, as I found that my grandfather's arguments, so clear and reasonable when he explained them, turned to dust and ashes in my mouth. It was only because my memory was poor, because I didn't know all the details, I was sure. If only I had been able to remember Sir's exact phrase and tone, I would have been able to persuade my parents as to the wrongness of their position, and there would be peace again.

Hiram had only meant the whole matter to be a hand of poker, a business scuffle in which the strongest and most alert would come out on top. But once the lawyers became involved, the language got uglier, and the situation became increasingly sticky. Everyone was keeping files; everyone was making copies. And after Amelia's daughter went home from her visit, Amelia began to refuse his phone calls.

At first she was only unavailable when he called. Drake's voice would sound on the line, hateful and smug. "I'm sorry, Amelia can't come to the phone right now," he would say, as if Hiram were a stranger.

Hiram told him bluntly one time that he didn't believe it.

"The truth is, she doesn't want to talk to you," Drake told him. "And she won't, until she feels like it."

It winded Hiram, it shook him with the first stirrings of impending loss. And then it enraged him. That he couldn't talk to his own daughter! Drake was obviously trying to destroy any family feeling here. If they couldn't talk civilly on the phone, of other things, family things, while the lawyers wrestled it out, there was no hope for the family's survival.

Hiram had implicit trust in his own charm, and in his devotion to his daughters. It never crossed his mind not to love his daughters. The fact that their lawyers exchanged blistering briefs had nothing to do with anything, was in fact irrelevant to their personal feelings for each other.

After the legal matters were settled, they would of course go back to being family again. That was the purpose of lawyers—they were like gladiators paid to go out into the ring and fight for the honor of the involved parties. This would spare everyone unnecessary blood and dust, and make it possible for them to continue on together afterwards.

But Amelia refusing to speak to him! It was Drake's doing, he was sure. He thought that Amelia might be somewhere near, struggling to reach the phone while Drake triumphantly held her away with one hand, and talked on the phone with the other, his handsome features set in a malignant sneer.

Amelia actually was near the phone, the times that Hiram called. But she was lying on the bed face down, with a pillow over her head. It had been her own decision not to talk to Hiram. He was so convincing, so persuasive, that all of her hard-won new independence of thought slid down into a swirling hole at the sound of his beloved voice, raspy, reasonable, loving.

The tidal pulls of her family were so strong, for Amelia, that even thirteen hundred miles of distance was not enough for her to escape them. The thing floundering in her to be free needed time to harden, and try its wings. It was yet so fragile and easily smashed. And it could not be born in conjunction with her family.

She didn't know when she realized that, but it was true. Her family held her to their own image of her, as powerfully as Anise had once pressed the mask to Hiram's face. Amelia could only struggle weakly against those molecular bonds.

But huge energies were needed to conjure up a transformation like the one that was hungry to begin in her. It needed rest, peace, and silence. It needed distance, and divorce from the people she had known. Hiram's compelling cheer pulled her back with a snap into what she had been, and she had grown too far to want to go back.

It was still an incoherent process in her. But she knew—her nerves screamed—that she could not go back. She would not. She would die. She imagined how it would be, going back to reunions and to Hiram's for Christmas, with his new bride presiding. Everything the way it had been, everything the same.

She would smile, and nod, and pretend to be the person she had been. She would exchange pleasantries with her family—Constance, who with her born-again fanaticism had become quite sincerely concerned that Amelia might go to hell for exercising with yoga, or studying Buddhism.

And there was Hiram's housekeeper, who had proclaimed that Drake's most beautiful painting was filled with the spirits of the Devil. The close-mindedness, the casual bigotry, the brutally stubborn belief systems would close around her, effortlessly.

And inside she would writhe and scuffle against the shell, and gasp for breath. It was impossible for her to go back, now. She could only go ahead.

Francine was horrified at the things that Hiram told her. It was a dreadful thing, when a daughter refused to speak to her own father. She agreed with him completely that Drake must have taken over Amelia's mind and turned her totally against Hiram. There was simply no other explanation.

And Francine failed to see why the girls were so intent on keeping the well for themselves. How selfish of them, when they knew that Hiram was so heavily in debt! They were asking of him things that he had worked his whole life for, things that he had built up with his former wife. They wanted to assume half his assets, but not half his debts. It was perfectly unreasonable.

They had always been insensitive to him, she thought. She remembered the time when she had told the girls to come and pick up the things they wanted. They laid all the crystal out on the table and were picking through it, striking bargains with each other, quite oblivious as to how it was affecting Hiram, to have the things of his life being taken away.

He and Constance had fought about something—some painting that she wanted. Afterwards Hiram had just stood there, at the top of the stairs. Francine remembered seeing him there, very white. He looked stricken.

And that was the night he had his first heart attack, the little one. Francine always secretly blamed Constance for bringing on that heart attack. But she didn't know about it at the time. Hiram only told Francine about it later, when it was all over.

"I feel kind of strange," he said, just like that. "My chest is real sore."

Well, of course she had insisted that he go to the doctor. He said he would but he wanted to go alone—wouldn't let her come. The doctor had gotten him into an ambulance and off to the hospital immediately. And as soon as Francine heard that, she called Constance and told her the news, asked Constance to pick her up since Hiram had left the car at the doctor's.

And this was the unbelievable thing—Constance had never showed up. Three hours later, Francine had arranged another ride. Three hours later! It was unbelievable to Francine that anyone would make a wife wait three hours while her husband was in the hospital, maybe dying. She had been washing her hair, Constance said later. Francine was too much of a lady to say what she thought of that.

Hiram never would admit that he had a heart attack. He was so stubborn. But the doctor had pulled Francine aside, and told her everything. Hiram had a congenital heart defect. A kind of leak in his heart. And the doctor said it was absolutely imperative to keep him from much emotional stress.

And here was his oldest daughter, refusing to speak to him as if she hadn't a care in the world, breaking his heart. Literally. Francine just didn't understand it.

Didn't those girls know anything about Hiram, after having lived with him and loved him all those years? Didn't they know that the oil money and his social security were the only income he had, and that it shamed him to have to depend on handouts from his own daughters? A charity case, he had said to her, over and over, walking the halls. He would be a charity case. "I'm at their mercy," he said. "If they get mad at me, I'll have nothing."

Drake had suggested that Hiram sell the land that Anise left him, and invest the money, and live on the proceeds. Well, that showed about as much knowledge as a turtle, Francine thought. She sniffed. Hiram was like any good Texan—he loved the land. It would kill him to sell even an inch of it. He would die first.

And now everything was in such a mess, and the lawyers were so expensive. But when a man's in a position like that, he has to stay in there and try to resolve it, and get something out of it.

Couldn't those girls see that Hiram was just trying to survive? All he was trying to do was come out with a living. He had worked all his life to pay for that property. He just wanted to salvage something.

And there was something else, something that Francine thought the girls were unaware of. They must be, or else why were they doing it? It was this: that no matter how much Hiram needed the oil money, nothing hurt him as much as having his relationship with the girls damaged. Nothing. It was like to kill him.

Francine had been beside him when he woke in the night, and had held him in her arms until he went back to sleep, mourning those girls.

She had been riding with him, horseback, the day that he went to the mailbox and pulled out the letter from Amelia that was a response to one of his offers to settle.

Francine had a bad feeling about that envelope, so square and white in his hand. It was a day in early spring, but the wind had suddenly seemed shadowed. She wanted very much for him to open it later, or not to open it at all.

"Let's go back, honey," she said. "You can wash up, and I'll make us lunch."

But Hiram was all afire at having a letter from Amelia, after so long not speaking to her. He thought it meant that she had come to her senses, that it was going to be all right. He ripped the envelope open, excitedly.

Francine watched his face as it crumbled and fell, leaving something dark behind. Then it wrinkled and cracked. He turned his face up, towards the sky, and wept. She had never seen him do that before. He sat on his horse and cried, long harsh sounds of loss and despair. She sat immobilized by shock, not even able to reach towards him. He dropped the paper on the ground and rode off towards the barn, whipping King to go faster.

She dismounted heavily, and went over to the paper. She picked it up, and flicked it open.

"Dear Hiram," it started out. She skimmed through it, saw Amelia's signature. What had upset him so? Then it struck her—Amelia had called him Hiram, and not Daddy. "You haven't treated me like a daughter, but like a business associate," the letter read. "I am disarmed by love and pity for you, and it seems that this is not returned. So I will call you Hiram now, as befits a business relationship."

Poor Hiram. Her heart hurt for him, and raged against the daughter who would treat him this way. Francine folded up the offending paper and put it away. She had never heard anything to match it. It was a dark day for the family, a dark day indeed.

36. Householder

The next time G.A. came back to the town of Patience for Mary Frank Masterson, he came with a gun.

During his years with the carnival he had thought long and hard about the whole thing, lying on his bed alone at night. He decided that it was her brothers who were keeping them apart, her brothers who had tainted her and made her scream when she saw his gift. They were talking at her all the time, he was convinced, turning her against G.A., making her afraid of him.

He would take care of them this time. No one would ever come between G.A. and Mary Frank Masterson, ever again.

He came to her house one evening, around dinnertime. He crept up to the window and looked in, feeling the metal of the gun pressed cool against his groin.

The family ate in silence, interrupted only by grunting sounds and the scraping of crock ware. They ate like beasts, her father and her brothers, wiping their mouths on the backs of their hands and spitting out bits that they didn't fancy. G.A. was glad they were like beasts. Beasts he understood. He knew the rules for beasts. Consume or be consumed, that was their lesson. His training would stand him in good stead.

Mary Frank's mother, he saw, stood shrunken in a corner in a dirty apron, waiting to serve her menfolk. She had grey skin and a look of long-cultivated invisibility. But G.A. could only see Mary Frank. It had been twelve years since he had last seen her.

She sat apart on the hearth, crouched with her thin arms around her knees. She, too, was waiting to obey orders, but she was not there, not really. She was somewhere else, G.A. could see that. The profanities and the rough talk did not touch her a bit. She would only do what she was told and then drop back to her place, her eyes wide with dreaming.

She was much older than when he had seen her last, and her body looked more like those of the girls in the magazines now, her breasts swelling out gently above the dainty waist. But the skin at her throat was still so thin that he could see a pulse there, and her hair still fell over her shoulder like silver cotton, so light that he could almost see it lift in an unseen breeze.

G.A. watched her. From the way that her lips moved and her eyes shone, he thought that she might be coming down that hill again in her mind, rounding the curve perfectly in control, her arms stretched out for the wind. She was such an inhuman thing sitting there, such a thing of air. His heart rose up in his throat and burst, and fell painfully at her feet with a dull thud. He was surprised that she didn't hear it.

He moved cautiously to the front door and made a scritching noise there, feeling the gun comfortably against his skin. He paused a moment, and made the noise again, and then a whining. He had seen a dog, a sorry-looking hound, out behind the house by the chicken coop.

Mary Frank's father shifted in his chair and lifted his eyes from his plate for a moment.

"Mary Frank, let in that damn dog," he ordered.

Mary Frank got up to open the door. G.A. watched her through a chink in the door, coming towards him just like in his dreams. She swayed softly, like a young palm. He imagined that her breath was sweet.

She opened the door, laying gentle hands on the doorknob and turning it. It was rusted, and took both her hands. G.A. sucked in his breath painfully, sweating in a delirium of pleasure and fear. In a minute he would see her, he would touch her! He had waited so very long.

The door swung open and he saw her, silhouetted against the light. Even as he leapt forward he saw the ripe outline of her body through the cloth of her dress.

He flung one hand around her mouth and neck, dragging the back of her head back against his shoulder. With the other he pulled out the pistol, and pointed the business end of it at the stunned family. One of the brothers let out an oath, and G.A. swung the pistol to point it right between the boy's eyes.

"We're going now," G.A. said. "And I reckon you shouldn't follow us, or it'll be the worse for Mary Frank, here. Ain't that right, Mary Frank?"

He looked down to see her eyes wide above the dirty back of his hand. She was curled against him, strangely complaisant and still.

"Well, goodbye," G.A. said awkwardly. He backed away, still holding the pistol steady and Mary Frank's head against him. She tried to bite him, and he winced and tightened his hold on her, so that she cried out, making a muffled noise.

"Don't do that," he whispered down at the top of her head. "I don't want to have to hurt you."

He took her and backed down the steps, letting the door bang closed in front of him. He could see the family sitting absolutely still, as if they were made of wax. He backed about fifteen paces away from the house, then cocked the pistol and fired at random in the direction of the back yard. The hound yelped, and whined.

Then he picked up Mary Frank and slung her over his shoulder. She was light as a bag of thistles. He could feel her starved rib cage against his shoulder.

"Be still now," he said, in an agony of love and fear. "Please just be still." And he started off into the forest in a dogtrot he knew could eat up many miles before morning.

From time to time that night, G.A. stopped to let Mary Frank down off his shoulder. She always held her ribs when he let her down, but she said nothing and did not complain. Once she indicated that she had to make water, and he let her go into the bushes, and then was seized with fear that she would not come back.

But she did, yielding to him like a child, as he put her back onto his shoulder, as gently as he knew how. She was far from home by now, and knew that she could not make it back alone. More than the crazy man— for man he was now, and no longer a boy, she could see that—she feared the dark woods that stretched around them, wakeful with strange voices.

G.A. ran until morning. In the first flush of his manhood he was huge and immensely strong, and he was driven by fear. The blood ran hot and clean in his veins that night, chanting strange things, and the sticks made runes before his eyes as he brushed them away, chattering messages that he could not stay to read. He was gripped by the need to get far away, so far that her brothers could never come between them again.

Finally Mary Frank begged him to stop. She spit into her hand and showed him the blood, cupped in her palm. He knew nothing of women's complaints and was frightened—was the blood from the inside of her cheek, or from some injury inside? He stopped and lowered her onto a bed of moss. They had halted in a clearing, not a bad place to stop.

She sat and watched him with wide eyes, slanting a little like a doe's, as he set up their camp. He was quick and efficient. He stripped a young sapling of its branches, tying down the tree to make an arch and weaving the leaves in and around it, to make a small green dome for a tent. He laid a circle of rocks for a fire, found dry wood and lit it with matches that he had carefully stored in his pocket, for just this minute.

He himself never needed a fire, ate his food raw. But he felt vaguely that Mary Frank was so delicate, she might need a fire, to keep warm. She must have every luxury.

He crashed off into the brush, to catch something to eat. He felt secure about her now, enough to leave her alone. There was nowhere she could go that he could not find her, no hiding place from which he could not flush her. His woodcraft was almost perfect. He killed a squirrel with a quick thrust of a sharp stick, and brought it back.

The glow of the householder possessed him. This was his, his camp! And he was bringing food back to his woman. It ran warm in him. He put his shoulders back and let his arms swing, and allowed himself to make noise coming back, so that she would know her man was on the way.

He came into the middle of the circle of stones, into the clearing that he had made, and stopped short. She was standing there, facing him. Her hands gripped each other at the wrist, moving over one another slowly, as if she didn't know them. Her face was swollen and her eyes bright. He saw that she had been crying.

He couldn't bear it, that she should be sad, when he was so joyful. Couldn't she feel it, what he felt? He had seen his mother cry many times, and he always hated it. He knew he was making her cry. Always his stupidity, his wrongness, his dirtiness made her cry. She was so pure, his mother, and his father was pure, and his sister. He, G.A., was the only one who was dirty, and so everyone around him always cried, no matter how he tried.

He stepped towards her, with his hand out.

"Don't cry," he said, and his voice was brokenhearted. "Don't cry."

She stopped crying, amazed out of her despair. She had never heard this tone in his voice before. She had never heard him speak, really, she realized, besides that one time on the road, with the mouse. It gave her hope, that there might be a human being there, besides a crazed animal.

"Please," she said, stepping towards him and holding her arms out pleadingly. "Please don't hurt me. Please let me go home. Can't you see that I'm afraid here?"

She came up close to him and laid her hand on his arm, looking up into his eyes confidingly. She searched for the sad boy she had heard in his voice. "Please be my friend. Don't hurt me."

Her sweet breath blew over him in a wash, and he reeled under it. He could feel the print of her hand on his arm, singeing right down to the bone. He felt as if the mark of that hand would be there forever, as if when she took away her hand the slim stamp would be charred black into his flesh. He smelled the scent of her hair, and her skin, and saw her breasts move underneath her dress, as she looked up at him imploringly. With a groan he pulled her into his arms, and buried his face in her neck, biting it to bring the blood to the surface.

Surprised, she struggled in his arms, and tried to push him away. But he had gotten the taste of her now, and was past stopping, past forgetting. Her skin tasted smoky, and he hungrily traced the line of it down, easily imprisoning both of her wrists in one hand. Her struggles only twisted her against him deliciously, and he felt the years of agonizing burning rise up in him, unrelieved.

He cried out incoherently and forced her to the ground, holding her wrists up over her head with one hand and ripping her dress down the front with the other, so that he could see her white breasts, traced with blue veins and tipped with nipples that were dark, surprisingly dark against her pale skin.

She struggled against him as he went down to taste those breasts, the ones that he had dreamed about so long. They tasted to him of raspberries, of sweet forbidden things.

Unable to wait any more, he ripped her dress and flung it aside, ripping and tearing her underclothes as well, cursing when they caught, until she lay naked under his hand, rigid and white and curved as a shell in the moonlight.

He forced her thighs apart, bruising them, marking them with the prints of his fingers, and thrust into her roughly, breaking her and rushing into her with a great cry, spending himself at once.

He lay on her heavily afterwards, staring at the ground. He noticed a mushroom growing close under his eyes, and saw an ant trying to drag something. His body had consumed itself in the flame of years, and now he felt that he was floating, hollow, content at last.

He was startled awake by muffled sobs, and the jerking of Mary Frank's ribs under his. He had released her hands and she had one fist stuffed into her mouth, trying to silence her cries.

He released her and sat up onto his knees. She stayed there on the ground as he had left her, her eyes averted from him, her knuckles pressed against her teeth. Her body twitched with suppressed sobs. He had pressed her into the moss so deep that it looked as if she grew there.

He was struck by how broken she looked, as if someone had dropped a doll from a great height, randomly. Her arms and legs seemed too thin, and crossed at impossible angles. Her hair lay scattered across her face, and from between her legs leaked the silver snail trail of his semen, and more darkly, blood. She would not look at him. He began to be uneasy.

"Mary Frank," he said helplessly.

She lay where she was, absolutely still. The tears leached out from under her eyes, running steadily. Her skin looked grey, and stained. He was struck, as he looked at her there, by the thought that he had cracked her. He had reached out for something humming in the air, and had gripped it in his hand, only to find that it was no longer the pure thing that he had loved, but something dirty and ruined.

He thought of the mouse that had died in his hand, and he was seized by great grief. He lay his head down on her and wept, great breaking sobs that tore out of the earth and through him, shaking him, the tearing sounds of an animal grief.

Startled by the noise, Mary Frank sat up to find his head in her lap. She saw that he was crying. Crying! She could not conceive it. It had an air of unreality about it, the whole night, the running through the forest, his hard sex thrusting into her, the silence of the space around them, filled with rustlings. Suddenly for some reason the black woods seemed not so frightening. She found them even comforting, a dark cloak wrapping close around her to hide her shame.

She found herself stroking his hair and murmuring to him softly, as she had done to her littlest brother, when he was very small and had hurt himself.

"There, there," she said, lamely. "There, there."

He lifted a great head to her, his eyes wildly swollen and still shaken with sobs. His eyes glittered in the half-light, and she stared into them, fascinated. His head was as large as the rest of him, almost leonine. Everything about him was large, and he had never fit in anywhere, she thought with a sudden stab of pity. He was too big for everything but the woods. He never fit in anywhere but inside her. She had felt his contentment in those brief moments afterwards. It had moved her strangely.

She looked into his eyes as if she would read all the secrets there, and she saw something in their distended, mournful depths that she had never seen anywhere, not in the whole of her brief life. He loved her, this glazed man-beast. For all of his noise and violence, he loved her, enough to take her away, loved her enough to do this to her.

Mary Frank had lived and swum in a sea of violence, and it was not strange to her. But she had never been loved before.

"There, there," she said, stroking his face, still staring into his eyes, as if hypnotized. "You didn't mean to. It's all right. I know you didn't mean to."

He laid his head back in her lap and wept again, this time from relief. She knew. She understood. He had broken something in her, but something else had risen up. He had made her to his image, shaped her woman body beneath him, and she would forgive him. It would be all right.

They sat there like that for hours, watching the movement of the light through the trees, and she stroked his hair gently, staring at his ear, which was all she could see of him. It was a marvelous ear, a perfectly constructed ear. It was the one part of G.A. that was not bestially overformed and too large. It was an absurd thing, a child's ear on a giant's body. It curled in a private and delicate pink spiral, showing vulnerable through his lank hair. She watched its whorls, watched the light change on it, and stroked the hair back from it so that she could see it more clearly.

He fell asleep in her lap, exhausted with grief, and release, his body curled around her protectively. She sat uncomplainingly under his weight as the sun rose through the trees. She learned a great many things about him in those hours, watching the edge of his brutish eyebrow and his ear, his mouth, which she saw was cruel and sensual in repose. His eyelids smoothed with sleep, and his breathing was even and regular. By nine o'clock she was drawn to him; by noon she felt she possessed him. She had never had anything all her own before.

So it was that the sheriff's posse found them, when they came crashing through the trees. Mary Frank's father was with them, and all her brothers. They had dogs, and rifles. They were furious and red-eyed, angry and crusted with whiskers from having searched all night.

The men were surprised, and stopped a minute to see the frail white body of the girl bent protectively over the sleeping form of the young man. The dogs whined and strained at their leashes. Then the men rushed forward to grab him, the hounds baying and the rifle safeties off.

They were even more surprised when they leveled the guns on the boy and began to drag him away, confused with sleep, and the girl put her body in front of his and held him away from the men, shielding him, so they had to shake her off roughly.

"He didn't mean to do it. Did you, G.A.?" she cried out, as her father yanked her away and angrily covered her with a blanket, averting his eyes from her nakedness. "Don't hurt him, Daddy. He didn't mean it. He didn't mean it."

37. The Mirror

When I was fifteen my grandfather came to Washington, where we lived, to ride with the Black Horse Mounted Patrol in President Reagan's inaugural parade. He came, coincidentally, during a weekend when I was being grounded for staying out too late.

The first I knew of his arrival was a phone call. The phone rang and my father answered it. I knew by the cold, queer sound of his voice that it was my grandfather. He spoke for a minute, and then held the phone out to me. I took it.

"Hello, punkin," said my grandfather's voice. I felt it rush over me, warm and vibrant. "Guess what—I'm in town."

"You are?" I said. "Where are you?"

"I'm riding in the parade," he said. "Right through the middle of Washington. And if you can come and see me here, I'll put you on the front of the saddle and we can ride together, right near the President. Ask your dad if you can come, all right?"

"I'll come," I promised him excitedly. "I'll see you soon. I'll be there."

"I love you, punkin," he said, and his voice cracked a little. "I've been pretty lonesome for you."

"Me too," I said. "I'll see you in a little while."

I hung up the phone, carefully, and went to run up the stairs to get dressed.

"He's here, he's here," I sang out joyfully. "I'm going to see him, and ride in the parade, all the way through Washington, right by the President."

My father was still standing, with a strange look on his face.

"I'm sorry," he said, "but you can't go."

I came back down the stairs, slowly. "What do you mean, I can't go?"

"I can't let you go," my father said heavily. "You're grounded, and you know that means you can't leave the house."

"I can't believe it," I said, spitting at him with all my rage. "He's in town, once in my entire life, and you're not going to let me go?"

"I'm sorry," said my father again. "You're forbidden to leave this house." He went into his bedroom and closed the door.

For half an hour I raged, for half an hour I wept, and for the rest of the time I destroyed all the furniture in my room that I could move. I hacked at things with scissors. Then I went back downstairs, and knocked on my father's door. He came out.

"I just want you to know this," I said. "If he dies, and I never see him again, I will never forgive you."

My father's face went white, and I had the satisfaction of seeing my shaft sink home. Then I went back upstairs to wreck the rest of my furniture.

I thought of going out the window and down the drainpipe, but I was too young to drive—though I had friends that could. If I could get to a phone and call one of them, without my father catching me. And even supposing I got that far, I realized I had no idea where my grandfather was. He could be anywhere in the city. The thought of roaming around Washington searching for him, against my parents' express orders, was too much for me. I cried myself to sleep instead.

And it was an odd thing, because it must have been some kind of foreknowledge I had that day. My grandfather did indeed die, before I saw him again. He died although my parents thought him in perfect health. And in fact, I never forgave my parents for keeping me from him that day.

It could have been a day, one more day with him. Perhaps I might have said goodbye. They took it from me, and they can never give it back, no matter how well intentioned they may be, or how sorry.

I told my father that, not long ago. I told him that I had never forgiven him for that day, and that I never would. He nodded, and took it well. We have done things, each to the other, that cannot be forgiven.

And my father confessed to me that he had kept me from my grandfather that day with rage, and for vengeance. I was the pearl of great price for my grandfather, the thing he wanted that my father could refuse him. I was my father's weapon; my forced absence was his revenge.

I never forgot that day. Nor, it seemed, did my grandfather. When I talked to his widow, Francine, many years after his death, she spoke of it.

"He never recovered," she said, "after that day in Washington. He thought that you might have found some way to get in touch with him. He never got over it. It just broke his heart."

Did I break his heart? He died of something like a broken heart, surely. His heart stopped working, and his doctors said there was no reason for him to fail, but that he chose to.

Some of the blood price for him is mine, I'm sure. I could have made it out of the house that day, if I had tried. I was weak, when the moment came, and I failed him.

He had set me challenges all my life, set the jumps on the fence gate higher than I thought I could ever reach. And each time I would take the gate, leaning forward and looking over my horse's ears, throwing my whole self over the fence because he told me to, and so I knew that I could. But when the last fence came, I faltered and failed. We all did.

transfixed. Against her will she looked into the mirror, deeper and deeper, drawn by the Indian woman's eyes.

Demeter saw G.A. loping through the woods with the frail, white body of a girl clasped over his shoulder. His face was set and russet, pointed like the face of the coyote mask from long ago. She saw him forcing the girl's legs apart, thrusting between them, hurtfully, so that the girl bled, and was broken. Demeter cried out in shame and disgust, her voice catching in her throat. She tried to close her eyes.

The Indian woman watched her still, her gaze as cool and firm on Demeter's face as fingertips. Demeter's eyes stayed open. She lashed her head from side to side, a screaming rose in her, but her eyes stayed fixed on the mirror.

She saw men with guns dragging her son through the woods as the girl's father covered her naked body. She saw the hounds baying, and smelled the blood. She saw G.A.'s terrified face, his eyes probing the woods for his mother, for someone to save him, and she shuddered.

She saw the men dragging G.A. into the jail cell, the iron walls looming up in front of him, grey and clanging, just as she had dreamed it before he was ever born. The shock of it, the truth of it, ran down her living nerves like flames. She felt her body convulse, and try to swallow her tongue. Her eyelids closed, seeking darkness.

But her eyelids were gently forced back open. She saw the Indian woman standing over her, pitiless as stone. The woman was holding some-thing under her cape.

The Indian woman passed her free hand over the mirror, clearing it for a moment, and then an image re-formed. It was G.A.'s face, pale and despairing, behind the grey maze of bars. The Indian woman spoke, for the first time. Her voice was cool, and liquid.

"Your son."

She swept her arm up from under her cloak, brushing it back, and showed Demeter what it was she held there.

"My son."

Demeter stared at the thing, withered and unborn, that the Indian woman held. She remembered now where she had seen her before. Demeter's guilt broke in on her, shattering the glass of her mind like a stone, so that the fragments floated in front of her eyes. She laughed and babbled, screaming and pinching dust motes out of the air with her fingers as she watched her memories go by.

Demeter was lying on the sofa, resting her eyes. She had the back of her hand across her forehead. Her eyes had been bothering her increasingly lately, especially when she tried to do close work like sewing or electrical circuits. She shifted on the sofa to ease her back. Seemed like everything was hurting. Demeter had held her body under the control of her will for seventy years now, and the whole thing was starting to rebel, like a horse held too long under the bit. Well, she had her day.

Bridget had just been to visit. How well that girl had turned out! Demeter cherished the thought of her daughter, upright and clean-limbed. Fid doted on the girl, and Demeter hadn't the heart to reprove him. If she hadn't known that too much affection could spoil a child, she'd have done the same.

And Bridget was so smart. She'd become an engineer, like all of them—except G.A., of course. Good with her hands, too. But Demeter could still keep up with her, Lord be praised. There weren't many women that could shingle their own roofs with real shake shingles when they were seventy years old as Demeter had done only a few months ago, and that was a fact. Demeter smiled to think of it.

She opened her eyes briefly and was surprised to see a woman crossing from one end of her house to another, an Indian woman. The woman was a stranger, and yet Demeter thought that she looked oddly familiar. The woman walked firmly and steadily, pressing the prints of her feet down onto the floorboards.

The Indian woman was aging and naked, with a heavy sagging belly and hairless pudenda. She wore only a short cloak around her shoulders, which hid her breasts and her crossed arms. Her black hair was touched with white where it fell down her back like water, and there was a slant to her eyes.

She stopped in her passage directly across from where Demeter lay, and looked at her, with a gaze that seemed lit from behind. Her eyes were very dark and sunken, but brilliant. She stood very straight, despite her age. Demeter struggled under her gaze, trying to remember where she had seen the woman before.

The woman took out from beneath the short cape a round mirror that caught the light. She held it up to Demeter's eyes. Demeter tried to turn her head away, but the level gaze of the Indian woman held her still,

Nakomas Sorrel drew the cloak gently back over the bundle that she held, and stood looking at Demeter for a moment with pity. For a long time, she watched. Then she pressed her palm flat on each of Demeter's ears as she sat rocking and babbling. She touched first the left ear, and then the right.

"Hear nothing," the Indian woman said, and in the wake of each of her hands there was a deafening silence.

Then she passed her hand over Demeter's forehead, which knotted with pain as she talked to herself.

"Forget," said the woman, and Demeter's forehead smoothed like cream in the wake of her hand.

The Indian woman stood for another long moment, watching Demeter sitting still, her eyes blank and a slight smile on her face, rocking gently. Then the woman turned, and was gone.

38. The Silence

There was something final that happened to Hiram after his trip to Washington. Amelia refusing to call him Father, refusing to talk to him at all, keeping him from his granddaughter. Something crystallized into a fighting fury in him.

It was too late now for soft words—the time for appeasement was over. He had tried to keep the family together, and work out the business details on the side. But Drake wouldn't let him—he had turned his daughter and his granddaughter both away from him.

It was all dirty pool now, and never let it be said that Hiram Jameson couldn't play dirty pool when the circumstances required. He was hurt, yes. But no one alive could take advantage of his softer feelings. They would see what he was made of, all right.

The day was nearing when the '77 agreement would be reversed in court. If no one protested it, the reversal would simply go through and it would be as if the agreement never existed.

The oil checks would be sent to the three daughters, the family would escape paying millions in taxes and Hiram would have lost his share of the well.

Ford Hatterly had advised Hiram to back away from the fee simple issue, afraid that it wouldn't stand up in court. But Hiram absolutely had to have at least some of that oil income. His debts to Francine shamed him, and he was desperate to provide her with some semblance of a comfortable life. He certainly couldn't do that with his social security money alone, not with the way that Francine spent money.

So time was growing short. He sent Amelia a letter. Although Drake was now doing all of the speaking for both of them, Hiram as a point of pride continued to address all his correspondence to Amelia. It was dated June 6, 1981:

Dear Amelia:

We, all four Jamesons, prior to any oil income, had some manner of income each sparked by our own individual efforts.

Now the oil income enters the picture, you girls claiming it because it was willed to you by your grandfather, and my claim being based on your assignment to your mother and her willing to me a life estate of the income. My suggested solution is to split the oil income four ways during the remainder of my lifetime. I know we could spend hours discussing the merits of this proposal, but as far as I am concerned that time has passed.

I have tried to keep a relationship between us that we could come back to, but your unforgiving and unbending attitude has made that impossible.

He put down his pen and thought a while, and then set his jaw and wrote on.

> If you do not wish to accept this arrangement I will instruct my lawyer to subpoena you preparatory to the suit that has been brought against me. I will inform all members of the Frankell clan, who stand to pay those heavy taxes, of the facts I have outlined here and let them be the judge as to whether it is your position or mine that will cause this lawsuit to come to trial. If you can live with their reactions on your conscience, I certainly can.
>
> I will expect to hear from you by the 10th of June. Agreed or not agreed.

He signed his name with a flourish. That should produce some results. He told himself that he was threatening to subpoena Amelia because that was the only way he could talk to her, now that she was refusing his phone calls. He read Francine the letter, and she sympathized with his position completely.

The truth was that the hard kernel of anger in him wanted to see Amelia broken. She had rebelled against him, against the family, and she would be brought to her knees again, one way or another. One way or another, he would see her again.

Fid found Demeter when he came in from working in the yard several hours later. The years had baked him close to the bone. He was as tall as ever, and dried. But he could still do a full day's work in the yard, and had kept all his hair.

Demeter was sitting in the darkened living room, humming tunelessly, a faint smile on her face. The silver in her hair caught the light that filtered in from the open door.

"Demeter," he said, leaning over her. "Demeter."

He looked into her eyes, and saw no one there he knew. He snapped his fingers by her ears and made noises, but she did not blink or start.

He dragged up another chair and sat beside her, holding her hand protectively in his. He sat there with her all night and the next day, not moving, and she stared straight ahead, humming a tuneless song that he had never heard before.

When Amelia received Hiram's letter, containing his latest offer and the threat to subpoena her, she went straight to bed and stayed there for three days.

The subpoena broke in her the last tie that had bound her to Hiram. To think that her own father would threaten to have her dragged into court, like a common criminal! And Hiram knew very well that they could not afford the plane ticket to Dallas to answer the summons.

The final strings frayed and parted in her, and a great weariness took over her spirit. She was exhausted, too exhausted to lift her arm or to eat. She lay in bed and looked out of the picture window, into the shifting shapes of the leaves outside.

There was a shifting inside of her too, as the elements of her childhood all broke apart and re-formed. It was absurd, unbelievable to her that this person who had written this letter was her father, the same man who had built the white playhouse with the blue shutters, who had taken her on his shoulders, taught her to dance and given her away in marriage, whispering just before she said her vows that it wasn't too late to come back to his house.

Now it was, indeed, too late. Her father was gone, dead, and in his place rested a cold stranger. She wondered tiredly if he had become this thing, this unfamiliar person, slowly, or if she had been a blind fool forever. The words ran in her mind, over and over, "agreed or not agreed, agreed or not agreed."

If she didn't agree to his proposal, would he truly oppose the reversal of the '77 agreement, and cost everyone all that money? The entire Frankell family, who had saved his life and been so good to him? Would he do it, or would he not? Was it a bluff, or did he mean it?

She had to decide whether he was bluffing, Drake had told her. She knew him, she was his daughter. Was he bluffing or not? She realized that she had no idea. She had never known this side of him, the gambler. She had no more clue as to his actions than she would have been able to guess the inner secrets of a total stranger, someone that she met on the bus, some man in a grey hat and a shearling vest.

How was she to know? And everything depended on it.

The day of the reversal was approaching. If he could only be lulled until that day was past, soothed into not opposing the motion—then everything would be safe.

She had two options, really. She could accept Hiram's proposal, and divide the oil income four ways. Then he would have control of the rest of Anise's estate until he died.

She imagined how that would be, pictured watching Hiram carefully until his death to ensure that he didn't gamble away the entire estate, wrangling with him to ensure that he didn't will all the heirlooms to Francine, struggling, arguing, chewing over every inch of gained ground. The thought made her faint with exhaustion.

And too, if she accepted his proposal, Hiram would consider it an invitation to put the family back together. They would all go back to the way they had been, family holidays together, everyone giving way to Hiram, laughing and joking as if nothing had ever happened.

Amelia would be smashed back into the mold of the girl she had been. She didn't want that, she realized suddenly. Even if it cost the family, she couldn't go back to the tiny life she had led before, the lying and deceiving and pretending she had no wants. Every muscle in her rebelled against the thought.

Or, she could simply wait. If she wrote Hiram a soothing letter, saying that she would consider his proposition and thought it sounded promising, perhaps the day of the reversal would just slide by, and the Frankell family would be safe.

Then the oil checks would come to her. She would be in control. Why, she wouldn't even have to give Hiram a fourth, if she didn't want to. She could just merrily wave goodbye to him, on her way to Europe, with the oil checks in her hand. Sorry, she would say. I changed my mind.

That was what Drake wanted her to do, undoubtedly. His ego was caught in this now. He was punishing his own father, all the men who had betrayed him, in the figure of Hiram. Nothing would be too much a punishment for Hiram, Drake thought. For him the war was wicked, and had been for some time.

But this choice left Amelia feeling ill as well. Some remnant of love, of daughterly feeling, remained in her. It was a tired shred, but it was there. To lull Hiram past the reversal date by seeming to agree, and then to betray him, simply wasn't in her.

Were these her only choices? To be victim or oppressor, to force him to her way or be forced to his? Surely there was something else. Surely there was.

She didn't want to break Hiram's pride, and humiliate him. She only wanted to be free of him, free of his heavy charm and heavy-handed manipulations. She only wanted to be alone for an eternity, to be alone in silence and heal. All of her nerves, the deepest inner connections in her, were outraged and broken. She only wanted to be alone.

And there might be a way, her mind whispered to her. There might be a third way that would leave her free of him, but leave him with his pride intact.

What if she were to take her third of the oil well now, and then give up any claim to Anise's inheritance after Hiram's death? Let them fight over her mother's portion like vultures, her two sisters and her father. She would be far away, in another place.

The more she thought on it, the more her shredded cells embraced it. You will be giving up your inheritance, a voice inside her said warningly. You will be disinherited. You will no longer be part of the family. You will be alone.

I don't care, she thought back unreasoningly. I want to be alone. I want to be all alone, in the silence. She drew the thought of the silence over her broken parts, like a blanket of snow, and slept.

And in the end, that is how it happened. My mother sent back her own proposal, in place of Hiram's. She would have her third of the oil well up front, and give up any claim to the rest of the estate. Hiram agreed, angrily and wearily. They signed documents to the effect.

And then there was a long silence. Two years, in fact. My mother and father nursed themselves and each other. My mother grew bitter over the fact that she had been disinherited. The fact blurred in her mind rather quickly that she had disinherited herself, by choice.

"We've been disinherited," she told me. Because, of course, my portion was with her portion, that portion she had given up. I would never have any of the things from my grandfather's house, the things I loved so much and wanted so dearly.

I wrote my grandfather one letter, asking why he had disinherited me. His reply was prompt and bewildered. "Disinherit you?" he wrote. "I would never disinherit you. You are my number one granddaughter, and I love you always."

I never wrote him back. The pain was too much, and the confusion, and I pushed it all away.

The oil money made our life easier. We took trips. And so it happened that, a year and a half later, we were away in Europe when the cable came that my grandfather was in the hospital, gravely ill. By the time we discovered it, the telegram was a month old.

When the men from the county jail failed to reach Demeter and Fid after countless tries, they contacted Bridget to tell her that her brother was in jail. She got in her red car and drove to her parents' house, skidding gravel as she went. She gripped the steering wheel hard, and rehearsed the words in her mind, practicing the best way to tell her parents the news.

She was absolutely furious at G.A. Such a disgusting thing to do. With all his advantages, and Mother and Daddy had been so good to them both. This would just break their hearts, she knew it. How could he have put them all in this dreadful position, have done this to the family name? It was a disgrace, that's what, a disgrace. She doubted they would ever live it down.

She pulled up outside her parents' house, stomped angrily on the brakes and went inside. In her fury she hardly noticed that the house was silent and the lights were out.

She was all the way into the living room before she saw her mother, staring blankly straight ahead, and her father sitting beside her mother, holding her hand grimly. The room was dark, and it stank. Had someone told them, then? But no, it was impossible.

Anxiously, Bridget snapped on the lights, flooding the room with a yellow glow. She saw that the room was dirty, that in just the few days since she had been there before, it had changed from a living room into a hole, an abandoned burrow.

"Good Lord, Daddy, what's wrong?" she said, coming forward. "Why didn't you call me? What happened here?"

"Your mother," said Fid. His voice was dull.

"Well, what's the matter with her?" Bridget said, in a fury of fear.

She went over to her mother and knelt down to take her hand. She was horrified to find that her mother, her lovely, tidy mother, smelled like a sewer.

"Mother?" she said, and snapped her fingers and waved her hands in front of Demeter's blank stare. "Mother?"

"It's no good," said Fid, in the same dull voice. "She won't move."

Bridget looked closer and saw that her mother was sitting in her own excrement. She gagged slightly. "Good Lord, Daddy," she said again. "Why is she sitting here like this? Here, help me carry her upstairs."

With her father's help she forced Demeter upstairs, bathed her and pulled a soft flannel nightgown over her head. Demeter sat limply, unresisting. Bridget got rid of the soiled clothes, went downstairs, heated up a can of soup and tried to force some of it between Demeter's lips. The hungry way that Demeter sucked at the spoon made Bridget think that her parents hadn't eaten in days, and when she questioned her father, he shook his head vaguely and admitted that he couldn't remember when he had eaten last.

Exasperated, she took him downstairs, leaving Demeter tucked firmly in bed, and heated up another can of soup. She watched him while he ate it. She was struck by how old he looked suddenly, like crumbling parchment.

"Daddy, I know this isn't the time, but you have to know," she said, hating herself for having to say it. "It's G.A., he's in jail. He's been arrested for rape. We have to go bail him out and find out about getting him a lawyer."

Fid closed his eyes wearily, and laid down his spoon.

"Thank God your mother's gone," he said. "She'll never have to know."

39. Horse Trading

Hiram's heart was acting strangely. Sometimes he would run out of breath, and would sway, and would have to grab something to hold him upright.

The Masons in the Mounted Patrol watched him with concern. They were practicing for the national tourney, which would be held in Denver. It was the biggest competition they had ever entered, and they'd been working towards it for a year.

After the practice drill at Waco, Hiram was so pale and so out of breath, sitting down and clutching his chest, that Ford Hatterly was afraid.

Hiram looked so feeble, suddenly. He had always been the heart of the drill, the buoyant, ebullient spirit that had driven the Masons to win. His illness cast a blight over the group. They let him alone, ostensibly unsaddling and caring for their horses, but watching him cautiously in case he should need them, leaving room for his pride.

Ford Hatterly walked up to him. My God, he thought. The man's going to die. Ford had never seen that shade of flushed grey in a man's face before, but he knew it was the color of death.

"Maybe you should take a little vacation," Ford said, sitting down next to Hiram. Hiram was still pulling his collar open, and struggling to get his breathing under control.

"I'm going to ride in the competition," Hiram said.

"Hiram, I won't let you do it," Ford said.

"Why not?"

"I don't like the way you look."

"Did I make a mistake?" Hiram said, looking up.

"No, hell, of course you didn't make a mistake," Ford said. His voice was rough.

"I don't make mistakes." Hiram wheezed. "You can't fire me if I don't make mistakes."

Ford went out behind the trailers and pounded his fist against a tree. Then he went back and unsaddled his horse.

The horses were trucked to Denver, and the Masons flew. Francine went with Hiram, sitting near him on the plane and holding his hand. She listened to the drawing in and out of his breaths, unconsciously counting them. She hated the way they sounded so harsh in his chest.

He looked over at her, squeezed her hands and smiled. Her heart contracted. He was strong, this man, and his eyes were so blue. He was stronger than this thing that threatened him, whatever it was, surely.

The Masons rode in Denver. They went into the ring, every red fez shining, every tasseled flag flying, the silver saddles and black horses glistening under the lights. The crowd roared to see them, the horses dancing in perfect rhythm, cutting past each other at harrowing angles, blending smoothly into the circles and moving out again to make patterns, triangles and diamonds of flying hooves and shining hides.

Ford looked up to find Hiram. He was weaving in his saddle a little, and his face was whiter than Ford had ever seen it. Ford muttered a little prayer under his breath that he wouldn't faint from the saddle and be minced under the eighty steel-sharp hooves that were thundering around the ring.

Hiram was looking bad, and everyone was watching him instead of concentrating on the drill. Joff Hooser, a young member of the team, miscalculated and came around with his horse a little too close to Hiram's horse, King, cutting him off.

Both horses were moving at top speed. King sheared out of line, spooked, and Ford closed his eyes for a split second in anticipation of the collision and the screams. But when he looked back Hiram had handled King smoothly back into the line in another place, without missing a beat. Goddamn the man, Ford thought joyously, tears stinging his eyes. Goddamn the man.

But Hiram was weaving in his saddle still. The colors and motion of the ring were blurring in front of his eyes. He turned the reins a little loose and concentrated on balancing himself in the saddle.

King knew the drill so well that he paced through it on his own, instinctively compensating for the slackened weight of his master's body.

"Good boy," Hiram whispered under his breath. He was desperately afraid that he was going to be sick right there on the horse. He imagined vomit coursing down the sides of his carefully polished saddle, and grimaced. Only a few more minutes now. If he could only make it through the grand quadrangle, they would be out of it.

The world swayed and spun sickeningly in front of him, and he hardly knew where he was. His breath rose faster and faster, as if an iron band were squeezing his chest. He felt pain shoot down his arm and out his fingertips. The pain rose to his brain, cutting off his sight and speech. He heard the roar of the crowd and saw with infinite gratitude the rough red wood of the gate. He had made it. They were coming out.

Francine was standing waiting there at the gate, and she caught Hiram in her arms as he slid off the horse in a dead faint.

"Ford, call a doctor," she called urgently, as Ford rode by. "And charter a plane."

Mary Frank wrote G.A. faithfully all the time he was in jail. She almost felt it was her fault he was there, since it was her own father who insisted G.A. be cuffed and imprisoned.

She ran through her mind again and again the moments when G.A. had looked into her eyes, weeping. She knew that he must love her. She had never seen a man cry before. For something to move a strong man so deeply, it must be true.

Besides, she discovered quickly, in the first few days that she hung retching and green over the washbasin, that she was going to have his baby. She thought of G.A.'s ear, the one that she had seen and studied so closely in the woods. It had been so pure, made him look so helpless. She thought that a baby might be like that, curved and pure, and she could love it.

Her father was disgusted with her, and refused to let her in the house during dinner. It infuriated him to see her swell with G.A.'s bastard in her, while she was still eating her father's food.

Her father would have liked to throw her out of the house altogether, but for once Mary Frank's tiny, tired mother put her foot down. No child of hers would be thrown out destitute. Her voice raised in insistence was such an uncommon occurrence that Mary Frank's father folded in amazement, and let her have her way.

But he grumbled audibly whenever Mary Frank was around, and she took to spending a good deal of time in the woods. She felt closer to G.A.'s spirit there.

As she wrote her daily letters to G.A., she wove him into the hero of her dreams. He was strong, he was forthright, he came and took what he wanted. Although there was a delicate, fervid part of Mary Frank that was repulsed by violence, there was another part of her that was compelled by it, and surrendered to it at once.

G.A. was her knight who had been driven mad with passion, misunderstood by common mortals, drunk and dizzy with love. And while a girl might wish for a little more gentleness, still, you couldn't argue with passion. It was hard for her, finally, to blame a man who had given up all his freedom for her.

In his absence she hung G.A. like a Christmas tree, with all the virtues she could discover. He was courageous, he was loving, he was virile. She sang as she spun her dreams for him, wrote him details of her swelling belly and her thoughts of the coming child, pressed kisses on the letters she sent him and enclosed locks of her hair.

When she could, she went to visit him herself. She brushed her hair silken over her shoulders, and put flowers in it. She could feel how his eyes drank at her hungrily, and she shivered under the inexhaustible flow of his desire for her.

Even the drab prison clothes came to sit on him, in her eyes, as a badge of honor. He waited in his chaste cell for her sake, undergoing a true trial of devotion. And he was becoming chastened, she could see that. Every visit, she thought she could see more gentleness in his eyes.

After the birth, she brought the baby to visit, too. It was a small, weasel-eyed thing, but she loved it. G.A. was very proud. He boasted of his son to all the men in the cellblock, who feared him for his enormous size and strength.

G.A. grew to his final bulk in jail, and he was a prodigious man. He became brawny, and cunning, and sly. He spent his spare time lifting blocks of iron to perfect his strength, and bashing his knuckles against the iron bars to make them impervious to pain.

He dominated the other men in prison easily. It was a world of beasts, and his early lessons had prepared him well. He was happy in jail, in a strange way. He would look back on it as one of the simplest times in his life. He fit there as he would never fit into the outside world. He knew the rules. They were his rules, and he was never bewildered by subtleties there, or things beyond his understanding.

He beat three men to whimpering pulps after he heard them making remarks about Mary Frank. After that the gangs of the jail stayed away from him. They whispered for many nights about the way he had picked up two men in one hand, and one man in another, and spun around to let them fly in different directions against the wall.

G.A. became something of a legend. Even the guards feared him. He would snake his hand out through the bars to catch hold of them as they passed by and make them admire his greasy, much-creased photo of Mary Frank and the baby. They would praise the woman and child with trembling, insincere voices.

"Only not too much," he would say, gripping the guards' uniforms tighter and breathing his animal breath on them. "I can't stand it if anyone looks at her in the wrong way." They would assure him that they had all due respect, and would hurry off, straightening their uniforms, relieved to be away.

G.A. married Mary Frank five months after he got out of jail. They were married by a justice of the peace, outside the trailer that Fid had given G.A. as his last gift.

G.A. put on a clean shirt. Mary Frank wore a light blue dress that she had made herself, to fit the dimensions of her belly, already swelling again. She held their stringy-haired, whining first child in her arms during the service, trying to shush it. Her face glowed with joy.

None of their family came; Mary Frank's parents had finally washed their hands of her as a whore and a fornicator when she continued to write and visit G.A. in jail.

Fid would not attend the wedding, which he considered a travesty, and Demeter could not. Demeter sat rocking silently, in the half-darkness of the home where they had put her, and did not blink when they told her the news.

The news that the Black Horse Patrol had won the contest was waiting for Francine and Hiram at the airport when they landed in the chartered plane. Hiram was under an oxygen mask, but he smiled and gave a thumbs-up when he heard it.

The doctor waiting for them at the best heart hospital in the state watched the machine monitoring Hiram's heart, and looked angry.

"I've told you this before, Hiram," he said. "You've got a damn hole in your heart. You've got no call to be getting excited, and you've got no call to be flying in a plane, or competing in Denver, where the air is thin. That's what happened to you—it was the air pressure.

"Now, I want you to stay quiet, or I can't answer for the consequences. You can have one drink or one woman per day, but not both. Do you understand me?"

"I understand you, Doc," Hiram said irritably. "Now get out of my way, because I'm leaving this hellhole."

Francine took him home, and they lived quietly for a while. There was still much that they didn't know about one another, things to be told from the long, long years they had been apart.

They measured it that way, now—everything before or after their marriage. They had been married only a year and a half.

Hiram was amazed at the pleasure he still got from seeing Francine in the kitchen, or coming around a corner. The curve of her neck, the way that her eyes lit as she saw him—it was worth waiting a life, he thought, for this. Odd to think that he was seventy-one years old. He felt fifteen. If you didn't count the tightness in his chest.

He tried not to think of Amelia, so far out of his reach now, and silent. He tried not to think of his lost granddaughter. When he thought of these things the band around his ribs would tighten and squeeze his heart until it ran up into his throat, and he thought he would choke.

He kept a file of his granddaughter's letters on his desk, always in front of him. Sometimes he would flip through it—the drawings, the poems she had sent. Sometimes he would be comforted by the longing in the letters, knowing that she wanted to be near him. Sometimes he wondered what Drake had told her about him, how her mind had been poisoned against him. He wanted to talk to her, just once. But she had never returned his letter.

Mostly he tried not to think of it.

There were other problems now, other difficulties to be faced. His two younger daughters, Constance and Sarsaparilla, were always around the house under his feet. It seemed that they were afraid that he would leave everything to Francine, and that they wouldn't get their share of the estate. The watch they kept over him made him nervous, and angry. For his whole life, some woman had been watching over him and controlling him, tying his hands, muffling his movements.

"When is it going to be my turn?" he asked Constance once.

She looked at him strangely. "Daddy, it's always been your turn," she said.

The three of them—Hiram, Sarsaparilla and Constance—drove out in the pickup one day to look at the lots of land Anise had left. They were going to split the land three ways. Hiram would leave his part to Francine, and the girls could do with theirs as they liked.

They got out of the pickup, and spread the lot map out on the hood, under the blazing sun. A vulture circled somewhere far above.

Hiram drew out the boundary lines with his fingers for them. "These two are the biggest," he said cagily, knowing quite well that there was water access on only one of the pieces of land, the smallest. The other two lots were almost worthless because without water access, no one could build.

Francine might build a little house there on the watered lot, he thought. Maybe after his death she wouldn't want to be in the big house. Maybe she would want to build a small place of her own, where she could still be near the places they had been together.

"I would let you two have the largest ones, and I'll take the little one. Plus I'll throw in this extra piece along the fence—you can split it," he said.

The two women looked at each other. "Isn't this small lot the only one with water access?" Constance said.

He shifted a little, and looked down. "That's right," he said.

Sarsaparilla started crying. Her blond hair shone like a halo around her face, which became instantly red and puffy. The tears went down her cheeks very slowly, one by one.

"Daddy, don't you want your daughters to have the best?" she said. "We're your children. What are you doing to us?"

"I don't know," he mumbled, uneasy. "I was just horse trading."

"Why are you horse trading with your daughters?" she asked him, through a glaze of tears. "Don't you want to take care of us? Don't you want us to have the best?"

Hiram stood there as the world rocked around him. He didn't know.

He didn't know what he had been doing. He climbed back into the pickup truck and put his head down on the steering wheel, and cried.

Harsh sounds came from him. The girls stood still outside the truck, frightened. Tears still rolled, forgotten, down Sarsaparilla's cheeks.

"I don't know what I was doing," Hiram cried out. "I don't know why I was doing that. I don't know why."

He wept uncontrollably, for the pieces of his life he felt shattering around him, in sharp edges that cut him so he bled. Somewhere he had forgotten something, he had lost something of great price, and he no longer knew how to find it. He wept his loss, and his shame, and the sounds went into the dry hot air and disappeared. The vulture dipped lower, hearing them, and then circled up onto a wind current, and was gone.

40. The Hole

Demeter never heard again, or remembered a single stroke of things gone by. Fid cared for her in the home where they had put her. He drove there every day, his old hands tight on the wheel, and shaking a little.

He would stop in the parking lot, and carefully set the emergency brake on the car. Then he looked in the mirror to check his hair, smoothing it down on both sides.

He straightened his collar, performing his toilette as gravely as a young man going courting. He shook out his ragged cuffs, and pressed down the lapels of his coat with his hands. Then he took the offerings he had brought for the day, candy or fruit or flowers, and went into the home.

Nurses recognized him, and nodded hello. He greeted them shyly, ducking his head. He paced the halls with an unconscious dignity, and did not know that many of them looked after him with admiration in their eyes, and pity.

Demeter's room was number twenty-four, at the end of the hall on the right, near the ice machine. He always knocked before he went in, although she could neither hear the door nor answer it.

She sat always in the center of the room. She had developed an almost magnetic insistence for being in the middle, although she was conscious of very little else. She would never look out the window.

The lack of exercise padded her once-stringy frame with fat that was round and smooth, the fat of childhood. Sitting wearing a diaper, with a blank smile and her bulk overflowing the chair, she seemed a large infant.

Fid would go in and greet her each day, laying his gift on her lap and holding her hand. Her temper was unsteady, and sometimes she would knock the gift off her lap. Sometimes she would tear it open, and eat the sweets greedily. Usually she only stared past his head, with a vague, sweet look on her face. She never once recognized him.

With hands that shook a little, Fid would take down her hair, and brush it smooth. He braided it back in two braids, one on either side of her face, and tied the ends with bright ribbons that he had bought at the drugstore. She seemed to like the red ones. He always marveled at the softness and silkiness of her hair. In her adult life she had cropped her hair short, after their marriage, but now it had grown out again, and had the same fat sleekness as her body.

After he had fixed her hair he would tidy her room, making it clean and pleasant for the day. Then he would sit by her and read to her, or most often, just stay silent. Sometimes she would let him hold her hand.

At mealtimes the nurse would bring in the tray and Fid would feed her carefully, watching for any spilled morsel of food that might fall onto her ribboned nightgown. After she was finished eating he washed her hands with rose water, and she let him, holding out her hands pliantly.

Most of the time she kept on her lap two baby dolls, which she bounced up and down in her chair. One was a boy, and one a girl. They were the only things that seemed to interest her at all, and sometimes she would bend them towards each other as if they were talking. Then Fid would lean close, to try to find out what passed in her blank and silent world. But he could never make out any of the words.

It was just as well. Because it would have been a grief to him if he had known that in her final hours, he crossed her mind not at all. She was not even aware of his presence, although he sat by her bed as always, holding her hand.

In her mind as she died Demeter was with Hiram again, standing on the stirrups of her pony as she swept over the land, marshaling the fields to her touch, running out over the plain with the speed of a young thing. She laughed with delight to breathe the wind. She saw Hiram before her, and he was riding, riding away, faster than she could go.

She set her lips stubbornly and refused to call out to Hiram to ask him to wait. But the last thing that she saw before she died was her brother's head bowed in her lap, and the flat blue bowl of the Oklahoma sky.

One day when Ford was riding by Hiram's property, he noticed a gaping hole in the fence. It looked as if someone had pulled some boards away, leaving a hole that looked just about big enough for a horse to get through.

He stopped at Hiram's house before he headed home, tied up his horse to the huge hitching chain and went in to find Hiram. He found Francine in the kitchen, mixing up a pitcher of lemonade.

"I think he's outside on the porch," Francine said. She was quite undisturbed at the sight of spurs scarring her kitchen linoleum. She had picked the pattern with spurs in mind.

"Thanks," he said, and accepted a tall glass of the lemonade. He sipped it as he walked. It was good. He thought how lucky Hiram was, to have found Francine. Even this late in life.

He saw Hiram through the glass before he reached him, and was struck by how odd he looked. Hiram was sitting in the porch swing, which swayed a little. His head was thrown back and his eyes were closed. It struck Ford as odd that he had never seen Hiram in that swing before, and very rarely seen him still, without whittling or something in his hands. He had most especially never seen Hiram's eyes closed during the day. He cleared his throat, to let Hiram know he was coming.

Hiram sat up at the noise, smiling. He shook Ford's hand, but didn't get up, Ford noticed. Ford was shocked again at how sallow and sunken Hiram's face looked.

"You didn't bring any lemonade for me? Damn you for a fool," Hiram said amicably.

"That's right, and damn any man who won't burn the shirt off his back at midnight, to make light to damn me some more," said Ford, and they laughed.

"What can I do for you?" said Hiram.

"I was riding along your fence line, and noticed you got a big hole down there near the Thousand Acres," said Ford. "You should better look at it—it's about horse size."

"Ah, it's okay," Hiram said. "Tell me about the drill."

They chatted for a few minutes, and Ford got up to take his leave.

"You take a look at that fence, now," he said, creasing his hat in his hand.

"Ford, you worry too much," said Hiram. "That's how come you're a lawyer."

Hiram thought he would get around to looking at the fence, but in fact he did not. Lassitude possessed him these days, creeping through his body with soft fingers and pressing him back onto the bed. He napped a lot, when he had never napped before. Just climbing from the barn up to the house would put him in a sweat, and he would have to stop and rest. And sometimes he would find himself drowsing off in his chair, in the middle of the day.

He would shake himself awake, irritated. "Only fools get old," he would grumble.

So it happened that the hole in the fence was still there, the night that King wandered over by the Thousand Acres. King pushed his nose around the hole and whickered, and led the other three black horses out the hole in the fence into the night. They roamed, milling and confused, until they were standing on the black road.

The young man driving the yellow convertible never had a chance to see all those black horses, on the black road. He drove his car at eighty-five miles an hour into the thick of them, and the first that Hiram knew of it was a scream, shrill and inhuman, coming from the road.

The neighbors came, too. Ford came, and the people from the other side. Fid would have come, but he was napping on a cot by Demeter's side at the home.

Ford came running out with his heart in his mouth. He knew even as his long legs paced out the distance between his place and Hiram's what had happened. He ran, praying as he went.

He arrived first, even before Hiram. The carnage was appalling. The yellow car was bent and twisted, and a dazed young man was wandering in the trees about a hundred yards away, looking lost.

Ford looked down at the mess on the road that had been four horses. He saw a head lying in the road near him, and a leg from below the hock. White tendons and entrails showed against the dark. He went and vomited in the bushes, quickly and noisily. Then he turned back to the road, searching the arriving figures with his eyes. He had to stop Hiram before he saw this.

But he was too late. When Ford looked back, he saw Hiram kneeling by one of the mangled horses on the road. He was holding the horse's head in his lap, bending over it.

It was King. There was a shrill screaming that was going on and on, piercing the night air with monotonous regularity, and Ford saw the noise was coming from King.

He went over and stood by Hiram, helplessly. The screaming went on. Hiram looked up. His eyes were dilated completely black in his white face. "You'll have to do it, Ford," he said. "I can't."

So Ford went back to the house and got his rifle, and came back and put a bullet through King's perfect head. Hiram stood away, at a distance, his shoulders squeezed up around his ears as if to block out the sound. There was one sharp report, and the screaming mercifully stopped.

There was another horse still moving, thrashing weakly in the dust and bleeding from the mouth, but Hiram seemed not to see it. The police had arrived by this time, and someone had called the horse doctor.

The horse doctor came in his van, and got out to silence the thrashing horse with sure fingers and a syringe. The neighbors began to load the bodies into the vet's van. More than one man wept that night, seeing the ruin of those horses. But Hiram was still, his eyes showing white around the edges, his silver hair standing up where he had run his fingers through it.

Ford watched him, and thought: Something is going to happen. Things are being wrapped up.

Hiram only interfered with the men loading the bodies when they came to take King away, and then he just stood there, blocking them with his body.

Ford stepped forward and said to them, "Leave this one. We'll take care of it."

They nodded, and went on with their work. The neighbors were there for Hiram. They didn't talk much to him, but only touched his arm or shoulder as they went by. It was their last act of devotion to him, and their greatest.

When they were all gone, Hiram and Ford and the body of King still remained in the dim light. Hiram looked up at Ford, and in his eyes was a naked question.

"I'll do it, Hiram," Ford heard himself promising. "You go back to the house."

So it was Ford who dug the grave for King, and called a friend back to help him drag the splendid, broken body into it, and cover it over with sod. It was the middle of the night by the time their work was finished. When they went to Hiram's house to tell him it was done, they found him on the floor, unconscious and face down, with Francine still asleep upstairs.

41. The Shell

The paramedics hit Hiram with the electric-shock machine, which made his body convulse. They took him to the hospital in an ambulance. They were due to operate at dawn, to try to find another way to get blood to his heart, which was fluttering like a lost bird.

Everyone came just before dawn. Constance and Sarsaparilla were there, Francine, Ford Hatterly, Fid, others of the Masons. Hiram was lying in bed when Constance walked in, with the back of the bed cranked up so that he could see his visitors.

Constance was horrified to see that everyone was gathered in one line along the wall looking at Hiram, as if they had been hired as a firing squad. They were frozen there, staring, and he looked back at them helplessly.

Constance went over and stood behind Hiram, arraying herself with him, against all the eyes. She looked at them, and then down at him. She saw the bones of his face showing through his skin, which was pale. As he looked up at her, she saw something that she had never seen before in Hiram's eyes. It was fear.

They came to wheel him away, and Constance had to restrain the impulse to run after them, to fight them away and take his stretcher herself, to run with it to a place where they would never be found.

Hiram survived the first operation, and lived in the hospital for three months. Francine was with him every day. She was with him so much that the head of the hospital, moved by her inexplicable charm, insisted on paying for a hotel room near the hospital for her, out of his own pocket.

Francine sat by Hiram. He was hardly conscious, although the machines forced life through his body. His kidneys had failed, and his face was puffed and swollen. His face and body were riddled with tubes. When Francine asked him for a kiss, he obediently puckered his mouth.

Amelia returned home from Europe, and found the telegram informing her that Hiram was in the hospital. She immediately flew to Texas. Constance met her at the airport.

Amelia had planned to stay in a hotel, and was surprised when Constance insisted that Amelia stay with her. Constance was surprised at her surprise.

"You're my sister," Constance said patiently. "Where else would you stay?"

"But after everything that's happened?" Amelia said.

"It doesn't matter," Constance told her.

Amelia prepared herself carefully for her meeting with Hiram. She told herself to be firm, to keep from being moved with so much pity that she would give up all the growth she had attained. She planned to be affectionate but honest. And careful of his heart, of course.

Amelia had gambled. She had used herself, and the wholeness of the family, as leverage against Hiram, to try to make him act the way she wanted him to. She had gambled even knowing that he might die in the meantime, without the family ever coming together again.

Now she thought perhaps the time had come that there could be reconciliation, and healing. The chapter would finish now. Hiram would see that she was a woman grown, her own person, no longer his child. She could afford to come back now. She had proved her point.

But she saw when she walked into his hospital room that it was too late. Francine was there, and she enfolded Amelia in a warm embrace, with tears in her eyes, and whispered, "He'll be so glad you finally came."

When Amelia went to the bed, she saw no one there that she recognized. The man under the oxygen tent was swollen and bulky, his face puffed with poisons. Tubes fed into him and bubbled out with green and yellow fluids. His face was dull, without the sharp fineness that she had remembered. It was a stranger who lay there. The father that she remembered, that she had wounded, with whom she had planned to reconcile, had gone.

She sat down by him anyway, and held his hand. "Daddy?" she said, trying out her voice. He opened his eyes briefly and looked at her, without recognition. She thought she might have felt a slight pressure on her hand, but then decided she had imagined it.

She sat there for a while longer, all of the unsaid words burning in her throat, choking her like dry bread. She sat with him until his even breathing told her that he was asleep. Then she got up to go, the words still in her throat, as they would always be now, making the sides of her cheeks ache as if someone were pressing there.

They laid Hiram on the metal table for a final operation. The doctors warned the family that the surgery they were about to perform was very high-risk, and might not work.

He was in surgery for ten hours. At the end of that time, the anesthesiologist reported that Hiram's vital signs had ceased to register.

From behind his eyelids, Hiram could hear the sounds of the operating room fade until they were far-distant, almost silent. In their place he heard the beating of ocean waves, lapping and receding slowly, with an old pulse.

He was standing holding close to his ear a shell that Fid had given Demeter long ago, with a curve inside that was as purely pink and satin as the elbow of an infant.

He held it to his ear for a long time, listening to the chant of the sounds inside, and then turned so that he could look inside.

Looking deep into the creamy heart of the shell, he saw that down its throat there was a tiny chamber, from which flooded an immense yellow-green radiance. The light rose out and surrounded him, shimmering as if he were under water.

He went to the place where the shell had been born. The greenish-yellow light was still there, stronger now, falling around him in sheets. By its illumination he could see that he was in a cavern, with wet dripping walls and rough crags of rock thrust out along the sides. The water covering the floor of the cavern was inky dark, as dark as oil. He knew that it went far, far down. It admitted no reflection of the light that danced along its surface.

He was drawn to the pool of water and looked down, deep into it. And rising slowly, like a fish, he saw a glimmer of something moving far below. It rose and rose towards his vision until he saw that it was a woman with green-gold hair, and arms the perfect white of a petal.

She rose towards him gracefully, dancing, and he saw that her arms were wound with pearls, and that there were pearls in her hair. He was struck suddenly by the familiarity of it all. He struggled to remember—it seemed to him that she should have a face he knew. He gazed down intently, trying to see if it was so.

And as he gazed he could see that her face was not the face of Francine, as he had first thought, or of Anise. It was the face of his sister that the figure wore, the hair dark and flowing down on each side of her pale face. It was the face he had seen pacing beside him and to his left, so long ago. It was the face of his memory, the face of his death.

He watched her come up through the rippling waves, and she broke the surface and smiled up at him, the bitter water running from her mouth. It was Nakomas Sorrel he saw there now, and she was as he had remembered her. She held out one arm to him, that gleamed above the inky surface of the pool.

And as she reached out to him the pool lit below her, as if a switch had been thrown. Hiram could see in it a wondrous city, a fabled place, far beneath her gently stirring fins.

It was a place of silver bridle paths and trees with bark of rough gold, where the fruits hung as true jewels over the way. Enchanted folk passed through, singing and marching towards the castle of crystal that stood in the center.

Hiram thought that all the treasures he had strained towards and lost were in the castle, which seemed to sit alone in the middle of a vast plain. He knew that somewhere below him was his son.

He saw the roads tracing through the places of that country, winding over hills with pleasant views. Fish the color of angels passed over, ridden as mounts and singing like birds in the trees, with the sweet high voices of women. There were serpents in the air, winged with fire. The things he had long forgotten came back to him in a rush, and he wept for joy.

The fish-tailed woman held out her hand to him again, her dark face shining with expectancy. Her glance was regnant, poised and watchful. He came towards her in the pool, sliding forward with hardly a ripple, and she put her arms out to receive him. He pillowed his face on her breasts, which were as cool and white as porcelain. And clasping him gently in her arms, smiling, she slid back under the water until it closed completely over his head.

42. Going Home

No one knew what to do with Hiram's ashes. No one was willing to undertake the voyage to Indian Bluff, to lay his remains there along with Anise, Wester and Lee. Besides, Francine didn't really want him there, so far from her.

Ford Hatterly finally volunteered an idea, and everyone agreed. So they all gathered on a soft spring morning, out on the Thousand Acres where Hiram loved to ride. Everyone was there except Francine, who could not bear to watch.

Ford was riding his great black horse. He carried with him the urn of ashes. With all the eyes on him, he spurred his horse forward, into a gallop. Faster and faster he went, until it seemed that the stretching hocks of the horse would lift off the ground in a blur.

He rode in a huge circle, the circle of the mounted drills, and he scattered the ashes behind him as he galloped, in a dusty trail. They glinted silver in the air for a moment, as the light struck them, and then settled softly to the ground.

My grandfather Hiram came hesitantly to me in a dream last night. I am so hungry for any sense of him now that I suck even my dreams dry as wood. He seemed unsure, changed, already become root and branch of what called him away.

I listen to his voice on the tapes I have, and close my eyes to see his face. I struggle that I cannot somehow arrange the walls of my room so that when my door opens again, it opens to him. It seems that with the slightest effort, it could be done, if I knew how. But my muscles are too stupid, too dense, my body too much dross to manage.

I see him often in my dreams, and wake from them longing, and bitter. Even asleep, I know to grip the dream moments, and test them: How did he smell? How did it feel to have my face pressed in his shirt, his arm around my shoulders?

These are the things I miss—the broad bluntness of his knuckles, the downward slant of his eyelid at the corner, the lines carved around his mouth.

But to evoke him now is a chancy thing—he has been long away, and wonders, I think, why it is that he has been called back with such urgency. Death has changed him, sunk him into himself, and when I dream of him now he is more pale and tranquil, less the man I knew.

I submerge myself in him, holding myself under water like a drowned man, looking up for the truth to appear in the broken prism of the water's surface.

I know a man of God who wrote this: "Remembering, and remembering truly, is the key to healing and reconciliation . . ." But I have forgotten whether any of my memories are true. I am crosshatched with light and shadow, random as a pile of sticks, and I can't trust even my own dreams to recall the truth of him anymore, how he was, his hands, the way his right hand floated, lifted above his thigh, when he rode his black horse —or was it his left hand?—the lap of skin under his jaw, the turn of his phrase. Just when I need them now, the memories give me no details, yield nothing but grief, and though I search, I cannot find him anymore in the shadows from the fire.

I never said goodbye to my grandfather. I heard of his death in Washington, and stared out at the hard, candy-colored town houses outside the window, and bit down on my tongue until it bled. I didn't cry then, or for ten years after.

Then I went to visit Francine, who had kept Lee's desk for me all those years. The desk, and a chair that matched it, were the only things my grandfather had left me in his will. I went prepared to resist Francine, having heard formidable stories of her ways. But she charmed me effortlessly, as she did everyone. We talked, and she told me stories.

She told me, among other things, that she thought my mother, Amelia, had broken Hiram's heart, when she stopped calling him Daddy.

She told me that I had broken his heart, when I failed to find him that day in Washington. She laid the blood guilt on us gently, with a strange care. I could not help but agree.

I drive to the site of Hiram's old house. Ford Hatterly and his wife live there now. They scraped together the money to buy it from Francine, not wanting the house to go to strangers.

I have the breathless feeling of recognition driving down the red-rock lane, past the scrubby leafless trees. It is all so familiar, just the way I had kept it in my memory all those years. They paved the street, but it still divides around the big tree that Anise and Hiram had refused to cut down when they first built their house and laid the crushed-rock road. "You can't leave a tree in the middle of the road," people told them.

"Why not?" they said, and built the road around it. Their only concession to public opinion was to adorn the tree with a glinting red diamond reflector, to show oncoming headlights.

I approach the house. The drive is still oval, wrapping around a central green. Driving up it, you see the house, long and low and brown. It was built, they told me, from the timbers of the barn at Indian Bluff, with pointed gables.

The heavy rusty hitching chain, as thick as my waist, still stretches between two posts. There is still the constant buzz of cicadas, and the red-stone path still runs down to the barn. I remember the particular jolt with which the horses would round up over the lip of the hill, climbing from the barn.

The red barn is still there, and the seductive sweet smell of hay and the tang of horse manure, the great cans of grain where I buried my arm to the shoulder, reveling in the richness and the smooth sliding feel of it. They have turned Sir's wood workshop into a weight room for the straw-haired, gap-toothed caretaker who shows me around the barn wearing unlaced duck shoes, dragging with mud.

He is persistent with his attentions, but I tell him that I want to walk alone. The feel of the place is rising up in my throat. All of it is pressed into my cells—the rusty color of the earth, the particular vertical grey scale of the bark on the knobby trees. The dead leaves underfoot surprise me. I remember this place always in summer, and the desolation is new to me.

I remember the leashed and sweating violence of the horses as Sir whipped them in circles with a rope, training them, shouting, "Hyaa, there, get along."

I remember galloping hard across the low scruffy ground, walking across the paddock, which seemed endless to me then. The earth here is particularly tender, as if it might hold a familiar hoofprint. I remember that as I galloped through the woods on a shining summer morning, I lost the belt that Sir gave me, with the buckle that said "Big Talkers Do Big Business." I had to go back over the ground carefully, to find it.

I don't remember the lake here, or the concrete walkway, or the barbecue pit. And I have never been here before when Sir was not here with me, swinging open the galvanized-steel gate with his monogram soldered on it, walking with his peculiar, long-limbed ease.

A goose lifts off and flies, strangely graceful, across the darkening sky. I don't remember geese here, but the sound is right. At twilight Sir would put three fingers in his mouth and whistle, three loud, high, piercing whistles to call the horses, like the cries of the geese somewhere through the trees.

I remember the harsh fragrant Texas heat, the downward motion of going fast with the clear, cold feeling of hawk flight. I didn't care then what evil Sir had done. I still don't. When I was with him the world was marvelous, limned with silver, flaming like endless rain on the trees.

He was the summer king. He held all the beauty of that burnt land in his hand. With all the words I know, I cannot explain it. I only know that now that he is gone, the gates of that place are barred to me forever. I can only stand behind them, looking through to the summer lands I used to own.

I never even said goodbye.

I can wear his hats down over my eyes, and smell his sweat and hair oil still on the band inside. I can look at his boots, propped now on my desk, and twirl the rowels of his spurs, run my hand over the picture frame he carved. But these are pale pleasures, and do not repay my losses.

I live in a place that could not be further from the place he knew. I wonder sometimes what he would think of it. My city is a wicked plume of a city, stacked creamy houses scattered over the abrupt hills and down to the water. We are short on land here, and I have lost the dusty reaches that would have been my birthright. Here I am surrounded by the sea.

The water is my land now, as the land was Hiram's ocean. And as I look over the water I have chosen, pressed flat with the spatulated hand of the wind, I see not the dreaming grey ghosts of ships there but riders, whipping their longhorns over the long plains, home.